Cover illustration and design by:
Rashed AlAkroka

Tower of the Four

The Dragon's War

Parts 4-6

The Nightmare, *The Resurrection* and *The Reunion*

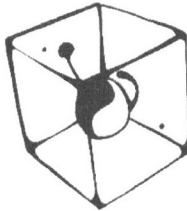

Todd Fahnestock

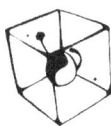

CONTENTS

THE NIGHTMARE

THE RESURRECTION

THE REUNION

Mailing List/Social Media

MAILING LIST
Don't miss out on the latest news and information about all of my books. Join my Readers Group

FACEBOOK GROUP

AMAZON AUTHOR PAGE

Part IV

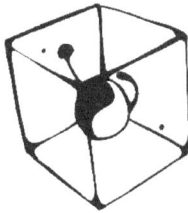

The Nightmare

1

VALE

Vale strode through the streets of Torlioch at night, alone. For *normals*, such a thing could be deadly. This city swallowed the careless, slit their throats, and left them to die in dark corners. No one braved these midnight streets unless surrounded by friends—protected by their crew, or by guards who knew how to handle thieves and murderers.

In Vale's time as an urchin, walking so brazenly would have been like baring her throat to the predators.

But she was a Quadron now. She reached up and touched the dragon amulet she'd received at her graduation from the Champions Academy, felt the lightning as its magic zinged into her fingers.

The petty concerns of *normals* didn't apply to her anymore. She didn't need a crew, and she certainly didn't need guards. She had power, more than enough to keep her safe. She had traveled the western coast alone, where desperate pirates would kill a person simply for stumbling across their hidden coves. She had traveled the snowy wilderness of northern Keltovar alone, where saber-toothed snow cats keened with the whipping winds, hunting humans. She didn't fear this dirty little city anymore.

Or at least, she shouldn't.

Despite her power, a recurring nightmare had plagued her these past weeks. It filled her nights and tainted her days until she could no longer find joy. Food tasted like mud. The sky weighed on her, gray and oppressive, whether sunset, sunrise, or bright noon. She woke with a sense of breathless failure every morning, like a hand was clenching her heart until she couldn't breathe. She went to sleep terrified that the nightmare would return. And it always did.

The last time Vale had felt this helpless, she'd been a struggling, dirt-smeared girl on these grimy streets. The nightmare had to be linked to this place, to this stupid little city that had tried—and failed—to grind her down.

She was going to purge it from her mind tonight, once and for all.

Fog swirled around her as she stalked through the city. Early spring brought mists to Torlioch every year. They drifted lazily down the streets, coiling around the lampposts, wrapping their guttering flames in stoles of glowing orange.

Finally, she reached the mouth of the alley where her mother had died, where the ghosts that haunted Vale's mind had been born. The mists lifted before her, as if they recognized the alley's importance.

The Wayward Inn rose to her left, its bottom half dark gray stonework and its top half brown-and-cream painted timber. Fendra's moonlight leaked through the mists above her, making the wet cobblestones glow. To Vale's right crouched the old tumbledown warehouse with its cracked wooden shingles, holes in the roof and crumbling mortar. So far as Vale knew, that warehouse had never housed anything except rats and spiders.

The scent of roasting meat wafted from the inn, but it couldn't completely cover the stench of animal feces and urine that emanated from the warehouse.

A shiver rippled through her even though her thick cloak kept her warm. Vale's mother had died right there, in that spot, and that's when Vale's helplessness had begun. A street thief named Jondry had closed in to loot the body while Vale had stood there stunned. He'd grabbed her wrist even as he rifled through Mother's meager belongings, obviously intent on keeping Vale too. But she'd broken his grip and narrowly escaped into the night. Afterward, Jondry had made it his personal mission to press her into his little gang of thieves. She'd spent years darting from shadow to shadow, hiding from him and stealing enough food to survive, but he'd eventually caught her right here, again, in this same alley. That time, he hadn't been so nice. He had stomped on her to slow her down, ripped a ligament in her leg so she'd always have a limp, so he'd always be able to catch her whenever he wanted. And he'd taken her food—a rich, still-warm half-a-steak discarded from the Wayward Inn. Gods, she could still remember the smell of it, the hoped-for taste of it, how that single half-a-steak had meant everything. And Jondry had chewed it in front of her as she lay crumpled on the cobblestones, permanently damaged. She'd never felt so helpless.

But in the end, Vale hadn't been damaged forever. Instead, she'd been healed by a recruiter from the

Champions Academy. The merciless city of Torlioch had swallowed Vale's mother, but it hadn't closed its jaws around Vale. She had gone on to the Champions Academy and become a Quadron, a user of magic who could do things that the urchins of this city could only dream of. She had claimed her power. She wasn't helpless anymore.

That's what she'd thought, at least, until the nightmare came.

The terrifying stranger in her nightmare had reduced her to that same frightened, shivering urchin again, had made her feel like she was pinned under Jondry's knee all the time.

The stranger in the dream had to be Jondry, a dark and twisted version that her mind had conjured. And here, in this place, she would banish him forever.

"Spare a copper, milady?" an urchin's quiet voice came from behind her.

The request was pitched to sound wretched, to play upon her sympathies and make her lower her guard, but Vale knew it for what it really was. She'd seen this ploy a hundred times. A gang would slowly surround a person—someone with wealth, someone out late at night in a place she shouldn't be, someone who'd foolishly walked these streets alone. The thief would offer a plea for help, would distract the mark long enough for his crew to close in.

After that, the mark was robbed or raped or murdered. Sometimes all three.

The thieves of Torlioch had come to work. And by Kelto, Vale knew that voice. She knew this crew. The gods were kind after all. It was as though they were assuring her that she would soon purge her nightmare and leave her helplessness behind.

"Hello, Jondry," Vale said softly. She turned, threw

back her cowl and opened her first Soulblock. Magic crackled through her. Her insides felt like a lightning storm, but none of this would be apparent to him.

He looked just as tall and rawboned as he'd been three years ago when he'd ruthlessly tormented her. He looked puzzled when she spoke his name, and that made her smile. He didn't recognize her.

But then, how could he? Jondry might be the same wiry thief he'd always been, but Vale had transformed. She didn't look like a stick-thin, ragged urchin with grime on her face and hands, a girl who wore piecemeal clothing stolen from laundry lines and rubbish bins. Vale's body had filled out with three years of good nutrition and full nights of sleep. And her clothes were rich by Jondry's standards: russet leather breeches, expensive black boots, a thick traveling cloak, and a bright scarlet silk tunic with silver piping. Her raiment, even scarred and dusty from her travels, cost more than Jondry could scrounge in a month. To him, she must look like a wealthy mark, a traveler too privileged and too stupid to know she'd walked into a trap.

He only hesitated a moment, then smoothly continued the facade, limping a step closer. Limping… Vale had given him that limp. "I…I was just wonderin' if you had a copper to spare, milady."

Vale used her magic and reached out, feeling for the emotions of Jondry's crew, who had to be close by. She found them. The six thieves were hiding in the shadows of the nearby buildings. With her Motus magic, she burrowed inside their bodies and held her ethereal hands over their hearts, but she didn't do anything else…yet.

"I am no mark, Jondry," she said. "It's Vale."

Jondry squinted, not understanding her or not believing her for one breathless instant. Then his eyes went wide as recognition snapped into place and narrowed in anger.

"Vale…" he breathed. He shook his head, and a raspy laugh escaped him. "Kelto must love me, to bring you back to me. That's what it is." He drew a long, straight knife. "Oh, I've dreamed about you. You know, I'll never run again thanks to you. Gonna settle our score, you and I. Gonna do it tonight. Gonna do it right now."

"Oh yes, we are," she whispered lethally.

He drew another dagger—curved and rusty with a wicked hook at the end—a fish-gutting blade. "I'm going to make the rest of your very short life a nightmare."

"You already did," she said, thinking of the stranger, that twisted Jondry doppelganger.

A smug smile spread across Jondry's face, like he was certain she belonged to him now, like he knew the trap had snapped shut, and it was too late for her to escape.

"Hold her," he commanded, his voice whipping into the darkness.

Jondry's crew emerged from their hiding places, lunging forward to grab her.

Vale tightened her grip on each of their hearts at the same time. The crackling lightning of her Soulblock surged through them, causing them all to twitch as though they were suddenly on marionette strings. In a heartbeat, she transformed their emotions; she made them adore her.

They stumbled to a halt, breathing hard, forming a gentle circle around her, and every one of them gazed at her in worship.

"Get Jondry," she said to them. "Grab him."

The group swept around her like a rushing river and seized Jondry. With a squeak, he tried to fight back, but they disarmed him in seconds. He struggled as they pinned his arms behind his back.

"I want him in the alley," she said, feeling the flush of victory. Finally, she could sleep in peace. She could live her life. She could be happy again.

"Let go, you turds!" Jondry shouted, but they hauled him bodily into the dark.

Vale followed, her open cloak rippling behind her like a queen's cape.

Jondry's initial surprise and outrage vanished. The impossibility that somehow his gang had turned against him had become a cold, shocking reality, and it exposed his naked fear. "Let me go! Are you crazy? What are you doing?" he said.

His crew said nothing, of course. Vale didn't want them to say anything, and they'd do whatever she wanted.

She closed in. Now she was the predator.

"You hunted me," she said in a low voice. "You hurt me. You made me feel helpless."

"You stabbed my leg!" he shouted as though that was some kind of defense.

"You made my life a nightmare, Jondry. I thought I'd escaped this place, escaped you. But just knowing you're out here has dragged me backwards. It's made me feel like that helpless girl I was. You burrowed your way into my nightmares, and I'm going to cut you out like a bit of rot."

She saw the whites around his eyes. "No! I wanted you on my crew, Vale, that was all. Would'a made both our lives better. That scuffle between us…it was just a tussle. I didn't mean to hurt you. Why would I? We have to look out for one another!" He was babbling now. "I mean, we're the same, you and I, right?"

"I'm nothing like you," she breathed.

"Gods, Vale, you got your revenge!" he squealed. "I

can't even walk right anymore."

"You won't even limp away this time."

He struggled vainly against the six boys who held him. "Vale, no!"

She let all of her rage flow into his crew, and they began to beat him. He cried out as the strikes fell hard and merciless.

But with each hit, Vale saw Brom's face, not Jondry's. It was Brom's face that got slammed to the side. Every time Jondry cried out, pleaded with her to stop them, she saw Brom reaching out to her, begging for help.

"Help me! We can beat them. Together!"

A sob caught in her throat.

"Stop…" she whispered, and she pulled her magic from Jondry's thugs. "Stop it."

The boys sagged, some of them falling to their knees, each of them looking bewildered. Jondry, blood on his chin, half of his face swelling already, looked up at her in sheer terror through his one good eye.

Why…why was she seeing Brom in Jondry's face? Brom was dead. He'd been gone almost a year now. Why had each strike upon Jondry felt like a strike upon Brom?

"Gods, I'm wrong," she breathed. "It's not you." Jondry wasn't the cause of the nightmare. He didn't have anything to do with it.

She turned with a flare of her cloak and ran into the night, leaving Jondry and his crew behind.

2

VALE

With her certainty in ruins, Vale fled the city, leapt upon her mare and galloped into the dark. She filled her mount with Motus magic, using her own emotions—confusion, anger, despair—to make the horse tireless. For three days, she rode hard and she did not stop.

The sun was setting on the third day as the Hallowed Woods hove into view. By the time she pulled her exhausted mount to a stop at the forest's edge, the orange light of day's end bathed the scaly green bark and purple-and-silver leaves of the fabled Lyantrees.

Their shapes varied wildly from one tree to another, as if the Lyantrees were each as individual as people. Some were long and tall like spears. Some were squat and twisted with burly roots breaking above the ground all around them.

She led her horse into the forest, searching for a good place to camp. Her eyes were blurry from fatigue, but she had done this time and again. Within moments, she came to a clearing by a stream and went through the well-ingrained motions of setting up camp. She removed the bridle, saddle, and saddle bags from her horse and turned her loose to find her own dinner. Vale knew her mare would roam, looking for juicy patches of grass, but she wouldn't leave. They'd spent months together and each had their routine when it came time to rest. Vale filled the water skins from the river, made a ring for a fire, and gathered enough wood for at least one night.

Once she had the wood stacked next to the fire ring, with her flint and steel perched neatly on one of the rocks, she stared unseeing at the ground. She knew she should pull her pot from the saddlebags, knew she should make dinner. She had barely eaten for three days, and she hadn't slept at all.

But instead of continuing her well-worn routine, she knelt at the base of the nearest Lyantree, looked up at the orange light filtering through the purple and silver leaves and wondered: *Am I going mad?*

She'd been sure Jondry was the reason for the nightmare, but he wasn't. And she'd seen Brom instead. Brom's face in place of Jondry's.

Was Brom... Was what she'd done to him the reason the nightmare had come?

In the nightmare, she and the stranger were lovers. She wanted him. She was eager at his approach just as she'd been eager for Brom at the academy. As the stranger neared, his mouth always quirked into a mischievous smile that ignited her desire. His hungry gaze devoured her, and she luxuriated in it.

Then the handsome stranger slowly reached up, took his jaw in his hand, and pulled it off his face. Vale's desire vanished as the stranger's eyes turned cruel, and little green flames flickered up from the edges of his eyelids. His gaping maw came closer with its exposed upper row of teeth—

And she would wake up screaming.

Vale twitched her head. Her hand gripped the scaly bark of the Lyantree like a claw. Her heart pounded. It couldn't be Brom. The stranger looked nothing like Brom. The man in the dream was…nobody. She didn't know him. And no matter how hard she searched her memory, she could find no recollection.

But who else could this torturer be, returned to haunt her for what she'd done?

She'd tried to banish that thought during her three-day ride, tried to tell herself Brom didn't matter. She didn't need her Quad anymore, didn't need those so-called friends. She didn't need to follow the rules of the Champions Academy. She'd taken the Test of Separation. She'd survived. Her power belonged to her and her alone.

But day after day as her horse had pounded south toward the Hallowed Woods, she had continued to see that moment during the Test. Brom reaching out to her from just beyond the mirror portal, begging for help as he was attacked.

"Help me! We can beat them. Together!"

And she'd turned away. She'd left him to die.

Another memory returned to her then, from just before the Test. They'd been in Brom's dorm room, and it was the last time Vale could remember being happy. That had been another time he'd reached out to her, gently. He'd said he loved her, and she'd turned away from him that time, too. She'd said love wasn't real. She'd made a hasty retreat out the snow-swept window, left him sitting on his bed with a mournful look and a broken heart.

She shook her head, trying to dislodge the memory.

She'd lied, of course. Lied to show him he was using a crutch. Love was real, but it was a weakness. It could only hold you back.

The last person Vale had allowed herself to love was her mother, and it had almost cost Vale her life. She had stayed too long sobbing over the body, and she'd barely escaped Jondry.

Since that moment, she had only ever wanted one thing: the power to protect herself, to stave off starvation, to be free from the predators who might devour her. She'd wanted that so much she could taste it like blood in her mouth. Once she had that power, she could be safe. She could be happy.

Now she had what she'd always wanted. She stood above *normals*. She'd never be that helpless little girl again, never have to fear a person like Jondry...

But the happiness she had expected never followed. Day after day, all she could think about was how much she hated her life. She hated the peace and quiet of this forest. She hated the clamor of a bustling town. She hated being with people and she hated being alone. She hated the thought of sleeping, and she despaired when she was awake.

Had she made a wrong turn when she'd left Brom to die? Was she to blame for her own misery? Had she conjured this twisted incarnation of Brom to torture herself?

I betrayed him... she thought. *But I couldn't have done anything else, could I? Brom wasn't my responsibility. We all knew the risks of the Test. We'd all been prepared to die. It was him or me, and Brom had simply drawn the short straw...*

Except *she* had drawn the short straw. She'd failed her Test. She'd been trapped in a cone of green fire that slowly sucked her magic from her. Her life had been ebbing away and she hadn't been able to get out. That had been the end. In moments, she wouldn't have known nor cared that she'd failed her Test. She simply would have been dead. But Brom had pushed her out of that green cone of flame. He'd taken her place.

Guilt flooded through her, and she keened.

"Was I wrong?" she asked the impassive forest. "Gods help me, was I wrong? Should I have died there?"

She sobbed against the Lyantree. Sunset became twilight, and she cried. Twilight turned dark, and still she cried. Finally, the tears stopped and exhaustion pressed down on her like a mountain.

"I'm sorry," she murmured, and she finally made the mistake of closing her eyes. Sleep rushed in like water, and the nightmare fell upon her instantly.

She was in a dark room sitting on a bed with soft sheets, and the handsome stranger emerged from the darkness. As always, she forgot he was her enemy, forgot this would end with her screaming.

Her heart fluttered in anticipation and she drew a happy breath as the man smiled at her. She waited eagerly for him, naked, ready. She wanted this.

He reached the bed and turned his emerald gaze down upon her. He was so beautiful. She felt like her fondest dreams were about to come true.

Then he reached up and plucked out his jaw, exposing his upper row of teeth. His eyes turned malicious, green flames flickering up from the corners.

Only now did Vale's memory of every other nightmare return in a rush. She scrambled to get off the bed, to flee, but the stranger caught her, pushed her down, and she screamed.

This was always when her terror jolted her awake. But

she didn't let it this time. She fought to stay in the nightmare. If this was her punishment for betraying Brom, she would face it.

She fought the stranger, but her arms seemed filled with clay. They moved lethargically compared to the stranger's swift, powerful attack.

He held her down with one hand and began to beat her. She twisted, casting about for a weapon, but couldn't find one.

Then she slipped his grip and won free. She rolled off the bed, slapped her feet on the floor. For one instant, she had hope. She saw the outline of a door in the dark, and she leapt toward it—

Crackles of fear struck her like lightning, and she stumbled. The stranger grabbed a fistful of her hair and threw her to the flagstone floor. He leapt on her, clenching her neck with an iron hand. Slowly, chuckling grotesquely through his jawless face, he pulled a silken cord from the pouch at his side. Vale's fear crackled so painfully she thought her heart would burst.

He hit her, harder this time, and she fell limply against the stones. Stars danced in her vision, and for a moment she couldn't move. As she regained her senses, she realized he'd looped one end of the cord around her wrist. Gods no! She couldn't let him bind her!

With a snarl, she lifted one lethargic leg and tried to kick him. She missed.

With that huffing, horrible chuckle, he hit her again. Her head smacked into the stones. Through half-lidded eyes, she saw him bind her other wrist, then her ankles.

When she was trussed up on the floor, he stood, surveying her with that vicious, glimmering gaze. With deliberate slowness, he reached down, retrieved his jaw, and put it back on. The skin molded together seamlessly and made it look as though this monster was human again.

She cried, hating the crackling fear that filled her, hating her vulnerability.

"Anything I want," the man said, "I can do to you."

She screamed defiance at him, but he reached down and slapped her across the face.

"Anything..." he whispered in her ear.

The monster flipped her over and he beat her again. The flame from his green eyes flickered across her cheek and neck as he whispered into her ear so softly it sounded like a prayer. She couldn't understand the words at first, but soon they became clear.

"You are helpless, Vale. You always were. Just a little girl. A weak little girl."

With every prayer the monster whispered, fear crackled through her like lightning.

Like lightning...

Like the magic of a Soulblock.

He whispered again, beat her again. And each time, he told her she was helpless. Each time he slapped her, she felt the lightning. She felt him driving fear into her...

...like Motus magic.

Finally, he was done torturing her. He rose and left her alone in the dark room like discarded garbage. She shivered on the cold flagstones, bleeding, fighting the fear.

The nightmare faded. The cold stone room dissolved away.

Vale jerked awake, opening her eyes to find she was still in the dark and quiet Hallowed Woods. She lay curled in the hollow of the Lyantree's enormous roots, and her clothes were soaked with sweat.

Shards of images came together in her mind, not quite

making a full picture. The stranger had used a heart-spike on her. He'd used Motus magic. She knew that spell. And she…remembered…

"Gods…" she whispered. This wasn't some twisted nightmare of Brom. This wasn't a nightmare at all.

It was a memory.

The moment that realization came clear, a compulsion tightened around her mind like a fist, trying to crack the memory apart, to make her forget what she'd just remembered. The compulsion was so immediate, so powerful that it almost worked, almost erased her hard-won knowledge.

But she clenched her teeth and fought it, scrambling and clasping the memory shards, trying to find one name—the stranger's name. It poised on the tip of her tongue, teetering there.

"Arsinoe…" she hissed, and it was like pushing a whole apple up and out of her throat.

The irresistible compulsion failed, and she gasped. More memory shards flew together in her mind, and she assembled them, forming the whole picture.

The cruel, green-eyed stranger was Arsinoe, the Motus of The Four!

"You…" she breathed.

Arsinoe had tortured her in real life. He had tied her up and beaten her. He'd burrowed into her emotions, dredged up her deepest fears and wiped her face with them. Over and over again.

And even worse…someone had made her forget the whole thing. Someone was *still* trying. And if the Motus of The Four had tortured her, it was a sure bet their Mentis, Olivaard, was making her forget.

A chill swept through her.

What else has been stolen? she suddenly wondered. *What*

else am I not remembering?

And if two of The Four had ensorcelled Vale, why not the others as well? What had Linza taken, parts of Vale's soul? Was Anima magic the reason Vale could no longer find any joy in life?

And what had Wulfric stolen?

She checked the urge to frantically pat her body to see if she was missing a toe. A finger. Something physical that her mind had forced her to overlook.

She got hold of those wild thoughts, clenched her fists in her lap, and tried to slow her hammering heart. She forced herself to think, to bring these horrors into the light so she could face them directly.

The Four used me, she thought. *They stripped me, abused me, befouled me and tossed me away like shit from a chamber pot....*

And when The Four discovered she'd unmasked them, they would wipe her memory again. They might know even now.

Her fear threatened to overwhelm her, but she poured boiling rage over it. No. She was not the helpless little girl Arsinoe wanted her to be. No amount of binding and beating would cow her. She wasn't going to give him what he wanted. She was going to give him a dagger in the throat instead.

Vale became deadly calm. This wasn't a mystery anymore, some soul-leeching nightmare she had conjured herself. This was an attack. And now she knew who the enemy was. The Four were living, breathing beings who could be made to suffer.

"I see you now," she growled into the night. "And you're going to die for what you've done."

3

VALE

Vale couldn't sleep for the rest of that night. She reeled with the implications, turning them over and over until morning light filtered through the purple leaves of the Lyantrees.

The Four had tortured her and they'd gotten away with it by making her forget. If they had removed memories from her mind, controlling what she remembered, why not also implant suggestions and control what she did?

Gods, she'd been traveling all over Keltovar this past year at their bidding, and she couldn't remember ever agreeing to do it. She'd simply...done it. Like it was the most natural thing in the world. The more she thought about that, the more she was certain her desire to please them was an unseen command given by Olivaard.

As she realized that, she could see the chain of events that had led to it, and she didn't think for a second any of those events were accidental. She thought of the Quadron who had plucked her out of Torlioch at her most desperate hour, given her a chance that only a fool would refuse, made her want to attend the academy at all costs. Then they'd forced her into a Quad with three others who were as unlike Vale as it was possible to be, letting them fight one another, tear at each other. And then, of course, the Test…

As she looked at The Four with her newly clear vision, she catalogued all of these memories. The Champions Academy didn't exist to train Quads. It existed to slice them apart. The Test of Separation wasn't meant to weed out weak students. It was meant to make weak Quadrons, to strip a Quad of its real power: the magical multiplying that came from union with one's Quad mates. It wasn't a trial by fire to bring Quadrons to their full potential. It was to ensure no Quad ever challenged the dominance of The Four.

Gods, it was so obvious! And the fact that no one had ever seen this before smacked of more mental manipulation. There had to be some spell shading the minds of every student when they arrived, making them overlook the glaring fact that the Champions Academy had never produced a single intact Quad—only Quadrons who, while far more powerful than a *normal*, were diminutive reflections of The Four and who lived to serve them.

But to maintain their spell from such a distance, she thought. *To control me as I traveled all over Keltovar, they'd have to do something to bolster that magic. They'd have to have given me some talisman that carried the spell within it to ensure their control was never broken…*

Vale's train of thought stopped dead. She swallowed heavily and looked down at the Champions Academy amulet on her chest, the mark of her graduation, the *talisman* that showed she was a Quadron.

She stared at the amulet and felt the ever-present magic crackling inside it, a magic that had always made her feel powerful, reminded her that she was a Quadron in a world of *normals*. It had represented everything she had ever wanted.

Now the copper chain felt like cockroaches crawling across her neck. She clenched it in her fist, ready to rip it off—

And stopped.

No. She couldn't do that. The Four were not stupid. If Vale took off the amulet, they would know. Of course they would. Of all the spells woven into this insidious thing, one of them had to be an alarm—something to alert its masters, who would teleport from their tower and attack Vale right here, right now.

The Four weren't street thieves like Jondry and his crew. She couldn't just kill them. They were the most powerful Quadrons in a hundred years. They'd overwhelm her. They'd steal her memory again, reduce her to a good little slave once more.

She had to be smarter than that. She couldn't afford to throw a tantrum for the horrible things they'd done. She had to ensure that when she threw off their slave's collar, they could never, ever be able to put it on her again.

With stiff fingers, she released the amulet. It thumped against her chest like an anchor.

Vale's paranoia blossomed as the sickening possibilities opened up before her. She, Oriana, and Royal had all received their Quadron's amulets after their Test. Oriana's was a white owl, Royal's a blue bear. Vale's was the icon of the Motus, a circular disk with a stylized dragon. It was wrought in such exquisite detail that the dragon seemed ready to stretch its miniature wings and fly away.

Every graduate of the Champions Academy had one of these. This… This was how they were controlling her—and probably every other Quadron in the lands.

Gods! Vale's former Quad mates were arguably the two most powerful people in all the lands. If The Four controlled Royal and Oriana, they could secretly be running everything.

Royal was now known as the Butcher of Gore Grove, the scourge of every Keltovari soldier in the kingdom. He was reviled and feared like some great monster from legend. Of course, in Fendir that made him a hero. They called him the Oaken Knight and said—if one believed Fendiran poets—that he'd single-handedly turned the tide of the war against Keltovar.

Royal had more influence than any man in Fendir now. If The Four were controlling him, the kingdom of Fendir would pivot at their whim.

And Oriana was the absolute ruler of Keltovar. She had ascended the throne half a year ago when her father had died. The Fendirans had painted her with the title "The Ice Queen" to remind their warrior druids how ruthless and inhuman she was. Intended as an insult, Keltovar had nevertheless embraced the title. They loved the strength of their Quadron Ice Queen. They would do anything for her.

Vale leaned against the magical Lyantree, fighting a sense of despair. How did one fight The Four? The more she thought on it, the more she realized how masterfully they had put the two kingdoms into the palms of their own hands and fortified their position. Defeating them seemed impossible.

She felt the tiny crackle of magic in the amulet against her chest, now hyper-sensitive to it. At the same time, she felt a tiny crackle within the Lyantree under her palm, as though it were responding. The magic of the tree was barely perceptible, but Vale had felt it before. Everyone in the two kingdoms knew the Lyantrees had magical properties. That was nothing new.

But this time, in the midst of Vale's despair, it sparked an idea. She blinked, turned toward the tree, and focused her attention on that little spark of magic within it.

Her mind began to race.

Lyantrees could be harvested to make weapons. It was why The Four had sent her here. She was to give a report of the war and how many Lyantrees were threatened by it. She was also to catalogue how many Lyantrees the Keltovari had harvested for their weapons.

The Hallowed Woods were sacred to the Fendirans, which was why they fought the Keltovari, who refused to surrender the forest because of the magical weapons to be gained.

Vale dredged up everything she could remember about the Lyantrees. She'd heard that the Keltovari could only make a single weapon from a single tree, and that the process often failed, producing no weapon at all. She remembered something about how the wood hardened, how it could be carved and shaped like normal wood right after harvesting, but when it dried, it became harder than steel, unbreakable. Sharpened properly at the time of creation, a Lyantree sword would hold its edge forever.

Vale moved her hands to the Lyantree's exposed roots and a plan began to form. As a Quadron, she could make a more powerful weapon than a *normal*. The question was: could she make a weapon powerful enough to kill The Four?

Under Oriana's expert tutelage, Vale had learned about the power of research. It could take painstaking hours—

even days—of shuffling through tome after tome to find a single kernel of wisdom. But sometimes that wisdom could be the difference between life and death.

Oriana had also taught Vale that great successes were built upon many failures, so it was best to get started methodically compiling those failures as soon as possible. Vale had to research the Lyantrees before she harvested one and tried to make her first weapon.

She reached deep inside the tree like she would reach into a person, letting her crackling magic seek its center— if it even had a center.

Finding and manipulating emotions was the easiest task for a Motus, so she'd start there first. She looked for human emotion in the tree, mostly to mark it off the list and move on. She didn't think she'd actually find any, of course. Human emotions were uniquely human. A Lyantree couldn't have such things any more than a rock could, so she anticipated beginning her stack of failures now. She would shape her knowledge of the Lyantrees through such experiments, which would eventually lead to success.

She sank into the Lyantree, deeper and deeper…

And gasped as a torrent of human-like emotions coursed into her.

4

VALE

Vale twitched her head, blinking, coming out of her hundredth communion with the Lyantree. It had been days since her initial startling discovery: Lyantrees had emotions every bit as complicated as a human's. The Lyantrees were sentient.

But after frustrating days and sleepless nights, she still couldn't communicate with them.

Her vision swam and her eyes burned with fatigue. She couldn't remember the last time she'd eaten. Her small pack of food had run out days ago, and her stomach had shriveled into a hard little knot in the center of her belly.

But she couldn't waste time foraging, hunting. She couldn't waste a single second. Since the academy, The Four had checked in with her by mental communication every week. They'd contacted her when she'd galloped along the Keltovari coast. They'd contacted her when she'd wandered the snowy mountains of the north.

They'd contacted her as she rode south toward Torlioch.

And this week's check-in was long overdue.

She expected that telltale tingling at the base of her skull every time she turned around, that tingling that hailed Olivaard's mental outreach.

Before now, she'd always looked forward to it, a good little dog waiting for her pat on the head.

But if Olivaard slithered into her mind this time, he'd know she loathed them, that she planned to destroy them. Her rage at Arsinoe—at all of them—would be obvious. He would know she had spent every moment of these past days desperately seeking a way to destroy them.

And they'd know she had found it.

The key to killing The Four wasn't a magical sword or axe. It wasn't harvesting the dead Lyantrees for a weapon at all. It was Soulblocks. The Lyantrees had Soulblocks within themselves, brimming over with magic.

That was the stunning revelation. Dividing one's soul into Soulblocks required intelligence. It required the most intentional and concentrated effort. It was why animals couldn't use magic and people could.

She didn't know what shocked her more: that the Lyantrees had Soulblocks, or that nobody seemed to know this. No one at the academy—masters, instructors, or students—had ever mentioned that Lyantrees were sentient creatures.

No one in the long history of the two kingdoms had ever tried to communicate with them as far as Vale knew.

Generations of Fendirans and Keltovar had warred in this forest, blithely unaware that they were fighting amongst "villages" of Lyantrees. The Keltovari harvested them, and if the Lyantrees had the ability to form Soulblocks from their souls, they surely had the awareness to know they were being killed. Cutting down a

Lyantree to make an enchanted sword was like hacking up a Quadron to use their arm as a club. Such a weapon was only a tiny fraction of the true power within.

If she could just communicate with the trees, she might have all the power she would ever need to destroy The Four.

The reason The Four were invincible wasn't their age or experience. It was because they were an intact Quad. When in close proximity, a united Quad doubled each Quad mate's number of Soulblocks, doubling their magic. In addition, Quad mates could lend Soulblocks to each other. Within an intact Quad, a Quadron could potentially wield twenty-eight Soulblocks. For a short time, she could become a god.

And that was with a link to only *three* other people. There were hundreds of Lyantrees in this forest, maybe thousands, each with four Soulblocks. If Vale could bond with them…

Well, if twenty-eight Soulblocks made a god, what would a hundred do?

But she couldn't get through to the Lyantrees. She had tried everything she'd learned at the academy about bonding with her Quad mates. She had used every bit of Motus magic to reach them. She'd attempted a Mentis' mind link and an Anima's ability to see into the soul, simply based on Oriana's and Brom's descriptions of those paths to magic.

Nothing.

She had even used an exercise Oriana had taught her which enabled her to recall memories that would otherwise have been long forgotten. She recalled every legend she'd ever heard about the Hallowed Woods, pieced together all the old wives' tales she'd ever heard in an effort to uncover something—anything—that might give her a clue.

The most common legends were about Lyancorpses, of course. Everyone had heard at least one story about the root-wrapped, undead corpses that wandered the lands, seeking vengeance on the living. It was said that if someone died in the Hallowed Woods, they became a Lyancorpse.

Vale's mother had also told her a story about a little girl who'd walked into the Hallowed Woods one day and emerged a year later with no knowledge that any time had passed. She'd neither aged nor suffered any kind of malnutrition, and she'd talked unceasingly about wondrous dreams and rainbows.

Vale also remembered a story Royal had told her about a Fendiran warrior druid who had become separated from his fellows during a battle. He'd run through the woods seeking to rejoin the fight but couldn't find it. He ran so far that he came to the edge of the forest, except it wasn't the edge of Hallowed Woods anymore. When he'd emerged, he'd somehow come a hundred miles to the northeast, to the uncharted eastern edge of Keltovar.

In her desperation, Vale even studied the physical configuration of the trees. She discovered a pattern in the way they were clustered. They always gathered together in multiples of four, the magic number. Obviously, they were communicating with each other. They had to be, but after days of frustrated attempts, she was no closer to understanding how.

And she was almost out of time. Olivaard would be checking in, probably today. He was already overdue.

"Come on, damn you…" she whispered. She slid to her knees, tears brimming in her eyes, keeping one hand on the scaly bark. She had kept physical contact with one tree or another constantly these past days.

She tried to review what she'd learned, but she was so tired and hungry that her thoughts felt fuzzy. "What is the secret? What am I missing?"

A distant rustle caught her attention, and Vale's head snapped up. She peered into the forest with fatigue-blurred vision. Nothing moved.

The noise came again, somewhere ahead of her, but closer now. Was it The Four?

No, she thought. *The Four wouldn't make some dramatic entrance, rushing through the trees. Olivaard would contact me mind-to-mind.*

Unless they already knew of her transgressions. Unless they knew everything that went through her head all the time. Perhaps they would toy with her like this, pretending to come from the forest, from all around her.

Calm yourself, she thought, and a fleeting smile came to her lips. Oriana used to say *"calm yourself"* to Vale all the time back at the academy, back when they were friends. Back when Vale had friends. She could almost hear the princess's voice in her head right now.

Look with clear eyes, Vale. Make your choices with your mind, not with your panic. Cut through your fears or they will strip you of your reason.

Vale calmed herself. If The Four were here, she would force them to step into the light. She would make her stand. She would die, but at least she would sell her life at a high price.

She slid quietly behind the Lyantree, hiding herself behind the trunk.

The noise grew louder, but no figure emerged. Vale began to realize how highly attuned she'd become to the forest. This rustling had been a long distance off when she'd first heard it.

The noise rose to a cacophony by the time a single

figure emerged between the trees, running desperately.

It was not The Four.

A nimble young man leapt bushes and dodged back and forth like a deer, a look of frightened concentration on his face. He wore only a brief tunic. His skin was darker brown even than a southern Fendiran, and it looked rough like tree bark.

Vale realized the young man also had the nubs of branches growing from his forehead…

He was a Sacinto!

The Sacinto were foreigners who had shown up in the two kingdoms recently, seemingly part tree and part human. No one knew exactly where they'd come from, but most assumed it was from somewhere across the Coral Sea. Vale knew almost nothing about them. Gods, she wouldn't even know what a Sacinto was if not for Oriana.

She would have used Oriana's memory-recall exercises to summon the princess's stories verbatim, but there was no time.

The Sacinto wasn't alone. A half-dozen Keltovari soldiers burst through the foliage behind him, weapons in hand. Each was flush with the hunt, murder glowing in their eyes.

And the Sacinto was their prey.

5

VALE

The soldiers crashed through the undergrowth like bulls, metal armor clanging as they pursued the young Sacinto. They whooped and hollered like it was a game.

Vale narrowed her eyes. She'd heard this same kind of whooping behind her as she'd fled through the streets of Torlioch as a girl. And that look on the Sacinto's face…she knew that as well: the panic of being prey.

There was only one way this kind of game ended.

"Don't let him get away!" gasped a stout Keltovari who lagged behind the group.

"Fan out," said another. "He's slippery. Don't let him duck to the side."

"Nowhere for him to hide now," a third huffed.

A fourth skidded to a stop with a blade pinched between thumb and fingers. He twisted his torso and hurled the dagger at the Sacinto.

It flipped end over end, a flashing blur in the sunlight,

and hit the back of the Sacinto's calf. It sliced and caromed sideways, bouncing to the forest floor.

The slender Sacinto went down with a cry, tumbling to the ground right in front of Vale's hiding place.

"Got him!" the knife-thrower shouted triumphantly.

"Nice throw," the lagging Keltovari huffed.

The Keltovari soldiers quickly encircled their prey, whooping in victory. The frightened Sacinto clutched his leg, looking around in terror.

The preoccupied soldiers converged on him, and they didn't see Vale as she stepped from behind the Lyantree.

"Hello boys," she purred. Her magic crackled through her, ready.

The soldiers looked up, stunned.

"Who are you?" one of them demanded, a tall gruff soldier with a blond beard.

"Where did she come from?" the lagging soldier huffed, finally joining the group. He drew his sword. "She some Fendiran priestess?"

"Wait," said a boyish-looking soldier with no beard. He was obviously the youngest, younger even than Vale, she guessed. "Valto, look at her."

"I'm looking," Valto huffed. "I'm supposed to see something?"

"She don't look like no Fendiran," the boy soldier insisted. "Those clothes. Red and the silver. Gods, Valto, I think she's a Quadron."

Vale's smile widened, and she let the boy's statement take hold of their imaginations. Everyone in the two kingdoms knew what a Quadron was.

And they knew that to cross one was suicide.

There were half a dozen things Vale could have done at that moment. She could have brought their sudden realization to a pointy terror, made them trip over each other in an effort to flee. She could have used the same terror to color her commands so that they would fear defying her.

She could have thrown a glamour over herself, made herself irresistibly attractive so that they would happily—desperately—do anything she asked.

Or she could have used the destructive aspect of the Motus, locking them inside their own petty minds with whatever emotionally charged nightmare she chose, for as long as she chose. The destructive aspect of the Motus was nasty. People under the sway of such an internal fantasy sometimes died of thirst, never raising a hand to take a drink because they didn't realize the dream was false. It was a good way to drive a man insane.

In the end, Vale chose rage. Magic crackled across the distance and sank into the boy's emotions.

"You." Her voice cracked like a whip. "Pick up that dagger."

"Yes miss!" the boy yelped. He jerked forward like he couldn't get to the dagger fast enough and snatched it up.

She looked at the young soldier, then at the dagger thrower. "Stab that man in the leg." She pointed.

"Hey!" the dagger thrower said.

The rest of the soldiers jumped to life. Half threw themselves between the ensorcelled boy and his new target, and the other half ran at Vale, drawing weapons.

"Boys," she said disapprovingly, like a mother to naughty children. She let her magic crackle into all of them, turned their desire to protect their fellows into a vacuum of apathy. "I want you to watch."

Their eyes went wide and vacant. As one, they turned and stared uncaringly at the beardless boy as he stalked the dagger thrower.

The dagger thrower backed away, his hands up in front

of himself. "Korlin, what are you doing? Put that down! Don't listen to her."

"You stay put," Vale commanded. She heightened his fright until it overwhelmed his instincts. He halted, shivering like a rabbit.

The boy named Korlin leapt frantically forward, driven by his fear of what Vale would do to him if he didn't please her. He plunged the blade into the dagger thrower's thigh. The dagger-thrower screamed and fell to his knees.

"Now," Vale said darkly, and she released all of them at once. The dagger-thrower howled. Korlin and the others staggered like drunks after a jug of ale. "Pick up your injured friend and run as fast as you can." She sent a heart-spike into each of them.

The Keltovari soldiers rushed at their injured friend, each of them trying to pick him up at once. As a jumbled cluster, they fled, holding the dagger-thrower on their shoulders.

In moments, the glade was quiet. The only sound was the rustling of leaves overhead and the quiet panting of the Sacinto boy.

When she was sure the soldiers were gone, she turned to the Sacinto and pulled her magic back inside herself. "Are you all right?" she asked gently.

He looked up at her with wonder. There were no pupils and no whites in his eyes, just huge, glistening black orbs.

"*Alari…*" he murmured. He rolled to his knees and prostrated himself. "*Systin vesh, Alari.*"

She knelt next to him, touched his chin with her hand and gently raised his head. He flinched, but held himself still, like he was expecting to be hit.

"I won't hurt you," she said. She had half a mind to

chase the soldiers down and kill them. She couldn't stand the strong who were cruel to the weak. They deserved to have their own cruelty visited upon them a hundred fold.

"Systin vesh, Alari," the Sacinto repeated.

Vale let her magic crackle into the Sacinto, but not as she'd done with the soldiers. A Motus could wreak havoc, to be sure, but she could also soothe. Vale had plenty of practice with the constructive aspect of her power. She'd bolstered Quad Brilliant daily.

With gentle, ethereal fingers, she soothed the Sacinto's emotions. He was surprisingly similar to a human. In seconds, he calmed.

"I'm sorry I don't understand you," she said. "But you are safe here. I won't let anyone hurt you."

"I…" he said hesitantly. "Do speak…the human. A small bit."

She smiled. "Well, good. Then understand that you have nothing to fear from me." She stood up.

"You are…the kind," he said. And he stood up with a simple grace, as though he had been lifted by invisible strings.

"Only to some," she said, thinking of how much horror she wished to visit upon The Four and how much she'd wanted to kill those soldiers. She'd almost commanded that the young soldier slaughter them all. She'd only changed her mind at the last second.

The Sacinto seemed to know what she was thinking, and he flicked a glance in the direction the soldiers had fled. "To kill is…a badness."

"The horrible should be visited by horror," she said.

The Sacinto blinked his big dark eyes as though he didn't know the word *horror*. But he seemed to understand the sentiment. "They are *Salisha,*" he said. "But the…killing?" he said it like a question, as if he wasn't sure he had the right word. "The killing is a…*horror.*" He tried the new word.

"There is always killing," she said. "Better it is them than you, don't you think?"

He glanced down, then back up. "If I come to the killing…" he struggled with the words. "If they are to kill me, I go back to the *aethern*…" He opened one nut-brown palm, indicating the ground. "But if I *do* the killing… The *feyri* does the dying…" He frowned, seeming to search for the word he meant. He pressed a hand to his slender chest, then reached out and pressed his palm against her chest.

She flinched and barely stopped herself from backing away. His touch was gentle, like the flutter of a butterfly's wings.

"*Feyri?*" he asked, and she knew he was asking for the human word.

"The heart," she said softly.

"The heart," he repeated.

She pieced together his meaning and said it aloud. "You return to the earth if you die, but if you kill, your heart dies."

"*Yes, Alari,*" he said happily, confirming she had understood. A big smile spread across his face.

"My heart is already dead," she said. "So I guess I don't have to worry about that."

He cocked his head to the side as though he didn't understand.

"What is your name?" she asked.

He watched her with his huge dark eyes. "If you are calling me, call me Tam. It is my human word."

"Tam…" She smiled. "Very well. My human word is Vale."

"Vale…" he said, as though tasting it. "I know the

word vale. It is *ythra*."

"*Ythra?*" she asked.

"It is a thing that is the thing." He frowned, seeming to realize that he hadn't made sense. He gestured in a circle with both hands. "A thing that comes back to itself." Then he shook his head, frustrated. "No. I do not mean this. It is something else." He tried again. "A vale is where many *lyan* live, yes?" He gestured around, and she realized his word *lyan* was meant to be Lyantree.

"Ah. Okay. I'm Vale in a vale. I see. Yes, a normal vale has many trees," she said.

"Why are you here, *Alari?*" he finally asked, gesturing at the trees. She noticed he didn't use her name, but rather the strange word he'd first called her.

The brief distraction of Tam's arrival leaked away. Her fear and fatigue returned. "Failing," she said.

"Failing," he said, again with that hesitation like he wasn't sure what the word meant. "You are trying, but you are not doing."

"Yes."

"What are you trying?" he asked.

"To talk to the Lyantrees," she said.

He cocked his head, and his wide mouth turned up in a smile again. "You wish to speak to the *lyans*..."

"Yes," she breathed. "But I can't do it."

"No humans wish to speak to the *lyans*. They close their ears. They shut their eyes. They do the killing. The *lyans* have been trying to talk to them for so long, but the humans do not hear."

"What?" Vale said, excitement thrilling through her. "The Lyantrees are *trying* to talk to us?"

"Many times. Many nights and many days. The moons pass over and pass over again, and still the humans will not hear."

"How do you know this? Are you... Can you speak to the Lyantrees?"

"Of course, *Alari*."

"Gods! Can you show me how?"

"Of course, *Alari*. Why are you frightened?"

"Another group of...humans...are coming for me," she said. "To do to me what those soldiers wanted to do to you. I want to stop these humans, but I need to speak to the Lyantrees."

"Then I will show you," Tam said emphatically.

Her hope, all but ashes moments ago, suddenly revived.

Tam took her hand and led her toward the copse of four Lyantrees where she had hidden.

"They will be so happy," Tam said excitedly. He was grinning.

They entered the hollow surrounded by the Lyantrees. He put his hand—warm and light—on hers, and pushed her palm against the scaly bark.

"It is this way," he said. "Your *feyri*. The *feyri* of the *lyans*." He left her hand pressed against the tree, then held his own hands apart, palms facing. "They become together." He pushed his palms together.

"How?"

"It is like this." He closed his eyes. Suddenly, she felt a tug at the center of herself, like he was coaxing the magic out of her. She sent it into him like she had sent it into the Lyantrees time and again. Once she did, it was as though the magic she had pushed into him had become a rope, and he tugged on it, begging her to come deeper.

She followed the sensation, closing her eyes and letting the "tug" pull her along. She dove deep into Tam and she could see colors like rainbow water flowing past her. She had the vague sense she was inside Tam's body, but that she was just passing through.

She flowed through his body, through his arm to where it now touched the Lyantree, and then into the tree itself. The rainbow colors suddenly became everything around her.

She stood in a glade of vibrating Lyantrees, but the world had utterly changed. It had become a landscape of rainbow colors. The sky was a rainbow. The sun itself was a swirling sphere of blues and reds and indigos and yellows and greens. Her mind could barely comprehend what it was seeing, but somehow this riot of colors made sense.

"What is happening?" she asked, but her words made no sound. There was only the…understanding that she'd said something. She gasped, but again the rainbow colors seemed to steal the sound away.

"This is the place," Tam said to her, but his words weren't words. She looked to her right, and he stood there, his body filled with pulsing colors. Somehow, instead of hearing his words, she felt the meaning of them. The sensation was odd and unsettling.

"This is the place the *lyans* made to talk to humans, but almost none have visited," Tam expressed to her, and his language was no longer stilted. It felt similar to how Oriana had talked mind-to-mind with Quad Brilliant.

"This is…amazing," she said.

"They were waiting for you, *Alari*. They have been waiting for so long."

"Show me how to—"

Her thought-speech was cut off abruptly. The rainbow land vanished, and she was jerked backward as though pulled by a rope. She couldn't breathe. The rainbow colors flew past her as she was ripped out of this beautiful land.

With a cry, she was back in her body, back in the normal forest with Tam standing next to her.

Her mind jangled with that telltale tingling. Olivaard was trying to make contact.

With a stab of fear, she tried to shut him out, but it was like trying to slam a door on a bear. Olivaard pushed through and filled her mind.

"Hello Vale," he said. "What do you have to report?"

6

VALE

Vale froze. For an interminable moment, she didn't know what to do.

"*Alari?*" Tam asked, concerned. Of course, he didn't know that Olivaard was in her head, didn't know that the "bad humans" had come.

"*Vale,*" Olivaard asked in her mind. "*Is everything well, my dear?*"

Not knowing what else to do, she began thinking a drinking song she'd once used to keep Oriana from reading her thoughts. She only hoped it would work.

Wiggling Will, he drunk the draught.
And spun his dagger by the haft.
The giggling maidens showed delight.
And spun his dagger through the night.

Wiggling Will, he drunk the draught.

And spun his dagger by the haft.
The giggling maidens showed delight.
And spun his dagger through the night.

"Vale," Olivaard said sternly. *"What are you doing?"*

She pushed down her panic. This wasn't going to work. The second he knew she was blocking him, he was going to stop asking and start taking.

Wet despair spread throughout her body. He was going to take her memories again. He was going to leave her a gutted and submissive slave.

Her gaze fell on the wide-eyed Tam. But it would be worse for the Sacinto. She felt a swift pang of guilt. When The Four came to punish her, they'd kill Tam just for being here, just for being a witness.

She thought of Brom, of how she'd let him die…

Well, maybe Vale was going to die today, but she didn't have to take Tam with her.

Her panicked indecision coalesced into certainty.

"Run," she whispered, hoping that if she whispered, it would somehow be quieter in her mind.

No such luck.

"Who should run, Vale?" Olivaard demanded.

"Alari—"

"Run!" she screamed.

The mind-stab hit her like a dagger of ice to her brain. Her entire body jerked, and she collapsed to her knees.

"Alari," Tam shouted, but his voice seemed far away, like her head had cotton packed around it. Vaguely, she felt Tam's hand on hers, tugging, trying to pull her to her feet.

"Run…" she whispered weakly.

Olivaard dug deeper, sharp fingers clawing into her mind. She shoved her revelation about the Lyantrees as deep as she could and she kept repeating that drinking song over and over.

"Vale..." Olivaard said like an instructor to a misbehaving student. *"I thought we had come to an understanding. What are you hiding?"*

She hummed through gritted teeth, trying to drown out his painful voice. She would have screamed, but it was beyond her. Olivaard's invasion had paralyzed her. Trapped within her own mind, she only vaguely felt her body crumple to the grass.

Vale had kept secrets from a Mentis before. When she and Brom had become lovers at the academy, they had practiced pushing that secret down, away from their surface thoughts where Oriana could pick it up. They'd been successful, and Oriana had never known.

But Oriana had been a friend. Olivaard had no compunctions about ripping apart her mind.

Vale was overmatched and she knew it. So she did the only thing she could think of. She opened her second and third Soulblocks at the same time, flooding her body with magic.

The crackling lightning burned through her, and for a moment her own scream of euphoria drowned out Olivaard's voice. The sheer power made her feel invincible. When she could think again, she realized her thoughts were still filled with his voice.

"That shall not help you," he said.

But it did help. She could feel her body again. She felt the grass pressing against her cheek, her legs draped over a protruding root. She could move her fingers. She could smell the leaves and hear Tam talking to her.

"Alari Alari Alari," the Sacinto repeated, gripping her hand, tugging insistently. She managed to sit up.

Olivaard redoubled his attack and his presence closed

like a fist around her mind, squeezing. She felt an overwhelming compulsion to lie back down and remain there.

"No!" she shouted. She took hold of the storm of magic within her and let her rage light her up. Olivaard's grip slipped. For a blessed moment, he was gone from her mind.

With a gasp, she leapt to her feet. Tam stumbled back.

Gripping her amulet, she started to rip it away…

But a deep resistance stopped her. No… This amulet meant everything, represented all she'd worked so hard to attain.

She released the dragon amulet.

It is vital to my magic, she thought. *If I rip it off, I'll be a normal again…*

Her hand hovered in the air, and a tiny voice—almost silent—spoke in her mind.

It's a lie. He's lying to you.

With a scream, she ripped the horrible thing from her neck and threw it onto the grass.

The moment she lost contact with it, her entire world changed. The bark of the trees became vibrantly green. The sky that peeked through the purple foliage became a deep, rich blue. She gasped, drawing in a breath that seemed to last forever, like she was tasting fresh air for the first time in her life. It was like she'd had a dirty veil hanging in front of her eyes, and it had finally been ripped way.

"Gods…" she murmured.

"We must run, *Alari*," Tam said urgently. "The *lyans* tell us we must run." He tugged her hand.

Vale snapped to action, and together they sprinted through the forest.

A horrible *clang* sounded behind them, evoking terror

in Vale's very bones. She knew that sound. That was the same sound she'd heard when she'd stepped through the mirror in her Test of Separation, right before the terrible cone of green fire had engulfed her and begun eating her soul. It was the sound of teleportation.

The Four had come to the Hallowed Woods.

She sprinted hard, straining to keep up with the fleet-footed Tam. But she knew this chase wouldn't last long. Even without the amulet, Linza could spot Vale's soul at a distance. She'd find Vale. Wulfric was an Impetu. He could run faster than a horse at full gallop. He'd catch her.

They had only seconds, then Vale would have to make a stand.

"Come, *Alari*. We are almost there," Tam said, still pulling her forward.

Vale's focus snapped back to Tam. "Almost where?" she huffed.

Tam's only answer was to lean his head forward, and she saw where he was going. It was another cluster of Lyantrees—eight of them this time—growing in a perfect circle. They always grew in fours, and those fours were usually in subtle circles, with brush and other trees obscuring what might have otherwise been obvious. But there was nothing subtle about this circle. The ground was clear all around it, and the pattern was perfect and unmistakable.

"What is that?" she asked between gasps.

Tam seemed to be done talking. He pulled her toward them, and she heard a crashing behind them like a bear tearing its way through the woods.

Wulfric.

She concentrated on making her burning legs move faster.

"She is here!" Wulfric roared from right behind her. Vale twisted, looking back. Gods, he was practically on top of them! His iron armor, rusted and pitted with corruption, covered every part of his thick body like a second skin, and his limbs moved nightmarishly fast.

The ironclad Impetu lunged at her, and Vale didn't see the tangle of Lyantree roots in front of her until it was too late. Her foot caught. She shouted as she tripped, tumbling across the threshold of the Lyantree circle.

"Alari!" Tam shouted.

"I have her," Wulfric boomed, presumably to the rest of The Four, somewhere in the woods behind him. He pulled his sword from its scabbard and chopped down through the air. The blade was huge—as long as Wulfric was tall, wide as a hand, and pitted with corruption.

He snarled at Vale. "You will never run again." The sword slashed down at her ankle.

Rainbow sparks floated all around her, lighting the air.

"Alaaaaaaaaarrrriiiii…" Tam's cry stretched thin, and time seemed to slow. The rainbow sparks swelled larger into spheres the size of apples, then larger and larger.

Wulfric's blade slowed, descending toward her leg, but it was like he was pushing through invisible mud. Vale couldn't seem to move either, couldn't yank her foot out of the way. All she could do was watch as the blade moved inexorably toward flesh and bone. The rainbow spheres swelled large enough to touch each other just as the blade touched Vale's ankle.

Rainbow lights engulfed her, and Wulfric and the Hallowed Woods vanished.

7

OLIVAARD

Olivaard strode through the forest, his steps slow and careful, but he seethed inside. Linza padded gracefully ahead like a skinny jungle cat draped in a black sheet. Even further ahead, Wulfric crashed through the trees after Vale.

Lagging behind Olivaard, Arsinoe sauntered lazily, as if this were a summer stroll. "So she remembered again," he said in his annoyingly cavalier tone.

Olivaard didn't reply.

"Is that *supposed* to happen?" he continued mercilessly. "When you wipe someone's memory? Does it just come back after a week or two?"

Linza stopped at a cluster of Lyantrees. "It's here," she said in her creaky voice, kneeling gracefully and snatching up Vale's amulet with its broken chain. She passed it to Olivaard.

"So," Olivaard said. "She has slipped her noose." She

should not have been able to remove the amulet. How was the little rat doing these things?

"She is here," Wulfric growled into their minds. They could also hear his muffled voice roaring from up ahead. He had no need to speak aloud when they were mind-linked, but he almost always did anyway. Sometimes, Olivaard's Quad mates were idiots.

"A momentary setback," Olivaard said into their minds. *"She will be in hand in a moment."*

"So?" Arsinoe said, also ignoring the mind link. "What are you going to do? Mind-wipe her again? Because that worked so well the last…" He counted off his fingers. "Three times now. And wasn't Linza supposed to suppress that vivacious soul of hers?" He winked at Linza. "Well done."

Linza hissed.

"Come now, dear sister. An Anima is supposed to look at the truth of things, so let's be honest. You suppressed her soul. She found it again. Olivaard wiped her memory. She brought it back. I even quashed her wild emotions, but she lit them on fire again. She's just a little bonfire of rage, isn't she?"

"Enough," Olivaard said aloud.

But Arsinoe continued blithely. "Wulfric believes we should have killed Quad Brilliant before they even graduated. All of them. I'm beginning to think he was right."

"Wulfric believes we should kill everyone in the two kingdoms," Olivaard said.

Arsinoe laughed. "My point is: Your theory about keeping the powerful ones alive seems to be…how should I put it? Bullshit. It seems to be bullshit. Are you overmatched by this little urchin?"

Olivaard clenched his teeth. He couldn't refute the

observation. Even Olivaard's excitement at Vale's power had waned these past months. The point of letting the powerful Quadrons leave the academy alive was to yoke their strength, to put them to work. But Vale had cost them more time and effort than she had saved them this past year. She was easily more work than all the other Quadrons combined. Arsinoe might be right.

If they couldn't control her... Well, what was the point of having a hound when it kept gnawing through the leash? This was the third time Vale had reclaimed memories Olivaard had locked away. Each time, he'd buried them deeper. She shouldn't have been able to restore them. Yet each time, she had.

"I have her," Wulfric said. Again, his distant, unintelligible roar reached their ears even as his growling voice filled their heads.

"Yes, we have done a poor job of checking Vale's rebelliousness, but this mess is your fault," Olivaard said evenly, keeping his temper.

Arsinoe had been furious for weeks after Quad Brilliant's upstart Anima had destroyed him in battle. The Motus had seethed because he couldn't bring Brom back to life and kill him again just for the satisfaction. Arsinoe had even wanted to desecrate Brom's body, pull it limb from limb, and Olivaard had been forced to stop him. The secrets of the academy had to stay secret, and it would be difficult to explain such a defilement. So Olivaard had given Vale to Arsinoe to play with on the condition that he leave her alive.

"You took out your frustration on her," Olivaard continued. "A product of your infantile need to salve your wounded pride."

"It was just a bit of fun," Arsinoe said, seemingly unfazed.

"You went too far," Olivaard said.

"Please. We've done worse to others and never had a problem erasing their memories. So I repeat: Are you overmatched?"

"Shut up, Arsinoe," Olivaard finally said.

Wulfric's roar of frustration cut off their banter, and Olivaard's heart sank. Linza flew forward, her feet barely touching the ground as she vanished into the trees, black robes flapping around her.

"That doesn't sound good," Arsinoe said, and even he started jogging. Olivaard strode after them awkwardly. Physical exertion was not his strength.

He reached the glade and found Wulfric in a rage, hacking wildly at one of eight Lyantrees with his sword. Arsinoe gave Wulfric a wide berth, watching with raised eyebrows as Linza—also at a safe distance—whispered softly to the big man. But her whispers seemed to have no effect.

Olivaard saw what had happened in an instant, and he saw the horrifying implications.

"Wulfric, stop!" he commanded, but Wulfric didn't listen. The idiot had killed the tree! He'd cut halfway through it. Olivaard gave the behemoth a tiny mind-stab.

That got his attention.

Wulfric's body jolted and he dropped his sword. He turned, his eyes glowing green through the tiny slits of his square helmet. That murderous gaze fell on Olivaard, and Wulfric crouched, ready to attack. For a moment, Olivaard thought he'd have to fell the big Impetu with a real mind-stab. But Wulfric mastered himself and quivered, fists clenched.

"She teleported!" he raged. "She can't do that! How can she do that?"

Wulfric's words confirmed Olivaard's fears.

Teleportation was one of the most difficult spells a Quad could perform, requiring years of study and the highest level of magic. Without a teleportation artifact, it required a full—and exceptionally powerful—Quad working simultaneously with all four paths of magic to transport the physical, mental, emotional, and spiritual parts of a person from one place to another. It also required at least six Soulblocks. Even if Vale had somehow acquired the knowledge to teleport, she didn't have enough Soulblocks to effect the spell. There was simply no way she could have done this alone...

Which suggested the only possible answer, and a foreboding spread across Olivaard's scalp like warm oil.

"What is going on here?" Linza creaked.

"She's opened the Soulblocks within the Lyantrees," Olivaard murmured, stepping past Wulfric to touch the Lyantree he'd hacked through. Purple sap dripped sluggishly down the trunk. With a groan, the Lyantree swayed. It gave a great cracking sound, shuddered, and toppled. Arsinoe lithely stepped to the side as the tree crashed to the ground.

"Idiot," Olivaard cursed at Wulfric.

"What?" he snapped.

"We might have been able to reconstruct the portal if the circle had been intact. Now you've made that impossible."

Wulfric swore. "I'll kill her—!"

"Except you won't," Arsinoe interrupted, "is what Olivaard is saying. Your tantrum has shut the door."

Wulfric rounded on Arsinoe. "You—"

"Enough." Olivaard cut them off. "Stop bickering and think. We have a larger problem now than one rogue Quadron."

"If she can access the Soulblocks within the Lyantrees

to teleport…" Linza caught on. "What else might she do?"

The repercussions now hit the rest of Olivaard's slow-witted Quad mates, and they fell silent.

"Yes." Olivaard nodded. No one in the two kingdoms knew about the Soulblocks housed within the Lyantrees, and no one was supposed to. It was one of The Four's most closely kept secrets. The power within the Lyantrees could turn one Quadron into a match for a full Quad. Possibly even a match for The Four.

"How could she know?" Arsinoe echoed Olivaard's thoughts. "How could she…" He trailed off, finally at a loss for words.

"Something is happening here," Linza whispered prophetically.

"Stop that," Olivaard said. Linza liked to turn everything into some mysterious, preordained destiny. "We have a clever girl. That is all. She's made an unlikely discovery."

"Which could kill us," Linza said.

"Then we kill her first!" Wulfric said.

Arsinoe rolled his eyes. "She's not here, thick-wit. You can't kill someone you can't find."

"Then we find her," Olivaard snapped, his temper flaring at their constant bickering.

"And we kill her," Wulfric growled.

"Yes," Linza hissed.

"By the gods," Olivaard agreed through gritted teeth. "This time we kill her."

8

VALE

The rainbow light swirled past Vale, then settled like a multi-colored blanket onto the landscape. The shapes of Lyantrees slowly poked up. They grew everywhere, and the ground was flat with no indication of grass or the knee-high shrubs that marked the Hallowed Woods.

Rainbow roots protruded from the ground at the base of the trees, and the multi-colored sky swirled overhead. There was no rustling of wind through the leaves, no chirping of birds in the distance, no squirrels scuttling from limb to limb. There was no sound at all. There seemed to be nothing else alive here except the Lyantrees, Tam, and Vale.

When Tam had taken her to this place before, it had only been in her mind—her...magical awareness. She'd only glimpsed this rainbow land. But now, somehow, she was physically here. She felt her feet touching the flat rainbow ground. She felt the air drawing into her lungs, and each breath seemed to fill her with hope.

"Gods..." she breathed. *"Where are we?"* Again, there was no sound, but she knew her words, or at least their meaning, were reaching Tam.

"This way, Alari." He replied in that odd mind-to-mind voice that wasn't quite the same as a mind link. He tugged her arm. She stumbled along behind him. *"The lyans are calling."*

"But I want... I want to see this." The rainbow lights pulled at her. Her thoughts stilled in wonder. This place felt...safe. It was perhaps the only place she'd ever been that felt completely safe. *"We should stay here,"* she said. *"We have to explore."*

"No, Alari."

"I want to stay forever..." she murmured.

He shot a worried look at her, squinting like he was trying to shut out the rainbow colors. He pulled harder on her arm. *"No, Alari. There is great danger here."*

Despite his warning, she felt no urgency. How could this place possibly be bad? *"I...love it, Tam."*

"It will take you if you let it, Alari. It will take you until there is nothing left of you," he said, still squinting his eyes. *"But the lyans will help you, if you listen. So do not look. Listen."*

Except there was no sound. She strained her ears, but still couldn't hear anything.

"Follow me, Alari. Focus on me."

Reluctantly, she tore her gaze away from the rainbow lights and focused on Tam's back, which was the only thing besides herself that wasn't swirling in rainbow hues. It steadied her, and only then did a tiny sliver of fear push its way into her heart. Her desire to lose herself in those colors... That wasn't her, that was...some outside force, some seductive magic coming from the Lyantrees.

"Do not look, Alari," Tam repeated. *"Listen."*

She shut her eyes, trusting Tam. He ran on, tugging her left, then tugging her right, as though he were following some distant music. She strained to hear it, but couldn't.

Finally, he shook her arm and pointed. *"There,"* he said.

She opened her eyes. Ahead stood another ring of trees, more than she could count at a glance. They swirled with that rainbow light, and once again she felt the need to cast away Tam's hand and rush forward, to dance among them. It was so…compelling.

Tam's tug jolted her, and she shut her eyes again.

He continued on with Vale in tow, and she began to hear a chorus of high female voices. They sang in words Vale felt she should know. Each one was recognizable as it began, but unintelligible as it finished. Each time the beautiful voices sang a new word, the meaning of the last somehow slipped away.

She opened her eyes one last time as Tam plunged across the threshold of the giant circle of trees. The beautiful chorus vanished.

The rainbow landscape contracted, breaking into giant rainbow spheres that became smaller and smaller until they were multi-colored fireflies. Vale felt like she was falling.

The impact of the ground knocked the breath from her. She raised her head and sucked in a lungful of air. It felt like she hadn't breathed the entire time they'd been in the rainbow land.

The last of the multi-colored fireflies faded away, and the sky became blue. Sound returned. Wind rustled. Birds chirped. The Lyantrees returned to their scaly green bark and purple-silver leaves instead of tree-shaped molds of swirling rainbow. Green grass and greener shrubs hunched in clusters all around.

"What…happened?" Vale gasped. She could barely lift her head, and she recognized the feeling immediately. This was soul drain; she'd opened all of her Soulblocks except the last. She searched inside herself for the crackling magic, but it was utterly spent. Whatever Tam had done, it had drunk her dry. She was sinking into oblivion from pure exhaustion and she fought it. If she slept, she might sleep for a week. Some Quadrons who opened their third Soulblock fell into a month-long coma.

With barely enough strength to lift her head, she looked around for threats but couldn't see any. Wulfric was gone. His fierce roars and chopping sword were gone.

Tam lay with his back against a tree trunk, and he looked to be in the same shape as Vale.

"We are…safe, *Alari*," he gasped.

"The Four?"

"Far away," he said. "We must…sleep."

His suggestion seemed to pull her down. Her head sank against the soft grass.

"Sleep, *Alari*," Tam encouraged, and he closed his eyes. His slender body went limp.

Vale made the attempt to rise, to wake. Her head only lifted slightly before thumping back. Soft… So soft…

She slept.

9

VALE

Make them brilliant...

They were the last words Vale's mother had ever spoken. She had told Vale a story about how the downtrodden—those like Vale and herself—were the dark horses of the lands, and that all those with privilege were the white horses. The white horses were well fed. They were brushed and pampered and given every chance in life. They took care of each other, but no one took care of the dark horses.

Mother had then said something that had stayed with Vale forever. The dark horses were special. She had said that when the sunlight hit the dark horses just right, they flashed more brilliantly than the white horses ever could.

There were none to help the dark horses realize they were special, to help them catch the light and shine, and as Mother lay there in that alley, she had laid a purpose upon Vale.

"Make them brilliant…" she had said, and then she had died.

Those dying words repeated over and over in Vale's dreams as she slept. She floated on a rainbow river away from the rainbow lands through which she and Tam had passed, and Mother's voice followed her.

Make them brilliant…. Make them brilliant…

Vale floated easily atop the water like she was a piece of driftwood. The river wound toward a distant line where the multi-colored sky became blue, where the flat ground became green with grass and shrubs, where the rainbow trees became the green-trunked, purple-and-silver-leafed Lyantrees.

As Vale moved inexorably toward that line, something tugged at her heart.

She jerked and looked down. A thread from the center of her tunic had been torn loose. It reached back behind her like the thin strand of a spider's web. Her shirt began to unravel as the river carried her further and further away from wherever the end of the thread was attached.

Again, her heart lurched, and she realized the thread wasn't just attached to her tunic. It went deeper. The thread was also somehow attached to her chest. As the river carried her further downstream, the tugging thread unraveled her skin and her breastbone like it was all made of flesh-and-bone-colored cloth.

Vale gasped and tried to stop herself from floating any further. She pulled at the string to try to break it, but she only unraveled it further. When the string opened up her heart, images began to float out of it as though they'd been caught in the fabric and were now finally released.

Stunned, she stopped struggling and watched the images rise…

She saw herself with Brom in his dorm room back at the Champions Academy. She sat behind him with her legs wrapped around him, and they were poring over old books. Stacks lay on the bed, on the floor, and two thick books sat on Brom's lap as Vale pointed out a passage.

Brom read it, then looked back over his shoulder. "Entire Quads have passed the Test of Separation," he whispered, stunned.

"Interesting, yes?" she asked. "But apparently only at the beginning of the school."

"What... What does that mean?" He leaned back against her. "Why wouldn't they tell us about this?"

"Why indeed?"

She brought another book forward and laid it over the top of the first two, flipped it open to a marked page that had recorded a report from a nearby village. A Quadron had died.

"He's from one of the full Quads that graduated from the brand new school," she said.

She laid another book atop the stack on his knees.

"Let me guess..." he said as he scanned the marked passage.

"Another Quadron dead," she said. "From the other full Quad that had graduated. They killed them. They went after them after *they passed the Test of Separation. And they killed them."*

She placed another book on his lap, flipped it open. "Here's another." She put another on his lap, open to another page. "And another."

"Gods, Vale..." he said. "You're saying..."

"That The Four are fucking murderers," she said.

The image floated up above Vale as the river carried her on, and she realized this was a memory. A memory she hadn't recalled until this moment, just like Arsinoe torturing her. She floated, stunned, as the thread continued to unravel her heart. A second memory floated up and out...

Vale and the rest of Quad Brilliant stood in Oriana's dorm room. The room's window was dark, and a lone candle illuminated the rich tapestries that hung on her walls, as well as her Quad mates' tense faces.

The image moved closer, becoming only Vale's face.

"I want to stick the dagger in these fucks," she snarled. "They lured me here, trapped me here. They never intended to let me leave…"

The image blurred, spinning, and then came close to Brom's face.

"I don't like the idea of forgetting what I know about The Four," he said. "It would be like turning my back to them…"

The image became the entire dorm again, showing all four members of Quad Brilliant.

"We will not forget forever," Oriana said. "I will…hide it. Then restore it."

"How do we get our memories back after?" Royal asked.

"A tripwire," Oriana said.

"What is that?" Royal asked.

"It's like an animal trap," Vale said. "A wire that triggers the trap. Likewise, a wire that triggers a spell."

"The last day of Summerdawn," Oriana said. "Year's end testing."

Vale snapped her fingers and pointed at Oriana. "When they give us the writ of passage. That is our trigger."

"What will you take?" Brom asked. "I want to know exactly. What are you going to remove?"

"I must remove your visit to the tower…" Oriana said. "All the relevant memories, otherwise your mind will go searching for them. The fewer gaps I leave, the less your mind will fight trying to recover what was lost."

"…what was lost…what was lost…what was lost…"

Oriana's voice repeated over and over as the memory

floated away.

"We knew," Vale whispered as she continued to float downstream in the dream. "Brom sneaked into their tower and discovered The Four were villains. We knew, and we erased it from our minds!"

Oriana had hidden the truth from them, intending to restore everyone's memories at the year's-end testing to ensure The Four didn't know it was Brom who'd invaded their tower. Except Quad Brilliant had never reached the end of the second year. They'd been advanced early to the Test of Separation.

"The tripwire never triggered..." she murmured. "We never got our memories back. We went like lambs into that awful building, and we didn't even know..."

That was why Vale couldn't find any joy in her new role as a Quadron, a servant of The Four. Deep down, she'd always known something was wrong. She just hadn't known what. Even before the Test, Vale hadn't felt right. She'd felt that feeling of missing something. She had accused Oriana of mucking with her mind, and the princess had denied it. But Vale been right. What she hadn't known was that she'd agreed to it. They all had. They had taken a terrible gamble.

And they had lost.

Vale continued down the river in the dream, and the thread of her heart continued to unwind. Another memory rose up and played out on the air before her...

She stood in an antechamber inside The Dome. They had just finished the Test of Separation. Brom was dead. Royal had just picked Oriana up by the neck, almost killed her, then dropped her again. Quad Brilliant was crumbling apart.

"I hate you!" Vale screamed at Oriana.

"Let Quad Brilliant die here," Oriana said coldly. "It has

served its purpose." Her eyes narrowed to slits. "Now…" she in a deadly tone. "If either of you try to touch me again, I'll burn your minds out."

"I will see you on the battlefield," Royal growled, fists clenched like he would attack her again.

"No," Oriana said through her teeth. "I have soldiers who do that sort of thing for me."

"I don't want to see either of you ever again," Vale swore. "The best of this fucking Quad was Brom."

"Indeed," Oriana agreed, and they turned their backs.

The memory faded away, urgently followed by another as though time was running out…

Vale stood in the great hall before the assembled students of the academy. To her right stood Oriana and Royal, and beyond them the assembled masters. The masters droned on about the accomplishments of Quad Brilliant, but Vale didn't listen. This was the culmination of everything she'd come to the academy for. This was the realization of a dream that hadn't seemed possible when she'd been a starving little urchin on the streets of Torlioch, and yet here she was. She was a Quadron.

But everything felt wrong. Something was…missing. She tried to tell herself it was because Brom had died and she was mourning. But it didn't feel like mourning. It felt like this victory wasn't a victory at all, but the worst thing that could have happened to all of them.

She looked at Royal, who stood like a statue, jaw clenched, towering over everyone. She looked at Oriana, who had reverted to the cold-blooded ice princess, replete in her shimmering-white high-collared gown. She wore her crown now, studded with purple gemstones, and her hair was braided back in a complicated pattern that must have taken a couple of servants an hour to weave. The princess was as poised as ever, back straight, chin high, cool stare surveying the crowd—

All except for her left hand. Vale's eyes widened. Oriana's long fingers gripped a scroll tightly, turned it, gripped it again, turned it again, over and over.

A chill scampered up Vale's spine. That was so odd as to be ridiculous. Oriana didn't even fidget in private among friends. Seeing her fidget at an official function was like seeing a frog smoking a pipe.

Vale couldn't imagine what that meant, but it added to her sense of unease.

The masters finished their litany of achievements at last and brought the Quadron amulets forth, placing the copper chains around Royal's neck first, then Oriana's, then Vale's, and Vale stopped thinking about Oriana's stupid scroll...

The memory floated up and faded away, turning into drifts of white on the air.

Vale knew why Oriana had been holding that scroll. It suddenly made sense! The princess had known something was wrong, something was missing, just as Vale had known. Oriana had unconsciously groped for the answer, latching onto that scroll.

Vale would bet her life that the scroll in Oriana's hand was the tripwire: a second-year writ of passage. If given to Oriana, it would have restored her memories. Except it obviously hadn't triggered the spell. The writ of passage wasn't Oriana's because she hadn't been given one. She'd probably taken it from somewhere, unconsciously knowing that a second-year writ of passage was important without knowing why. But by taking it instead of receiving it, the conditions of the tripwire hadn't been met. Oriana had not regained her memories.

The rainbow river deposited Vale onto the shore in the normal world where there were no rainbow colors. She lay there on the wet muddy bank, dumbstruck. She remembered everything now. She remembered it all. Quad Brilliant had been torn apart, but they'd done half of it on their own.

We were such fools, she thought. *And Brom paid for our arrogance.*

It was too late to escape the clutches of The Four, too late to undo the destruction of Quad Brilliant. But it wasn't too late for vengeance.

She closed her eyes. When she opened them, she awoke and the dream vanished.

10

VALE

"Alari…" Tam's voice warbled to her. *"Alari…"*

Vale slowly awoke. Her eyes were crusted with sleep, and she blinked as she sat up. Her head felt lopsided. She touched her cheek, which had indentations from where it had pressed against the grass.

"We were fools," she murmured. "We knew, and we threw our knowledge away."

"Alari?" Tam asked quizzically.

They had discovered The Four were evil back at the academy, but they hadn't put that knowledge to use before The Four tore Quad Brilliant apart. And the Quad could never come back together. Royal and Oriana would try to kill each other on sight. They both hated Vale. And Brom was dead.

Quad Brilliant was gone, but maybe Vale could return the favor to The Four.

"How long have I been asleep?" she murmured.

"The sun has passed twice, *Alari.*"

"Two days?" she asked incredulously, and the memories of how she'd come to this forest came back to her. She'd walked through that rainbow land, and it had drained her magic just like the green cone of fire. Except it had left her final Soulblock.

"Gods…" she murmured. Using her third Soulblock should have meant a month-long coma, not just a couple days' rest. But her Soulblocks brimmed with magic, fully restored.

"Two days," Tam said. "Yes, *Alari.*"

"How…can that be?" she murmured.

As her mind cleared of sleep, everything they'd done flooded back. The Four were looking for her, and even two days of sleeping was dangerous and reckless.

"We have to move," she said, struggling to stand. "We have to go right now, as far away as we can. The Hallowed Woods aren't safe."

"We are not in that place," Tam said. "This…*Hallowed Woods.*" He said the words like he was trying them out for the first time.

But Lyantrees surrounded them as far as she could see, and there was no other place in the two kingdoms where Lyantrees grew. She shook her head, blinking again.

"Tam, we're in the Hallowed Woods," she argued.

"No, *Alari.*"

"Then where?"

"The *lyans*…moved us. They took us elsewhere. We are higher than we were before," he said, then made that frustrated face like he hadn't used the right words. "Not higher. We are…colder. We are…further away from humans."

She tried to understand what he meant. Higher? They were both still on the ground. Colder? And she suddenly realized that it *was* colder. The Hallowed Woods had a warmth to them, like it was perpetually early summer. But here the air was crisp like autumn.

Then she understood. "You mean they moved us to the north?"

"North. Yes, north. And away from humans."

The hearts of the two kingdoms were closest to the coast. Tam was saying the Lyantrees had teleported them northeast of the Hallowed Woods, into unexplored lands. It was said that the wilds at the eastern border of Keltovar held fierce beasts that hunted humans. Like dragons.

"There's *another* Lyantree forest besides the Hallowed Woods?" Vale asked.

"Yes," Tam said. "Come, *Alari*, we must find food."

The moment he said it, she realized she was ravenous. Gods, it felt like there was a hollow chasm where her stomach should be. She'd never been so hungry.

She followed him deeper into the forest.

Vale wasn't sure what Sacintos ate, and as Tam led her between the trees, she envisioned that he was going to find a nice little clearing and then stick his feet in the ground, turn his face to the sun and plant himself like a tree.

But it turned out that Tam ate the same things she did. He found a bush of delicious berries to start. They were a swirled blue and yellow color, like two different paints poured into a bucket, and they tasted glorious. While she was plucking berry after berry and popping them greedily into her mouth, Tam vanished into the forest. He returned moments later with an armful of thick red roots, crusted with moist soil. After washing them off in the stream, she and Tam crunched through the whole bunch. They were juicy and tasted like sugared lemons.

"These are amazing," Vale said. She'd never eaten anything like them before.

"They are the good for stomachs," Tam replied in his stilted way around mouthfuls of root. "Much feeding. Sacintos eat *teshran* each day. A great giver of strength and life."

"*Teshran?*" she asked.

"In Fendir, humans call it redroot. But most do not know of it at all. It grows only near the *lyans*."

"Well, it's delicious."

After eating a dozen *teshran* roots and what had probably been a couple bowls worth of berries, Vale finally rested her back against a scaly-barked Lyantree and let out a long sigh.

"Gods, I'm full," she said. "That is a good feeling. If I'd known Lyantree forests were full of such fantastic roots, I'd have left Torlioch as a child and lived like a beast in the woods."

Tam smiled. "Torlioch?"

"The city where I grew up," she said.

"Ah. A human grove?" Tam said.

She laughed, realizing that Tam had probably spent exactly no time in any human cities. "Yes. A human grove."

He wrinkled his nose. "Human groves in Keltovar smell bad. They are stone and they have no trees. Stone paths. Stone houses that block the wind. Too many people. Too close together. Keltovar human groves feel like cages."

After spending so much time in the wilds, she couldn't disagree. Except she'd still been caged that entire time, an unwitting slave to The Four.

"I'm free for the first time," she murmured.

"*Alari?*"

"That man who came for me, he and his friends had me in chains."

He glanced at her, looking for the chains.

"Invisible chains," she said.

"But you are free now?"

"I am, thanks to you."

"And a thanks to you, too," he said. "With the Keltovar soldiers."

"That was my pleasure," she said. "I hate bullies."

"What is a bully?"

"Someone strong who hurts someone weaker."

"Ah."

They sat in silence for a moment, then Tam said, "And are you still hungry?"

She patted her stuffed belly. "No."

"The *lyans* are wanting to talk to you. They are…eager," he said, trying out the word. "Will you talk with them?"

Vale sat up. "Yes."

"Now?"

"As soon as possible."

Tam stood up and came to her, knelt in front of her. "Good." He extended his hand. "I will show you."

Vale took his hand, and Tam showed her how to reach into to the Lyantrees.

11

VALE

Tam explained that the Lyantrees did not use human words to communicate. They used colors.

For all the things Vale had readily learned while on the streets of Torlioch, at the Champions Academy, and finally in her travels throughout Keltovar, she couldn't seem to learn this.

Colors! How did one speak in colors? She couldn't seem to wrap her mind around it. That first day as Tam put her hand on the nearest Lyantree's bark, then put his hand over hers, there was nothing. After traveling through the heart of the Lyantree "world" to get here, she thought she'd be able to see those rainbow colors instantly. But apparently using the Lyantree circles to teleport from one place to another had been the will of the Lyantrees, guided by Tam, and it had little to do with actually talking to them.

It took until the third day before she could actually see

the colors Tam, ever patient, kept mentioning. She finally gasped with relief when she saw a stream of yellow trickle through her mind, just as Tam had described it.

But that huge accomplishment soon seemed tiny. Seeing the colors was only one part of it. Understanding the colors was something else entirely, and it was simply impossible.

Day after day she struggled, trying in vain to translate colors into words that she could understand. She pushed down her fears that, despite ridding herself of the insidious amulet and teleporting a hundred miles to the northeast, The Four were going to suddenly appear and gut her. She reminded herself that if she didn't figure out how to make the Lyantrees her "Quad" and utilize their Soulblocks, nothing else mattered. Whether The Four found her today or a year from now, she couldn't stop them from killing her unless she had her own "Quad" to fight back. If Vale couldn't figure out how to access that idle magic within the trees, there was no Quad for her.

But that was easier said that done. She couldn't form a Quad with the Lyantrees if she couldn't talk to them!

After nearly a week of failure, even the mild mannered Tam began to show his frustration. He'd given up getting her to talk to the Lyantrees directly and instead told her to try to talk to him using Lyantree language. He said that once she could communicate with him, then she could try again with one of the Lyantrees.

And even at that, she was failing.

"*Alari*, no," Tam insisted. "You are trying to use human words. They are not the same. It is a..." He tried to find the human words to explain to her what she was doing wrong, but Tam's mastery of human language was limited. "It is this," he said again, and he made a frustrated gesture with his hands. The barest hint of blue and yellow colors flickered behind Vale's eyelids, but that was all.

"I *see* the colors, Tam," she shouted. "But it doesn't make any sense! It's just stupid floating ribbons of blue and yellow. They don't *mean* anything."

He sighed. "It is not to *mean* anything, *Alari*. It is not to be 'blue' and 'yellow.' Those are being human words. It is to…" he said, and he gestured again. Blue and yellow lights again flickered in her mind.

"This is ridiculous," she spat. "If '*it is not to mean anything*,'" she mimicked him acidly, "then it's not communication!"

Tam bowed his head, which she had come to understand as the Sacinto's expression of extreme frustration. He closed his eyes, opened them, then raised his head. "You give the colors. You keep the colors. Then the colors are the same colors."

The colors are the same colors… Of all the stupid, nonsensical…

"Please. If you will to try again," he said.

She clenched her teeth. She didn't want to try again. By the gods, learning to be a Quadron hadn't been this hard. She'd come at this for days and days, and she was no closer to deciphering the language than she'd been at the beginning.

"Try, *Alari*."

"Fuck you," she growled.

"What is to 'fuck you?'" he asked.

"Never mind."

She imagined blues and yellows going to him. He watched her steadily, and after two full minutes of trying, she realized he wasn't getting anything.

"Try, *Alari*," he said again.

"I *am* trying!"

"It is not with words. It is…" He gestured again, and those fucking blue and yellow lights glowed behind her eyelids.

She threw up her hands and screamed in frustration. She screamed at Tam, screamed at the sky. She even stood up and spun in a circle, screaming at everything. She screamed so hard her vision went red.

Tam flinched like he had been hit, then his face split in a grin.

"Alari!" he said excitedly. "Yes! You gave me…" He hesitated, as though reluctant, then he said. "Red. But it is not red. Because it is not a human word. It is…" A ribbon of red slithered through her mind like a snake.

Vale froze, and her anger vanished.

"Red is not correct, though. It was…mean." He shook his head. "No, that is the wrong word. It was…anger?" He looked up at her hopefully. "You sent me your anger."

A door opened in Vale's mind, and a realization that she'd—ridiculously—missed suddenly came to her. As a Motus, she should have seen it immediately. She'd been thinking about this kind of communication with the Lyantrees—with Tam—as being akin to talking mind-to-mind with Oriana. Something that had to do with thoughts, something that could be translated to words.

But the Lyantrees had no words. Tam had been trying to tell her for days. What if there was no way to make this communication into words? What if there was only emotion? Vast emotion, raw emotion, each a color in the mind, but for which there was no true translation?

But how could someone converse that way? The anecdotes or full pictures attached to a single word was what made communication possible. What dialogue could possibly be created through spurts of colors based on emotion?

Vale began thinking about her own emotions and what colors she might attach to them. Red made sense for anger. She'd always thought of rage as red. Green meant forests and grass to her, and she'd always had a sense of peace in such places. Green was calm. Serene. She thought she might attach yellow to joy, to the shining sun overhead, to a feeling of freedom, traveling under the open sky. Orange made her think of fire, of warmth and safety.

She sat down again and exhaled, letting all of her frustration go and sought a sense of peace. She imagined it as a rich green. And this time, she let that sense of peace include Tam. She "sent" it to him.

Suddenly, it seemed similar to using her Motus magic to manipulate the emotions of others. But in this case, she wasn't diving into Tam. She wasn't pushing the crackling lightning of her Soulblock into him. It was more like she was…breathing on him. There was no attack. No force. No agenda. Only the "breath" of her mood.

"Yes, *Alari*," Tam said. "It is…green, yes?"

Yes… But when Tam said it, the word "green" suddenly seemed clunky and awkward. It was nowhere near capable of describing the entirety of what she'd meant to convey, and she suddenly understood Tam's previous frustration. She'd insisted on cramming a square peg into a round hole over and over and over again like some idiot child.

"I understand now," she said. And then she decided to try to put that feeling into a color. She sent it over. It was orangish brown.

"Yes, *Alari*," Tam said aloud. A golden glow of admiration and satisfaction flowed back to her, lighting the backs of her eyelids.

A thrill of excitement rushed through her. She let the rich blue and sparkling white flow to Tam. He giggled.

"You have it, *Alari*... You are speaking like a *lyan*."

That was the largest barrier, and once she'd broken it, Vale was able to improve. It was clunky at first. There was far more nuance to the speech of the Lyantrees than just "a primary color attached to a primary emotion." And of course the color Vale assigned to an emotion wasn't the same as what a Lyantree might assign. But slowly, with Tam's help, she began to understand basic meanings sent by the Lyantrees.

The most common color Vale received she came to refer to as "sunlight happiness." Most Lyantrees sent a steady stream of "sunlight happiness" all the time. The color was a yellow floating on a molten river of gold with tendrils of green and blue threaded through it. To receive "sunshine happiness" from a Lyantree meant that all was well. There was sunlight and blue sky and the growing of green things. If Vale were to reach out to talk to a Lyantree, "sunlight happiness" was what the tree always sent back first. It was their general state of being.

But when a tree had something specific to say, a dozen different colors would come at her in streams. Blue mixed with green. Then solid green followed quickly by another burst of blue mixed with green. Then a splash of red thinning into pink. Then another blue mixed with green. And finally the color they always finished with: a steady stream of "sunlight happiness."

It was overwhelming at first. With the exception of "sunlight happiness," the colors made no sense to her. But she took that in stride. She'd found the key, and she could muddle through the rest.

She soon determined that "sunlight happiness" at the end of every attempted communication was like a punctuation mark. It was as if the Lyantrees had told her something, then finished with, "Okay? Did you understand that? Is everything 'sunlight happiness?'"

Vale's frustration turned to the delight of constant discovery. Mostly it was little things. She didn't worry that she didn't understand every communication. She just spoke. They answered, and she made a pile of failures that led to little understandings. With Tam's help, she narrowed down the nuances with all the fervor of the researcher she had become during her days with Oriana at the Champions Academy.

Over the next few days, Vale began to truly understand the Lyantrees.

She soon realized that most of the Lyantrees actually had no interest in talking to her. Only a select few wanted to communicate with humans at all. Lyantrees were as diverse as people, and each had different desires and agendas. Most of the trees simply wanted to bask in "sunlight happiness" and ignore Vale's presence. A few wanted her to leave, and she received dark, foreboding colors when she came near those trees. But there were some who were keenly interested in her presence, excited that she was in their forest, and these were almost always the older, taller trees, or the obviously ancient squat and gnarled trees. The youngest trees were far more interested in just being trees, basking in sunlight and reaching toward the sky.

The elders were the ones concerned about humans.

She came to understand that every single Lyantree in the lands—whether in this place or the Hallowed Woods—was connected to all the other Lyantrees. The pain of the harvesting in the Hallowed Woods was felt by every Lyantree in this hidden northeastern forest.

And the elder trees wanted to stop the slaughter. They

wanted to talk with humans so they could tell them to stop chopping down Lyantrees.

Vale soon learned that the color for humans in Lyantree speech was an oily brownish color mixed with "sunlight happiness." A tree who did not wish Vale to come close would shoot a muddy river of color at her. Once she'd learned the language, the repulsion was strong—a shout of, "Go away, human!"

But the elders who were curious about her wanted nothing more than to help her, to understand her and to have her understand them. They sent the same oily mud color mixed with "sunlight happiness" that, to them, meant "human." But Vale felt lured toward them, not repelled, and she suddenly realized that the force with which the colors were sent was vital to understanding the true meaning. The same color could mean opposite things depending on *how* it was delivered.

Vale spent most of her time with these elder trees, learning. She called them the "elder trees" in her mind, and at first she thought of them like the elders of a village, venerable and revered, leaders among the others. She soon realized that there were no leaders in the forest. Neither the elder trees nor the younger trees seemed to be "in charge." There was no discussion about "where to go" or "what to do." These were already known quantities. There was no "where" to go. Trees did not move. There was no question of "what to do." Trees soaked in sunlight and grew tall, widening their leaves to catch more sunlight. Why have someone telling you what to do when it was already obvious?

After a month living in the forest, Vale became fluent in Lyantree speech. She greeted each of her favorites when she came near and sat with some all day long, telling them stories of humans as best she could, conveying the legends she'd grown up with, of the gods Kelto and Fendra and the great heroes and Quadrons of old.

In turn, the elder Lyantrees told their stories. There were no Lyantree heroes, no tales of great deeds or empires. To a Lyantree, a life well-lived was based on the amount of "sunshine happiness" it experienced. It had nothing to do—as in the case of humans—with how many accomplishments, how much wealth or how much power a tree gained.

Vale realized this was why so many of the Lyantrees ignored her. They were exclusively focused on living within "sunshine happiness."

Soon, during their conversations, the elder Lyantrees came up with a color for Vale specifically. When she greeted them, they sent her a flowing river of red wrapped around "sunshine happiness," interwoven with tendrils of a sad-feeling sea green. Deeper, at the very center, was a steel gray-blue. This entire combination of colors meant "Vale" in their minds, and it came to be how she thought of herself when she spent time with them.

These hazy days of learning blended together, one into the next, and Vale unwittingly began to use the Soulblocks of the Lyantrees. It happened completely by accident at first. She was talking with the Lyantrees about the Hallowed Woods and didn't realize until halfway through that some of the elder trees in the conversation were a hundred miles away in the Hallowed Woods themselves.

The Lyantrees in her present location had bolstered Vale's magic—and her ability to talk their language—with their Soulblocks. This magic enabled her to span the distance just like the Lyantrees did.

When Vale realized what had happened, she explored more about the Soulblocks and found that, unlike humans, Lyantrees shared their Soulblocks freely. It was like an ocean of magic that ebbed and flowed between all Lyantrees, depending on who needed it at the time. The sunlight and the rain replenished the Soulblocks, and so there was always more than enough of a reservoir of magic to fuel whatever communication—or other endeavor—a Lyantree needed.

And Vale could use it too. She could use as much magic as she wanted.

One morning, she woke up and found herself thinking in Lyantree colors instead of in words. At first, it seemed perfectly natural, but as she came more fully awake, a little warning sounded in the back of her mind.

She'd discovered what she'd come here to discover. She had learned to communicate with the Lyantrees and she'd gained access to an unfathomable amount of magic that could give her the ability to destroy The Four.

And what had she done with these discoveries? Nothing. She'd simply begun to live life like a tree, content with walking through the forest, talking with her friends, essentially seeking out the human equivalent of "sunshine happiness."

How long had she even been here?

She tried to count the number of days and she couldn't. She remembered the first few weeks with Tam, but many days had passed since that time. Even weeks.

In fact, it could be months.

She tried to remember how long it had been since she'd spoken any human words aloud at all, and she couldn't. Even Tam spoke to her only in the color speech of the Lyantrees now.

I am... She tried to think in human words, but it

fizzled out.

She blinked and sat up. A cold fear prickled her scalp.

I am not a Lyantree, was what she'd wanted to think, but she had to force the human words to form in her mind.

"I am Vale," she said aloud. Her voice was raspy with disuse, and the words seemed crude and ugly compared to the elegant communication of flowing colors.

I'm changing, she thought. *Gods, I'm turning into a Lyantree.*

In fact, she was so deep in her transformation that she couldn't consider human ways without judging them.

"What am I doing here?" she murmured.

"Alari?" Tam asked, also aloud, matching her choice of language. He sat up from where he had been leaning against one of Vale's favorite Lyantrees, the elder tree she'd first spoken with. Back then, she'd called him Crookbranch because of his lowest branch—thick and crooked at a right angle like a human arm.

She realized she hadn't called him that human word in forever. In Lyantree speech, Crookbranch was a river of green-gold with different-sized flecks of black.

"Why am I here?" Vale said. "I came here with a purpose, Tam, but now…" Her rage at The Four, her fearful escape from them in the Hallowed Woods, these emotions had faded. She didn't burn with thoughts of Arsinoe and what he'd done to her. She didn't swim in guilt over Brom's death.

She had lived with the peace of the Lyantrees so long she'd forgotten her purpose. She remembered when she'd traveled here with Tam through the rainbow world. During that intense escape, she'd wanted to give herself over to the rainbow light, and Tam had said it was dangerous.

How was this any different?

This Lyantree forest, in a slow, seductive way, was

doing the same thing. Vale longed to continue her days here with Tam and the elders. She simply wanted to seek "sunshine happiness," like they did.

"You came to learn the speech of the Lyantrees," Tam said.

"But that's…not why I came here. I came to find a way to destroy The Four," she said.

Tam's brow wrinkled over his huge dark eyes. He obviously remembered their harrowing flight. Vale recalled Wulfric's freakishly fast movements as he tried to chop the foot from her leg, how he'd almost done it.

"To kill them," Tam said sadly, like he wished she hadn't brought that up.

"Some people deserve killing," she said.

"*Alari…*" Tam said, concerned.

"I can't stay here, Tam," she whispered. "I can't be…this. I didn't escape The Four so I could be a tree. I have debts…" She thought of Brom, of him reaching out to her.

"But your *feyri*—"

"The Four are villains. They are capturing all the powerful young people in the two kingdoms. And they either castrate them or kill them. And those they don't kill they turn into slaves."

She paused and felt the weight of her next words, felt how horribly true they were.

"I'm the only one who can stop them, Tam."

"*Alari…*"

"If I don't do something, more people will die. More Broms."

"Broms?"

"I have to do what I came to do," she said.

Tam sighed. "The *lyans* say a right decision is marked by its amount of sunshine happiness, but this decision makes you so sad. You are so sad. Are you sure you wish to do this?"

Brom's face rose in her mind, and she blinked away tears. "My life isn't supposed to be sunshine happiness."

"I do not believe that, *Alari*."

"You should. I made a horrible mistake. I killed someone I loved, and I can't ever undo it. But maybe I can save someone else. Maybe I can save hundreds of people."

She didn't say anything for a moment. Then, "I can't just stay here and float away on the colors of the *lyans*. It's not…right. Not for me."

Tam still looked solemn. "What is right, *Alari*?"

"I'm going to save the two kingdoms," she whispered.

"With death?"

"With four deaths," she said. "That's all I need."

Tam shook his head.

"Will you help me, Tam?" she asked.

He kept shaking his head back and forth, but he said, "Yes, *Alari*." His dark eyes glistened with tears. "I will help you."

12

VALE

Once Vale escaped the beautiful distraction of the Lyantrees, her plan started to come together. She'd need a trap—something to separate The Four so she could strip them of their Quad advantage and then face them one-on-one. Using Motus magic against each of The Four individually was possible, but she'd have to ensure that the battlefield gave her every advantage it could. She planned to use her familiarity with the forest and her ability to communicate with the Lyantrees.

She had all the magic she would ever need, but she needed more than that. She would need to transform her part of the forest into a gauntlet of traps that would keep three of The Four busy while she fought one.

As she set about creating booby traps throughout the woods, Vale stumbled across a discovery that changed everything.

She was jogging through the forest to sketch out part

of a trap. She had been running for hours before it occurred to her that she should be exhausted, but she wasn't. She stopped, trying to understand how this was possible, and she realized it was the Soulblocks of the Lyantrees. Somehow, they had bolstered her stamina as if she were an Impetu.

She sat down right in the middle of her run, stunned by the possibilities. This opened an entirely new avenue of research, and she delved into it immediately.

Over the next few days, she abandoned her pedestrian, tree-based traps. Instead, she pushed this new Impetu power, running all day—nearly a hundred miles at once. Not only did she not tire, but her feet didn't blister, her muscles didn't ache. The magic was boosting her strength, and it was healing her.

As she experimented with this glorious Impetu power, she discovered some things.

First, while she was obviously using Impetu magic, she wasn't nearly as powerful as Royal. At the academy, he had once uprooted an entire tree and tossed it aside to gain his first-year writ of passage. Vale tested the limits of her brute strength and found she could barely lift one end of a deadfall.

Second, when she disconnected herself from the Lyantrees, cut herself off from their Soulblocks and used only the magic from her own Soulblocks, she lost all Impetu abilities. She tried it a dozen different ways, but it was clear that her own intrinsic magic was purely Motus.

With Tam to use for practice like the Invisible Ones from the Champions Academy, Vale tried working Mentis magic and Anima magic as well...

And she found that she could. She worked on speaking mind-to-mind with Tam, worked on seeing into his soul.

It was exhilarating. The sheer power of being able to work the other three paths of magic, however muted, made her a kind of super Quadron. Her hopes grew.

She could do this. She could take on The Four.

But as with the Impetu path, when she tried to use her own Soulblocks, each of the other paths was inaccessible to her.

It made her think about the nature of the four paths of magic. The Lyantree Soulblocks were pure and uninhibited, whereas hers had been created in the regimented structure of a Quad.

She tried to retrain her Soulblocks, to have them— even in some small way—work another path of magic. They wouldn't, not even a little bit. It seemed that once her Soulblocks had been trained to do Motus magic, that was all they knew.

It appeared that the only place Vale could ever be a "super Quadron" was within the Lyantree forest. It was frustrating, but her disappointment didn't come close to eclipsing her excitement.

She never tired until she was finished for the day and let the magic go. She could pick up Tam's thoughts if she concentrated, could talk to him mind-to-mind far more quickly than using the Lyantree color-speech. And she had begun to feel everything in the forest—the trees, the animals, even the shifting of the breeze and the heat of the sun—through a light connection to what she assumed was the thing Brom had called the Soul of the World. It was like the forest was now an extension of her body.

One day while Vale was eating *teshran* with Tam, she decided to use Motus and Mentis at the same time, feeling Tam's emotions while simultaneously reading his thoughts. It worked, and she suddenly wondered why she hadn't tried to do this before. If she was going to fight

The Four, she'd have to know how to use all the paths of magic together.

As she held the Motus and Mentis connections, she noticed a shimmering in the air between herself and Tam.

Tam jumped, seeing it also. He scooted back. The shimmering writhed like a mirage of heat.

"*Alari*… What…what is it?"

Vale's eyes were wide. "I don't know." She focused on her connections with Tam, and the shimmering air intensified. "Gods, I'm affecting the actual air!" she said.

"You are doing this?" he asked.

She explained what she had done, using two paths at once, and she cut herself off mid-sentence as a lightning strike of inspiration hit her.

"This is how they do it…" she murmured.

"Who, *Alari*?"

"The Four," she said.

"What do they do?"

She paused before answering, running through her thoughts. Students at the academy could read minds, change emotions, see souls, or heal a person, but only a person. Magic was based upon what a Quadron could do to themselves or to another. Quadrons couldn't make the wind blow, light a fire with their minds, or build a stone tower with pure magic. No Quadron could.

None except The Four, of course.

The wondrous constructs of the academy had been built by The Four: the giant wall, the Dome, the automatons in the library, the looming tower.

"They make things," she murmured. "They shape reality by using multiple paths at once. They bend the elements, not just other people. *This* is how they do it."

New possibilities arose, opening magic that went beyond her wildest dreams. She reeled from the discovery, but as she set to work, exploring those possibilities, she realized that the knowing was far easier than the doing. Using two paths at once used more than twice the magic. Four paths used more than four times as much.

When Vale first tried to bend the elements to her will—by transforming a large rock into a stone bowl—it took six Soulblocks! It depleted two of her own Soulblocks in an instant, and four from the Lyantrees. They gave to her freely, of course, but the sheer amount of magic required raged through her body. And it hurt.

Still, as she knelt in the grass, breathing hard with her heart on fire and her hands around the smooth stone bowl, she couldn't help but buzz with excitement. She was going to destroy The Four. She was going to take them one-by-one...

She abandoned her previous plans and came up with an even better one. She became adept at shaping rock and started a labyrinth of tunnels far beneath the Lyantree Forest. She sank it deep, past the topsoil and the roots, past the packed earth into the bedrock. There, she laid her traps.

The process was exhausting. Day by day, channeling so much raw magic took its toll. It felt like it was trying to pull her apart. It yanked at her muscles and tendons, tried to separate her skin. She found herself fighting to hold herself together as she worked. After the first two weeks, she began sleeping ten or even twelve hours a night to recuperate.

"This place?" Tam asked as she lay exhausted against Crookbranch after another full day of melting rock and creating tunnels. "You will kill The Four here?"

"Yes," she said for the dozenth time, too exhausted to have this argument again. She needed sleep, needed to rest and let the sublime nourishment of the Lyantrees flow through her, replenishing her Soulblocks even as they replenished their own.

She'd wielded the magic of twenty Soulblocks today. A lightning storm of power had raged through her. And twenty Soulblocks yesterday. And the day before that. Her body felt like an old clay pipe that was starting to crack after much water had been shoved through it day after day. Would her body begin to fail? Had it already begun?

Even as Tam helped her build the maze, the Sacinto continued to try to convince her not to kill The Four. He just wouldn't shut up about it. He repeated that such a thing would harm her *feyri* forever.

She didn't care about that. She didn't expect to survive this fight, and if she could do just this one thing, nothing else mattered.

After I destroy The Four, she thought, *it doesn't matter what happens to me. I just have to hold on until then.*

"What will you do now?" Tam asked.

"Rest," she said, already beginning to drift into pleasant slumber where her dreams would become Lyantree rainbow colors.

"And after?"

"We bait the hook," she said.

"They will come to you?"

"They've been looking for me since we escaped them in The Hallowed Woods," she said.

"Perhaps they will be content that you vanished into the *lyans.*"

"No, they'll come for me. They have to kill me. They can't risk me wandering free, telling someone else what I know. My very existence threatens them."

"How do you know this?"

"Because they're predators. And I know predators."

"Alari—"

"Please Tam," she said. "I have to sleep now."

The Sacinto paused, then said in a resigned voice, "I will look after you while you rest."

"Yes," she said as she drifted off. "You always do.".

13

VALE

"He is coming, *Alari*," Tam said, though he didn't have to. Vale knew. She felt it.

They had been inordinately lucky. When she had asked Crookbranch to teleport her and Tam to the Hallowed Woods to entice The Four to follow her back to the northern Lyantree forest, she'd hadn't imagined she'd find one of The Four here already, and alone. But Wulfric had been searching for her, scouring the Hallowed Woods from one end to the other. Apparently, the other members of The Four had relegated the hunt for Vale to him.

Now, she waited outside a ring of eight Lyantrees with a makeshift trap laid between her and the direction from which Wulfric would come. Just outside the circle, Vale had created four standing stone monoliths in a square formation about six feet apart.

Every one of her senses crackled with magic, alert. She

was part of the Lyantrees now, felt what they felt, sensed what they sensed. They were her...Quad. Anything magical within the Hallowed Woods was like heat on Vale's skin, and Wulfric was a bonfire. He plowed through the undergrowth, trampled bushes, cracked branches and even entire tree trunks in his mindless passion to reach her. He'd caught Vale's scent because she'd wanted him to. He followed the trail she'd placed for him.

Vale grit her teeth as his bonfire presence neared. His careless flinging of Impetu magic hurt the Lyantrees around him. It hurt her, too. She could feel his hate—the force of it and the textures.

Wulfric hated...everything. If it were up to him, he would kill everyone and everything around him. His continuous rage for Arsinoe in particular was like a smoky red dragon perched on his shoulders, digging in with sharp talons.

Wulfric even longed to kill all of his Quad mates, but he fought his desire because he needed them. If he killed them, the vastness of his power would vanish, and he hated that need most of all.

Only pure action gave him respite. When he ran fast enough, when he leapt over gorges or broke a tree trunk in half, and especially when he killed, his anger thinned, tapering out behind him like a ribbon. But when he stood still, the ribbon piled up within him, coil after coil until he thirsted for blood.

And right now, he wanted Vale. His rage lashed him onward and it would only stop when he found her and tore her limb from limb.

Come and get me, Vale thought.

Tam began to shift from foot to foot as he felt the tension mount within Vale, felt the moment nearing.

"It is time for the killing, *Alari*?" the Sacinto asked.

Annoyance flared up in her.

"Shut up, Tam," she said.

"Alari Alari Alari..." he murmured over and over again, hands against his head.

She checked her anger. It actually served her purpose to have him whispering. With his Impetu ears, Wulfric would hear, and it would drive him harder, sure that his prey was almost within reach.

Vale had opened herself to the Lyantrees. She was so full of magic that, every now and then, a little crackle of lightning arced from her neck to her arm or between her hands, visible from the outside.

Now she could hear Wulfric's crashing and cracking of branches with her human ears, rather than feeling it through her connection to the Lyantrees.

Seconds later, Wulfric burst into the glade at inhuman speed.

Part of an Impetu's power was heightened animal instincts. Sight, sound, smell, touch. And the sense when danger was near. Vale had thought Wulfric would charge right at her in his mindless rage, but he skidded to a halt, digging deep furrows in the grass. He sniffed the air as though something wasn't right.

His glowing green gaze, nearly hidden behind the slits of his square helmet, flicked to the four standing stones between him and Vale. Then he looked at the circle of Lyantrees behind her.

She had meant to act frightened and step back toward the Lyantree circle when she saw him, as though she was going to teleport away again. She'd intended to trigger his chase reflex, entice him into the center of the standing stones.

But he had sensed the trap. He saw the stones and

seemed to realize they were intentional.

The idea flashed through her mind that she should taunt him, try to bypass his caution by igniting his rage.

Instead, she laughed. None of it mattered now. He was close enough. He'd come here thinking she wasn't going to escape. But it was Wulfric who was trapped. The magic lanced through her, crackles of lightning racing all over her body. It made her feel invincible.

"Has it sunk through your thick head yet, you animal?" she asked.

Wulfric glanced at Tam, who continued his litany, "*Alari Alari Alari…*"

"What is this?" Wulfric growled.

"For you?" she said. "The end."

He snorted. "You think yourself clever that you set this little hook, lured me here? But you're going to die. I'll stick that hook through your neck!"

"You're not the fish, you steel-clad moron," Vale said darkly. "You're the bait."

He roared and lunged at her.

Twenty Soulblocks of magic spit and forked through her. Lightning lanced into the standing stones. They rose into the air and slammed into Wulfric from all sides, smashing together and then melting into a boulder ten feet in diameter.

But even with her own Impetu-enhanced reflexes, he almost reached her before the trap slammed home. His meaty, iron-clad forearm stuck out from the perfectly round boulder. His hand went wide in shock, then clenched into a dying fist.

It twitched, then went still.

Vale fell to her knees, spent. Her sense of invincibility fled, and she felt like a cracked pitcher, barely able to keep enough magic inside herself to raise her head.

But she looked up at the monstrous boulder encasing the Impetu of The Four. She looked at his limp, dead fist hanging pitifully out of the rock, inches above her head.

"We did it, Tam," she breathed. "The Four are broken. Wulfric is dead, and that means the rest of them are just shadows of what they were. We will take them. One by one."

She raised her head—

"*Alari!*" Tam tackled her.

Wulfric's hand swiped at her head, five iron fingers scraping through hair and flesh and narrowly missing catching her in a grip that would have crushed her head like an egg.

The agonizing pain shot through her even as warm blood trickled down her scalp. She and Tam looked up, aghast, as Wulfric's hand thrashed this way and that, seeking anything it could grab.

Vale pressed her hands against the raw wounds, shocked.

He almost had me, she thought. *Gods, he almost killed me. How could he be alive? How was that possible?*

The next thought struck her hard. There was more here than she understood. She'd been arrogant to think she knew what was possible or impossible for the Impetu of The Four. It was a serious miscalculation, and everything could unravel if she didn't act quickly. If Wulfric could somehow survive being crushed by her boulder, if he could somehow fight his way free—

Gods, that wasn't even her biggest problem. If he was still alive…he might have summoned The Four, mind-to-mind, from within his prison. The Four could arrive any second, and Vale was spent. This was not her chosen battleground to fight all of them.

"Tam! We have to go," she croaked, so exhausted she

could barely speak.

With Tam's assistance, they limped toward the circle of Lyantrees together, toward safety.

But before Tam could activate the teleport, Vale hesitated.

"Wait, no," she said. "I can't leave him."

The most recent plan had been to kill Wulfric and leave him here in the Hallowed Woods to strike fear into the hearts of The Four, then lure them northward to the labyrinth. But if Wulfric wasn't dead, that wasn't going to work.

"If I leave him, they'll free him," she said. "And I'll be back where I started, except they'll know I can do this." She gestured at the boulder with Wulfric's desperately grasping hand. "We have to take him with us."

"How?"

"I have to try." Without another word, without another wasted moment, she reached out to the Lyantrees. Plentiful magic rushed into her, but she felt like a tattered sail trying to catch the wind.

"Gods!" she said, fighting the pain.

"Alari!"

Feeling like she was raking a knife down her insides, she forced herself to take the crackling magic and to send it out to do her bidding. Slowly, she forced the boulder to roll into the center of the Lyantrees.

"Take us…" she gasped to Tam. "Take us through."

"You will not make the journey, *Alari!*" Tam said.

"Do it!" she demanded.

The rainbow spheres grew around them and took them away, and Vale screamed. It felt like the magic was going to tear her apart. She kept screaming, but she stayed focused. She used the magic to force the boulder to roll after them. It felt like she was shoving a mountain with her bare hands.

She remembered traveling through the rainbow realm, remembered seeing their destination, that perfect circle of rainbow-swirled Lyantrees ahead.

But she didn't remember reaching them.

14

OLIVAARD

"Wulfric is missing," Olivaard said. He hoped his statement of the obvious would show his disappointment. "That is what you're saying."

"I...tried to find him," Linza said hesitantly. "But it is...difficult."

Ever before when Linza spoke, it was with authority. Her slightest whisper commanded attention. Her connection to the Soul of the World gave her words an oracular strength. In limited ways, she knew the future and could share it with them.

Right now she sounded like a frightened grandmother. Linza couldn't find Wulfric. It was bad enough she hadn't been able to pinpoint Vale. But now she couldn't even find her own Quad mate? Olivaard clenched his teeth. That meant losing Wulfric wasn't their only problem. Was Linza also somehow...faltering?

Arsinoe pretended not to care. Or maybe he actually

didn't care. Or maybe he was insane. Olivaard had grown tired of guessing.

The handsome-seeming Motus lounged in a red doublet and silken hose on one of the divans in their meeting room, eating thin slices of Fendiran dragon fruit, one after the other.

"Good riddance," Arsinoe said flippantly, settling back into the cushions. "Wulfric is boorish and he's constantly yelling. He's been a drag on us for years." Arsinoe flung a slice of dragon fruit into the air. It spun, reached the top of its arc, then fell directly into his open mouth. He chuckled and chewed.

There was no love lost between Arsinoe and Wulfric, but their Impetu was still part of The Four. Take away one member—even the most abrasive, disgusting member—and the magical ability of The Four dropped precipitously. They might as well become *normals*.

Arsinoe acted flippant, but he wasn't. He was scared.

They all were. For a hundred years the two kingdoms had danced to a tune played by The Four. In the last three years, though, things had mysteriously begun to go wrong. It had been little things at first. A few random portals opening from the Beneath. The nameless little Quad The Four had killed that had formed outside the academy in the Hallowed Woods. The noticeable increase in potential academy recruits; children with magic talent popping up everywhere. Initially, Olivaard had dismissed these as troublesome coincidences. But the problems had grown. Like Quads within the academy that had been set up to fail but somehow still managed to bond. Like the portals from the Beneath increasing in frequency. Like that upstart Brom actually defeating Linza and absolutely dismantling Arsinoe during his Test of Separation.

Elements that had been in hand for almost a century

were suddenly slipping out of control. And now Vale had not only thrown off Olivaard's mind-wipe spell and somehow cast away her amulet, but she'd vanished into the Hallowed Woods. Even Linza couldn't track her.

What had once seemed like a smattering of coincidences was beginning to look like an attack, like some crafty enemy trying to put a noose around their necks. But who could it be? If they were under attack, if this really wasn't just bad luck, Olivaard couldn't see the enemy.

And now Wulfric was suddenly missing. He'd gone to the plains north of the Hallowed Woods to see about another portal from the Beneath. The Four had been hunting for and closing these portals, keeping the One Beneath in check. The portals had been opening more frequently, all over the lands—sometimes in a back alley in Keltan, sometimes in a remote spot in the wilderness where humankind had never been.

With Linza's ability to feel disturbances in the Soul of the World, the portals were easy for her to spot. Wulfric had gone on dozens of these missions. This was supposed to have been routine. And it had been, right up to the moment he vanished.

Each of The Four had ivory necklaces that Olivaard and Linza had crafted. They were much like the Quadron amulets, and they allowed The Four to talk mind-to-mind over any distance.

On the first day Wulfric was overdue, Olivaard had assumed—with great annoyance—that their beastly Impetu had decided to spend more time looking for the missing Vale since he was so close to the Hallowed Woods. Olivaard had reached out to him mind-to-mind. When that hadn't worked, he'd commanded Linza to use the Soul of the World.

And now, just like Vale, Wulfric had vanished. And now, just like Vale, Linza could not find him. Olivaard felt a creeping fear. Wulfric should have been as easy to spot as a bonfire at midnight.

So either Wulfric was dead or…

Or Linza had somehow lost her connection to the Soul of the World.

Until now, Linza's power had been as immutable as the rising sun. She was the Champion of the Soul of the World, the most powerful Anima alive. She was the favored one, the first and foremost to whom the Soul of the World spoke. Her connection to it made her immortal. The Soul had resurrected Linza when Brom had killed her during that ridiculously sloppy and disappointing Test of Separation.

So while Wulfric's death would be a horrible blow, the thought that Linza might somehow have lost her magic might even be worse. It could mean she was no longer the Champion of the Soul of the World. It could mean the Soul had chosen a different Anima as its favored one.

That, as impossible as it seemed, meant Linza was no longer preeminent in her path of magic.

And if one of them could fail, how soon before the others did?

Arsinoe probably hadn't even noticed Linza's struggles yet. But Linza knew it. Her hesitancy gave her away, though perhaps she thought—or hoped—Olivaard hadn't noticed.

But if some powerful Anima had risen and claimed the mantle of the Champion of the Soul of the World, who was it? If such a person existed in the two kingdoms, Linza would have spotted them and brought them to the academy long before they could become powerful enough to challenge her. If it had been someone from across the sea come to Keltovar or Fendir, they'd have shown up in Linza's mind the moment they set foot upon this continent.

There had only been one Quad in the last fifty years with that kind of ability, and Quad Brilliant had been dealt with. They had sent Brom home in a pine box. Oriana and Royal were carefully planted in their respective kingdoms, lashing out at each other and doing exactly what they were supposed to do. They were in hand.

Vale had gone rogue, but she was alone. And she was a Motus. She couldn't become the Champion of the Soul of the World.

Could she?

Olivaard tried to wrap his mind around that concept. Could it actually be Vale? Could she somehow have disrupted Linza's connection to the Soul of the World?

"Maybe Wulfric finally just left." Arsinoe broke the prolonged silence. "He's always hated us. Every last one of us."

"You'd have me believe he has broken the Quad on purpose?" Olivaard replied.

"I would have you believe," Arsinoe mimicked Olivaard's voice. "That maybe it's good riddance."

"Your wisdom is a comfort," Olivaard said acidly. "I shall keep it in mind the next time I see a mere student reduce you to a pile of children's blocks."

Arsinoe's smile melted into a scowl. "Now why would you have to go and say that?" he asked in a low voice.

"Because this is serious."

"Serious?" Arsinoe said. "Wulfric has gone away on journeys ten times this long without checking in."

"Not when he's on a mission." Olivaard pointed out.

Arsinoe waved one hand negligently while grabbing

another dragon fruit slice with the other. "I don't think—"

"I have him!" Linza creaked suddenly.

Olivaard whipped around. Her cowled head twitched, and her hands gripped the air in front of her like she had ahold of a fishing pole. After a brief second, her fists jerked open like the pole had been ripped from her grasp. "I lost him."

Olivaard pulled a teleporting coin from his pouch. He reached into Linza's mind, and she let him. There, he saw what she had just seen. Flattened long grass. The edge of a forest.

He knew exactly where that was. He knew it like he knew his own name.

He flicked the coin at the floor. A loud "clang" sounded, and a copper circle grew up from the ground, creating an archway.

One after the other, they leapt through the portal. Arsinoe jumped from the couch so quickly he went through the portal before Linza.

Olivaard landed on the matted long grass of the plains that led up to the great and hidden eastern Lyantree Forest. Wulfric wasn't there.

Linza pointed. "He was right there. He was…encased in stone," she said uncertainly.

"Wulfric!" Arsinoe called. "Is this one of your 'hunting the hunter' games?" He sauntered toward the trees. "Don't be an ass."

But Wulfric didn't emerge. Either Arsinoe was right—this was one of Wulfric's hunting games, particularly insensitive and poorly timed—or someone had dangled him outside the Lyantree Forest to catch Linza's attention, then pulled him back in.

Arsinoe glanced at Olivaard, confused. "Do you really

think someone could kidnap Wulfric?" he asked.

"What about a member of Quad Brilliant?" Olivaard responded.

Arsinoe stopped walking toward the trees. "Vale? She ran like a squirrel from Wulfric the last time!"

"Can you think of anyone else who might be so audacious?"

"But she knows nothing!" Arsinoe protested. "She's barely a Quadron."

"And Brom was barely a student," Olivaard said.

"If it is her, she's signed her death warrant," Linza creaked. "Showing her face. Bringing us here."

Arsinoe began laughing. "Oh, I hope it *is* her."

Olivaard didn't feel Arsinoe's confidence. There were simply too many questions without answers. He didn't like this one bit. This unnamed Lyantree forest was supposed to be a secret. The Four had kept it a secret for a century because of its immense power. In this place or in the Hallowed Woods, The Four could become a hundred times more powerful than normal.

So could Vale, if she had a Quad to help her.

But she had no Quad. Without her Quad mates to help her contain the power of the Lyantrees, her body would come apart.

Again, more questions and no good answers.

"Let's teach her the last lesson she will ever learn," Arsinoe said. He cracked his knuckles.

"Yes," Linza hissed.

"Stay alert," Olivaard warned.

They entered the forest. The moment Olivaard strode underneath the thick canopy of purple-silver leaves, he reached out with his mind and his magic. Linza sighed deeply, obviously connecting to the limitless Soulblocks within the Lyantrees.

Olivaard felt the Soulblocks in the forest—
And found Vale's mind already connected to them.

15

VALE

The Four had come at last, and Vale was ready. When she stepped between the trees and saw the look of shock on Olivaard's stupid, elongated face, it was the closest thing to happiness Vale had felt since she'd lain in Brom's arms in his dorm room back at the academy.

"Your time is done," she said through her teeth.

Linza hissed, crouching to leap forward, but Vale had no intention of letting her do anything. The magic crackled through Vale, a half-dozen Soulblocks at once, and a hole in the earth opened beneath Linza. Her crouched legs sprung futilely with nothing beneath them. She fell, wailing, into the darkness.

Vale opened another hole beneath Olivaard, who wasn't nearly as fast as his Quad mate. He only opened his enormous mouth into an enormous O before he tumbled silently from view.

The holes slammed shut over Linza and Olivaard with

the crunch of stone. Vale sent them straight down into her prepared maze, drove them deep and far away from each other, breaking their Quad bond before they had a chance to respond.

Let the arrogant Olivaard use his Mentis magic on solid rock for a few hours before she put an end to him. Let Linza run through the maze, looking for the way out. Even with the Soul of the World, it would take her time to find the surface. And Vale only needed a minute to do what she'd been aching to do since the moment she had ripped the veil away from her nightmare.

"Hello, Arsinoe," she said. Arsinoe wasn't going to have to fight the maze. He was going to face Vale's anger and a hundred Soulblocks' worth of power.

He narrowed his eyes and took a step away from her, looking confused. The sudden vanishing of his Quad mates had cracked his smug expression.

Vale unleashed half a dozen Soulblocks. With a thought, she made the Lyantrees behind Arsinoe lean toward him, branches extending, creating an intertwined wall of foliage.

His head twitched, looking back and forth, seeing his escape cut off. The sleazy villain wasn't going to get out of this forest alive. He snapped his gaze to focus on Vale. She could feel his heart racing.

"Ah Vale…" he said and, despite it all, his voice came out smooth and confident. "You are delightful."

"Delightful?" She showed her teeth. She wanted to kill him right now. She should just do it, but she couldn't let it be that simple. He'd sliced her open and made her suffer in the way she'd most feared. That wound still bled, and she needed to look into his eyes and see them light up with terror and helplessness. She needed more than Arsinoe's death. She wanted him to beg for his life first.

"So…revenge?" he asked. "Is this whole…" He waved a hand at the trees. "…production an angry response to our last meeting? Really, Vale…" He shook his head like she was a petulant child, like what he'd put her through wasn't important.

"You're going to die here, Arsinoe," she hissed. She needed him to react, to show some sign of fear.

"You still think what I did was designed to hurt you?"

"You *did* hurt me," she shouted. "You beat me bloody!"

He chuckled. "Tell me you're not that dumb." He raised his arms and turned slowly, as though gesturing to the entire forest. "Look at you. Look at what you've accomplished. Do you think that's an accident? What do you think our meeting was?"

"I know what our *meeting* was."

"Of course I beat you," he said, unrepentant, and his emerald gaze held her. "Of course I did," he repeated in a whisper. "I was supposed to."

"Supposed to?"

What was he talking about? He spoke as though her torture was normal, natural. She shook her head.

"Every Quadron must be strengthened before they are allowed to leave the academy."

"You didn't test me. You *tortured* me."

He gave that dismissive head shake. "Everyone who passes the Test must be tempered before they can go out into the lands, before they can be allowed to wield such power among *normals*. We have to make sure you're strong enough."

"That's a lie."

"We do it with every newly made Quadron," he said.

She shook her head, but his words made sense to her. Quadrons were so powerful compared to normals. So potentially dangerous. "I…I don't believe you."

He chuckled. "Yes you do. We can't just let anyone become a Quadron, even if they pass the strenuous Test of Separation. It would be incredibly irresponsible. Can you imagine what might happen if we graduated weak-willed Quadrons? What if some ruthless Keltovari duke or Fendiran priestess druid manipulated or tortured a Quadron into doing their bidding? It would be a disaster."

"Stop talking," she said. "That's… That's what the Test of Separation is for."

"The Test identifies a Quadron's greatest weakness. We use that knowledge. We strengthen our Quadrons."

"No. The Champions Academy is a lie…" she said. "You…split Quads. You make…slaves." But she didn't feel confident about that anymore.

"Slaves? Really?" Arsinoe said, and she felt embarrassed.

"You tortured me…" she repeated softly, but her argument, which had seemed so strong before, suddenly seemed petty. The Four had been helping Quadrons for a hundred years. They knew far more than she did.

"Vale, I tempered you like a sword in the fires of a forge. And you emerged as the strongest Quadron we've ever seen," he said. "Power comes with a price. You of all people should know that. Now you've paid that price. And look at you! Look what you have done. You are *magnificent.*"

His praise felt like warm sunshine on her shoulders. Gods, he was right. It was because of her revelations about him that she'd pushed this hard, learned how to speak to the Lyantrees, learned how to wield their magic.

"And there are so many more secrets to reveal," he said, moving closer to her, away from the curving wall of branches. "You've exceeded all of our expectations, but you've barely scratched the surface of what there is to know."

Excitement thrilled through her. The Four knew secrets. They knew things no one else in the two kingdoms could fathom. And she could have those secrets. She could be brought into that power.

"We'll unlock the tower for you," Arsinoe murmured. "You've proven you're ready." He stood next to her now, and she felt comforted by his nearness. "We'll show you everything." He lifted her chin with his slender, beautiful fingers.

She luxuriated in that feather-light touch and gazed up at him. His emerald green eyes glinted.

"Yes..." she said dreamily.

Just beyond Arsinoe, at the edge of the small clearing, stood Tam. He watched her with concern, hands clasped in front of himself.

"Alari?" he said.

Arsinoe twitched, shooting a quick glance to the Sacinto.

A spike of horror cracked Vale's euphoria.

Gods! Arsinoe was using magic on her! He'd slipped past her defenses somehow, and she hadn't even felt it. She'd actually *believed* his lies, had felt embarrassed that she could ever doubt him.

Arsinoe only looked away for a split second before he snapped his focus back to Vale. The euphoria, the hope, the excitement rushed into her again. But this time, she saw it for what it was.

She drew her dagger and jammed it into his side.

He gasped. Her euphoria popped like a soap bubble.

Rage boiled up inside her as she realized just how close she'd been to losing this battle. If Tam hadn't distracted

Arsinoe, he'd have had her. She'd have laid down and let him truss her up again, all the while believing it was a good and wonderful thing.

Arsinoe staggered back, the dagger sticking out of his side, fixed there like she'd driven it into a block of wood. Instead of making a wound, it had pushed a chunk of his body out of place, leaving a square hole right through the middle of him.

"You bitch!" Arsinoe cursed, trying to shove the block back into place. He pointed at her, and a crackling ball of fear exploded within her. A heart-spike. "You're playing with fire," he growled.

"No," Vale growled back at him. "You are."

She opened her body to the Lyantrees and filled herself with magic. Four Soulblocks. Six Soulblocks. Twelve. Eighteen crackled through her. She could feel the strain in her bones, like they were being bent to the breaking point. She could feel the pull on her muscles as though the magic was trying to yank them from their anchors. She felt her skin stretching, like it would rip in a hundred places.

With a shout, she turned her magic on Arsinoe, weaving together Mentis, Motus, Impetu and Anima. She twisted reality.

Arsinoe blew apart.

His rich red clothing ripped away like cobwebs as chunks of him flew in every direction, but there was no blood. No flesh. No bones. It was as though he'd been a child's toy, a painted wooden man made of blocks. His head separated into a dozen squarish pieces, each thunking onto the grass. His arms and legs and torso divided and tumbled across the forest floor. The exterior of the chunks still looked perfectly human—stunned eyes still wide, fingers curled—but the insides of the blocks were as smooth as polished wood and as green as though they'd been painted the same color as Arsinoe's eyes.

Vale fell to her knees, then onto her side, spent. Tam rushed to her, cradling her head in his arms.

"Alari Alari Alari!" he said, obviously seeing she'd used too much magic.

"I had to," she gasped. "I thought...I could stop him from enslaving me. But he had me. Gods, if you hadn't been there, Tam... If you hadn't been there, I..." She didn't even want to think about that.

"You must rest, *Alari*. You must sit with the *lyans* and recover."

"It's done. Arsinoe is dead. The power of the Four is broken forever. They have no Quad anymore."

"What about the other two? In the maze," Tam asked.

"It will keep them separated long enough for me to rest."

"Come, *Alari*." Tam rose, putting her arm around his neck. "I will take you to the circle with Crookbranch."

"Wait." She winced. "Just...let me lie here for a moment. I just need...to lie still."

He hesitated, then gently put her back down, his brow furrowed in concern. She looked up at the silver and purple leaves overhead and allowed herself a moment of triumph. It was over. Gods, it was over! No matter what The Four did now, even if somehow Vale failed to kill the rest of them, their real power was shattered. Their reign was over.

"This...was for you, Brom," she murmured.

"You...are...laughable..." Arsinoe said.

Vale sucked in a long, thin breath. Painfully, she pushed herself up to a sitting position. Tam spun, shocked.

Arsinoe stood in the center of the glade. Or rather,

most of him did. His legs were full of squarish holes and he was missing his right foot, but he stood more-or-less upright. His torso was also missing pieces, and he hunched over. His left arm was missing, but his right was almost fully formed and, as she watched, he picked up the last piece of his head and shoved it into place.

"You think…you can kill one of The Four?" he said. "You think…you're the first to try?"

Vale's breath seemed stolen away. She wanted to leap to her feet, to flee, but her body was on fire with pain. If she stood, she was sure one of her arms or legs would tear loose, just like Arsinoe's.

"*Alari!*" Tam said.

Arsinoe shambled toward them, limping with his missing foot even as body pieces flopped toward him over the grass, eager to reassemble. He picked up a mostly-assembled left arm and put it back in place.

"Gods…" Vale said.

"You think because you unlocked a secret about Lyantrees it makes you a match for us? We've been unlocking secrets for a hundred years." He picked up the piece of his side she'd stabbed, with the dagger still sticking out of it. He yanked the blade free and contemptuously threw it to the grass at her feet. "You're pathetic," he said as he shoved the piece back into place.

Vale swallowed. She had to run. She had to get away from here. If nearly twenty Soulblocks of magic weren't strong enough to kill him, what could?

She didn't know what to do. And she knew Arsinoe was playing on her fear. He was elevating it, trying to strip her ability to think, but did it really matter? She was spent, her body nearly ripped apart from using so much magic, and in moments, Arsinoe would be at full strength.

"We'd hoped to use you, put your talents to work,"

Arsinoe said. He loomed over her. "We won't make that mistake twice." He reached down, grabbed her by the throat and lifted her.

"Alari!" Tam threw himself into Arsinoe's side. Arsinoe's grip faltered and Vale fell to the ground.

"Kelto's teeth," Arsinoe swore. He grabbed Tam by his tunic and slammed him into the ground. Tam gasped as Arsinoe took hold of the Sacinto's throat. "I can see I'm going to have to kill you first, branch head." Tam struggled, but he couldn't get Arsinoe's hands off. His face darkened to purple as Arsinoe choked him.

"No!" Vale screamed, and she did the only thing she could do. She opened herself to the magic of the trees again.

Lightning crackled into her and she screamed. It felt like a hundred daggers stabbing into her body all at once, into her arms and legs, into her chest.

Arsinoe snapped his gaze up, releasing Tam and reaching for Vale, trying to disrupt her spell.

The magic ripped through her, but Vale opened the ground beneath Arsinoe just as he leapt at her.

With a grunt, his waist hit the edge of the hole and one of his flailing arms snatched Tam's wrist. Tam jerked and slid toward the hole as Arsinoe went over.

"Tam!" Vale leapt onto her belly, catching Tam's waist, stopping them both. Vale strained under the weight, willing herself to hold on, but her strength was fading. Her body felt like it was held together by bloody strings. She couldn't even feel her legs anymore. If Arsinoe made it out of that hole, he'd won. She wouldn't have the strength to fight him again.

Her gaze fell on the dagger Arsinoe had contemptuously cast away. It lay right next to her.

She snatched up the weapon and twisted around.

Arsinoe scrambled up Tam's body like a giant feral squirrel, eyes ablaze with green flame. As he reached for her, Vale stabbed the dagger into Arsinoe's elbow, into the arm that clung to Tam. The joint separated and the arm came away. Arsinoe's reaching hand swiped right in front of her face, missing by inches.

He screamed in rage as he plummeted into the darkness.

Vale hauled Tam back up, onto the grass. He batted at the hand and forearm that still gripped his wrist until it came away, then kicked it into the hole.

Pushing the last of the crackling storm of magic out of herself, Vale slammed the hole shut.

Tam gripped her shoulders, and she slumped into him. Faintly, she heard his words warbling to her. "*Alari*, stay awake. *Alari*!" But she couldn't feel his touch. She couldn't feel the pain anymore. She couldn't feel anything.

Her eyes rolled up into her head, and the world faded to black.

16

VALE

Vale kept her eyes closed, focusing on the maze below and far away, closing off yet another passage, opening up more to shepherd her captives along. She let out a long breath as the magic crackled away. Her hand trembled on the bark of the Lyantree. Her skin had begun to split on the surface again.

It had been a week since she'd fought Arsinoe and imprisoned him with the others. She almost hadn't woken up after that last fight, but between Tam and the Lyantrees, they'd nursed her back to health.

When Vale had discovered the ocean of magic within the Lyantrees, she'd thought it was limitless. But there was a limit—Vale herself. She could only channel so much before her body started coming apart.

And The Four knew it.

They were fighting her fiercely now, and she was losing the battle. While Vale had been unconscious, Linza had found a way to rejoin Wulfric and she had broken him out of Vale's boulder. That reunion had made them both stronger, and they'd begun hunting through the labyrinth for their Quad mates.

Vale had been forced to close off tunnels, create new ones, and continue to keep Arsinoe and Olivaard far away from their fellows.

But it turned out The Four also knew the secret of the Lyantrees. They were too far below the earth to be able to pull the kind of power Vale could, and that was the only reason she was still alive. If they could all access the magic the way Vale could, they'd have broken out of the labyrinth and converged on Vale already.

But Vale suspected one of them, at least, could pull some kind of magic from the Lyantrees, probably Linza. Every time Vale walled off Linza and Wulfric from their fellows, they managed to break through in another area that connected to the tunnels where Vale kept Arsinoe and Olivaard, and Vale had to close down those pathways, shift the rock again, create a new prison.

And it was slowly killing her.

Linza had pushed Vale into an impossible choice: to keep using the magic until it tore her apart, or to stop fighting and let Linza and Wulfric reunite their Quad.

Death or death, and nowhere else to turn.

In desperation, she had constructed a sanctum to bolster her strength. It was a small island in the midst of a fast-flowing river. The river fed a circle of twelve friendly Lyantrees, including Crookbranch, who had agreed to continuously heal her. Her sanctum was the only thing that had kept Vale alive this long. But it wouldn't help her forever. It couldn't heal Vale faster than the magic did damage to her. And Linza simply would not stop. She forced Vale to continuously fight her.

She had begun to believe the fight was essentially over. She'd go until her last breath, but it was just a matter of time.

Then, as though the gods had seen fit to give her one last chance, she had felt the presence of a group of Keltovari touch the western edge of the forest today, and a plan formed.

So she had come here, to the place the Keltovari group was about to enter the forest. Vale had risked leaving her sanctum to entertain this one final hope.

"They come, *Alari*," Tam said. "Please don't, *Alari*. Please…"

"I have to, Tam." She raised her head and finally opened her eyes, sparing a precious bit of her attention to focus on the here-and-now instead of the maze below, where Linza and Wulfric even now chipped through rock, straight toward Olivaard like they could feel him.

Yellow light filtered down through the purple-silver leaves. Gods, it was a new day. That meant she'd been standing here with Tam for almost an hour, yet it had only seemed like a few minutes. Her grasp on reality was slipping.

"But the magic, *Alari*." The nubs of branches growing from his bark-brown forehead twitched. "You are already—"

"Be quiet, Tam."

The Keltovari rode horses, wending their way single file between the scaly trunks. Vale counted twelve of them, armed like soldiers. A dozen mules with wagons had been tethered at the edge of the trees, the wagons too wide to come deeper. It was a Keltovari harvesting expedition, come to chop down Lyantrees and turn them into magic weapons.

"You will scare them?" Tam asked. "Just scare them?"

"No killing," she said, and Tam fell silent, wringing his hands.

Vale clenched her fist against the Lyantree trunk and opened her connection to the magic again. It crackled into her. For just one instant—before the excruciating pain tried to rip her apart—she felt the ecstasy of it all.

Images of Brom flashed through her mind. His dorm room. His pale neck and dark eyes. His lips on hers. She could almost feel the brush of his whiskers against her skin. During that split second of euphoria when the magic crackled into her, she could imagine she was still back at the academy. During these moments, she remembered what it was to be happy.

Then her body shook as the pain hit and she keened through clenched teeth. The cracks in her skin pulled open a little more. Blood oozed out.

Tam whimpered. Vale closed her eyes and changed reality with the power of her will. The trees twisted and groaned, interweaving to form an enormous dragon.

Screams of fear and shock rose from the Keltovari.

"Careful, *Alari*! Please to be careful!"

Vale opened her eyes, and the tall straight trees surrounding the expedition were gone. In their place was a churned-earth clearing upon which stood the dragon, silver and green with scales and horns tipped in purple. The Lyantrees had bound together, twisting into the shape Vale had imagined. Silver tendrils of roots stretched up from the ground to every part of the dragon—its hind legs, its barrel chest, its underbelly, and its neck. Its long tail wound back, slithering beneath the churned earth.

The echoing hoof beats of the horses and the frantic thumping of wagons faded away as the party fled from Vale's monster.

Only one man remained, caught in the claws of the

dragon. The man twisted and writhed, struggling to free himself, but the dragon held tight.

"Kelto! Kelto!" the man cried in a high, panicked voice. His whole body shook violently. But despite his shock, he seemed to realize that the dragon had stopped attacking. "Please!" He managed to blurt, trying to communicate with the thing. He pushed feebly at the giant silver-green claw, but it didn't budge. "Please..."

"*Alari Alari Alari,*" Tam murmured, intense and focused on her.

Vale ignored him and limped forward, hunched over at the pain. She needed to get back to her island or she would die here. Linza and Wulfric were digging frantically, tearing great chunks of stone away with fists and magic. They had sensed her vulnerability, had sensed she'd used her magic on something other than fighting them.

Or perhaps they sensed her intentions, that she was going for help, that she was reaching out to perhaps the one person in the two kingdoms who could make a difference here.

Queen Oriana.

When Vale had sensed the Keltovari come to her forest, it had triggered the dream she'd had just after she'd come through the rainbow land from the Hallowed Woods—the dream that had restored her memories. The forgetting spell. Oriana's fidgeting. The scroll.

That second-year writ of passage, if given to any one of Quad Brilliant, would bring their memories back, would show them that The Four were villains.

Vale had come here to deliver a message. She had bet her life that Oriana still had that scroll, still kept it close to her at all times, still wondered why she needed it so badly.

If Vale could ignite Oriana's mind with the answer to

that mystery, if she could trigger the tripwire and bring Oriana's memories back…

It just might be the difference in this battle.

Vale grunted and hobbled forward alongside the dragon. It lowered its claw so that the shuddering, sobbing Keltovari man was level with her. His eyes were wild, whites showing around the edges.

"I have a message for Queen Oriana," Vale said hoarsely. "Tell her you saw me, that you saw what I could do. Tell her Vale says the answer is the writ of passage. That's what she's missing. That's why she can't remember. The scroll is the tripwire."

"Please! Please!" the man said.

"Do you hear me?"

"Yes! Yes!"

Vale felt faint, and her vision swam. She stumbled, but clenched her teeth and forced herself to focus on the man.

"The writ of passage," she said through her teeth. "It's the tripwire. Say it."

"The writ of passage. Yes! I'll do it!"

"It must be taken from her, then given back to her. Then you tell her where I am. You tell her to come."

"I will!"

Vale nodded, her vision blurring. She had to get back to her island.

The dragon opened its claw, and the man fell to the ground, lurched to his feet, and backed away.

"Thank you. Thank you thank you!" he babbled. He fled, scrambling over the churned earth toward the light at the edge of the forest where all of his fellows had gone.

Vale watched the fleeing man, watched the burst of sunlight engulf his dark silhouette as he broke the edge of the   forest.

Part V

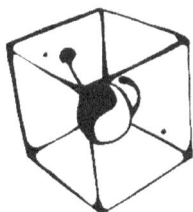

The Resurrection

1

BROM

AFTER SIX DAYS OF RUNNING, Brom finally stood on the rise overlooking the Champions Academy, breathing hard and holding his side. His feet were blistered and bleeding inside his boots. His dirt-crusted clothes hung loosely on his bony frame, and the claw wounds on his back and arms burned. He'd barely eaten since he'd fought his way out of his grave and killed the monster who'd tried to destroy him.

The white walls of the Champions Academy loomed in the distance. Seagulls gave their thin cries as they floated above a setting sun, and the scent of the lilac fields before him combined with the taste of blood at the back of his throat.

His skin crawled at the idea of going back inside the academy, but he had to. His friends were unaware, vulnerable, their necks exposed. And Brom might be able to save them. That single unlikely hope had driven him all the way here on ragged feet, praying with every painful step that he'd be in time.

His vision blurred, and he shook his head to clear his fatigue.

The Champions Academy's gate was an impregnable latticework of iron, and the entire place was bound with magic. But Brom had one advantage. He'd been a student there. Once, those protective spells had allowed him to enter, to walk the academy's halls without molestation.

If the protective magic still recognized him as a student, he needed only to sneak past the human guards. If not, Brom surmised the spells would repel him, alert The Four, and he'd be caught. And he knew the next time The Four tried to kill him, they'd make sure it was permanent.

He edged down the slope. Using the tall grasses and long shadows for cover, he slunk forward until he reached the packed and rutted road that led up to the academy's walls.

Scooting gingerly into the roadside ditch, he watched as a trade wagon rolled across the drawbridge through the open portcullis a hundred yards to his left. To his right, in the distance, two more wagons crested the hill and started down toward the academy. There. That was his way in.

Brom hunched down, fighting fatigue, until the two wagons trundled up alongside him. Their tired mules pulled and their bored drivers stared straight ahead. Just as the second wagon, full of bushels of wheat, reached Brom, he lurched from his hiding spot, grabbed the tailgate, and pulled himself underneath the wagon. His feet dragged—making so much noise he was sure the wagon drivers would stop—as he grappled with the spare wagon wheel chained to the undercarriage.

But the wheels kept creaking and rolling. Brom lifted

his right foot and jammed it into a crack in slats of the wagon bed. His muscles bunched tight with effort, and he lifted his left leg so it stopped bumping on the ground.

Aching seconds rolled by. The driver still didn't stop.

Please, Brom thought as his legs and arms began to quiver. *Please let me hold on long enough to get through the gate.*

He gritted his teeth, trying to keep his breath even and quiet as he wedged his other foot atop his shin to keep it from trailing in the dirt. The slices in his arms and back felt like they were splitting open again. He bit his lip to keep from gasping and focused on his trembling muscles.

Hold on, he demanded of them. *Just hold on.*

The wagon rolled interminably forward, and just when Brom thought he could no longer hold on, the iron-shod wheels thundered over the thick planks of the drawbridge. He permitted himself a gasp in the midst of the noise, shifted his grip and redoubled his efforts.

Just a little longer. A little longer…

The wagon stopped at the guard post, and by then Brom was shaking so badly he feared they'd hear the rattle of the spare wheel's chain. But the wagon driver talked briefly with the guards, and then the wagon rolled into the academy. Brom felt the telltale tingle of the academy's protection spell wash over him.

It didn't hurt him. *By the gods, it had worked!* It had accepted him as a student of the academy.

Beyond the gate lay a road of crushed white gravel. He craned his neck and saw the legs of the guards as they returned to their posts inside the wall—

Brom's foot slipped.

His legs thumped to the ground and his arms gave out at the same instant, dropping him right in the middle of the white gravel road. He rolled painfully to his knees, expecting a shout go up from the wagon driver or from the guards at the wall. Kneeling in the middle of that white road, he'd be as obvious as a fly in a bowl of milk. He raised his head, preparing to run…

…but no one shouted.

Bewildered, he looked at the guards. Both were faced away from him, their focus on the purple lilac fields beyond the drawbridge. Neither had seen him fall.

He craned his neck in the other direction. The driver faced the heart of the academy. They hadn't heard him either.

Astounded, Brom scrambled behind the nearby stables. He sidestepped to the south side until he was hidden from the tall wall and the road. The deepening shadows laid a dark cloak over him, and he huffed until he'd regained his breath.

When he could finally make his exhausted muscles move, he shuffled across the campus to Westfall Dormitory, sticking to the shadows. With his dirt-stained clothes, his unwashed face, and the brutish beginnings of a beard, he didn't look like a Champions Academy student. He clung to the shadows, hoping not to be noticed.

Students came and went through the front entrance of the dormitory, but the east side of the building was dark. As Brom had done a hundred times before, he painstakingly scaled the drainpipe until he reached the ledge outside the row of third floor windows.

What had been a regular adventure for him mere days ago was a trial he almost couldn't manage now. He almost fell twice, but he finally made it up, scooted carefully along the ledge, and pushed open Vale's window. He fell through onto her floor, breathing hard.

He had hoped she'd be there, that she would rush to him with a cry and embrace him. He longed for that, but she wasn't in the room. It was empty and…

A feeling of foreboding prickled up his spine.

The room was completely different.

She had changed…everything. In the place of her academy-provided pine wardrobe was now an ornate mahogany one. And she had hung a tapestry of a unicorn on the wall. Even the bed was different, draped with soft blue blankets and fine, light blue sheets rather than the dun-colored sheets and gray wool blanket given to each student as a matter of course. This kind of finery had been brought from outside the academy.

Like a ghost, he moved to the expensive wardrobe and opened the doors with an increasing sense of doom. Inside, there were more than a dozen dresses and skirts.

In the years Brom had known Vale, she'd never owned nor worn a dress. Everything she wore had been provided by the academy. And she had worn her academy-provided skirt only once. She'd had no money, no family outside to send her clothes or fancy sheets, let alone a mahogany wardrobe.

Maybe these were the spoils of becoming a Quadron. Maybe a stipend was given to newly made Quadrons. But why would Vale redecorate her room?

It simply felt wrong. Even if she would redecorate her student's room days after her Test of Separation, the more he looked around, the more this all felt like someone else's touch. He knew Vale. And even if they'd given her a chest of gold, she'd never spend it like this. She wouldn't buy frilly dresses, and she'd never have put a unicorn on the wall.

He pushed aside the dresses, looking for the academy-assigned clothing every student possessed, the clothing that indicated their path of magic: Mentis, Motus, Anima or Impetu.

He stumbled back from the wardrobe. The uniforms were blue! Impetu blue, not Motus red…

He cast about, certain that somehow he'd climbed into the wrong room. But no. There was the familiar thin crack in the mortar above the bed, snaking up to the ceiling. He had stared at that crack night after night in this room, Vale's naked body next to his.

This *was* Vale's room, but Vale didn't live here anymore. She'd left the academy, and they'd put someone else here.

But even that seemed wrong. Why would they move a new student into this room a week from the end of the year?

He calmed his racing mind and forced himself to look at the room differently, to look at it as some other student's room rather than Vale's.

His prickling sense of foreboding increased.

The desk in the corner was scattered with papers, some shelved in little slats. There were crates in the corner, stylish women's boots with dried mud on their heels at the foot of the bed.

He heard voices approaching the door. Quickly, he backed toward the window and climbed onto the ledge, ducking from view just as the door opened.

"…so frustrating," a haughty young woman's voice said as she strode into the room. "As if I should already know the width and breadth of pain control in my first year."

"They're just trying to expel you because of who you are," a wheedling voice responded.

"You're right, of course," said the first voice. "It's because of who my father is. They're pressing me harder, throwing obstacles in my path and making outrageous demands. They didn't do this to Queen Oriana. They built a road straight to the Test for her. They let her pass in her second year. Second! But me, no. They won't even give me a chance to learn."

Brom pressed his back against the marble wall. Who were these women? As an Anima, he could have looked into their souls, could have seen their desires and likely life paths. He'd have been able to glimpse something of their background and possibly why they were in Vale's room.

But his magic was gone.

Where Brom's magic had once been, there was only a hard little pebble, as though his Soulblocks had all been melted down to a useless lump. He'd spent every spare moment of his journey trying to coax his magic out, trying to recreate those Soulblocks. But Brom had failed to conjure even a whisper of magical confidence, let alone soul-sight. Night after night, day after day, every time he tried to use magic, the most that damned pebble ever did was vibrate.

He suddenly realized the voices in the room had gone silent.

"By Kelto, what is happening here?" the haughty girl suddenly demanded, her footsteps stomping toward Brom's hiding place. "If I'm damned to live in this drafty little cell, the servants can at least close the window! These academy drabs ought to be punished! How many slights am I to endure?" With an indignant huff, she slammed the window shut and locked it, never seeing Brom clinging to the ledge just outside.

Her muffled voice continued inside, but Brom couldn't make out her words anymore. It didn't matter. He'd heard enough. Clearly, this was the wrong room or...or something else was happening here that he didn't understand.

Quietly, Brom slunk back to the drainpipe and slid down to the ground. His rubbery legs collapsed, and he slumped against the base of the wall, breathing hard. He wanted to fall over and sleep for a week. His exhaustion pulled him down like he had stones tied to his body.

He looked back up the wall toward where Oriana's room would be, and he cursed himself. He should have thought to check Oriana's room before he slid down, but the idea of climbing up the drainpipe again made him quail.

For the first time since he'd begun his journey, despair crept over him. Too many little things didn't feel right. That haughty Impetu girl had referred to Oriana as "Queen Oriana." But Oriana was a princess, not a queen.

His stomach growled, and the cuts on his back burned horribly. Even the warm summer breeze seemed icy to him. He shivered.

I'm feverish, he realized. *My wounds... I should have taken care of them. I should have eaten something. I should have...*

A female student rounded the corner of the dormitory, close enough that Brom could have flicked a pebble and hit her. Her tawny hair bounced about her shoulders. When she glanced up at the darkening sky, her face was clearly visible, and he recognized her.

Caila! She was the first student he'd ever connected with at the academy, back when he and his Quad were struggling to bond.

She was dressed in black breeches, black boots, and a black tunic—the school uniform for an Anima—and she moved like a breeze, fluid and graceful. It was unmistakably her, and yet...she was different. Caila had been long-limbed and lean the last time he'd seen her, but now she had curves to her hips. Her breasts were larger, and her face rounder, as though she'd put on weight. As though she had…grown up.

In two weeks? What was going on here?

A chill crept through him.

New students in Vale's room. Caila looking older.

He had assumed he'd been buried and had awoken the next day. Or perhaps the day after. But what if he'd lain there for longer than that?

The hard pebble in his belly twisted, and Caila stopped, as though sensing him. She turned, spotted him and cocked her head. Brom must have looked a fright with his matted black hair, black scruff, and dirt-stained clothing, but she came forward unafraid. And why should she be afraid? She was a third-year student, practically a Quadron. She was a match for any ragged beggar.

"Caila," he said hoarsely.

She squinted. "Do I know you?"

"It's me," he said. "It's Brom." He pushed his matted hair away from his face.

She watched him for another breathless second, eyes narrow, then those same eyes went as round as coins. Her mouth formed an 'O'.

"Caila…" he began, but realized he didn't know what to say. He hadn't stopped to think about the effect he'd have on her. Brom was supposed to be dead.

Her calm courage had vanished, and she did look scared now. Her body tensed like she was about to flee.

"Please, Caila…" he said, and she hesitated, tight as a bowstring.

"Are you…a ghost?" she whispered.

"I don't know what I am," he said hoarsely. The strain of the last week crashed down on him. The hunger. The pain. This horrible confusion. He felt like a ship in a storm, sails in tatters, rudder broken. He'd been hanging on to one single certainty: if he could just rejoin his Quad, all would be mended. But his Quad wasn't here.

"You're... How can you... We saw your body. Your...coffin. They took it back to Kyn."

"They buried me," he said.

Her chin rose, her eyes widening. "In the Hallowed Woods?"

"I'm not a Lyancorpse," he said quickly.

She swallowed again, and she wrapped her arms around herself like she was cold. "Then what are you?" she asked.

"Just Brom. I'm just..." He clenched his fists, trying to marshal some meager strength, but tears burned his eyes. "Please. I need to...find out what's happened. How long...has it been?" he asked.

She swallowed, hesitating. Then her mouth set into a line, as though she'd come to a decision. She stepped toward him, into the shadow of Westfall Dormitory. "Since you died?" she asked. "You want to know how long it's been since you died?"

"It's been more than ten days, hasn't it?" he asked.

The surprise on her face told him more than words could, a surprise that quickly softened into compassion. "Oh Brom..." she whispered, and she descended to her knees next to him. "It's been a year. A whole year."

The last of his strength left him, and he leaned his head back against the marble wall.

"No..." Everything clicked together, and now it made sense. He had failed before he'd even begun his journey. He wasn't just late. He was far too late.

Whatever had become of Quad Brilliant, it had happened long ago.

2

BROM

BROM LET HIS EYES SLIDE SHUT. His strength trickled away, and he slumped against the wall. He had failed.

"Are they…okay?" he murmured to Caila. "Royal and Oriana. Vale…"

"What do you mean?" Caila asked.

"I mean… Are they in danger?"

"Royal, probably. Because of the war. He has been on the front line since he left the academy, as you'd expect. But the queen doesn't participate in battles."

"The queen?"

"Queen Oriana. Sorry. Yes. She took the throne earlier this year."

"*Queen* Oriana…" Brom repeated what the haughty Impetu student had said. "And Vale?"

"I don't know, Brom," Caila said. "They all left the academy as Quadrons. Just like the Quadrons before them. I suspect she is on a mission for The Four. I've

heard nothing about Vale. I hear a lot about Queen
Oriana, of course. Struggles with the war. The Butcher
has turned the tide in the Hallowed Woods. There are
worries he may encroach on Keltovari lands soon."

"The Butcher?"

"Sorry. That's Royal now. That's what they call him
ever since the battle of Gore Grove last Springdawn.
Well, the Fendirans officially call him the Oaken Knight,
but almost nobody uses that title. So yeah, I know a bit
about Royal, too. But I don't know about Vale. Did
anyone even know where she came from?"

"Torlioch," he said.

"Maybe she went back to Torlioch, then?"

"But you don't know."

"Only The Four would know," she said.

"The Four," he said, remembering those bloody last
moments of his Test, how Olivaard had promised he
would punish the rest of Quad Brilliant.

Caila took his hands in hers, and gave a little shake to
them, like she couldn't believe she was holding them.
"Your hands are warm," she said. "In my Anima sight,
you're not a ghost. You're as alive as anyone."

Brom had been lying in a grave for a year. A year! How
was that even possible?

His Quad was scattered across the two kingdoms.
Oriana and Royal had become blood enemies again. Vale
had vanished. Brom was just a ragged beggar with no
home and no friends. And no hope of reassembling his
Quad. No hope of reclaiming his magic.

He could barely keep his eyes open now. It was all too
much, and he just wanted to rest. He'd tried. He'd failed.
It was over.

"You're a fourth year now," he murmured to Caila,
and he thought of at least one thing he could do. He

could warn Caila.

"Yes…" she said, as though she didn't understand what he was getting at.

"You take the Test this year."

Her eyes narrowed. "I'm supposed to."

"Don't," he said. "Don't do it."

She cocked her head, suspicious. "Don't take the Test?"

He was about to tell her that becoming a Forgotten was far preferable to becoming a Quadron, but he faltered.

How much should he actually say to her? How much could he really trust her? How much could he afford to say to *any* student of the academy? Caila hadn't seen Brom pull away the veil that hid The Four, revealing them as villains. She hadn't seen them come after Brom with murder in their eyes. She still believed The Four were benevolent demigods, and he doubted anything he could say would change her mind.

"What do you know?" she asked. "Do you know something?"

"I…" She might be reading his soul right now, gleaning bits of the information.

"Do you know where they are?" Her eyes lit with interest.

That wasn't the question he'd expected. "Where they are?" He glanced in the direction of the looming Tower of the Four.

"You *don't* know," she said, now a little confused. "You weren't talking about the fact that The Four were missing?"

"Missing?"

"The Four have disappeared. That's what we think, anyway. No primers have been announced. We're three and a half weeks past the end of the school year and no Tests of Separation have been taken. And the masters have been holding secret meetings. A lot of them have left the campus, too. I haven't seen The Collector or Master Tohn Gelu all week. Master Saewyne isn't saying anything, but…" She shrugged.

Brom winced at a hunger pang in his belly, then shifted to sit a little more comfortably against the wall. Caila reached into her pouch and pulled out an apple. She handed it to him.

"Here. Please. You look ravenous," she said.

He tore into it like a mongrel dog. The sweet juice burst in his mouth. It seemed to fill his whole body with light.

"Gods…" he murmured as he chomped and chewed. "Gods, thank you."

"You're welcome." She went quiet for a moment, which was fine with him. All he could think about was the juicy…crunchy…gods it was good! He devoured it down to the core and then, after a moment's consideration, ate the core, the seeds, everything.

She handed him a slice of bread wrapped in wax cloth.

He took the bread from her and devoured it just as quickly.

"Kelto's teeth, Brom. Slow down," she said.

His stomach had already told him it was full-to-bursting, so he stopped. Immediately, he felt a lassitude. His body had gotten sustenance. Now it demanded sleep.

"Thank you," he said. "Thank you for your kindness, Caila. You have no reason to be sweet to me."

"No reason?" she said, and she gave a tentative echo of the saucy smile she'd given him so long ago in Quadron Garden. "Hey," she said, winking. "How often does a legend come back to life?"

"Legend?" he murmured, but words sounded distant to him. This piece of hard ground against this hard wall suddenly seemed like a great place to sleep. His eyes slid shut.

"Hold that thought, Brom," Caila said. She took his wrist, wrapped his arm around her neck and pulled him to his feet with a grunt. "Up you go. Let's get you to my room. Then you can rest."

With the darkening twilight he could barely see the shapes of the buildings as he stumbled along. She guided him quickly through the quiet campus until they reached a row of small, identical marble houses. He recognized it as the fourth-year housing. The first-year class mostly lived in Westfall Dormitory. But each graduating class lost about half of their students between the year-end test failures and students simply dropping out, taking the path of the Forgotten. By the time a whittled-down class reached its fourth year, there were only a handful of Quads remaining. The fourth-year accommodations were far fewer and far more private.

Twenty of these tiny marble houses lined the white gravel road, with sculpted gardens and twisting trees in their front yards. Caila led him inside the third house from the right.

There were only two rooms inside the small house: the main room and the bathroom. Caila's bed was to the left and her desk against the near wall. A stove and a table with a hand-washing basin stood to the right. The doorway to the bathroom was behind that, open. He could see a giant tub full of water.

Brom staggered toward the bed.

"Oh no you don't," Caila grabbed his wrist, led him to the bathroom. "I had a bath waiting. It was going to be mine, but now it's yours."

"I just need to sleep," he said.

"Not like that, by Kelto. Not in my bed."

Barely able to stand, Brom staggered to the tub. She helped him strip his clothes away and led him to the warm water.

"Gods Brom, what happened to your back?" she whispered, looking at the lacerations. She eased him into the tub, and he hissed as the water touched his cuts. It lanced through his fatigue, waking him up.

With her sleeves rolled up, she washed his back thoroughly as he gritted his teeth. When he was finally clean, she helped him out of the filthy water, dried him off and laid him face-down on her bed.

She pushed a new candle into the candlestick on the nightstand and lit it. The soft glow drove back the darkness, lighting her kind face.

The smell of the fresh soap and the melting wax was comforting. He felt Caila press soft cloths against his cuts. He was so tired, so ready to fall asleep that it barely even hurt.

"You're a mess," she murmured, and her voice seemed to be getting more and more distant. "You're going to need more than I can give you. I'll speak to the masters."

The pebble in his belly vibrated, and he forced his eyes back open. "No," he tried to say, but it only came out as a mumble.

"Brom?" she asked.

"No," he managed to say.

"Brom, you need a healer. These cuts... They're inflamed—"

"No masters," he said. "The Four are..."

"The Four are what?" she asked.

"The Four are evil," he murmured into her pillow. He didn't want to tell her about The Four, but he couldn't risk her bringing any of the masters here. "They wanted me dead... They...tried to kill me during the Test."

"What?" she whispered. "That's crazy."

"Evil..." he murmured. He had to say more. He needed to make sure she understood what he meant. But his words swirled away on a tide of darkness. He simply didn't have any strength left.

"Sleep, Brom," Caila's sweet voice floated down to him. "I'll take care of you. I'll stay right here. All through the night."

"No masters..." he insisted.

"No masters," she replied. Her promise was like a knife severing his last line to consciousness, and he fell into sleep.

3

BROM

BROM SLEPT SO DEEPLY he forgot about his pain. He didn't know how long he drifted there, but soon he became aware of that damned pebble in his belly, twisting, vibrating, insistent.

Let me sleep, he thought.

The twist became a stab. He gasped and sat upright. The sheet fell away, and he stared around the dark room, blinking. It took him a long moment to remember where he was. Caila's house. He was inside Caila's house at the academy. The stumpy, guttering candle told him it had been several hours since he'd fallen asleep.

And Caila was gone.

He rolled off the bed onto his feet, wincing at the pain in his back. He hobbled to the chair, grabbed his dirty breeches and pulled them on. The cuts on his back felt enormous—giant ridges pulsing with heat—and his head still seemed fuzzy. He staggered to the bathroom, the cold tile of the floor helping to wake him up. The tub was still full of dirty water. No Caila.

I'll stay right here, she'd said. *All through the night.*

The pebble in his belly vibrated again, and Brom's ears perked up as he heard voices approaching.

"It'll be all right, dear," a woman's smooth voice—not Caila's—came from outside.

"He needs help," Caila answered. "I just… I didn't know what else to do. I mean, he's supposed to be dead! We saw his coffin."

"You did the right thing, dear," the smooth voice said again, and this time Brom recognized it. That was Master Saewyne.

"He was raving about The Four trying to kill him."

"Was he?" Master Saewyne said.

"Is he… Is that possible?"

"Oh dear. It sounds like his paranoia infected you. The Four? Hurt someone?" She gave a throaty chuckle. "The boy obviously needs help. And we're going to help him." Brom didn't like the sound of Saewyne's voice, and neither did the agitated pebble in his belly. Saewyne sounded like a liar, but Caila wasn't picking up on it.

"Maybe it's a fever dream," Caila said.

"Dream?"

"Those cuts on his back. They're infected. I think he was attacked by an animal."

"Undoubtedly the case," Master Saewyne said.

Their footfalls crunched on the gravel in front of the house, and there were more than just two of them. Three or four sets of feet crunched up the walk. Saewyne had brought healers.

Or guards.

"Thank you for helping me," Caila said. "For helping him."

"He's to be a bit of a celebrity soon, isn't he? The fourth who survived the Test. So many stories to tell, I'm sure," Saewyne said. The master's placating, oily tone should have been apparent to Caila, as well as the unspoken threat. Saewyne didn't intend to have Brom tell any of his stories. And he was suddenly sure that Saewyne wasn't going to let Caila talk about any of this afterward either. The masters wouldn't allow a witness to someone surviving their rigged test.

Caila sighed happily, as though everything was going to be all right. She wasn't hearing the same thing in Saewyne's voice Brom heard because Saewyne was using magic on her.

Saewyne was a Motus. She had the power to manipulate the emotions of those around her. Brom remembered how she'd liked to cause chaos in her students' emotions. He remembered the conflicting emotions he'd always felt in her classes. She would be icy, aloof, and then she'd saunter across the room like she was trying to draw the gaze of a lover. He'd find himself spellbound, watching her sensual movements, watching the pull of her tight clothes. Then she would turn and lance him—and every other student who had been caught by the same spell—with a glance. Every time Brom had left one of her classes, he'd felt half scared of her and half smitten with her.

Caila was undoubtedly hearing just the right tone to keep her docile and obedient.

Brom froze in indecision. There was a window in the bathroom. He could leap out and try to run, but then what would happen to Caila? She already knew enough to make her inconvenient to The Four—and to Master Saewyne if she was a knowing part of the horror of this school. What would Saewyne do to Caila after Brom

142

escaped? They'd mind-wipe her.

Or kill her.

"Dammit," he swore under his breath. Caila had done what he'd told her not to do, but he couldn't let her die because of it.

He lunged at the chair, snatched the dagger belt hanging there, then shrank into the bathroom just as the front door opened. With soft hands, he opened the bathroom window, hunched through it, gritting his teeth against the pain of his cuts, and dropped to the ground. The air was cool, and he shivered.

"Caila," Saewyne said, irritated. "There is no one in your bed."

"He was right here," Caila said, surprised. Brom heard her footsteps running to the bathroom.

He didn't hear the rest of what she said because he sped around the outside of the house, crouching low as he reached the front. He peeked around the corner at the front porch.

A grey-clad guard stood there, peering watchfully left to right. Brom ducked back behind the corner just before the guard's gaze swung in his direction. Thankfully, the man was just a normal guard, not a Quadron. But…was he alone? Had Saewyne brought more than one?

As emaciated as Brom was, he'd have to take the guard by surprise and end the fight quickly. If he stumbled even once, took too much time, Saewyne would come running, and Brom was no match for a Quadron.

One strike. So quiet no one would hear.

Brom came around the corner like a wraith. He took two quick steps, leapt onto the porch and jumped into a spin kick, flinging his leg out at the guard, who was looking in the other direction.

The guard spun at the last second, saw Brom, and his

eyes flew open—

—just as Brom's heel caught him in the temple. The guard's head snapped to the side, and his eyes rolled up. With a quiet little puff of surprise, he crumpled to the porch.

Brom landed with a thump, unable to believe that had actually worked.

He'd trained to throw that kick over and over when he was a student here, but only after opening a Soulblock, when magic and an Anima's certainty flowed through him.

The thump of his landing made Saewyne, Caila, and a second guard inside the dark house spin about. They saw Brom through the open door.

"Brom!" Caila cried.

"So it's true," Saewyne hissed.

The second guard didn't hesitate. Maybe he didn't know who Brom was. Or maybe he was simply unimpressed by the living dead. He charged, long sword ringing from its scabbard.

Brom lunged toward the house like he was going to attack. The guard took the bait and swung his sword overhead, just as Brom ducked to the side. The long sword, too large to effectively use inside a small room, hit the doorjamb and stuck. The guard cursed and yanked on the blade, but before he could pull it free, Brom reappeared and rabbit-punched him in the throat.

The guard coughed, trying to back away, but Brom grabbed the man's tunic and yanked him forward. Brom dropped to his back, shoved his feet into the man's belly and vaulted him overhead. The man cried out as he crashed headfirst into the steps, tumbled to the ground, then lay still.

Brom rolled to his feet, stunned he had disposed of

both guards in about ten seconds.

A stupid little chuckle escaped his throat. That was the most ridiculously lucky thing he'd ever seen.

He tamped down the sudden giggle and turned his gaze on Saewyne. Two *normals* was one thing. A full-fledged Quadron was something else entirely.

Master Saewyne stood in the main room, eyes narrowed, tense, like she was afraid of him.

It suddenly occurred to him she had no idea he'd lost his magic. She probably thought he was using it right now. The kind of luck he'd just displayed was exactly what Animas were known for.

Maybe he could use that! Maybe he could frighten her into fleeing.

"Don't make me hurt you," he growled in his hoarse voice, pointing his dagger at Saewyne's throat.

"Brom, what are you doing?" Caila blurted.

"Come with me, Caila." He held out his other hand. "Come with me right now."

"How did you survive?" Saewyne asked breathlessly.

"Brom, you're hurt," Caila continued. "You're talking crazy. Let us help you."

"Caila dear," Saewyne said in a sweet voice. "I think it's best if Brom and I talk alone."

The pebble in Brom's belly vibrated.

"Don't listen to her, Caila!" he urged.

"He's just confused and scared, dear," Saewyne said. "Let me handle it."

Caila hesitated, as though maybe she sensed Saewyne was manipulating her. Brom held his breath, hoping she would shake off the spell.

"O-Of course," Caila stammered and headed toward the bathroom.

"She's using magic!" Brom said. "Don't listen to her."

Caila came to a stop in the bathroom doorway, facing away, hand on the door. Her head twitched.

"Caila please!" Brom urged, but Saewyne cut him off.

"It's for the best, dear," she reinforced in her oily voice. "Don't you think?"

Caila's tense shoulders relaxed, and she nodded. "Okay. Let me know if you need me."

"I will, dear," Saewyne said.

Caila went into the bathroom and shut the door, and Brom's heart sank.

Saewyne studied his face, as though searching for something. Apparently she found it. Her wariness vanished, replaced by a smile.

A real Anima would have leapt into action with unshakeable confidence. He wouldn't have whined at Caila to believe him.

And Saewyne knew it.

"Brom Brom Brom…" she clucked. "I honestly didn't know what I was going to find when Caila came to my study tonight, talking of ghosts. I had to come look, of course. Strange days, these. But it *is* you."

"If you hurt her, I'll kill you," he said.

"If you could have, you would have." She tossed the edge of her cloak over her shoulder, revealing a floor-length nightgown beneath.

Suddenly, Brom couldn't look away from that nightgown and the body beneath it. Sheer fabric, Saewyne's curves. The pebble in his belly vibrated wildly, as though urging him to flee.

Saewyne began to chuckle.

"Well you're not a ghost at all, are you?" she murmured seductively, cocking her hips and pointing a finger at him. Brom began breathing faster. He wanted to approach her, to run his fingers along her toned arms, over the curve of her hip.

The pebble vibrated, but Saewyne's magic spread throughout his body, electrifying him, making him want her more than he'd ever wanted anyone.

"Stop it," he gasped.

"Make me." She sauntered forward, vibrant and sexy. And she wanted him, too. She was his for the taking.

He took a step toward her.

"Come to me, Brom," Saewyne purred.

His cheeks felt hot, his entire body felt hot. He needed to tear the rags of his clothes off and leap on her. She raised her hands to touch his face, and he leaned forward, aching to feel those fingers on his skin. The pebble in his belly twisted hard.

He threw up on her.

Saewyne jerked backward, cried out in disgust. The threads of the spell snapped, and Brom gasped. For a moment, his mind was his own again. He shook his head, momentarily stunned.

Gods! He couldn't fight her. Even with his full Anima powers, he wasn't sure if he could have pulled away from such a glamour. Without them, he had no chance.

His heart wrenched as he realized that, if he didn't flee now—and leave Caila behind—they'd both be captured.

Vomit dripped down Saewyne's glorious hair, turning it into dangling wet ropes. She glared up at Brom, enraged.

He bolted.

"Brom," she called. Her power returned like a warm caress across the back of his neck. "Come back," she commanded.

He stumbled and paused.

Come to me. Touch me. We will do all the things you want to do…the spell promised.

Brom dove deep inside himself, concentrated on that twisting pebble in his belly, letting its pain be a knife that cut Saewyne's bonds. He managed to keep his gaze off her, and he jolted into a staggering run again.

"Brom!" Saewyne's voice cracked like a whip. Fear lanced into him, and he went down to one knee, scrambled upright, stumbled, and kept running.

He sprinted across Quadron Garden.

A whistle pierced the night behind him. Saewyne had finally called for help. In moments, the campus would be crawling with guards.

Brom dropped down to the path near the river, strapped his dagger belt around his waist, sheathed the dagger, and ran for all he was worth. The water rushed alongside the path, and he finally made it all the way to where the river plunged underneath the great white wall.

There was a grate that let the churning waters pass beneath the wall, and Brom knew there was a hole in that grate, deep beneath the surface. Or, at least, there had been a year ago. He knew where that hole was, had found it while exploring the campus with Vale, and it was just large enough for a person to get through.

He dove into the river. The current pulled him down, shoving him at the grate. He aimed for the hole and twisted at the last second, corkscrewing through the rusty opening.

The water rushed him onward, beneath the wall and out to the delta leading to the sea. He swam hard for the sandy bank but couldn't reach it. The current had him, and his muscles were beginning to fail.

And then there were no riverbanks at all, only a shrinking shore as the current swept him out to sea.

4

BROM

BROM FOUGHT. He pushed to reach the shore, but with every swipe, with every feeble kick of his legs, the shore drifted farther away. The ripples of the river turned into small waves, then to large ones. He could see the coastline, but it became thinner and thinner against the horizon.

His arms burned, and his legs felt like weights.

Soon he gave up his futile efforts and concentrated on keeping his head above water. Maybe if he stopped fighting the current, it would sweep him along to a place where he might regain the shore.

But the crests just became larger. He had to work to ride them. He paddled up one side, then down the other. Up, then down.

Breathing hard, he mis-timed a wave and swallowed a mouthful of water. He coughed, kicked frantically, and fought to keep his head higher. Now he could only see the coastline on a crest, and it vanished as he slid down into the trough.

I'm going to die, he thought. *After all this, I'm going to drown at sea.*

The pebble in Brom's belly vibrated as though in agreement.

He craned his head around, searching—

A log rode down the slope of the wave right on top of him. With a weak cry, he twisted, but the thing caught him in a glancing blow to the head and shoulder.

He plunged under the water. He hadn't had a chance to take a breath, and almost immediately white dots appeared in his vision. His legs felt like sacks of wet sand that he could barely wiggle, but he forced them to the task, kicking as hard as he could, grabbing water desperately with cupped hands. Up up up.

He broke the surface and gasped for breath, taking in almost as much water as air. He coughed and fought to keep himself above the water. The log that had almost ended him was already a dozen feet away, climbing another wave, then sliding out of view.

That had been close. So close—

"No…" he huffed, his sodden brain finally catching up. That log had not been his doom, but his salvation.

The little pebble vibrated nervously, as though it were saying "Go go go."

He pulled at the water with cupped hands, kicked with heavy legs, and chased the log. This time, the gods smiled on him. The current that had pushed him away from the shore pushed him toward the log, and his little bit of effort was working. Slowly, crest after crest, he closed the distance. Just when he thought his aching body would give out, he crested the final wave, putting him right above the log.

With a coughing cry, he bore down upon it and grabbed one of its nubby, broken branches. He wrapped his arms around the log and leaned into it.

"Thank you…" he murmured. "Thank you thank you…"

He clung to it, his dead legs finally just hanging in the water.

I'm still going to die, he thought. *I'm going to fall asleep. I'll let go, and I'll slip under the water. And that will be the end of me.*

With one hand, he held onto the log. With the other, he reached down and undid his dagger belt. He almost dropped it.

Shivering, clinging desperately to the log, he buckled the belt around a hooked branch nub on the log, then wriggled his head and arm through the loop.

It wasn't perfect, but he didn't have the strength for anything else. The belt pinched his body against the log. The sodden bark bit into his side and armpit, but even when he went completely limp, his head stayed a few inches above the water.

Slowly, he relaxed, letting his beleaguered muscles rest. His head thumped gently against the log as he drifted in and out of consciousness. Sometimes he'd jolt awake, water splashing into his mouth and making him cough. The night above smeared into a blur of stars and moons as he reeled between dreaming and waking.

Up the waves, down the waves. He began to shiver uncontrollably.

Something hit his foot, and he imagined a giant whale beneath him, tapping him with its nose.

The tap came again, this time on his calf. Then again on his thigh, moving up his leg.

It's eating me, he thought. He didn't feel teeth, though. Whatever it was had brushed up against his entire side,

151

abrasive like sand. A shark?

He felt like he should care, but he just didn't have the strength.

When the thumping settled against his entire side, all he could think was: *I'm not bobbing up and down anymore. I can sleep.*

When he slipped into unconsciousness this time, no water jumped in his mouth to wake him.

HE AWOKE TO THE GENTLE ROCKING of the log and his body against the sand.

Sand?

He opened his eyes. The sun was bright overhead, but he shivered uncontrollably. The light breeze poked him with pins of ice. He was still lashed to the log, but it had hitched up against a driftwood pile along a beach. He lay half in and half out of the surf, which lapped up to his waist, causing the rocking of the log.

I need to crawl farther up. I need to get away from the sea so it can't drag me back in.

But all he could do was crane his neck about. The rest of his body simply wouldn't move.

I'm tied to the log, he thought. *I have to untie myself.*

He tried to move his hand, but it was like trying to lift one of Father's quarried stone blocks. His arm barely twitched. With supreme effort, he got his hand onto the buckle, but his fingers fumbled with it and slipped away. His hand splashed back into the surf, and he simply couldn't muster the strength to lift it again.

I can do it...later.

He drifted in and out of sleep. The sun beat down on him, and though he felt his skin burning, every shift in the breeze made him shiver. Night fell, and he shivered even more.

He came to his senses when he felt himself moving.

"No…" he moaned. The current had him. It was pulling him away from the shore.

He blinked open his gummy eyes, prepared to make a last valiant effort to save himself. But…he wasn't in the water. Someone was carrying him.

He looked up at the man. Tanned face. Short, dark hair, a cowl drawn over his craggy features. Long, thin arms, and they were strong, so strong. They seemed to carry Brom with no effort.

He didn't know if the man was here to help him or hurt him. For all Brom knew, this man could be a servant of the Champions Academy, come to take Brom back for torture. But the pebble in Brom's belly was quiet. If this had been one of the masters from the academy, he was sure it would be bouncing around.

"Thank… Thank you," Brom said.

The man gave a gruff chuckle. "You're a tough son-of-a-bitch," he said. "I'll give you that, Brom Builder. But you're not much of a seaman, are you?"

Cold fear washed through Brom. The man knew him. Had the academy sent him? "Who…are you?" Brom asked. His lips felt three times too large.

"Quiet now," the man said. "Save your strength." He lowered Brom into a small boat with oars sticking out each side. "Right now, you stay alive. Questions later."

"Who…are you?" Brom persisted.

The man smiled a little, shaking his head at Brom's stubbornness. "I am Undilayne. The queen sent me. Rest. You're safe."

"The queen…"

"That's right."

"Not...the academy."

"I'm not from the academy."

Brom laid his head back against the bottom of the boat, and it felt as though he'd fallen into a deep well. Oriana had found him... His Quad hadn't abandoned him.

He let himself go. Let himself fall the way to the bottom.

5

BROM

Tap tap…

Tap tap tap tap tap…

Taptaptaptaptaptaptaptap…

The rain created a staccato rhythm, and Brom opened his eyes. He was bundled up in dry clothes, two cloaks, and a thick blanket. A fire burned low in front of him, and a tarp had been stretched over him. Rain pounded on it, creating the tapping sound. He could feel the fire's heat wafting toward him, but somehow it didn't make him warmer. His whole body shook.

He took a deep, shuddering breath of the night air, and it smelled like smoke, rich earth, and wet leaves.

He tried to ask where he was, but it came out as a moan.

"Yeah," a gruff voice replied. "Gonna be a storm, sure enough."

Brom's eyes felt crusty, like little grits of sand had

collected in the corners. He blinked and looked at the man hunched just outside the makeshift shelter. The man was huddled in his cloak in the rain, cowl pulled down as the water poured off him. Only Brom and the fire were protected beneath the shelter.

"Where... Where am I?" Brom finally managed to ask.

"Torlioch River," the man said as though he'd answered this question before. Rain streamed off the edges of his cowl.

"I have to save..." Brom began.

"Your friends. I know," the man replied, like he'd also said that before. "Your Quad."

"Vale... Oriana..." Brom said. "...they're in danger."

He couldn't see the man's eyes beneath the shadow of the cowl, but he could see the smile.

"Vale lives in Torlioch," Brom said.

"I know," the man said, as if by rote, as if he'd reassured Brom about Vale before. "I'll take you there. You just rest. I've got you."

"What's...your name?"

The man chuckled as though that wasn't new either. "Undilayne."

"You... You told me that before," Brom said.

"I won't hold it against you. Fever's got you. Make anyone forgetful. But Kelto's not done with you." The man shook his head like he couldn't believe Brom was still alive.

"Kelto?"

"Rest Brom. Gonna sort you out."

"I'm sorry," he said.

"I know," the man said, again like he'd said those same words before.

"I wasn't fast enough," Brom said. "Came...to warn them. But I was too late. I'm sorry."

The man gripped Brom's shoulder gently, then pulled the blanket farther up, all the way to Brom's chin. "You did what you could," he said softly. "Sleep, Brom."

Brom slept.

When he woke next, the sun was shining, huddled in the bottom of the boat. The man—what was his name?—rowed smoothly and steadily above him. The tops of trees hung over the river, passing overhead as the boat moved along the coast.

The man seemed indefatigable. He just kept rowing and rowing, his sleeves rolled up, cords of muscles in his slender forearms bunching, relaxing, bunching, relaxing.

The man noticed Brom was awake.

"Still alive, I see," he said, again with that little head shake, as though he'd bet himself that Brom was going to be dead, and that he'd lost.

"Where...are we?"

"Torlioch River," the man said as though he was reading the answer from a piece of paper. But he smiled and continued rowing.

"I have to save my Quad."

"Yep. Going to save the Quad."

"Th-Thank you, uh..."

"Undilayne," the man said, smiling.

Brom fell back to sleep.

Brom woke again, and this time the man was carrying him. Then he lifted Brom up higher, like he weighed nothing, and put him on a horse.

"Steady. You're not going to like this, but we need to make better time," the man said.

The man swung up behind Brom, put an arm around him and adjusted the thick blanket wrapped around Brom. He made a clicking sound, and the horse trotted forward at a brisk pace. Brom's head bounced around on his shoulders like it was barely attached. With every bounce, it felt like the strings that made up his entire body were getting yanked over and over. He moaned.

"Lean back," the man said. "I got you." The bouncing got a little better when Brom did as he was told. The man's long-armed embrace was steady, reassuring. Brom passed out.

THE NEXT TIME HE AWOKE, the bouncing had stopped. Everything was still and quiet except two hushed voices. He was in a blessedly soft bed with thick covers pulled up to his nose. He cracked open his eyes. A fire crackled in the hearth on the far side of the room, which had a low ceiling with thick wooden rafters and a thatched roof, and everything had fuzzy edges like he was dreaming. It had to be a dream. He almost felt warm.

"He's a good lad," the man's voice said, and Brom moved his gaze to his right. The man was talking with a woman who looked like a barmaid. She was pretty, with large brown eyes, curves on display, and shiny, shoulder-length brown hair. She wore a skirt slit all the way to her waist, exposing the entirety of one shapely leg. Her white peasant shirt was frilly and low cut, bosom pushed up by a tight bodice, giving an ample view of cleavage.

"All he talks about is helping the queen and his

friends," the man continued. "Queen wants him. Top priority. I'd take him with me, but I can't risk it. He's got a dead man's fever. Seen a dozen like this, and not a single survivor. But I dragged him all the way from the coast, and he's still hanging on. It's like Kelto won't let him die. But I'm not gonna tempt fate taking him all the way to Keltan. Priority is that he lives."

"He'll be safe here, sir," the woman said confidently. "I promise."

"Anyone here suspect you?"

She leaned her head to one side then the other, like she was stretching her neck, preparing herself to perform.

"'Spect me, love?" she asked in a completely different voice. It was huskier, with a thick peasant accent. A moment before, she'd stood straight, shoulders back, chin high like a soldier ready for inspection. Now she cocked her hips and put her hands on her waist as though to present her cleavage. A mischievous smile curved her lips. "Nothin to see here." She winked. "'Cept the obvious. You just leave this handsome lad in my hands. I'll have him up and about in no time."

He seemed satisfied with her transformation, and not at all surprised. "This one's worth more than your life and mine combined, the wrong people get hold of him," he warned. "It's the most important thing you've ever done. Quadrons are looking for him. Quadrons, Faline. They find him, they'll take him. They'll walk right over your corpse—or mine—to get to him."

Faline paused. "The Butcher?" she asked, and the peasant accent vanished.

"She didn't say, but... Queen says Quadron, I think of The Butcher."

"We all do," she said.

"Faline, you have the resources to keep him safe and

hidden. If someone comes searching—and they will—I made the trail impossible to follow. No normal person could track us. No *normal* person."

"If The Butcher is involved," she interrupted, "you don't need to inspire me, sir. I'm up to the job. *My life is Hers.*" She spoke the last words like she'd spoken them many times before.

"*And we make that life count.*" The man intoned with the same reverence, as though he was finishing a motto they both knew by heart. "Get him warm, Faline. He hasn't stopped shivering this whole time. And make sure he eats. He's only had gruel since I found him, and far less before that, by the look of him."

"Sir."

"I'll return if I can," he said. "Eight days at most. If I don't, it'll be someone else She sends. Whoever it is will have this." He showed her something that Brom couldn't see. "If they don't, you know what to do."

"Yes, sir."

He glanced at the door, impatient. "Queen's waiting."

"What if *he* wants to go somewhere?" She nodded toward Brom.

"Fever will keep him here. If not, you do."

"Sir."

The man clasped her shoulder like he'd clasped Brom's. Warm. Genuine. "Keep your wits about you," he said.

"Godspeed," she murmured.

"Queen's luck," he replied.

The man left the room, and the woman turned to look at Brom. She noticed his eyes were open a crack, and she smiled.

"Morning, handsome." She winked, and now she had the peasant accent again.

"Am I…dreaming?"

"I think we's both dreaming." She leaned over him and pushed his lank hair back. Her hands were callused but gentle.

He swallowed down a dry throat. She noticed and brought a cup of water to his lips.

"Gonna get you on your feet in no time."

He gulped the water, but after a few swallows, he didn't want any more. She put the cup back on the nightstand, then picked up a little bowl of burning coals. She dropped a handful of dried purple leaves over the coals. Purple smoke curled up from the little brazier. She inhaled some, then put it under his nose.

"It's medicine, love. Set ya right," she said.

The smoke filled his nostrils with the bitter sting of orange rind, then settled into the coppery taste of blood at the back of his throat. He swallowed to get the foul taste out of his mouth…

And suddenly he felt much better. The pain of his cuts drifted away. The woman leaned close, her ample cleavage hovering before his face.

"This dream is better than my last one…" He smiled.

"Aren't you the sweet one?"

She put the bowl of burning purple leaves on the nightstand, then moved around the bed behind him, vanishing from view. Clothing rustled, and he heard her skirt fall to the floor. He wanted to turn and look at her, but that was far too much effort.

She slid under the thick covers with him, careful of his cuts. Her bare arms wrapped around him and her bare legs spooned against his. She was warm. So warm…

"Gods…" For the first time in days, he stopped shivering. "Thank you…" he murmured.

"Just doin' my job, love. You sleep now."

He slept.

6

ORIANA

QUEEN ORIANA TURNED the well-worn scroll in her hand, rubbed it with her thumb, turned it, rubbed it again. Warm sunlight slanted through the high windows of her throne room, casting great squares of yellow across the gray flagstones and the hundred people waiting for her judgment. One of them was talking, but Oriana had listened to the first few words and had determined Edmure could handle it, so she let her mind wander.

It was preoccupied with prophecy. The fours were stacking up. The number four was the magic number, the number of fate, and it was appearing in all the wrong places. And now The Four themselves were missing. She felt a pressure in her ears like the coming of a storm.

Oriana wasn't an Anima. She didn't look for portents, didn't feel the Soul of the World. Her strength was analyzing, calculating the odds, seeing the plain truth, not deciphering signs and omens. But the fours had turned up

163

over and over, glaringly obvious this past month, as if the very lands were trying to tell her something.

A movement to her right caught her attention, just beyond the stoic figure of Dantolis, one of her two personal guards. The door to her private audience chamber opened, and one of her pages entered the throne room. The boy, dressed smartly in a white doublet with gold trim, white hose, and golden shoes, hesitated at the edge of the dais, then walked swiftly and quietly up to her throne as he had been trained. He leaned close to her, ignoring the hundred people staring at him.

Next to her, King Edmure pretended not to notice the interruption and he finished with the man who was talking about his goats, which he was certain were being stolen by his neighbor to the west.

The assemblage—courtiers, commoners, supplicants and guards—also pretended there had been no interruption, but their attention was on the page. Edmure asked for the next supplicant to be brought in as the page whispered in Oriana's ear.

"A man waits for you in your private audience chamber, Your Majesty," the page said.

She turned her head ever-so-slightly and gave the page a narrow, sidelong glance. The boy was supposed to state who was waiting, and he knew it.

The boy flushed. "I don't know who he is, Your Majesty, and he wouldn't tell me," he whispered. "I asked three times. But… Well, the guards let him through, Your Majesty. So I thought…" He swallowed, then hurried to finish. "He bade me give you this." He handed her a small envelope. It was sealed with a special signet ring— one of only a pair, and Oriana had the other.

"Thank you," she said and waved the page away. He bowed and hastily backed away, never straightening or turning until he was off the dais.

She slid one of her long fingers under the seal and broke it, pulled out the single piece of paper only far enough to see the single line of written words.

You were right. I found him. I have him. He is safe in Torlioch.

Her heart began to race. She wanted to stand up and leave the throne room immediately, but she couldn't. There was a line of people expecting her attention on their issues. But what Undilayne had just sent her, it was... Well, in short, it was impossible. The note told her that the dead had, indeed, come back to life.

Brom was back.

So many feelings tumbled over themselves, threatening to reach her face. Incredulity. Remorse. Fear. And the lightning thrill she felt whenever she thought of one of her Quad mates. She stringently kept all of these emotions tucked away.

She sat still for so long that the next supplicant had been speaking for some time before she realized it, and she hadn't heard a word he'd said. The assemblage watched her expectantly. Apparently this wasn't something Edmure could handle, and everyone in the room seemed to know it.

She blinked, forced herself to focus on what the man was saying. He was babbling about dragons and magic.

Using a mental exercise her father had taught her when she was a child, she recalled who the man was instantly, recalled everything she knew about him. He was an academic, sent to follow up on the rumors of an entirely new forest of Lyantrees that had suddenly appeared on the eastern edge of Keltovar. This academic had begged to be sent, and she'd agreed. An alternate forest of

Lyantrees could end the war with Fendir, which badly needed to happen. And, of course, anyone sent on the expedition would go down in history.

The man had returned long before he should have, and he knelt before the dais. King Edmure rose and called for a chair for the academic.

Oriana checked her annoyance as two attendants jumped up and ran to fetch one.

You don't have to stand up to give a command, Edmure, she thought. *Just…give the command. Sit there and look like a king, for Kelto's sake.*

Ruling was mostly observation, but Edmure was one of those men who only equated action with effectiveness.

Oriana looked at the great swaths of dried dirt on the academic's clothing, like he'd rolled through the mud. His shoes were broken at the seams and his tunic in tatters. He had scrapes on his face and his exposed elbows. At first glance, one might have thought the man was set upon by brigands, but Oriana had seen the injuries of battle before. These were the injuries of a man who'd fallen repeatedly, scrambling up a steep slope or while running in terror.

He kept claiming that his fellows had been attacked by a dragon.

And the academic actually seemed to believe it. Oriana wondered at whatever actual horror he'd experienced to force him to see a dragon in his mind's eye. Perhaps some beast had frightened him during the night, even tagged him with a claw, and the terror had eaten away at his mind, replaced the truth with a monstrous story. The mind was a swamp of mystery. She had seen this before: men and women whose minds had snapped, erasing the line between reality and imagination.

"An actual dragon?" Edmure posed the question on

everyone's mind. Dragons were myths.

"It came out of the trees," the academic babbled. "It was…the trees themselves. Tall as a castle. Commanded by a Quadron."

And there it was. *Normals* assumed anything inexplicable was the result of some faceless Quadron.

Edmure nodded sagely as though the babbling academic was actually making sense. He glanced at Oriana, a neutral glance, but she could see his question plainly. She actually *was* a Quadron. And a Mentis. If she wanted to, she could pull the truth from the man's head.

She didn't acknowledge her husband's look. *Normals* assumed all Quadrons did was walk around flinging magic all day. Therefore, why spend time teasing out an answer when one could simply magic up the truth?

What Edmure didn't understand—what most *normals* didn't understand—was that magic exacted a price. Reading the academic's mind would take two seconds, yes, but the burden of the leftover magic would then need to be dealt with. Oriana would need to spend time hearing the thoughts of everyone around her to drain the rest of the opened Soulblock. And if she didn't drain it, the lightning within her would attack her body. If she went to sleep with unused magic, she would wake with soul-sickness. For a simple mind-reading, opening an entire Soulblock was far more trouble than it was worth, especially when she could find the answer with two minutes of keen observation.

"She gave me a message," the academic blurted.

"The dragon?" Edmure asked, and Oriana wanted to sigh.

"Uh, no," the academic said. "The…the girl. The Quadron. She said the answer is the writ of passage."

Those three words jolted Oriana, and her hands

stopped turning the scroll. She felt the pressure in her head return. The fours. A waft of prophecy. She focused all of her considerable attention on the academic now.

"What about a writ of passage?" Oriana asked.

"She said...that it is the answer. And you can find it in the vale."

Cold lightning crackled through Oriana. Vale...

"Vale?" she asked.

"Y-Yes," the academic said. Oriana rarely spoke at audiences, except to make a decree or hand down a decision. She almost never asked questions. It was said the queen didn't need to ask questions because she already knew the answers.

"The writ is in the vale?" Oriana said. "Or the Quadron's name was Vale?"

"I..." the man hesitated, and his face went red. But she already knew the answer. In his terror, he had botched the message. Oriana's Quad mate Vale had sent this man. Another crackle of lightning went through Oriana.

Against all logic, she suddenly believed the dragon might be real, as ridiculous as that sounded. Vale had always had a way of...overstepping her bounds. If anyone in the lands could summon a fairy tale dragon, it was her.

"Your Majesty," the academic said. "That-that might have been what she meant."

"Tell me the entire message," Oriana said, and her frustration must have shown on her face, because the academic blanched and shrank away from her. He began shaking.

"S-She said that was what you were missing, Your Majesty. The writ of passage. She said you would remember."

Oriana looked down at the scroll she was forever

twisting in her hand. It was, in fact, a second-year writ of passage from the Champions Academy. She had stolen it after her Test of Separation and had kept it. If she didn't have it in hand, she kept irrationally casting about for it—like she was missing her arm—and she had no idea why.

It sounded like Vale did.

That sense of premonition prickled across Oriana's scalp, and she thought of the fours.

Sixteen days ago, commoners in Kyn had found a dug-up grave in their cemetery—the grave of Brom Builder, a student of the Champions Academy and Oriana's Quad mate. His grave had not only been defiled, but his body was missing.

Four days after that—twelve days ago—Oriana had received the news.

Now, Undilayne had returned from the south to tell her that Brom had been found, and that he was alive. And though Oriana had not yet confirmed it, she would bet that Undilayne had left Brom only four days ago.

Sixteen. Twelve. Four. And here, with this academic, the final four in the sequence had almost certainly fallen into place.

"You were attacked on the twelfth of Summermarch," Oriana murmured. "Eight days ago."

"Uh…" The academic paled, no doubt assuming she had invaded his mind. "Yes."

"What did the Quadron look like?" she asked.

Edmure glanced at her, surprised, and she realized she had unconsciously stood up in front of her throne.

"She had eyes like the bottom of a w-well," the man stammered. "She was…enormous, Your Majesty, with blood painted across her arms and face like some…like a Fendiran. I think it was the blood of her victims. To fuel her dark magic."

Oriana frowned. Vale was five-feet-tall—a foot shorter than Oriana herself—and Quadrons didn't use blood to work magic. She suddenly knew she wasn't going to get the truth from this man. Vale had scared him so badly he probably couldn't remember his own mother's name.

Oriana opened her first Soulblock at last.

The magic crackled through her, a euphoria unlike anything else. A sense of invincibility filled her, and she plunged into the academic's mind. The man was half-starved, and his mind was a river in flood, swollen and brown with the mud of fear and confusion, carrying images and thoughts like broken branches and swirling leaves.

Oriana deftly found and plucked the image of the academic's "enormous" blood-painted Quadron.

It was Vale, but the woman couldn't have looked more different from when Oriana had known her at the academy. Her hair was longer, tied into crude braids matted with dirt. She wore a little wooden circlet, like she was the queen of the woods. Her tunic had been tied into a barely-decent covering for her breasts, and her midriff was bare. Her breeches were cut short below the knees, and she was barefoot—she had become some wild thing of the forest. Her body was covered with open wounds, like she'd taken lashes from a cat-o-nine-tails.

But by the gods, that *was* a dragon next to her! The image was blurred by the academic's terror, but there was no mistaking what he'd seen.

Oriana went further, finding the exact words Vale had spoken.

"I have a message for Queen Oriana. Tell her the answer is the writ of passage. That's what she's missing. The scroll is the tripwire."

Tripwire!

Oriana's heart rose into her throat. She quickly searched for anything else that might be relevant, but the man's mind was a mess. What Oriana had found might actually be the entire message. If it wasn't, Oriana couldn't find the rest, or it had been obliterated by the chaos of that swollen river. She slipped out of his thoughts and considered her own.

A tripwire was the trigger for a spell that had been prepared but left unused. It was something only a Quadron could do. It was something only a Quadron would know about. But how was the writ of passage a tripwire? In what way? And for what?

She turned the scroll faster in her hand.

The mystery chewed at her. Vale was trying to tell her something, but Oriana didn't know what it was.

She suddenly realized the throne room had gone absolutely silent. She must be a sight, the ice queen blazing like a general about to lead soldiers into battle. A hundred subjects stared up at her, mouths open, curious, afraid.

Without a word to any of them, Oriana strode from the throne room, leaving her husband to deal with the stunned audience, with the babbling academic. Her personal guards, Dantolis and Reela, quickly fell in stride next to her.

She felt like she was twenty steps behind and twenty days late. Urgency throbbed in her body. She didn't even have time to visit Undilayne in her private meeting chamber. He would have to follow her.

For more than year, she had been waiting for something to happen, something she couldn't define, and now powerful events were smashing together one after the other, so fast she felt like a slow student trying to understand the meaning. The Four had vanished. Brom had risen from the dead. Vale had resurfaced with a dragon, and she had spoken of tripwires and this writ of passage in Oriana's hand. It was like Oriana was back at the Champions Academy, filled with excitement and fear and the inescapable knowledge that the storm was already here.

Quad Brilliant was calling, and she must answer. She must bring them together again.

7

ORIANA

ORIANA WENT STRAIGHT DOWN the hallways leading to her bedchambers, bleeding off the magic of her Soulblock as she went, reading the minds of everyone within a thirty-foot radius.

"They said there was flour in the pantry. There was no flour in the pantry," a scullery maid thought as she hurried by. *"Oh sure. Send Galina. She don't mind. She likes wasting her time…"*

The thoughts passed through Oriana as she continued on. Around the next corner, she saw Count Bertegran's son, Lucios, loitering at the end of the hall.

He was flirting with the castle's new chambermaid, but his shifty gaze spotted Oriana. He stooped into a flourish of a bow, dropping the chambermaid's hand as though it were a hot pan. He murmured a polite greeting even as his lascivious thoughts brushed across Oriana's mind like tentacles. She cut them off, listening instead to the chambermaid's shocked thoughts as she blushed.

"Gods! It's the queen!"

Oriana gave Lucios a quick nod as she passed him and moved on. She read mind after mind. The ambitious courtier, composing and committing a clever joke to memory. The angry washer woman, cursing her lazy children in the quiet of her mind.

And of course, she heard Reela and Dantolis's thoughts, but they were the same as always, bent on how they might anticipate their queen's needs to better serve her in this sudden and unknown goal.

One after the other, she let their thoughts flow into her and out, slowly diminishing the reservoir in her Soulblock. She saved some magic, of course. She was going to need it in a moment.

Oriana strode into her royal bedchambers. Reela and Dantolis took up posts outside on either side of the door as she closed it. She crossed the floor and shook a golden velvet rope that hung by the bed. A bell rang, summoning Cintia, her room attendant.

Cintia entered through the side door where her little apartment lay. She curtseyed deeply. "Your Majesty."

"Fetch Undilayne. He is in my private audience chamber. Tell him to attend upon me immediately."

"In your bedchambers, Your Majesty?"

"After you've delivered your message," Oriana said, ignoring Cintia's obvious question. "Fetch a pastry for yourself from the kitchen. Your choice. Have them bake it fresh for you, on my orders." Cintia loved pastries. The idea of having the royal chefs bake whatever she wanted would thrill her. That would keep her out of the way long enough.

"Your Majesty." Cintia bobbed into a second curtsey, smiling excitedly, and ran from the room, her yellow skirts flapping.

Oriana sat down at her desk. This past year, she'd swum in a soup of mystery, waiting for some sign of what she ought to do. Now she knew and she was suddenly rushed. She turned the old scroll over and over in her hand, then set it on the desk and took out a sheet of paper and an envelope. She uncorked her inkpot, dipped the quill and began writing. The first part was easy, and the words flowed from mind to hand to pen. Then she paused over the sheet, thinking about the next, about Brom, about how she should phrase it. Her quill hovered over the paper, and then she simply wrote it down. Plain and simple. Royal Peronne—the Butcher of Gore Grove, Oaken Knight, hero of Fendir and scourge of Keltovar—and Oriana's former Quad mate—was plain spoken. Best to get to the point.

She sealed the note just as a knock sounded on the door.

"It is Undilayne, Your Majesty," Dantolis said through the thick wood.

"Let him in, Dantolis," she commanded.

Undilayne slipped inside, and if she hadn't been watching for him, she wondered if she would have seen him. Her master of spies had a way of blending with his surroundings.

He was cloaked and cowled, though it was the height of Summerwatch. He pushed his cowl back as he knelt before her. Dantolis shut the door behind the spy.

Undilayne had a nondescript face that could blend into any crowd. It made him invaluable as a scout, a spy, and a messenger in hostile terrain. He could pass for a Keltovari peasant or a Fendiran warrior druid. He had mastered half a dozen regional accents, and he'd served her father for years before he had come to serve her. She trusted him almost as much as she trusted her personal guards.

175

"You found him," she said.

"Yes, Your Majesty."

"Think of him. Show me everything." Oriana didn't have time for talking. If Brom was actually alive, she had to know everything, and she could no longer wait. So she dove into Undilayne's mind.

Obediently, he thought of Brom. She saw Undilayne pick him up from what looked like the wreckage of a ship on a beach. She saw Brom bundled in blankets beneath a makeshift tarp in the rain. She saw him in a bed with a roaring fire, a pretty barmaid standing nearby.

"Kelto…" she murmured. "It *is* him." It was impossible, but there he was. That was her dead Quad mate.

"He's in a room above a tavern called The Wayward Inn, Your Majesty."

"And the woman?"

"Faline. One of our own."

"Faline?" Oriana was impressed despite herself. She knew Faline, but hadn't recognized her at first glance. The girl was the youngest of Oriana's spies. She had only been assigned to Torlioch six months ago. The last time Oriana had seen the girl, she'd been standing at attention in a green and white doublet and breeches, sharp lines, chin up, eyes fierce and dedicated. She'd barely been sixteen when she'd begun her training. But her father and two brothers had died in the Battle of Gore Grove, and Faline had sworn to give her life in service of the queen. She'd learned surprisingly fast under Undilayne's tutelage, like she'd been born to it. In less than a year, she had become one of the deadliest women in the kingdom.

But the woman in Undilayne's memory looked like a busty barmaid, not that fierce-eyed girl. Of course, that was the point.

"Well done." Oriana gave Undilayne a rare bit of praise. "You warned her?"

"Of course, Your Majesty. I explained we are dealing with Quadrons, though I did not hint that Brom was such. Further, the young man exhibited no magic I could detect, aside from having the luck of the gods. He's a hard man to kill. I've never seen anyone so lucky."

"That's the way Anima manifests," she said. "His type of magic can seem like luck."

"Your Majesty." He bowed his head in deference.

"She knows to keep a close hand on him? Brom is...slippery."

"She knows, Your Majesty. She will nurse him to health and introduce Lyanleaf smoke to keep him tractable. Time can stretch when in a Lyanleaf fugue. It is a temporary solution. Still, it should be enough for me to return."

"You won't be returning," Oriana said.

"Your Majesty?"

She handed him the message she had just penned to Royal.

"Deliver this to Royal Peronne," she said.

Undilayne's eyebrows rose in disbelief. "The Butcher of Gore Grove?"

"Bring him to Torlioch."

The spy's brow furrowed in concern.

"You heard me correctly. Deliver it with all haste. Use the fastest horse in the royal stables. Don't stop to eat. Don't stop to sleep."

He might think it was a death sentence she was handing him. Even if he did get past the numerous sentries that would stand between him and Royal, there was no guarantee that, after reading the note, Royal wouldn't simply kill Undilayne. No guarantee, except

Oriana knew Royal would never do that. Everyone in Keltovar knew the legend, but Oriana knew the man. Certainly, he'd proven deadly on the other side of a battlefield, but he would never kill a messenger.

"Your Majesty..." Undilayne hesitated. Most of Oriana's subjects did not know the queen had been friends with the Butcher of Gore Grove at the Champions Academy. What happened behind the academy's white walls stayed there, and even small things—like the fact that students must bond with a Quad to earn magic in the first place—were completely unknown to most *normals*. But somehow Undilayne understood the nature of Quads and how they worked. More than that, he had discovered that Royal and Oriana had been part of the same Quad.

He knew that the emotional attachments of a Quad ran deep, and emotions could be a distraction in war. He was worried his queen was making a poor decision because of sentiment.

"He won't hurt you, Undilayne," she said.

"I'm not worried about that," he said. "It's just..." Undilayne was worried that Oriana was, for some reason, trying to make an ally of a notorious enemy. But her master spy couldn't fathom their connection. No *normal* could. No matter what else Royal and Oriana were now, they would always be Quad mates. And Brom changed everything. Royal would have to come.

"Won't he think it is a trap, Your Majesty?" Undilayne asked.

"No," she said. "When he has finished reading the note, you tell him Brom is in Torlioch, and I will meet him there."

"You?" Undilayne said incredulously. "No, Your Majesty!"

She gave him a flinty stare.

He bowed his head deeply. "My apologies. But…" He looked up. "You? And The Butcher? I'm sure he would like nothing more than to be alone with you."

"I can handle myself, Undilayne," she said.

"He is an Impetu—"

"I know what he is," she said frostily. "Go now. This may be the most important thing you ever do. Do not fail me."

Undilayne gave her one last pleading look. She returned it with a cold stare, then returned to her writing.

Quietly, Undilayne left the room.

She wrote a second note for Edmure, left it unsealed on her desk. Then she pulled all the items she would need from her wardrobe and chest of drawers and threw them onto her bed. She called Reela into the room. Together they hastily undid the many buttons of Oriana's royal gown and stripped it away. Reela never questioned, simply helped Oriana don her commoner's attire, which she'd had specially made to help her blend in with the lowborn folk of her kingdom, complete with a kerchief for her silver-gold hair and a deep cowl to conceal her indigo eyes.

When she was dressed, she called Dantolis in and commanded he put together a travel pack with the items she'd thrown on the bed, in addition to anything else he felt she may need for a week's journey.

"Once you're finished, meet me at the royal stables," Oriana said.

Both Reela and Dantolis were stunned by the announcement that Oriana was going on a journey.

"Your Majesty," Dantolis acknowledged, and he immediately set about packing.

"Shall I organize an entourage for you, Your Majesty?"

Reela asked.

"There will be no entourage."

Reela hesitated, then nodded. "Your Majesty."

Oriana snatched up the old writ of passage from her desk, left her bedchambers, and strode down the hall. Reela followed gracefully. Oriana only had so much time, and she must make every moment of it count.

She had left the throne room swiftly. For appearances' sake, Edmure would finish up the audience with the academic and the next two or three petitioners before sending someone to look for her. That would take half an hour, if she was lucky, and she'd already burned fifteen of those precious minutes.

She wound her way through the palace, cowl low. Outside these walls, the commoner's clothes would serve to hide her. Within the palace, the clothes made her conspicuous. If anyone spotted her and recognized her, it would cause a scandal.

She went down to the courtyard, then around to the royal stables and paused at the closed doors. She put her long slender fingers on the grooved wood, and her heart fluttered. This trip would likely claim her life. She could say goodbye to Edmure with a note, but she couldn't leave without seeing Ayvra one last time.

"Stay here," Oriana told Reela. The guardswoman moved silently into the shadows of the eaves, practically vanishing from view. Reela knew what was expected of her; she'd done this many times before.

Oriana's personal guards had been assigned to her when she was eleven years old. They had been specially trained since they themselves were eleven, and they could kill a person in fifty different ways. They could literally sleep on their feet, and could sense a threat to the queen like a hound could smell blood on the air. Sworn to absolute secrecy, they knew nearly all of their queen's secrets.

Including that the queen had a lover.

8

ORIANA

ORIANA ENTERED THE STABLES and closed the double doors behind her. The warm midday sunlight slanted in through the side windows, the hay dust sparkling in the shafts. Stalls full of horses lined each wall. The stables were tidy, but it was still a place of horses. The smell of horse dung and leather hung in the air.

Ayvra stood in a pool of warm, glittering light, petting the nose of a tall gelding in the fourth stall down. The fourth stall. Of course it was the fourth.

The beautiful woman didn't look up as Oriana opened the door, though the flood of light had certainly alerted her.

"The middle of the day," Ayvra said, letting go of the horse's face and turning toward Oriana. She cocked her head and leaned against the gate. "Either you've thrown caution to the wind, or something has happened."

Ayvra's keen gaze dropped to the scroll incessantly

turning in Oriana's hand. She pushed off the gate and moved forward, sunlight flashing over the smattering of freckles across her nose and cheeks, glinting in her huge brown eyes.

Ayvra came very close to Oriana, so close she could feel the heat from Ayvra's head near her cheek.

"What is it?" Ayvra asked softly, laying a light hand on Oriana's arm, so light it felt like the touch of a moth.

"I...need a horse," Oriana said. Her mouth had suddenly gone dry, and she swallowed.

"If all you needed was a horse, you'd have sent someone," Ayvra said.

"I needed you." Oriana forced the words out. She had been trained to lead, to look and act perfectly. But she had never been trained to be vulnerable. She felt awkward.

Ayvra nodded as though she'd known.

"And...I came to say goodbye," Oriana finally managed to say.

Ayvra raised her head and her eyes narrowed. She didn't say, "Where are you going?" didn't say, "You're leaving me?" Instead, she searched Oriana's gaze, perhaps seeing that her words were true, and Oriana could see a flash of anger there.

"You'll need three mounts," Ayvra said. "Or are Reela and Dantolis staying behind?"

"Of course. Three."

"But not four?" Ayvra let the unspoken question hang in the air.

Oriana swallowed. "I...came to say goodbye," she repeated.

Ayvra's nostrils flared, and she turned to the wall where the tack hung. She began taking down bridles.

"Distance?" she asked.

"Ayvra…"

"I must know how they are to be equipped, mustn't I? Saddle bags or no?"

"The fours are stacking up," Oriana whispered, not knowing what else to say.

"Just not *this* fourth." She pointed at her chest.

"I cannot say more."

"Will not." Her dark eyes flashed.

"Ayvra, if I leave information with you, it could put you in danger."

"And what of your danger?" Ayvra asked. "Of my worry?"

Oriana hesitated. She didn't expect to live through this adventure. She had no right to expect such a thing. Ayvra didn't want to hear that, and Oriana didn't want to say it.

But Ayvra must have seen something on Oriana's face.

"You've come to fare-thee-well me," Ayvra whispered.

Oriana swallowed, "I—"

"Take me with you," Ayvra cut her off, finally saying it outright.

"The danger—"

"I don't care."

"I do," Oriana said.

"So they are Quadrons from your academy days. I don't care."

Oriana had only once spoken about her Quad mates to Ayvra, and it had been a mistake. Edmure had been out of the kingdom that night. She and Ayvra had had a unique moment together within the palace.

They had eaten smoked salmon, Fendiran cheese, and shared a jug of Chaledrienne wine. They'd picked at the delicacies, drank, and made love on the balcony beneath the moonlight. It was the most selfish moment Oriana could remember taking for herself, and she'd fallen into it with abandon. She had never drunk more than half a glass at a time. She had never confided so many secrets to one person.

She'd told Ayvra about the academy, those strange two years of her life. She told of how closely she'd bonded to her Quad mates. To Oriana's credit, she'd never mentioned names. Not even a jug of wine could pry those from her lips.

"We will always be bound together," Oriana said. "But everything changed after the Test. We made our choices. We did what we had to, and it tore us apart. I have to see if I can put us back together. The time is coming when the lands will need our magic. I may already be too late."

"All the more reason you need my help," Ayvra insisted.

She simply didn't understand. She was a *normal* and she never would. Having Ayvra along—worrying about her safety—could only weaken Oriana.

"Ayvra, magic comes with a price, and I feel…" She trailed off, her heart warning her she'd already said too much.

"You feel what?" Ayvra asked.

"We… My Quad mates and I, we each had our different prices to pay…for our magic. Some paid more heavily than others, and I feel that I have not paid all."

"What does that have to do with me?"

"It has everything to do with you," Oriana whispered.

"Why—"

"Because you could be that price," Oriana cut her off.

Ayvra stared at her, speechless.

"Since the moment I left the academy, I have felt an axe poised above my head," Oriana said. "When it falls, I don't want you near me."

"You cannot know that," Ayvra said.

"I cannot *risk* that."

"I can help you," Ayvra said.

"You don't understand. You're...."

"What? A *normal?*" Ayvra practically spat the word.

"Kelto's teeth, yes," Oriana hissed. "What would you do if The Butcher picked you up by your neck? Would you slap him? Stab him with the dagger in your boot?" she demanded, and the moment the words left her mouth, she wished she'd kept silent. She should not have said that.

"The Butcher..." Ayvra murmured, eyes wide.

"I simply meant—"

"He was one of your Quad," Ayvra guessed.

"Ayvra..." Oriana considered scoffing like it was ludicrous, but she had never lied to Ayvra. Instead, she sighed. "Now do you understand? This journey will test the limits of my power. Royal will not hurt me." She waved a dismissive hand at that. "I...am not even sure if he can. But I fear there are far greater dangers than Royal Peronne. Any enemy I uncover may decide to hurt you to get to me. I cannot allow that."

"I can take care of myself."

"You can't."

"No?" A blush crept across her freckled cheeks.

"Ayvra..." Oriana began. Why had she ever thought this would go well? Even if a more thorough explanation would sway Ayvra—which it wouldn't—Oriana was out of time.

For a moment, Oriana couldn't form any words. She had craved one last moment of being the person she was in Ayvra's arms. One last moment of wine and moonlight. But it wasn't to be.

Ayvra's gaze softened as she watched Oriana, as though she could read the struggle. She pulled Oriana down into a kiss. Ayvra's strong, calloused fingers worked into Oriana's fine hair. Oriana clasped her back.

"I will return to you," Oriana whispered into Ayvra's cheek. "If such a thing is possible, I will return. But you must promise me you won't follow."

"If you must go, then why must I—"

"Promise me."

Ayvra pushed away, eyes flashing. "I'm to wait for you like some noble's lady? Fretting, working needlepoint, staring out my window until your horse clops over the rise, bearing you or your body?"

"Do you remember when we first kissed?" Oriana asked. "The very first time, I told you I would always be bound to my duty. I told you the good of the kingdom must come first. Always."

"I remember your lips on mine," Ayvra said.

"Do you remember your oath?"

"I remember our bodies entwined."

"We vowed we would take what we could take," Oriana pressed. "And you swore that would be enough."

"I never promised to let you go to your death."

"Yes you did."

"Oriana!"

"Don't make me…" Oriana trailed off, but the threat died on her lips. A Mentis could ensure Ayvra wouldn't leave the castle. Just a twist of magic and Ayvra would never know nor care why she had abandoned her desire.

And such a betrayal would destroy them as surely as Ayvra's death.

"Promise me," Oriana urged.

"Then this is all we get?" Ayvra asked. "A few seasons of joy?"

"And even those were stolen," Oriana said.

"Stolen…" Ayvra echoed bitterly. She turned her head

away, a curtain of dark hair falling to cover her face. Oriana waited.

Ayvra turned back, tears on her dark lashes. "Three horses," she managed in a husky voice. "With stocked saddlebags. I will see it done, *Your Majesty.*" She bowed low, and when she came up, her face was stony.

The line had been drawn—No, the line had always been there. Oriana had simply refused to see it. She and Ayvra had been divided from the start. And they always would be. Oriana was queen, a Quadron. Ayvra was not. This was how it was always going to end.

Oriana's heart hurt so much she wanted to gasp. She wanted to relent. She almost took Ayvra into her arms and told her to saddle a fourth horse, to ride out with them.

Almost.

"Thank you," Oriana said, her voice under control, her emotions locked away. Without another word, she strode from the stables.

9

BROM

BROM AWOKE. This time, the room didn't seem so cold, and the aches in his body were gone. Gingerly, he levered himself up to a sitting position, putting his back against the headboard. Gods, he was weak. But the cuts on his back were bandaged, and he could feel the scabs underneath. They were healing.

And he was starving.

Faline had diligently forced him to swallow spoonfuls of broth every time he'd awoken, but he'd hated every minute of it. He'd only done it because she was so unfailingly sweet and unfailingly persistent. But now the scent of cooking food that wafted up from downstairs smelled amazing.

As though thinking of her had conjured her, Faline opened the door and backed into the room. She turned, bearing a wide tray. It held a plate of golden roasted chicken, a plate of steaming vegetables, and a tall flagon of foamy ale.

"By the gods," he breathed. "You're the most beautiful thing I've ever seen."

"Talkin' to me or the chicken, love?" She winked and deftly bumped the door shut with her hip.

Her slitted skirt swished as she walked to him, giving him a fine look at her legs. She set the tray on his nightstand and smiled. She had a dimple on her right cheek, but not on her left. Just the one dimple.

"I'm still not convinced this isn't a dream," he said. She'd slept in the same bed with him every night, keeping him warm with her body heat. It was like they were lovers, except she hadn't done more than hold him and occasionally kiss him on the forehead.

Faline hadn't just healed his body, she'd made him feel safe and secure when his entire life had been torn apart.

He bit into the chicken with vigor, and she laughed. He chewed and gulped, chased it with a swallow of ale, then chewed and gulped more. Faline went to stoke the fire.

Around a mouthful, he said, "No. Please. It's fine. I'm sweating."

"Fever broke, did it?" She stopped fussing with the fire and stood up. "That's good." She picked up the little brazier from the mantle and brought it over to the nightstand.

"What is that?" he asked. She'd given him a little of the purple smoke every day, but he'd never thought to ask her what it was.

"You've never had Lyanleaf before?" she asked, seemingly surprised.

"Like from a Lyantree?" he asked.

"Exactly like that."

Brom knew of magical weapons and armor harvested

from Lyantrees. But he'd never even heard of smoking the leaves.

"That's what's been healin' you, love." She set the brazier down, took a deep whiff herself, then waved some of the smoke his way. She tapped the edge of the brazier, and it rang lightly. "Kept you alive." Again, he tasted that acrid tang on the back of his throat, then a coppery taste. Then, almost immediately, the flavor of the chicken he'd just eaten increased, filling his mouth.

He stuffed a spoonful of potatoes in after it, closed his eyes as he tasted them. Salty and buttery... Gods, they were amazing!

Faline sat on the edge of the bed, put a hand on his knee and watched him eat. They both stayed quiet while Brom wolfed down his meal. He ate all the vegetables. He drank all the ale. He ate every single chicken leg until he tossed the last bone onto the platter with a clink.

That haze of the purple smoke seemed to float about his brain, making everything fuzzy, taking away the harsh edges of the world. The room. The hearth. The nightstand. Even Faline herself. He sat back and closed his eyes with a sigh.

He felt the bed move, and then warm lips press against his forehead.

"Goin' to make you better, love," she whispered. "You're safe here."

He wanted to ask her who she was, and who Undilayne was, and why she was being so nice to him. He'd wanted to ask her about that first night, when it seemed she'd spoken with a different accent, but the thought circled in his mind on purple smoke and never seemed to make it to his lips.

Instead, he said, "Thank you."

"I steals a kiss and he says thank you. You're a

nobleman, you are." The bed moved as she stood up, and his eyes fluttered open.

"Where are you going?" he asked.

She pushed back his hair. "Give you your rest. You need to feel better," she said, letting a finger linger on his chin. "That's what's important."

"I do feel better."

"And we're going to keep it that way. Sleep."

"I'm tired of this bed," he murmured, but it suddenly felt so soft that he just wanted to sink right into it.

"Soon enough, love, we'll have you up and around."

"Tomorrow?"

"O' course." She winked and made the dimple appear again.

The purple smoke hovered around him, throughout him, and he closed his eyes. She was right. Sleep was wonderful. Sleep was perfect.

10

BROM

FALINE KISSED BROM on the forehead, soft lips brushing his skin. Her bosom hovered in full view, mesmerizing him. He felt like he should be thinking about other things, but whenever he awoke and his muddled thoughts began to clear, she appeared. Then there were glimpses of that bosom, flashes of her shapely legs, and a knowing gaze directed at him from beneath her long eyelashes.

Then whatever he'd been thinking about strayed to daydreaming of what she might look like naked.

She seemed to like that his eyes followed her as she bustled about the room. It seemed, almost, that she expected it, but just when he was sure she was going to disrobe and join him in the bed again…she didn't.

Her sultry smile promised more…but then he fell asleep. At least, he thought he did, because he never remembered anything after that.

In fact, he tried to remember exactly what he'd done

yesterday or the day before...but he couldn't. The days seemed to blend together. Had it only been one day since he'd recovered? He'd had chicken for dinner yesterday... But no, he had a vague memory of a ham hock. So that had been a different dinner. The chicken meal had been the day before.

Then he had a memory flash of three differently shaped tankards of ale. So three meals? Had he been in this bed for three days since his fever had broken?

His thoughts flew away as Faline finished kissing his forehead, then kissed him softly on the lips. It was the first time she'd done that, and it stoked his desire. Her every gorgeous move and touch seemed irresistible.

She sat up, reached out and pressed her thumb on his bottom lip like a signature.

"What a thief I am," she said, moving her hand to his chest. Brom wanted to sit up, take her in his arms, but his desire prickled with frustration. He'd been thinking of something. Before she'd kissed him, he'd had something to say.

What was it? There had been something about meals and tankards of ale...but now he couldn't remember. All he could think about was her kiss and the hazy purple smoke in his mind.

What day is it? He wanted to ask her. But he'd already asked that question, hadn't he? She'd told him. And he'd just forgotten.

"You're nearly well," she murmured.

"I'd like to take a walk," he managed to say, and he felt good that he'd been able to express that.

"'Course, love. Fresh air'll do you good. Tomorrow."

"Tomorrow..."

A stray thought drifted up on the haze. She'd said that before. He was sure she had. He had asked to go for a walk, and she'd said "Tomorrow." Was that yesterday she'd said that? The day before? He couldn't remember.

He blinked. His eyelids were so heavy.

"I'm looking forward to tomorrow," she said. She wasn't sitting on his bed anymore. He hadn't felt the bed move—didn't remember her getting up—but she was now at the door, that glorious skirt flashing her bare leg.

"Sleep, Brom," she said, and she left.

He began to drift off, but his stray thoughts became words floating in his head, disconnected. He felt that if he could just put the words together in the right order, he'd know something important, but when he tried to grab for them, his fingers would hit them numbly, and they'd bounce away, drifting out of reach.

Who was Faline, really? Why was she kissing him? Undressing for him?

No. She hadn't undressed for him, not since that first night. He just *wanted* her to do that.

The pebble in his belly vibrated. Brom blinked. He suddenly realized the pebble hadn't vibrated in quite some time.

He fell to watching the words floating about in his mind, and two of them came together, bumped together, and they stuck. They became larger and larger, and finally he could read them: *She's lying.*

"You always were a beautiful fool," a voice said. He sat up and looked around the room. That wasn't Faline's voice. He knew that voice... That was Vale's voice!

"So trusting," Vale said. Her voice sounded like it was coming down from the rafters.

"Where are you?" He looked around, but all he could see was wafting purple smoke.

"Of course, you always had a weakness for liars. You fell for me, didn't you?" Vale chuckled ruefully.

"Liars... You mean Faline?"

"Oh please. Every time you ask her questions, she fills the room with Lyanleaf smoke and pushes her boobs at you. Tell me you noticed."

"Vale…" He peered through the smoke, but it was no use. He couldn't see where the voice was coming from. Maybe it was coming from the smoke itself.

He closed his eyes and imagined Vale was right next to him, wished for it with all his might, then opened his eyes again.

The drifting purple smoke moved toward the center of the room, thickening into the smoky figure of a girl. She sat on the floor, leaning her back against something invisible.

"Vale!" Brom said.

The smoky Vale raised her head as though she could see him too. She stood up, her indistinct body taking on more detail. Now he could make out her nose, the shape of her shoulders and arms.

She turned, like she was regarding the room. *"This is the Wayward Inn,"* she said, and she let out a little breath. The front of her face came apart, like her breath disrupted the smoke of her body, but then it coalesced back into shape.

"So I'm punishing myself. Ouch," she murmured. Then her head turned toward him. Her smoky form gained more definition. Now he could make out the shapes of her eyes and the details of her clothes.

It was Vale, alive and vibrant and standing right in front of him, except everything about her was in shades of purple. And she didn't look quite the same. Her once short hair now went past her shoulders, wild and twisting. A half dozen little braids framed her face, and a wooden circlet coiled around her forehead. She wore strips of cloth across and under her breasts, with thongs attached to her neck and around her torso. Her tight breeches had been cut off below the knee.

"I'm dreaming." She chuckled, like that was funny. *"Let's pretend it's real, though. Please? Let's pretend that all the awful things I've done, I never actually did."*

"Vale—"

"Tell me about Lady Swishy Skirts." She looked around the room. *"Why is she drugging you?"*

"I came looking for you," he said. "To warn you about The Four."

That brought a sad smile to her face. *"Gods, I've missed you, Brom,"* she said breathlessly. *"I was wrong. I was so wrong. I'm sorry…"*

She cleared her throat, and a little wisp of purple smoke came out of her mouth, though this time her face stayed intact. Her flesh continued to solidify. Now he could see even smaller little details. Her thick leather belt, scarred from use, the rips in her breeches, her bare feet. He could even see the freckles across her nose, darker purple than the lavender of her face.

"So, you came looking for me," she said. *"You forgave my betrayal and you came to save me, but you ended up held prisoner by a pretty girl who flirts with you,"* she said.

"Uh…yes."

"That is so you." She gave him the same grin she'd given him many times at the academy. It was full of mischief, except this time there was a deep weariness to it, too, like she hadn't slept for a week. *"So apparently she wants you to stay in the room?"*

"No. She just wants to make sure that—"

"You asked to go for a walk. She blew smoke at you."

"Maybe you're right."

"Then let's break the rules like we used to. Come on."

She went to the window and opened it. He joined her,

and they looked down together. There was a small ledge on the other side, a rafter built into the stone wall, sticking out about three inches, and she crawled onto it. He hesitated. It was a two-story drop to the wet street.

Vale balanced on the tips of her toes, her smoky body leaning gracefully into the wall. "There's a lantern pole," she said. "All you have to do is get to the corner and jump." She edged across the wall, reached the corner, and leapt out into space. She caught the pole, swung around it, trailing little wisps of purple smoke as she spiraled gracefully to the ground. Her feet puffed when she landed, then she looked back up at him.

He hesitated.

She laughed. *"Are you actually scared?"* she asked from below. *"It's a dream, silly."*

The breeze was cold on his bare chest. The ledge was rough against his bare feet. Vale said it was a dream, but he didn't think so.

"Look, I'll catch you." She walked back to stand directly under the window and held out her smoky purple arms. It was a ridiculous gesture, and it made him smirk. Teeny tiny Vale, two stories down. She was five feet tall if she was an inch, and she barely weighed a hundred pounds. Even if she wasn't made of smoke—even if she was solid enough to catch him—he'd crush her.

"You're kind of mean," he said.

"Yeah, but I'm good in bed," she replied. *"Come on."*

He scooted along the edge of the protruding rafter. With his magic, he wouldn't have hesitated to tiptoe deftly along it, but he barely felt strong enough to stand, let alone perform acrobatics.

The fresh air cleared his head, and the farther he went, the more he realized he didn't want to go back inside. He inched forward.

"Maybe you could sit down and scoot on your butt like a little boy," she said, rolling her eyes. *"I want my money back. This dream is broken."*

His legs got shakier with every step, but he made it to the corner of the inn. Clinging desperately, one hand splayed on each wall, he looked at the expanse between himself and the pole. He took a deep breath and leapt. The alley flew beneath him. He managed to grasp the pole, and his momentum flung him around it. He circled it once just like Vale had done, but then his strength failed. His hands sprang off the pole, and he cartwheeled through the air. He landed on the cobblestones and skidded sideways.

Vale doubled over in laughter.

The fall knocked the wind from him, and at first he just lay there, stunned. His whole body ached from the impact. Finally, he rolled to his back, wincing.

Eventually, gasping through giggles, she went over to him. *"Oh, Brom. Gods, I've missed you."*

He worked his shoulders in a circle. He didn't seem to have broken anything.

She held out a hand. He reached out to grab it, but his fingers passed through hers.

Her giggles faded. *"That figures."* She sighed. *"I can dream, but I can't touch..."*

"Where are you?" he asked. "How are you here?"

"Want to know something?" she asked abruptly, cutting him off. *"My mother died here. Right there."* She pointed to the back of the alley.

"What?"

She looked around, up at the misty night above them, and she nodded. *"I understand it now, why I'm here. This place is both of you, really. The mother I couldn't save. The lover I killed."*

"You didn't kill me."

She slid her smoky hands around his neck and gave him a ghostly kiss he couldn't feel. When she finally stopped, she slid her smoky cheek against his and whispered in his ear. *"Forgive me, Brom,"* she said. *"Tell me you forgive me."*

"I do."

She gave a little half-sob. *"Thank you,"* she whispered. *"I can't kiss you, so that'll have to be good enough. It's all I—"*

She cut herself off and raised her head from his shoulder. Something in the dark had caught her attention, and she moved deeper into the alley. The shadows swallowed her, and he hurried to keep up.

She stopped in front of a sapling that had grown up between the cobblestones. The sapling was about as tall as Vale, and she stared at it like it was a bear wearing a dress.

"It's a Lyantree..." she murmured, touching the tiny dark leaves. *"Here..."*

"What if this isn't a dream, Vale?" Brom asked. "I don't think this is a dream."

She turned, letting go of the Lyantree sapling. *"Oh Brom.... You are a terrible avatar of vengeance. You should be stabbing your finger at me, flinging portents of doom. You should hate me."*

"What if it's not a dream?"

"Then when I wake, stay with me. In my forest."

"Show me how—"

"I wonder if this is my reward," she said to herself. *"You being nice to me. Forgiving me."* Dark purple tears appeared on her lavender cheeks. *"I killed you."*

"You didn't."

"Oh, I did. I destroy everything I love."

"That's not true."

She chuckled, but there wasn't any mirth in it. *"Oriana knew. She always did. And Royal found out in the end, what kind of person I am. They both saw."*

"If that's what they saw, they didn't look deep enough."

"Stop it…" Her voice broke. *"Just stop…being nice to me."* She hung her head. *"You should hate me. I would, if I were you. It's what I deserve."*

"Tell me how to find you."

"I tried to make it up to you, you know. I did what you would have done. What you did *do at the Test, that we were too stupid to see. The Four had us even then and you knew. They had us collared and chained."* She shook her head. *"I was a fool. And they're just too strong. And now Tam is going to die too, because of me. I won't last much longer."*

Vale's once clearly-defined body became smokier. The stark details of her face, her clothes, were already hazy. The pebble vibrated in Brom's belly.

"Don't go. Who's too strong?" he demanded. "The Four? Are you fighting The Four? Tell me where you are!"

"We'll see each other soon enough, lover," she murmured. *"After The Ragged Man, I'll come find you…"*

"Vale!" He tried to grasp her hands, but they curled around his fingers and became nothing more than purple smoke. Her body drifted apart. Legs and arms dissipated. Tendrils floated away in a dozen little drifts. In seconds, she was gone.

Brom fell to his knees on the muddy cobblestones in front of the Lyantree sapling. He didn't know how long he knelt there, but soon the purple haze returned. He raised his head, looking for Vale.

"Easy, love," Faline said. He spun about, and she stood behind him with a brazier of burning Lyanleaf in her hand. Thick curls of purple smoke rose from it, encircling his head.

"No!" he said. He swung at the brazier but missed. He lost his balance and fell onto his back, blinking up at the night sky. The haze swirled around him, obscuring his vision and laying that pleasant blanket over his mind. His eyelids felt heavy.

"No…" he murmured. "Vale…"

His eyes closed.

11

BROM

WHEN BROM AWOKE, he wasn't in the alley anymore. He lay in his soft bed at the Wayward Inn, the wooden rafters high above. It was still dark outside, so either he hadn't slept but a moment or he'd been asleep for far too long.

Had that moment with Vale actually happened? It had seemed so real.

He pulled his hands from under the covers and looked at them. Scrapes on both hands, elbows. He yanked the blankets off and found he was naked. Casting about, he found his breeches draped across the chair. There was mud on the knees.

It *had* happened. The pebble in his belly began to vibrate.

The door opened, and Faline entered, skirt swishing, and bumped the door shut with her hip. "You all right, love?" she asked, a little out of breath as though she'd run up the stairs.

He narrowed his eyes. "I'd like to go for a walk."

"'Course, love. Soon as you're better."

He said nothing.

"Tomorrow," she said, and his chest tightened.

"You're keeping me here." He glanced at the softly burning brazier on his nightstand. Her gaze went with his, and the utterly innocent look on her face sent another cool slither of fear across his heart.

She was a liar. He knew it, but she was still so convincing. That meant she was a good liar. A professional one.

He swatted the brazier away, spilling burning purple leaves and glowing coals across the wooden floor. "It's not medicine," he said. "It's a drug."

She looked annoyed but tolerant, a vexed nursemaid. She drew a breath, no doubt about to tell him the same story: that the Lyanleaf was to help him heal, that he needed to rest. That he should sleep, that they'd go for a walk tomorrow.

But she stopped halfway to the spilled brazier, and her flirty swagger also stopped. Shoulders back, chin high, she turned to face him. She looked like a soldier now, suddenly out of place in her sexy garb.

"You're not a barmaid," Brom said.

"No," she said without a trace of her thick peasant accent. "I'm not."

She came toward the bed, this time without her smiling, languid advance. She simply sat down on the edge. He recoiled from her, scooting to the other side.

Her hand, which had been reaching out to him, dropped to the covers. "I'm not a barmaid, Brom. But almost everything else is true. My job *is* to heal you, and to keep you alive at all costs. As to Lyanleaf, yes, it's a drug. But it is also a pain killer and a healing herb, just like I said it was."

"Except I'm well now."

"Maybe. But you're still in danger. Letting you wander around Torlioch at midnight…I can't allow that. You're too valuable."

"Valuable? To whom?"

Faline hesitated.

"No more lies!" Brom said.

"To the queen," she said.

Oriana… Echoes of Brom's fever dream came to him. He remembered the thin man bringing him to this inn. He remembered the man saying Oriana had sent him.

"You work for Oriana…" he murmured, and he felt the truth of it in his heart, like he'd known that but between his fever and the Lyanleaf fog, he'd forgotten.

She didn't respond to that, but the tightening of her lips confirmed his guess.

"Why drug me?" Brom asked. "I was looking for Oriana. I would have gone to her willingly."

"Following orders. I'm to wait for Undilayne."

"The man who brought me here," Brom murmured as the name surfaced in his memory. Undilayne.

I am Undilayne. The queen sent me. Rest. You're safe.

"Where is he?" Brom asked.

"Overdue."

"How overdue?"

"Four days."

"How long have I been lying here?"

"Twelve days."

"Twelve— Gods!"

A knock sounded on the door, and Brom jumped. With a frown, Faline hesitated, as though she didn't want to be interrupted. But she reluctantly strode to the door. No swaying hips and swishing skirts this time. She opened the door a crack as though she didn't want Brom to see who was on the other side. Or perhaps she was keeping the visitor from seeing Brom.

A high-pitched voice talked in hushed tones, and the angle of Faline's head indicated she was talking to someone small. A child?

Brom threw off the covers and, stark naked, walked toward the door. Faline shot him a warning glance and held up a hand to stop him, but he only stopped when he was close enough to hear both sides of the conversation

"…big as a house," the child was saying.

"You're sure, love?" Faline asked, switching to her peasant accent.

"Ran into town fast as a horse. And he wasn't out o' breath or nothin'. Never seen anything like that. Quadron, methinks."

"Fendiran?"

"Maybe. Skin on his hands was dark, but I didn't see his face 'cause of his cloak. He saw me, though. Looked right at me. I thought for sure he was going to kill me, but he just looked away and started searching houses."

"Where?"

"Dockside. Was that the kind of thing you's looking for?" the child asked expectantly.

"Just the kind of thing, love." She produced a pouch from her skirts, counted out three coins and put them into the little outstretched hand. The hand vanished and she closed the door.

"We have to leave," she said. "Now."

12

BROM

"NOW YOU WANT TO LEAVE," Brom said.

"What I *want* doesn't matter. The Butcher of Gore Grove is here," she said. "Put your clothes on."

The name rang a bell in the back of Brom's mind, but he couldn't remember where he'd heard it.

"Who is that?" he asked.

"The Oaken Knight. The leader of the Fendiran warrior druids," she said.

The pebble in Brom's belly vibrated.

"Royal!" Brom exclaimed.

Faline hissed and made a slicing motion with her hand. She shot a nervous glance at the door. "Don't you know *anything* about Quadrons? Say his name and he'll hear you."

"That's ridiculous," Brom said. "Quadrons can't do that."

She frowned and threw his breeches at him. "Put your

clothes on. I didn't nurse you back to health just to get caught by The Butcher."

"He's my friend," Brom said, but he shoved one leg then the other into his breeches.

"Your *friend?*" She went behind the wardrobe and picked up a new pair of traveling boots. "The Butcher has no friends."

"He wouldn't kill me," Brom said.

"What do you know of The Butcher?" she asked.

Brom found himself reluctant to answer.

Faline shook her head. "If Queen Oriana wants you alive, The Butcher wants you dead. That's sure." She opened the wardrobe and withdrew a full pack attached to a coil of rope. "He will do anything to destroy Keltovar."

Brom hesitated. That actually *did* sound like Royal. He had always hated Keltovar and her royalty.

"Royal is a good man," Brom protested, but could he actually know that? A year could do a lot to change a person.

"Tell that to the hundreds dead at Gore Grove," Faline said, striding to the window.

"Hundreds? I don't believe it." Brom tried to imagine Royal killing hundreds of people.

Faline took a loop of the rope—close to where it was tied to the pack—and tied a slipknot to a thick nail that had been driven into the windowsill. She threw the rest of coil out the window, then threw the pack after it. It dangled from the short end of the rope just outside the window. "The Butcher waded through the bodies of two hundred soldiers at Gore Grove," she said. "Slaughtered them using Quadron magic. Including my father. And my brothers."

Brom paused, stunned. Royal had always been

intimidating, sure. At nearly seven feet tall, he towered over every other person. But he'd never been a killer. He was a protector.

"The Butcher slaughtered them all," she repeated, her voice barely a whisper.

Her confession was so raw that Brom doubted his friend. After all, it *had* been a year. Caila had changed. Oriana was no longer a princess. Brom didn't know what the Test of Separation had done to Royal. Brom's own Test had scarred him forever. What had it done to his Quad mates?

"Come on." Faline grabbed a brown cloak from the open wardrobe, tossed it to him, grabbed a green cloak for herself, then took his hand just as he finished lacing up his final boot.

They went to the door, where she stopped and turned to face him. She took his face in her hands gently and, for a moment, he thought she was going to kiss him. She didn't. Instead, her brown eyes searched his, as though looking for something.

"My job is to keep you alive," she said softly. "To keep you safe. Do you believe me?"

He hesitated. He did believe that. Though she had drugged him the entire time, if she'd wanted to kill him, she could have done so at any moment. And she hadn't. Slowly, he nodded.

"I will spend my life to that purpose," she said, still holding his gaze. "Do you believe *that*?"

Her conviction rattled him. He nodded again.

"We do not discuss The Butcher, not while he is after you. First, we make sure you are safe."

"I don't think Roy—"

She put a finger on his lips before he could complete the name. "Safety first. Please."

Brom hesitated. Faline seemed genuine. His instincts told him she was telling the truth, or at least she believed what she was saying.

But Brom had gone to the academy to find his Quad mates. Finding Royal was something Brom wanted. The big man would have so many answers. Like what had happened to The Four. Like what had happened to Quad Brilliant after the Test.

And Brom simply couldn't imagine Royal hurting him. At least, not the old Royal.

The old Royal...

But I'm not dealing with the old Royal, he thought. *It's been a year.*

What if Royal had become something Brom wouldn't recognize? What if the Test of Separation had twisted him? What if The Four had? Brom couldn't know for certain.

What he did know, without question, is that he'd be dead if not for Undilayne. He'd be dead several times over. And Undilayne had left Brom in Faline's hands. That meant Oriana had too.

"Okay," he said.

"Good." She gave one nod. "Now, we go through the main room downstairs. Holt's the owner of the Wayward, and he works the bar during the evenings. He likes to talk, and he likes me. So he's going to say something as we leave." She touched Brom's chest with her index finger. "You say nothing. He thinks you are a friend of my brother's, come south from Seldyn. You got sick on the road, and I've been nursing you to health. I'm going to say we're getting some fresh air, and we'll be right back. That's what I say." She paused with a meaningful look. "And you say?"

"Nothing," he murmured.

"Smart boy." She winked.

Brom glanced over his shoulder at the pack hanging out the window.

She caught his glance and said, "We'll get that in a second." She opened the door.

They exited onto a landing that overlooked the tavern floor. Half the tables were full, and the air was thick with the smell of roasting meat, pipe smoke, and raucous conversation. Faline led him down the stairs like they weren't in a hurry. Hips swinging and leg flashing, she flirted her way across the room, tossing greetings to a few patrons and slapping away a few playful hands aimed at her bottom.

Just as they reached the front door, a bald man with thick forearms and a prodigious belly called out from behind the bar.

"Faline!"

She swung about, hips and head cocked to the side. She fixed a winsome smile on the man. "Is that destiny I hear?"

The bald man chuckled. "So he's up and around. Good news!" Then, to Brom. "You're a lucky lad."

Brom opened his mouth to say something, and Faline pinched his arm.

"A bit 'o fresh air, I says," she interjected. "Then back to bed."

A ripple of chuckles went through the room, as though they all knew what *back to bed* meant if Faline was saying it.

"Go on with ya." She gave an exaggerated wave of her hand, like she was swatting down a fly. Shaking her head in mock disgust, she left the bar with Brom in tow.

Once they were out of view, her saunter turned into a stride and they turned the corner once, twice, then came to stand beneath Brom's window where the pack bulged against the side of the inn. The rope dangled down into the alley, and Faline gave it a quick yank. The slip knot came undone and the pack fell like a bag of bricks. She caught it and undid the rope, coiled it, and handed it to Brom.

"You take this."

She opened the pack and pulled out a dagger, sheath, and belt. She strapped the belt around her waist. It was an odd contrast to her sexy barmaid skirt and bodice. Then she pulled out Brom's dagger and belt, which he hadn't seen since he'd lashed himself to the log in the Coral Sea, and handed it over to him. He hastily buckled it on.

She closed the pack and shouldered it.

His doubts about running from Royal suddenly returned. The Fendiran was one of only three people who might answer Brom's questions. Was he making the right choice to flee?

"Maybe we should wait for him," he said.

She glanced at him like he was insane, then she frowned. "We had a deal. Talk later. Safety first."

"What if I'm not in danger?"

"You are."

"Do you know what a Quad is?" Brom asked.

"A Quadron?"

"No, a Quad."

"No," she said softly.

"It's the way Quadrons learn magic. Four Quadrons bond together in a Quad. That bond transcends friendship, even family. Only once we're bonded can we unlock our magic."

Faline stiffened. "We?"

He looked at her steadily.

"Kelto…" she murmured. "*You're* a Quadron."

"I was. Me, a woman named Vale, Roy…the, uh, the Oaken Knight," he said, trying to assuage her mistaken fear that a Quadron could be summoned by saying his name. "And Oriana."

Faline's eyes widened. "No…"

"She was a princess when I knew her. We were friends. She and I and Vale. And…the Oaken Knight."

"That's impossible." Faline shook her head.

"It's true."

"That's…" She held her hands out, splayed, like she was going to grab something or gesture. But they just hung there. Finally, she let out a breath. "That's…" She couldn't seem to come up with the words to follow, and she cleared her throat.

"Maybe we *should* let him find us," Brom said. "I'm part of his Quad. There are magical reasons he wouldn't want to kill a Quad mate. But more than that, I simply don't think Royal would hurt me."

Faline's lips were pressed hard together. Brom realized he wasn't likely to convince her to trust the man who'd killed her father and brothers. "Brom, if you trust me at all, let's go see the queen first. She's part of your Quad too, right?"

Slowly, he nodded.

"If she doesn't convince you, you go to The Butcher. Is that fair?"

He hesitated, but the pebble had gone frantic in his belly. A warning. Did it mean he should resist Faline? Or did it mean that Royal—bent on hurting him—was actually closing in on them, and that he should run?

"Okay. Let's go," he said.

"This way."

She jogged up the alley. When they reached the intersection, she turned left down another dark alley and

213

headed toward the brighter, lamplit street ahead. "We'll buy a pair of horses at Vyndell's stables," she said. "Then head north to Keltan—"

A dark figure stepped in front of them, blotting out the light. The giant's muscled bulk filled the alley from wall to wall, dark clothes and dark skin seeming to grow from the shadows themselves, a wild beast birthed from the shadows.

"You didn't really think you could escape, did you?" the Quadron asked.

13

BROM

"BUTCHER," Faline spat, crouching. Her dagger flashed out. The pebble in Brom's belly went crazy.

The cloaked figure at the end of the alley was huge and probably weighed as much as Brom and Faline combined. The hands that emerged from the cloak were dark-skinned, Fendiran, but... Something was wrong.

"That's not Royal," Brom whispered. The figure wasn't...tall enough. Royal had wide shoulders, arms as thick as Brom's legs, and legs as thick as tree trunks, but he was also over seven feet tall. This person was huge, but not Royal-sized.

"What?" Faline said.

The figure chuckled, reached up and pulled back her cowl. Long fat braids of black hair fell down to her shoulders. Thick rectangular eyebrows crouched over her squarish eyes, which glowed green in the darkness.

"Well-spotted," she said in her throaty voice. "But

then, you would know the difference."

"Master Jhaleen!" Brom said.

"Who?" Faline said.

A cold shiver went up Brom's back. "She's from the academy," he said. He'd almost looked forward to being caught by Royal, but not by an academy master. This was like facing Saewyne again, except worse. Master Jhaleen was an Impetu, and Impetus didn't bother with persuasion. They didn't need to. "She's come to take me back."

"Oh, I'm not taking you anywhere," Jhaleen said. "You're not leaving this alley. You're supposed to be dead, and soon it will be true."

"You'll have to go through me first," Faline said.

Jhaleen gave a dark chuckle. "I do so love brave *normals*."

"Faline, get out of here," Brom said.

"Run, Brom," Faline said, never taking her eyes from Jhaleen. "I'll hold her. Run!"

Faline lunged at Jhaleen's belly, a feint. She spun at the last instant, ducking to avoid any attempt to grab her, and brought the dagger around behind Jhaleen's leg to hamstring the Quadron.

When Faline's blade swept behind Jhaleen's thigh, the master shifted her stance with such speed and power that the cobblestone cracked beneath her foot. Faline's strike slashed through empty air and she stumbled forward. Jhaleen grabbed Faline's neck and pulled her off the ground.

Faline's legs swung out, kicking. Her blade clattered across the stones. She grappled with Jhaleen's gauntleted fingers, trying to wrench them apart.

She might as well have tried to bend steel.

Brom leapt forward, ramming his shoulder into

Jhaleen's belly with all his strength—

He bounced off and skidded across the cobblestones.

For a pain-filled moment, he thought he'd broken his shoulder. Stunned, he raised his head in time to see Faline struggling frantically, bare legs wrapped around Master Jhaleen's thick arm, every muscle in her body tight, fighting for her life.

Jhaleen regarded the barmaid like she would a struggling moth. The green light from Jhaleen's eyes cast a sickly glow across Faline's reddening face. The master gave a quick twist to her hand.

"Don't—!" Brom screamed, but he heard the sickening crack, felt it in his body as though it had been his own neck. "No!"

Faline went limp. Her arms and legs fell away from Jhaleen, dangling down. The master threw her to cobblestones. Faline's boneless body tumbled to a stop against the wall.

"Gods damn you!" Brom shouted as he got to his feet.

"They damned you first," Jhaleen growled. She threw back her cloak, exposing both of her muscular arms. Each bore a blue-enameled steel gauntlet. She showed her palms and smiled, waiting for him.

His heart felt ripped in two. He could still feel Faline's kiss on his forehead. Now she was dead. Just like that. That was what happened when a *normal* fought a Quadron.

Gods, he wanted to lash out at her, this murderer, wanted to kill her and avenge Faline. But he could never win without magic. Not against an Impetu. If he was really going to hurt the master, he had to be smart. He had to think.

An interminable moment dragged by while Jhaleen watched his internal struggle with amusement. He came up with nothing. He glanced at his dagger, sheathed at his waist, but didn't touch it. The only reason she hadn't killed him yet, he imagined, was because it amused her to watch him squirm. If he threatened her, she'd come for him, and he wouldn't be able to stop her. Drawing the dagger was useless.

He stood up out of his fighting crouch and tried to calm his racing heart. He began to circle her, like he was looking for an opening. She would expect him to sidle away, trying to escape, so he didn't. "What happened to your eyes?" he asked.

Her thick eyebrows raised a little.

"That green glow," he clarified. That same green glow had lit Linza's eyes during the Test of Separation. Gods, it had lit her entire body. And it had lit the body of the monster that had tried to dig him out of his coffin. That couldn't be coincidence. "You're one of *them*, aren't you?" he said, not even knowing who 'they' might be. He just wanted to get her talking. If he could get her talking, perhaps he could think of a way out of this.

Jhaleen straightened. Her cloak slipped forward over one shoulder, covering half her body.

"We've already alerted the queen. She knows all about you," he continued, bluffing.

Jhaleen's eyes narrowed.

He'd actually hit upon something. Maybe there actually was a connection between Linza, the monster at the grave, and Master Jhaleen.

"The queen will expose you. She knows what you're doing at the academy…"

Jhaleen grinned, and her hesitation vanished. He realized he'd gone too far, showed some ignorance in his words.

"You don't know what you're talking about, do you?

You're playing for time."

She moved then, lunged across the distance so quickly Brom didn't even have a chance to put a hand on his dagger, let alone draw it.

She grabbed him around the neck like she had Faline and lifted him off the ground. He choked and grabbed her bulging arm.

"Die, spawn of the Soul," she said. "It's too late for your world. The doorway is open." Jhaleen's arm tensed. Sparkles danced in Brom's vision as she cut off his breath. He waited for the inevitable crack—

—but Jhaleen's muscled arm started to vibrate, as though she was struggling with herself, like she wanted to snap Brom's neck but couldn't.

"Put him down," Queen Oriana said as she strode out of the darkness.

14

BROM

GROWLING, EYES WIDE AND TEETH CLENCHED, Jhaleen slowly lowered Brom to the ground and let him go. He sucked in a blessed breath, hands going to his throat as he stumbled backward, hit the wall, then slid to his knees.

Oriana lit up the darkness like a silver-and-gold torch as she came forward, her hair braided and twisted atop her head. It seemed to catch all the light from the street behind her. Even in the near darkness, Brom could see her telltale indigo eyes.

She wore a commoner's clothing, but the intentionally-brown breeches, boots, tunic, and cloak did nothing to hide her imperiousness. Brom suspected that, even if Oriana had wrapped herself in rags, she would still look like a queen, shoulders back, eyes blazing, voice sharp with command.

Two formidable-looking people flanked her—a man with long hair that fell across his right eye, and a lean woman with a series of silver rings around her neck, stacked halfway up to her chin. Like Oriana, they both looked like they'd intentionally dressed in common clothes. Also like Oriana, they didn't look common at all. They moved like snow lions, lithe and graceful. Their gazes surveyed the alley with professional coolness. They couldn't have looked more like bodyguards if it had been written on their foreheads.

"Oriana!" Brom rasped, pushing the words past the terrible burning in his throat. The pebble in his belly vibrated, and he felt a tingle in his arms and legs, close to the telltale surge of lightning he used to feel every time he was close to his Quad mates.

"It appears I've arrived just in time," Oriana said. Her gaze never left Jhaleen.

Brom ran to Faline's twisted body and fell to his knees. "Don't be dead," he said. "Please—"

"Leave her, Brom," Oriana commanded.

"But she—"

"We aren't done yet."

Brom glanced over at Jhaleen. The master stood where she was, arm extended, hand like a horseshoe around empty air, as if she were still choking Brom. Her entire body trembled, the cords of muscles bunching beneath her skin as she fought whatever Oriana was doing to her.

"Back up," Oriana said to Jhaleen, striding closer. Oriana's guards fanned out.

Jhaleen growled in frustration. With jerky motions, she stepped away from Brom and Faline. Her legs trembled with each step, and Oriana's fierce concentration told Brom that controlling the master was not an easy task.

"You...will die," Jhaleen growled.

"Obviously," Oriana said dismissively. She spared a glance at Brom. "So... You're alive." She spoke as though they were conversing in the practice room back at the academy.

"It's a story," Brom said.

A smile flickered at the corner of Oriana's mouth. "You never fail to deliver mysteries."

"But no answers."

"Let's find out." She turned her focus back on Jhaleen and narrowed her eyes in concentration. Jhaleen clenched her teeth and her fists. As the two struggled in a battle that Brom couldn't see—a battle for Jhaleen's mind—the master's green eyes glowed brighter.

Finally, Oriana let out a little breath, and her delicate brow furrowed. "Your thoughts are...." Oriana trailed off. Then, "Who is protecting you?"

"You're all doomed," Jhaleen growled, and her voice sounded deeper, darker. "It doesn't matter what you do now."

"You're not human," Oriana whispered.

"Not human...?" Brom thought about the monster that had dug him up, that green flame around it. "What is she?"

"More questions," Oriana said. "Well, if I cannot read your thoughts, 'Master' Jhaleen, I suppose you're just going to have to tell me." Again, Oriana narrowed her eyes.

Jhaleen growled, clenching her teeth.

"What are you?" Oriana demanded.

Jhaleen gasped, bowed her head as though trying to turn away from Oriana, but the rest of her body didn't move. "M-Master Jhaleen," she said, breathing hard.

"What else are you?"

"You..." Jhaleen huffed. "...will never...know..."

"Oh, I think we both know that's not true," Oriana said, but sweat now glistened on her pale forehead. "It simply takes…time."

"You…are out…of time," Jhaleen huffed.

Oriana's eyes suddenly went wide, and she turned her head as though she'd seen something no one else could see.

Something hit her, invisible and swift. She gasped, pain flashing across her face, and she fell to one knee.

"Oriana!" Brom turned desperately, looking for the enemy, but there was no one. Still, he knew a mind-stab when he saw one. There was another Quadron, a Mentis, somewhere nearby.

Oriana's bodyguards snapped into action. Steel weapons flashed into sight. The woman drew two curved short swords. The man drew a longsword, and they both leapt at Jhaleen. The long-haired guard went high, the woman dropped into an artful slide behind the giant woman.

But the mind-stab had broken Oriana's hold. With a triumphant keen, Jhaleen leapt into action, moving so fast she blurred.

The male guard's sword, which was meant for Jhaleen's heart, went through her meaty shoulder instead. The female bodyguard's flashing daggers, meant to hamstring the master, instead sliced deep into her calves.

Jhaleen roared, crashing to her knees, but she was an Impetu. The bodyguards needed to have killed her with the first strike.

They hadn't.

Now it was the same battle Faline had faced. A Quadron versus *normals*. They'd have no chance, no matter how well-trained. They simply didn't have enough speed, enough strength to match Jhaleen's magic.

Brom had to find that Mentis.

He might not have magic, but he had knowledge. A

strong Mentis could attack from a distance. But to bring down someone as powerful as Oriana, the Mentis had to be close.

Brom sprinted toward the mouth of the alley, the direction from which Jhaleen had arrived, and he drew his wide-bladed dagger. He burst into the street and saw the figure immediately. Fully cloaked and cowled in white, the Mentis stood by the wall just around the corner. It was Tohn Gelu, another master from the academy!

Brom leapt at the figure—

"No." Tohn Gelu held up a hand.

Brom grunted as a thick, oozing hand spread over his mind, holding his body still. He tried to resist, and the oozing feeling turned to fire. Brom screamed and fell to his knees. His dagger clattered to the stones.

"Watch," the master commanded.

The fire burned his mind, and Brom jumped to his feet like he was on strings.

His legs walked his body stiffly back to the alley's mouth, turned him so he could watch Oriana.

"No…" he whimpered.

Oriana crawled toward Tohn Gelu, one slow limb at a time as though she were pushing against an invisible wind. Her head hung down between her arms in concentration, her hair undone, silver-gold braids dragging in the mud. But still she came, as though getting closer to the other Mentis would give her some advantage.

Behind her, Oriana's female bodyguard lay face down on the cobblestones, as still as Faline. Jhaleen now focused on the male bodyguard who had, miraculously, managed to escape the master's first attack. He danced back, trying to draw her away from Oriana.

Jhaleen laughed thunderously, lunging at him so fast

she became a blur in the darkness. The male bodyguard whipped his sword up to meet Jhaleen's charge—incredibly fast for a *normal*—but she batted it aside with her blue gauntlet, shattering the blade. She punched the male bodyguard in the chest so hard, he flew through the air. He hit the street twenty feet away, rolled to a stop, and lay still.

The master leapt the distance to the crawling queen, raised a gauntleted fist and brought it down—

The darkness behind Jhaleen blurred, and the master flew forward like she'd been shot from a catapult. Her fist came down just in front of Oriana's head, missing the target and cracking the muddy cobblestones instead. Jhaleen somersaulted and crashed to the stones on her back.

For a breathless moment, Brom didn't even know what had happened. He stared past Master Jhaleen—

—to see a dark figure loom behind Oriana. Time seemed to slow as the giant stepped gracefully around the queen and interposed himself between her and her attacker. The shadows fell away from him, revealing long wild hair, a thick beard, and that telltale tattoo that went down the left side of his rugged face.

15

BROM

"ROYAL!" Brom exclaimed. The pebble danced excitedly in his belly.

Royal had always been large, but the Fendiran was enormous now. His friend had filled out, and Brom was astonished to realize that the man he'd known at the academy had been some gangly adolescent version of Royal, despite still being twice the size of every other student. This was the adult Royal, every bit of him bulging with muscle and laced with battle scars. He was all bulk and wild hair and beard.

The big man's presence filled the alley. He'd just tossed an Impetu *master* across the street, yet his face was calm, certain, like there was no danger here, like he wasn't afraid of Jhaleen.

Royal had always been the naïve one in the Quad. But this wasn't a student looking to his fellows for assistance, as Royal so often did at the academy. This was a veteran of war and death, quite ready to kill.

"You are far from the academy, Master Jhaleen," Royal's deep voice rumbled.

Jhaleen hesitated. Clearly, she hadn't expected him.

Brom wanted to help, wanted to shout that Tohn Gelu was right around the corner, but he still didn't have command of his body or his voice.

"There's...a Mentis," Oriana said, still on her hands and knees. It looked like it was taking all of her effort just to speak. "Tohn Gelu."

"You would have killed her," Royal said to Jhaleen, like he was trying to understand. "You'd have crushed her skull."

Jhaleen didn't say anything, and that seemed answer enough for Royal. He nodded.

"Then fight," Royal said. "Or run. Either way, you won't leave this alley alive."

Jhaleen showed her teeth. "You're a fool—"

Royal charged, blurring forward. Jhaleen leapt back, turned, and reached out to grab Brom, who *still* couldn't make his body move.

She'd intended to kill him before Royal could reach them, but Royal was faster. Jhaleen's huge hand whistled by Brom's face as Royal hit her. They crashed past Brom like a pair of tumbling boulders, cracking the cobblestones where they landed.

They rolled and came to their feet, both moving so fast Brom had trouble seeing them.

Jhaleen snarled and whirled, slugging Royal in the side with her gauntlet. Bones snapped, but Royal didn't make a sound. He hauled Jhaleen over his head like she weighed nothing, and hurled her away from Brom.

Jhaleen hit the building and the wall cracked, crumbling down upon her. Royal dove on top of her. The entire two-story brick building shuddered, and screams arose from inside as its occupants awoke in terror. Brick dust billowed out.

Flames engulfed Brom's mind, and he fell to his knees screaming. It wasn't just a mind-stab to stun him or scramble his thoughts. Tohn Gelu was attempting to burn out his brain.

Everything that made Brom who he was—his memories, his hopes, his fears—became words written on scraps of paper, and Tohn Gelu set those papers alight. Brom screamed again—

Then suddenly the pain stopped. A loud ringing filled his mind, like his head was made of metal and someone had struck it with a mallet. The ringing went on and on.

He forced his eyes open.

He was curled into a fetal position on the muddy cobblestones. Oriana stood over him, back straight, head high as she held her palm toward Tohn Gelu.

With a gasp, Brom rolled over, feeling like a baby just learning to use his limbs.

Tohn Gelu's head was bowed, and the opening of his cowl was filled with green light. He clenched his fists, fighting whatever Oriana was doing. The ringing died down in Brom's head, and he realized he could hear their voices.

"...nice little ambush," Oriana was saying. "But you've lost the element of surprise. Whatever will you do now?"

"You...will...die..." Tohn Gelu said, his voice shaking.

"Clearly," Oriana said dismissively. "Tell me, you both seem so interested in killing Brom. Why?"

Tohn Gelu just growled.

"You can tell me," Oriana said. "Or I can rip the memories from your head."

"You…can't…" he gasped.

"Is that so?"

Tohn Gelu cried out.

Brom got to his hands and knees, wobbly and disoriented. He fell back on his side. The Impetu battle raged twenty feet to his left.

Royal and Jhaleen hammered at each other. Giant fists blurred as they rose and fell, thudding against meat and bone. The two Quadrons spun, tumbled, tearing through the building like it was made of brittle clay. The entire western wall had crumbled away, exposing rooms filled with dust and scrambling, screaming people. Royal slammed Jhaleen into the ground so hard the entire alley shook. Jhaleen lashed out with her gauntlet, striking Royal in the face. Bones broke with each blow, but the combatants healed as fast as they were injured. Brom could feel the crackling lightning in his chest—could feel their magic—even from this distance.

Oriana's voice became implacable as she continued her interrogation of Tohn Gelu.

"Tell me," she demanded.

"No!" Tohn Gelu cried.

Oriana's eyes were the barest of slits. Her extended hand closed into a fist. Tohn Gelu's cowl lit with bright green light, and a strangled cry erupted from his mouth.

Oriana's indigo eyes snapped open. She lurched forward as though she would reach the master.

But before she'd even gone half a step, Tohn Gelu's white robes exploded into green fire. He screamed, back arching, hands curled into claws. He became a tongue of emerald fire that reached twenty feet in the air. Brom and Oriana shielded their faces as the flames licked outward, but instead of the expected wash of heat, a chilling cold whipped past them.

Tohn Gelu vanished. A patch of greenish frost remained where he had stood.

Brom stared, stunned. Oriana also hesitated, then turned toward the sagging building where the Impetus battled.

Royal flew backwards out of the building and crashed heavily into the alley, cobblestones and dirt flying as his sliding body carved a trench in the ground. He rolled to his feet. His left arm sagged, broken and dislocated, but as Brom watched, the arm mended, twisting and thunking into place, broken bones and ripped flesh healing. Royal rushed back into the billowing dust of the building.

For a long moment, the only sound was the shouts and running feet of those escaping the crumbling building. No further thuds echoed from the billowing brick dust. A moment later, Royal emerged, shaking his head.

"She's gone."

He glanced about, cocking his head as though he was also listening, but Jhaleen did not reappear. Apparently, with Tohn Gelu's demise, she'd fled.

Brom finally managed to stand up. His disorientation faded, and the horror of what had happened fell into place.

Faline!

He staggered to her crumpled form, slumped against a wall across the alley from the destroyed building. He fell to his knees, tears brimming, and hesitantly touched her shoulder.

"Don't move her," Royal's deep voice rumbled from behind him. Brom craned his neck to find the giant Fendiran towering over him. "Her neck is broken, but she lives."

"She's alive?" Brom gasped.

The big man descended to his knees next to Faline,

and Brom got out of the way. One of Royal's giant hands slipped beneath her head, the other beneath the small of her back. His thick fingers were so gentle, so different than the brutish fist-pounding that had just destroyed a building.

Each path to magic—Mentis, Motus, Impetu and Anima—had four aspects within it. The internal, external, constructive, and destructive. Impetus were primarily known for their destructive aspect: the ability to uproot trees, crush rocks, or do battle beyond a *normal*'s ability to thwart. But there were three other aspects of the physical path to magic, and one of them was healing.

Lightning crackled through Brom, and he knew that Royal was pushing his magic into Faline.

She gasped, her chest rising and her back arching as though all the pain of her snapped neck hit her at once. She wailed, and her hands reached up, grabbing nothing, then fell back to the muddy stones.

She blinked, twitched.

"Easy," Royal rumbled. "Move slowly. You will damage yourself if you move too quickly. Let the healing settle."

Eyes wide, Faline stared up at Royal like she was seeing the Ragged Man himself.

"You…" she growled. "What have you done?"

Royal didn't reply. He stood up and stepped back.

Brom rushed in, grabbing Faline's hands. "Gods, I thought you were dead."

She didn't seem to see him, though. Her gaze was fixed on Royal.

"That's The Butcher," she hissed.

"He just healed you," Brom said.

"What?"

"Master Jhaleen…broke your neck. Royal healed it."

"No," Faline said, shocked. "No, he didn't. No…"

"Put your personal feelings aside, Mistress Faline," Oriana said. "We have much to mourn today. Your injured pride can wait."

"You haven't changed at all," Royal growled at Oriana.

"You prefer I let her stab you?" Oriana asked. "I assure you, that's what she wishes to do."

Oriana strode to where Dantolis and Reela lay. She stared down at them, her face an impassive mask.

"I can't do anything for them," Royal said softly as he joined her. "They're gone."

"I know," she said.

Brom started toward her, but she held up a hand as though she had eyes in the back of her head. He stopped. "Oriana, I'm so sorry—"

She shook her head, and he stopped talking.

"We must get away from here," Oriana said.

"If you need time," Royal said, "then we will take the time."

Oriana turned away from the bodies to face Royal. She was six feet tall, taller than Brom, but still she looked up at Royal. "That will not be necessary."

"You are as cold as ever," he said, frowning.

"And you are larger and hairier," she said. "Though just as sentimental."

Royal's jaw muscles clenched.

"This isn't a game, Royal," Oriana said, talking to him just like she had back at the academy. "Every mistake. Every delay offers only more consequences like this."

"I know that better than you do," Royal growled.

"I'm glad to hear it. Because these won't be the last casualties," Oriana said. "The fours are stacking up."

Royal raised his bushy eyebrows in surprise, and Brom recognized the phrase as one Royal used to use—an homage to the goddess Fendra, who was said to speak to her chosen through the repetition of the number four in nature.

"You read the fours now, do you?" Royal rumbled.

"Despite what you may believe, I do not turn away from knowledge of any kind," she said. "No matter the source."

"So we are allies again, is that what you're saying?" Royal asked.

She held his gaze, and Brom couldn't decipher her expression. Was that anger? Hope? Mourning? It flashed across her beautiful face and was gone. If he'd blinked, he'd have missed it. Then it was just Oriana again, imperious and expectant.

Royal extended his hand. After a moment, she put her slender fingers in his, and they gave one shake.

"Fendra damn me for a fool," he said. "Why does it make me feel better to see you again?"

"Because you are smarter than you look," Oriana said, and Brom couldn't tell if she was joking or not.

"And do you bring information, Mentis?" Royal rumbled. "Or just the same pile of mysteries I already have."

"I brought Brom," she said.

Royal glanced over at Brom, and the big man's gaze didn't seem friendly. "If he is Brom."

"It's me, Royal."

"It is him," Oriana said.

"Simply because he does not have the green eyes of the enemy doesn't make him Brom. We saw him die."

Green eyes of the enemy... Brom suddenly wondered what Royal knew about the cold green light that had infected the masters, that apparently had immolated Master Tohn Gelu.

"In point of fact," Oriana said. "We did *not* see him die."

"We saw the body."

"Which is not the same thing."

"I think I *was* dead," Brom said. "If that helps at all."

Oriana turned her cold gaze upon him. "And why do you think that?"

"When I woke in the grave, a year had passed. In my head, that time is just…missing. If I wasn't dead, I was simply not there."

"Or deeply asleep," Oriana said. "How did you wake?"

"The first thing I remember was the scraping of claws as some creature tried to get to me. The creature had the same green fire the masters had."

"Yes," Royal said, like he was not surprised.

Oriana caught the big man's tone. "What do you know?"

But Royal looked down on them with a stony face, like he was reluctant to say anything. Oriana continued to burn a hole in him with her eyes. She must hate the idea that he knew something that she didn't. Knowledge was her hallmark as Mentis of the Quad, not his.

"Very well," he said finally, seemingly more to himself than to them, as though he'd overcome an internal struggle. "Perhaps I am a fool for not reaching out to you earlier, Oriana. I simply…" He shook his wooly head. "It doesn't matter now. We are here, against all reason. And if this is really Brom—"

"It's me, Royal," Brom repeated.

"If it is really Brom, then we have work to do."

"We each have pieces of these mysteries," Oriana said. "Together, we may assemble the entire picture. Tell us what you know."

"Let's see to the injured first." He glanced at the

crumbled building. "Then we can talk."

Oriana glanced in annoyance at the rubble, as though it was beside the point. For a moment, Brom thought she would insist he leave the *normals* alone, crack the whip with her imperious voice, but she didn't.

Hope suddenly welled up inside Brom. He was here. He was actually here with his Quad. Despite the year that had passed, despite his harrowing, disappointing visit to the Champions Academy, he'd found them. And they were, in the end, the same friends he'd known: Royal, who never passed up a chance to help someone, and Oriana, who'd always been smart enough to know when her orders would be ignored.

The stone in his belly bounced about happily, and a laugh escaped him.

Both Royal and Oriana turned to him in surprise, and their confused expressions made him laugh harder.

Oriana gave a little shake to her head. "If you needed proof this is actually Brom," she said, gesturing toward him, "there you have it."

Royal cocked his bearded head contemplatively, as though he might be willing to believe Brom was actually who he claimed.

The only thing missing from the moment was Vale. She'd have winked at Brom, let him know without words that she understood him in a way the others never could.

"Let's get about it," Oriana said, striding toward the rubble.

16

BROM

MANY HOURS LATER, miles away from the city, the campfire popped and crackled. Brom had to concede that, outside the academy walls, this was one of the most bizarre groups ever assembled. The Butcher of Gore Grove and the Ice Queen of Keltovar sat across the campfire from each other and actually seemed to be enjoying each other's company. Brom would bet that no one in the two kingdoms could have imagined these leaders staring at each other without opposing armies at their backs.

Mists hung thickly over the plains and Brom tried to shake off the chill. His cuts had healed, his fever had gone, but he was still practically skin and bones from his death—or long sleep—and his undernourished trip to the academy. He wrapped his cloak tightly about himself and leaned closer to the fire.

They had just finished burying Dantolis and Reela. The

funeral had been short. Oriana had given a eulogy, ending with a promise that she would pay proper tribute to her guards upon her return to Keltan. Everyone had agreed the bodies should not be buried anywhere near a forest. Even this far from the Hallowed Woods, no one wished to risk them turning into Lyancorpses. Oriana had also recommended they go far enough for it to be difficult for anyone to track them. So they'd ridden until they reached the plains.

Faline, who had been flirty and talkative since Brom had met her, had become withdrawn. She hadn't spoken a word to Brom since the fight, since her…healing. He didn't know if this was her true personality emerging at last, or if her silence was due to Royal's ministrations. Brom wondered if she would rather have died than have The Butcher help her. She stood away from the fire, almost in shadow. Her face was a mask of conflict as she stared at Royal.

"We have much to discuss," Oriana finally said.

Royal grunted.

"I honestly wondered if you would come, Impetu," she said. "I had faith, but not certainty."

"Did you?" Royal said.

"I thought you might assume it was a trap. An attempt at assassination," Oriana said.

"You're the one who taught me how to find a Mentis's weakness. If it came to a fight, you'd lose, Princess."

Faline stiffened, put her hand on her dagger. "You will address Her Majesty properly," she said.

Oriana barely lifted her hand, but Faline caught the gesture. Reluctantly, she settled back.

Royal didn't look at Faline, but a small smile grew beneath his beard. "It still amazes me, the knack you have for inspiring such obedience," he said softly.

"We call it loyalty," Oriana said.

"Only because Keltovari do not know the difference," Royal said.

Oriana smiled in response, a genuine smile. "Kelto, it's good to see you, Royal," she murmured. "Of all the Quad, I didn't think I'd miss you. But I have."

Faline shot a stunned look at her liege, which Oriana ignored.

"I would never admit I missed you," Royal said.

Oriana laughed this time. It was a light, attractive sound. Brom had always loved her laugh. "Well said. Shall I add diplomacy to your ever-expanding list of skills?"

"A lot has happened this year," he said.

"Mmmm," she murmured, and her smile faded.

Royal turned to Brom. "I nearly believe you could be telling the truth about who you are. If you would please tell us your story, I would hear it."

Oriana nodded. "As would I."

Brom relayed his adventure, starting with his Test, The Four's attempt to kill him, his "death," and then the moment that he'd awoken in a coffin with the *scratch scratch scratch* of the monster's digging. He relayed the fight, the greenish tint of the monster, his discovery that his magic had been stripped from him, and his narrow victory afterward. He described the harrowing journey to the Champions Academy—which included running into Lyancorpses on the road, sneaking into the academy, talking to Caila, and the fight with Master Saewyne. He relayed his journey with Undilayne, arriving at The Wayward Inn, Faline nursing him back to health, drugging him with Lyanleaf, and finally the strange dream about Vale. And that perhaps it wasn't a dream.

"The rest you know," Brom said.

Royal sat back, pulled a pipe from the large satchel at

his waist, filled it with tobacco, and lit it with a stick from the fire. The campsite was deathly quiet.

"Royal smokes a pipe now?" Brom lobbed the comment at Oriana in a light tone, trying to get her to smile again.

She acted like she hadn't heard him, her gaze now on Royal.

"The Four weren't trying to kill you," Royal said.

"I know you don't want to believe it," Brom said. "But they were. It wasn't just a test. They *told* me they wanted to kill me. And they said they were going to do horrible things...to all of you."

"Yet obviously they didn't," Royal argued. "Because here we all are, with everything they promised us. The Test was hard, yes. But it was supposed to be. We knew it would be."

"Have you ever actually thought about the Test, Royal? Nobody at the academy seems to really think about it, but somehow my eyes were finally opened and I did. And it's ludicrous. No full Quad has ever passed the Test. *None save The Four themselves.* You don't find that hard to believe?"

"None have ever been strong enough," Royal said. "The Test of Separation is the most difficult test there is. Not everyone could—or should—become a Quadron."

"Or The Four are sadistic bastards," Brom said.

Royal's blue eyes flashed. "The Four have done more to shepherd the two kingdoms than anyone in history."

"They *killed* me, Royal."

"Except obviously they didn't."

Brom rolled his eyes. "I was there. They acted like assassins, not teachers. They wanted me dead. It was their objective."

"It's part of the Test," Royal repeated.

Brom had forgotten how stubborn Royal could be, and how much he and Oriana wanted to believe in The Four. Only Vale had shared Brom's skepticism about authority, had gleefully joined him in breaking the rules at the academy. Royal and Oriana *wanted* to believe in the rules. It was a conviction they'd both always shared.

"Okay, let's set aside The Four for the moment," Brom said. "I'm alive. Why is that? Why would that be? I've been trying to piece that together, but I can't figure it."

"You were gone a full year," Oriana said. "You awoke amidst a flurry of fours. That is not a coincidence. It feels like the gods are at work. And yet…you awoke with no magic?" She shook her head like that was the one piece that made no sense.

"There's something…almost magical. It feels like a pebble in my belly," Brom said. "I think it's what's left of my Soulblocks. I was hoping it would…revert to normal when I found you again, when I rejoined the Quad. But it hasn't."

"You may not have Soulblocks, but I can still feel your presence as if you did," Oriana said. "When you are near, my magic increases, just as it did back at the academy."

"It does?" Brom asked.

"As does mine," Royal rumbled.

"Have you ever heard of a 'pebble' Soulblock?" Brom asked Oriana. "Did you ever come across anything in your studies that mentioned someone coming back from an injury where their Soulblocks seemed to have collapsed like this?"

"No," she said, looking thoughtful. She folded her long-fingered hands in her lap, and Brom instantly doubted her answer. She had often folded her hands just like that when she'd figured out something she didn't yet want to share with the Quad.

He thought about pressing her, but Oriana had reasons for everything she did. It's possible there was a good reason for her. He decided to try to draw it out later when he caught her alone.

"Okay," Royal rumbled in his deep voice, sounding disappointed. "One mystery. No answers. Let's move on to the next. Oriana, you believe The Four have vanished?"

"Yes," she said.

"How do you know?" Royal asked.

Oriana gave him a withering look. "Keltovar has an extensive information-gathering apparatus. I am privy to everything that happens in my kingdom, most of what happens in the academy, and some of what happens in your own country, Royal. The Four left the academy weeks ago. They never returned."

"And you do not know where they went?"

"No."

"So not that extensive, in the end."

She ignored the jab. "My spies report that The Four vanished exactly four weeks ago."

"You sound like a priestess druid," Royal said.

"I wonder if their disappearance has to do with the piece of information you hold," she said.

"My piece," Royal said softly, and he tossed the stick he'd been holding into the fire. He glanced past Oriana at Faline.

"She is loyal to me," Oriana said. "Speak freely."

"That green glow in Tohn Gelu's and Jhaleen's eyes…" Royal said. "It means they've been infected."

Oriana narrowed her eyes. "Infected?"

He set his pipe on the edge of the fire ring. "We're under attack, Oriana. By an enemy I don't know how to fight. I've been thinking on it for months, and your note finally prodded me into action. I've not dared confide my fears to the Council of the Wise, for I fear one or more of the priestess druids are also infected."

"Your council has been infected?" Oriana asked.

"It is possible. While some of the infected reveal themselves with green eyes, some do not. So there's no one I can trust for certain, except you. I knew the moment I saw you I'd be able to tell if you'd been infected," Royal said. "As your Quad mate, I'd *know*. But I couldn't think how to contact you, what message I could send that you'd respond to. I've been wanting to talk to you since the Battle of Gore Grove—"

"Gore Grove?" Faline stepped into the light of the fire.

"Faline, please." Oriana held up a hand, and Faline stopped her advance.

Royal glanced at Faline and his eyes became haunted. "You had friends in the...at Gore Grove," he said.

"My father," Faline said through her teeth. "My brothers."

Royal looked down at his hands, and for a long moment, he didn't speak. Finally, he raised his wooly head and held Faline's fierce gaze. "I am...sorry, Faline," he said. "Perhaps you should hear this most of all."

"You killed them," Faline said.

"What happened in Gore Grove?" Oriana asked.

"Everyone thinks they know. Everyone is wrong."

"You slaughtered them, Butcher," Faline spat. "That is what happened."

"Faline," Oriana said coldly.

"I had sixteen warrior druids with me when two hundred Keltovari soldiers caught us at Gore Grove," he said softly. "I killed them all, including my own."

That got Oriana's attention. "What?"

"There was…a pit." Royal looked into the fire like he was looking back to that time. "It wasn't made of dirt or stone, but of green light, coming right up out of the ground. Wisps of light tentacles wriggled out of the pit, a thousand of them, and every person they touched…they changed. Those infected glowed green. Eyes, skin, fingernails, hair. Each was different, but they weren't human anymore. They weren't…themselves. Because of my magic, because of my speed, I was able to avoid the tentacles. But every other person in Gore Grove was taken, and they came after me with a bloodlust I've never seen before. The Keltovari soldiers. My warrior druids. They said things like 'the door is open' or 'you will die' and 'your time is over,' just like the masters." He paused, looking at each of them in turn.

"You're lying," Faline whispered, and this time Oriana didn't reprimand her. She seemed deep in thought.

"They were no longer the people you knew," Royal told Faline. "Nor the people I knew."

"Tentacles of green light?" Oriana asked.

Royal nodded. "The whole thing felt like a spell. But I couldn't find the Quadron. I looked. I scoured that part of the Hallowed Woods for days afterward."

"A Quadron could not do something like you describe," Oriana said. "A magical infection? I've never read of such a thing."

"It wasn't any Quadron we've ever seen or read about," Royal said. "Perhaps it's something different than a Quadron. Whatever it is, it doesn't show itself. It works through others. Friends. Family. An enemy who can infect those loyal to us, turn them against us. How do I fight that? I can't stop thinking Gore Grove was the first skirmish in a coming war. That's why I wanted to talk to you, Oriana. That's why I felt the need…for my Quad. Fendir's and Keltovar's endless war in the Hallowed Woods suddenly seemed like a distraction from the true danger, this secret war that threatens *both* kingdoms." He spared a quick glance at Brom, then settled his gaze on Oriana. "We must find The Four," Royal said. "Only they can expose this enemy—"

"No," Oriana said.

"No?" Royal frowned.

"I am inclined to believe you are telling the truth," Oriana said.

"Why thank you."

"This secret war you speak of, it could be exactly what all the fours are pointing to. But finding The Four isn't our priority. Finding Vale is," Oriana said.

Brom sat up. "What about Vale?"

"We have a full Quad, Royal." Oriana ignored Brom's question. "Quad Brilliant could come together for the first time as full Quadrons. That hasn't happened in a hundred years. If you are right and this unseen enemy is infecting entire armies—infecting Quadrons, for Kelto's sake—we must reunite with Vale."

"You're saying that us forming a Quad is more important than finding The Four?"

"I am."

"Oriana… Even you couldn't be that arrogant," Royal shook his head. "*They're* the protectors of the two kingdoms. Not us."

"The Four might be behind this entire thing," Brom said.

"Stop it, Brom," Royal growled. "Just stop it. You're being ridiculous." He turned back to Oriana. "You know we need them. Whatever we could do is inconsequential compared to what The Four could do. We go to the academy. We find out what happened to them. Then we find them."

Oriana shook her head. "The academy is a dangerous waste of time. If Tohn Gelu and Jhaleen are infected, the rest surely are. We'd be wading into a battle we would lose. But not if we had Vale."

"Where is she?" Brom asked. He was tired of being ignored.

"She attacked the expedition I sent to look for the rumored new Lyantree forest," Oriana said. "She scattered it, sent a message back with one shivering academic she'd scared half to death. Unfortunately, she frightened him so badly his message was garbled."

"What was the message?" Brom asked.

Oriana reached into an oblong pouch tucked against her ribs and removed a scroll.

At the sight of it, the pebble in Brom's belly bounced so vigorously that he coughed. "What is that?" he gasped.

Royal seemed as spellbound as Brom.

"This is a second-year writ of passage," Oriana said.

"We never got second-year writs," Brom murmured.

Oriana nodded. "I stole it."

"Why?" Royal asked.

"I don't know," she said.

Brom felt a strong compulsion to snatch the scroll from Oriana. Royal had leaned toward Oriana, elbows on his knees. It looked like he had the same urge.

"You took it," Brom whispered, trying to shake the compulsion, but he couldn't. "Because you had to. I want it too. There's something…important about it."

Royal nodded in agreement. The scroll seemed to emit invisible lightning, like a Soulblock—like something that connected them all together.

"I was hoping perhaps one of you could tell me why,"

Oriana said.

"What did Vale say about it?" Brom asked.

"She knew I had it, for one," Oriana said. "And she'd have no reason to know that. She said the writ of passage is the answer. She said it was a tripwire."

"A tripwire!" Brom said.

"For what spell?" Royal demanded.

"That is the question," Oriana said.

Now the compulsion to possess the scroll was so strong, Brom opened his mouth to demand it. But Royal beat him to it.

"Give it to me." The big man held out his hand.

Oriana's fingers curled possessively around it. Faline put her hand on her weapon again and moved closer.

Royal flicked a glance at Faline and shook his head warningly.

"Oriana," Brom said. "From the moment you took it out, I wanted to grab it from you. Completely irrational. It has to be part of the spell."

"Perhaps you should give it to one of us," Royal said. "Perhaps one of us is supposed to have it."

Oriana brought the scroll closer to her body.

"Oriana…" Brom said softly.

She matched gazes with him, and he could see the struggle in her—and Oriana never let such things show on her face. Finally, she nodded. "Very well. I will give it to you, Brom."

Frustration flashed over Royal's face. He clenched his fists and sat back, but he didn't protest.

With a shaky hand, Oriana held forth the scroll. It seemed like she wanted to yank it away, and it was all Brom could do to keep himself from snatching it. Instead, he forced himself to reach out, palm upward, and wait.

Oriana's hand shook so fiercely when it hovered over Brom's, it seemed she'd been taken by a sudden palsy.

"Oriana?" Brom asked.

"It's…difficult," she breathed.

She hesitated a moment longer, then dropped the scroll into his palm.

The scroll touched his skin, and something cracked inside Brom. It felt and sounded like a twig had snapped inside his head. He twitched, pressed his palms to his temples.

Royal leapt to his feet with a roar, hands on his head also. Faline surged forward to catch Oriana, who had drooped.

Memories flooded into Brom's mind, as if the snapping sound had been a dam breaking, releasing an ocean of knowledge. Memories flooded into him.

The Four *were* evil, and all of them knew it, not just Brom. The entire Champions Academy was a trap, a web to collect all the young magic users of the two kingdoms. And the Test of Separation was exactly what Brom had said—it was designed to ensure that no Quad ever graduated intact. It was designed to ensure The Four maintained their preeminence as the most powerful Quadrons in the two kingdoms.

Brom saw the memory of himself invading the tower of The Four in secrecy, seeing The Four in all their grotesqueness. He saw himself jumping through a stained glass window into a snowstorm, fleeing The Four as they sought to kill him. He'd opened his fourth Soulblock to escape, risking almost certain death, and he saw how the rest of his Quad had risked their lives to bring him back. He saw himself sitting with Oriana, Vale, and Royal in Oriana's room, discussing what must be done next. Instead of fleeing, they'd decided to hide in plain sight by using a forgetting spell to erase these memories from all of their minds.

"By Fendra!" Royal roared, and Brom knew he must be regaining the same memories.

"We did it to ourselves," Oriana gasped. "I made us forget. But we were supposed to remember. We were supposed to remember at the end of the year when we received our writs of passage."

"But we never got them," Royal said. "They sent us to the Test of Separation early."

"Kelto…" Oriana murmured.

Brom reeled with the implications, at all they had lost, at how they'd walked into the Test of Separation like the good little lambs they'd been duped to be.

Royal clenched his fists at his sides, muscles flexing, as he stared into the darkness.

"Vale knew," Brom suddenly said. "She found out the truth somehow, without the spell and the scroll. She remembered all this. That's why she reached out to you, Oriana." The realizations kept coming, striking Brom one after another like lightning. "I know what she's doing…" he murmured, astonished.

"Speak if you know," Oriana demanded.

"If Vale discovered that The Four were villains, what's the first thing she'd do?" he said.

"She would find us," Royal said. "She would warn us."

"Don't be absurd," Oriana said, seeing what Brom meant. "*You* would. *I* would. Maybe even Brom would. But Vale wouldn't. She'd attack them."

"She'd want blood," Brom said. "You remember—she wanted it at the academy, when we first uncovered this."

"You think she *attacked* them?" Royal asked. "Attacked The Four alone? That's suicide."

"Perhaps not," Oriana said.

Royal's face was screwed up, like his head was being pressed between two heavy stones. "How is that *not* suicide?"

"How could Vale command a dragon?" Oriana countered. "She's discovered something. Some new power."

"But she's losing the fight," Brom said. "My dream… She said that *they* were too strong, and that she was going to die soon. She was talking about The Four."

"When I mind probed the man who delivered her message," Oriana said, "Vale looked haggard. She had cuts all over her arms and face."

"She was calling for help," Brom said. "That's why she sent the message."

"She said nothing about needing help," Oriana said.

"But she wouldn't, would she? If she'd told you The Four were your enemies, you'd have ignored her. You saw how Royal reacted. She had to get you to remember!"

"She's fighting The Four," Royal marveled.

"Kelto's teeth, that girl…" Oriana said.

"But she's losing," Brom said. "We have to help her."

Royal raised his chin, looking to the east, fierce pride on his face in the flickering firelight. There was nothing more romantic to a Fendiran than fighting ridiculous odds for a noble cause.

"We go to Vale," Royal said.

Oriana nodded. "Pack up the camp," she said. "We ride tonight."

Hold on, Vale, Brom thought. *Hold on. We're coming for you.*

Part VI

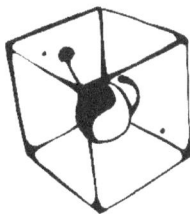

The Reunion

1

VALE

VALE WANTED TO SLEEP. She wanted it so badly her eyes burned and her chest constricted, like someone had grabbed her heart and twisted, pulling all the strings of her body tight. She huddled against Crookbranch, drawing strength from him and all the Lyantrees nearby. Their magic kept her alive. If not for them, she'd have died already. Her mind would have been overthrown by Olivaard. Her soul would have been sucked away by Linza. Wulfric would have clawed out of the tunnels and torn her limb from limb.

The Four had tried to kill her, and she'd stopped them...so far. Gods, they were strong! Even with all her carefully laid traps, she'd been unprepared for how powerful they were. She'd lost count of how many times she'd almost died.

And now they'd gone quiet. They hadn't attacked for hours. A desperate part of her wanted to believe she'd cowed them, beaten them, that one of them had died in their struggles against her, but that was a childish hope. They'd gone quiet to deceive her, to lure her into a sleep from which she'd never awaken.

Despite her almost endless supply of magic from the Soulblocks of the forest, Vale had quickly turned from aggressor to defender. The Four had attacked and attacked and attacked, even from deep underground where she kept them. When she'd realized her maze of tunnels—filled with magical traps—and her direct assaults weren't going to be enough, she'd fled, hastily constructing this island, her "fortress" in the midst of the river. There were no walls or guards or swords here. Instead, Vale had surrounded herself with water, had forced the river to flow around her sanctum, around Crookbranch and her most loyal Lyantrees. This, and only this, had saved her from certain death.

Vale had learned much these past months, from discovering the secret of the Lyantrees to understanding how The Four manipulated the elements of creation themselves. The Four had created their tower and the entire Champions Academy by molding stone and air, fire and water, but no one had ever known *how*. Not even the masters, Vale suspected. Of the four paths to magic, only an Impetu could affect the physical world, and that was only by brute strength, a magical elevation of what *normals* could already do.

The Four could levitate chunks of stone from the earth and shape them into a tower or a wall through the power of their intact Quad. An individual Quadron could never master such a thing. It required more magic than one person could muster.

And of course, The Four had ensured that no full Quad had ever survived the Champions Academy. That was its secret purpose, unbeknownst to all who trained there. The Four gathered ignorant youths from the two kingdoms and pierced them with psychic hooks, binding them to servitude forever.

But Vale had broken free of their bonds and uncovered an even greater secret, one that The Four had hidden for a hundred years: the Lyantrees provided a nearly limitless supply of Soulblocks. And those Soulblocks meant Vale could wield the power of an intact Quad all by herself.

For Vale, it had opened a whole new world of magic with its own rules and difficulties that had led, in her moment of panic, to creating her sanctum. Of all the elements, rock was the easiest to shape and water the most difficult. Water's wilder, unpredictable nature wreaked havoc with the steady, organized implementation of magic. Water could be a barrier or a bolster to magic, depending on how it was used. Before she'd attacked The Four, Vale discovered that a circle of water enhanced magic within and repelled magic without. This was undoubtedly why The Four had put a moat around their academy, and it was Vale's first desperate thought when she'd fled to this place where the flowing water of the river shielded her from The Four's attacks.

After she'd sunk them deep into her labyrinth, she'd tried to separate them, tried to suffocate them, to crush them. But the best she'd been able to do was hold them, confound them, and drive them deeper down as she extended the tunnels. Her greatest success—perhaps her only success—was denying them a return to the surface where they could face her head-on.

But now those slithering snakes were hatching something new, and she didn't know what. She didn't know which was worse—fighting another relentless onslaught or waiting for one.

They were alive down there, still together, and Vale was alone. Every part of her body hurt. She kept thinking that if she could have killed even one of them, she could have cut their power in half. The battle would be over.

She'd made so many mistakes. This battle would have gone so differently if she hadn't been so damned foolish, if she'd just secured an ally beforehand. If she'd only gone to Oriana ahead of time, told her about the writ of passage and stood there while the queen recovered her memory, everything would be different now....

Now Vale was trapped. She could never leave her sanctum until The Four were dead. If she did....

She twitched her head, forcing herself not to think about it. She still had one thin thread of hope. Oriana might have received Vale's message. She might—just might—be coming to Vale's aid, and that's all Vale would need. Even at this point, one ally could make the difference.

She'd sent Tam west to see if there was any sign of the queen. Vale's desperate mind had also dreamed of Royal, of how he might somehow sense Vale was in trouble through the bond they'd once shared. It was a foolish dream, but wasn't that what Fendiran warrior poets wrote about incessantly? A true Fendiran hero always arrived at the last moment to save the day.

Gods, she had even dreamed of Brom, had conjured a meeting with her dead lover. He'd been in Torlioch at The Wayward Inn, "held hostage" by a beautiful barmaid. That part had been so very Brom. In fact, everything Brom had done in the dream had been so authentic that she'd allowed herself to believe that he was actually alive. It had been a glorious fantasy, but it made waking to her predicament that much more painful. It was like she'd lost him all over again—a spike of emotional pain to go with her slow physical destruction.

Her fingers hovered shakily over the rips in her skin. She couldn't remember what it was like not to be in pain.

She knew now that she was going to die. It would happen one way or another. Either The Four would finally get her, or she'd tear herself apart trying to stop them, forcing more magic through herself than a human body could endure.

It wasn't so much her own looming death that bothered her. It was that if she died, The Four would continue their villainy. The truths Vale had dredged to the surface would slip below the murk and become secrets again. None would know about Vale's last stand except for Tam. Only the stalwart Sacinto would remember that one woman had stood against The Four for the sake of the two kingdoms. And who would listen to a Sacinto—

"Vale," a voice called from behind her. "By Kelto, Vale…"

Her head snapped up. Brom stood before her, and her breath caught in her throat. He was just as she remembered him from the Champions Academy, that graceful stance and slender neck she had loved kissing. His wavy black hair curled over his forehead, his dark eyes….

"Oh Vale… What did they do to you?" Brom whispered.

"You…" Her disorientation bordered on vertigo. She felt like she was leaning sideways. Was she dreaming again? Had she fallen asleep and hadn't noticed?

She stared for a long moment, blinking, but Brom didn't vanish. She moved her arms, pulling at the rips in her skin. She winced at the fresh wave of pain, but she didn't "wake up." Brom stayed where he was.

"You're fighting The Four, aren't you?" Brom asked. "All of them. All at once. What were you thinking?"

"You're dead," she murmured.

"Not...exactly. It's a story worth retelling, I can assure you, but we can talk later. Right now, we need to get you to safety."

"Safety? Where—"

"The Queen of Keltovar received your message," Brom said. "She's here. The Oaken Knight is here, too. We've come to help you."

Tears welled in her eyes. They'd come for her. Her Quad had come to rescue her at last. She pushed against Crookbranch's scaly bark, trying to get to her feet, and Brom rushed to help her. His hands were warm on her arms. Gods, he was actually here. She wasn't dreaming.

"How...?" she murmured.

"Time enough for stories later," he said, cradling her head in the curve between his shoulder and his chest, a perfect fit. When they'd lain in bed long ago, back at the academy, this was how she'd always rested.

She could barely assimilate what was happening. "Gods, Brom. I'm so... *How* are you still alive?"

"They tried to kill me," he murmured into her hair. "But they failed."

She gave a weak laugh. "We have that in common." A lassitude fell over her like warm oil poured over her scalp. "It's so good to see you, lover. I missed you. I dreamed about you."

"Let's get you out of here," he said, leading her away from Crookbranch. "The queen awaits at the forest's edge. We have to get you off this island."

Vale wasn't alone anymore. Gods! Her ordeal was nearly over. With her Quad mates, she could turn this battle around.

And yet…that same question nagged at the back of her mind.

"How… How did you survive?" she asked.

"You're not going to let it go, are you?" Brom smiled wryly down at her as they moved toward the river.

"I just—"

"You," he said. "Whatever you did worked."

"What *I* did?"

"With the trees," he said.

Vale's confusion bubbled up within her slowly, sluggishly. "Opening the Soulblocks within the Lyantrees brought you back?"

She'd finally gotten her legs under her and was able to stagger forward on her own. He strode confidently without answering, pulling her through the Lyantrees.

"Brom?" she prompted.

"It's…complicated," he said. "Getting you to safety is my top priority right now."

They reached the edge of the water, and Vale felt a reluctance to cross it. This rushing moat protected her from The Four.

"What is it? The water?" Brom asked.

"This river…. My sanctum consolidates power," she said.

He gave her a lopsided smile. "Your Quad is here now," he said. He tugged her into the water, and together they sloshed across it to the other side. The river wasn't too deep and the current wasn't bad. It only went thigh-high at the deepest.

"So you…awoke when I accessed the Soulblocks?" she asked as they emerged on the other shore. "Does this have to do with my dream about you in Torlioch?"

"It does," he said.

"Were you actually *in* Torlioch?"

"I was." He tugged her along.

"Somehow I knew it. It felt so real!"

"It was."

"But I don't…understand how that works," she said.

He laughed and stopped walking, turned to face her. "You're the same as ever. Will you let go of the puzzle for one second so I can help you? We have to get to the others. Come on." He tugged her arm again.

She went with him, and even though she knew she was going into the arms of her Quad, drawing away from her sanctum made her stomach uneasy. "You rose from your grave?" she asked.

"Right out of the ground," he said.

"With…Lyanroots?"

"The queen will explain everything," he said.

"The queen?" she said. "Why do you keep calling her the queen? It's Oriana, right?"

"Why aren't I…" He hesitated. "Well, she's the queen now."

Brom had always been irreverent, especially with titles. He had never called Oriana "princess." Vale had. Even Royal had. But Brom had always called Oriana by name. Why would he call her "the queen" now? Why would he…?

The answer solidified in her mind like water freezing. He wouldn't. Brom wouldn't. Not the real Brom.

"Oh gods…" She yanked her arm from his grasp as a horrible chill raced up her spine. "You're not Brom…"

Brom's body cracked and fell to pieces like glass, vanishing in little shimmers before they hit the ground.

"No!" Vale spun about, almost lost her balance, and fled.

Somehow, Olivaard had broken through the barrier of her sanctum. Somehow, he'd infiltrated her mind and planted an illusion there. Planted *Brom* there.

"Die bitch," Olivaard said in her mind. The words became a spear, plunging into her skull.

She screamed and lost all connection to her body. For an instant, it felt like she was floating, and then her face, chest and legs smashed into the wet earth and grass. It jolted her awareness again, and she raised her head.

The river was right there, barely a hundred yards away. She imagined herself running to it, splashing through the water. She imagined herself reaching Crookbranch.

But the pain of Olivaard's attack had caused her arms and legs to seize. She wasn't running anymore. She was lying on her face.

This was it. They had her now. She was going to die.

She heard cracking timber, the groaning of roots ripping from the earth, and she looked up. Overhead, a giant Lyantree shook itself as though coming awake, stretching. Its branches rose up like arms.

Eyes wide, Vale froze. She didn't know what to do.

Jondry flashed through her mind. Her final test before seeking the life of a Quadron had been to overcome Jondry, the unbeatable urchin who had tortured her when she was a girl. He'd been bigger, faster, and he'd had a gang. She had lived in terror of Jondry. It was as though her life had rested in his cruel hands, like she was alive only because he allowed it. She had fled from him, had given up her food to him, and when he'd caught her, she'd endured his beatings.

But the final time they'd met, that had changed forever. Before Vale had gone to the Champions Academy, she'd lured Jondry into a dead-end alley. When he'd come close enough, she'd leapt upon him like a feral cat and stabbed him in the back of the knee with a sharpened spoon. That night, she had severed his tendon...and his hold on her. Jondry had feared *her* after that, rather than the other way around.

It was the most important lesson she'd ever learned: that her fear of Jondry had made her less than she really was. And she'd only learned it at that last moment, after years of being a frightened little slave.

Despite Jondry's advantages—his strength, his ruthlessness, his gang—he had never been her greatest foe. *She* had been. Her belief in Jondry's supremacy had made her smaller than she really was.

Somehow she'd forgotten that lesson. She'd allowed herself to believe in The Four's supremacy. She'd run from them, waited for them to do their worst, and she'd clung to the idea that she could make herself safe in her sanctum.

Except there was no such thing as safety. That was just another word for cowering. Freedom from cruelty required risk. It required daring. It meant showing the predators they must turn and run away from her, not the other way around.

Face down in the dirt, paralyzed by Olivaard's strike, with a tree poised to crush her, Vale tore through her fear. If she was going to die, she'd die clawing at their faces.

With a guttural cry, she shoved back Olivaard's attack—just a little at first, just enough—and rolled to the side. A thick branch stabbed the earth where she had been, driving deep and showering her with chunks of grass and dirt. She rolled toward it and grabbed hold of the branch as the tree rose again to its full height.

Vale screamed as she clung to the branch, wrapping her arms and legs around it. It raked her hands and her thighs raw and pulled at the rips in her skin.

But when the tree snapped upright, she let go, and the tree's power flung her through the air. Her sudden, unexpected flight dislodged Olivaard's mental attack. Suddenly, Vale could think again. She gasped and cast about, trying to get her bearings. She sailed through the air, arcing toward her island sanctum.

She cackled madly.

In the scant seconds before she would smash into the ground and break her bones, she opened her mind, reaching out to the Lyantrees who still served her. She opened up their Soulblocks and let their magic rush into her.

Her body fluttered like a curtain. Her skin ripped, the tiny cuts growing longer as her body strove to contain more magic than a human was meant to have.

But now she had more than enough power to save herself.

Vale released the magic into the wind, calling to it, commanding it. Malleable but capricious, air was difficult to tame. Trying to make it do what she imagined was like trying to form dry sand into a ball. She had to keep grasping, keep scooping, keep pushing until it obeyed.

Vale hurtled toward the river that surrounded her island, then slowed, then hovered over the water as the wind lifted her.

She laughed again and let the magic go. The wind dropped her and fluttered on its way. She splashed into the water and turned, stared back at the tree that had tried to kill her. It slowly straightened, branches reaching toward the sun as they normally would, then went stiff, becoming a tree again. The Four had released it.

The euphoria of the magic coursed through her, made her invincible. But the nature of Lyantree magic was that she couldn't keep it. She could not refill her own

Soulblocks with it. She could only bring the magic in and push it out again, using it for whatever spells she had ready. None of the magic stayed within her, and after it left, only its devastation remained.

The Four had taken their shot, and they'd failed. She could only imagine what it had cost them. Orchestrating that spell, strong enough to pierce Vale's sanctum, would have taken all of their combined strength.

They had gone quiet again, and this time, she knew it wasn't because they were planning; it was because they were recovering. She felt no attack on her mind, her spirit, or her emotions.

She turned and walked out of the shallows of the river onto her island. The magic churned through her, and now she let it go. It rushed out of her, flowing back into the trees.

Vale had longed for her friends to show up and lift her burden, and The Four had exploited that weakness, and if she held onto that weakness, they'd do it again. She could never let that happen. It was time to admit the truth. No one was coming for her. Not Oriana. Not Royal. And Brom was dead.

It was just her and The Four.

2

BROM

BROM AWOKE to the starry night sky overhead. His eyes flickered open as the pebble in his belly twitched, and he rose silently. To his right, Royal snored. The big Fendiran only had two states of being, it seemed: wide awake or loudly asleep. The first couple of nights of this journey, that grinding noise had kept Brom awake, but now it was strangely comforting. That rumble meant Royal was nearby, that any danger would have to go through the formidable Impetu before it could reach anyone else.

To Brom's left lay Faline, who felt the exact opposite about Royal's presence. She had refused to sleep the first three nights because she was determined to protect her queen from The Butcher of Gore Grove when he finally "reverted to type" and tried to slaughter them all.

But it looked as though Oriana's insistence had finally swayed Faline...or the beautiful spy had simply collapsed from exhaustion. She lay slumped on her side, her head close to the cold and quiet fire ring.

It was Oriana's watch, but as Brom scanned the campsite, he couldn't find her. The queen would have stayed within view.

Brom reached out to shake Royal's mountainous shoulder, but he stopped as he spotted her.

Oriana's slender silhouette was barely visible against the dark purple of the horizon. She had to be at least a hundred paces away, sitting atop a small rise.

Brom shivered and wrapped his cloak tightly about himself as he stood up. It was summer, but the mornings were chilly this far east in Keltovar. Something about the way the winds flowed over the plains, Oriana had said.

He drew closer to her. The queen sat cross-legged, eyes closed, head up, chin high. A rosy pink blush marked her pale cheeks and nose. Her slender hands, also pink with cold, rested on her knees, and her cloak had blown open. It lay back on her shoulders as though she were posing for a portrait.

She was clearly casting, and he wondered how far away her mind was. He crouched next to her and pulled the edges of her cloak over her shoulders, covering her body and her crossed legs.

Her eyes cracked open, and she looked up at him with a frown.

"Sorry," he said. "You, uh, you looked cold."

"I am Keltovari," she said.

"Well, I'm Keltovari, too," he said. "And you looked cold."

The corners of her mouth turned upward. "You're the oddest combination of annoying and sweet," she said.

"That almost sounded like a compliment."

"It almost was," she said.

He chuckled. "Any luck?"

"She is there. I can feel a swell of magic ahead, but the distance makes it difficult for me to sense anything beyond that. Her mind is cut off from me. I suspect that is either because Olivaard is blocking me from getting to her, or because Vale is blocking anyone from entering her mind."

The very first night, Oriana had tried to reach out to Vale mind-to-mind. Keeping a mind-link with someone close by, according to Oriana, was a simple matter. But the further a person was from a Mentis, the more difficult it became. Oriana had said her outermost range was about a mile, but that took a great deal of power.

"So we're going in the right direction," Brom said.

Again, Oriana gave her half-amused smile. "Yes."

They'd been traveling for three days at a ridiculous speed. Their horses had practically flown over the flat fields of eastern Keltovar. What would have taken any normal person five days to cross had taken Royal and his Impetu powers three.

As an Impetu, Royal could infuse others with strength, endurance, and agility beyond a *normal*'s capacity, and he had done this for their horses.

"So," Oriana said. "We will not be able to tell her we're coming. She cannot prepare for us. She cannot...hope for us to help her."

Brom swallowed his disappointment. "She'll think you didn't get her message, that you aren't coming. That she's all alone."

"Yes."

Brom knew what that was like.

Oriana's cold fingers touched his chin, lifted his head.

"But we *are* coming," she said softly.

"What if she gives up before we get to her?" he asked.

"What if the sun rises in the west tomorrow?"

He smiled at that.

"This is Vale, remember," she said. "The woman doesn't know how to quit. She will fight until the last trickle of her life bleeds out on the ground."

"What if we are too late?" he asked.

"Then fate is cruel," Oriana said. "But such speculation helps no one. Put it from your mind. Worry will not make us go faster. It will not strengthen us for the upcoming battle." Oriana drew a deep breath of the crisp air. "Soon, we will be able to feel the conflict between Vale and The Four without trying. It will be like a great fire in the distance."

She said "we," but she didn't mean him. She meant herself and Royal. Brom wouldn't feel it. Without his magic, he couldn't feel anything—

Oriana pinched his chin again with her long fingers, and he blinked.

"Find your heart, Anima," she said. "It is your purpose within our Quad, and we need you. It does not do for our Anima to sulk."

"I'm not an Anima any longer, though," Brom said, hating the words. "Am I? I'm just another *normal* for you to protect."

Her touch lingered, and he realized this was probably the longest Oriana had ever touched him. Finally, her fingers slipped away and vanished inside her cloak.

"I suppose we shall see," she said.

He cast his gaze down.

Oriana stood up in a swirl of cloak, and the pebble in Brom's belly vibrated.

Royal stopped snoring abruptly. He grumbled, rolled over, and scratched his beard. Faline drew a swift breath and sat up, blinking. Brom realized both had been mentally prodded by Oriana. That was why the pebble had vibrated. That was the extent of Brom's *magical* abilities.

Faline looked bewildered.

"Your Majesty," she said, horror dawning on her face. "My apologies…I fell asleep." She leapt to her feet and turned a scowl on Royal, who sat up, his bushy hair flat on one side of his head. He looked lopsided.

"You *should* apologize," Oriana said to Faline, indigo eyes flashing. "For not taking care of your physical needs."

"I must protect you," Faline countered.

"Which you cannot do without sleep. When you insist on being obstinate, you force me to take a hand."

"You…made me sleep?" Faline trailed off.

"Do not make me do it again," Oriana said.

Faline was angry, but she bottled it up. Her gaze fell to the ground. "Yes, Your Majesty," she said.

"Good," Oriana said.

Royal stood up, put his arms over his head and stretched. His cavernous yawn sounded like a lion's roar.

"Animal," Faline muttered under her breath. She glanced at him with all the venom she'd obviously wanted to send at Oriana.

"Are you ready to ride, Impetu?" Oriana asked.

"I am ready," Royal said.

"Today, we reach her. Let us make haste."

3

OLIVAARD

OLIVAARD GROWLED. He wanted to leap to his feet and throw a chunk of rock at the wall, but he couldn't spare the energy. As it was, he could barely hold himself upright.

He had fooled Vale. He'd gotten her off her damned island, but somehow she had evaded the Lyantree. That branch should have stabbed her through the heart. They'd had her. They'd *had* her! But she'd slipped through their fingers. Again.

The little bitch was miraculous. How could she possibly keep going?

He glared around at his Quad mates. Their haggard, shadowed faces reflected his own failure, and with that failure, he had run out of time. He was going to have to tell them the secrets he had kept back. He was going to have to tell them what was happening out there in the two kingdoms while they'd been blind and deaf down here in these gods-forsaken tunnels.

And then he was going to have to tell them the dangerous gambit he'd already set in motion.

The only light source in this benighted hell came from Olivaard's magic opal ring. It gave off a glowing white light that cast long shadows, making nightmarish parodies of their bodies on the jagged walls. Its glow had diminished over these past weeks, an apt reflection of how the fight with Vale was going.

Wulfric lay unconscious a few feet away, his wounded hand bound up with white cloth that had turned almost completely red. When they needed him, they'd have to yank him back to consciousness with a wash of Lyantree magic. The Impetu had incautiously used up his third Soulblock weeks ago, and without an influx of Lyantree magic, he dropped right back into a coma. At this point, he was like a marionette on strings. When they forced Lyantree magic into him, he came to life. When the Lyantree magic was spent, he collapsed again.

Arsinoe sprawled on the rough, rocky floor, exhausted but still awake. The rest of them had stopped pulling from their personal resources at the second Soulblock, which was tiring enough. But of course to keep up with Vale, they'd had to borrow magic from the Lyantrees as well, and that took its own toll. Arsinoe's head leaned against the wall, barely connected to his neck—like a stacked block about to topple. His leg had disconnected completely and was a good six inches from his hip. One of his arms lay on the ground beneath his shoulder. There was no blood, of course, and each of his limbs would connect back up to his body once he caught his breath. Arsinoe's body—each of their bodies—had been different ever since they'd made their pact with the One Beneath.

Despite his insufferable personality, Arsinoe had done his part with the latest deception. He'd hooked into Vale's emotions just enough to heighten her longing for help, to force her to believe that her lover, Brom, had returned for her. Olivaard had done the rest, had crafted the illusion that Vale was actually seeing Brom, hearing him, feeling his touch.

It just…hadn't been enough. It seemed that the gods themselves didn't want the girl to die.

"How is she this powerful?" Linza creaked in her weak voice. She leaned against the rocky wall opposite Arsinoe, orange light flickering across her ghoulish features.

Olivaard didn't answer. That was the obvious question, wasn't it? Vale had learned more than Olivaard had imagined possible, and all in a matter of months. These past weeks, The Four had fled from Vale's vicious attacks, running down tunnel after tunnel. She had kept them tightly within her trap. She had changed tunnels, collapsed tunnels upon them, opened holes beneath their feet. The Four had only narrowly avoided being crushed by tons of falling stone, or broken from hundred-foot falls. Every time they tried to create a new way out of her labyrinth, she found a new way to foil their escape.

And despite what everyone in the two kingdoms thought, The Four were not invulnerable. Because of the insidious deal they had made with the One Beneath, they were immune to the ravages of time, but they could still die by violence.

In fact, they'd have been dead at Vale's hands weeks ago if Olivaard hadn't tapped into the Lyantree forest and cut the little bitch off from half the forest.

"How can she…keep going?" Linza huffed. "She should be dead."

Olivaard sneered. It seemed all Linza could do was point out the obvious. And then whine about it. Even Arsinoe had contributed more than Linza during their captivity. Their Anima's magic was weak. It came and went like a flickering candle about to go out, and Olivaard feared he knew the reason why.

Arsinoe offered little more value than Linza. Mostly, he nattered at them, picking and picking until Olivaard wanted to take Wulfric's sword and separate Arsinoe's head from his body for good.

And when Wulfric was awake and not in the midst of spell casting, he was worse than useless. He had lost his mind. Before he fell into his coma, Wulfric had stopped talking altogether. Oh, he made sounds, but they could hardly be called words. He growled, gnashed his teeth, and muttered unintelligibly as he compulsively clenched and unclenched his fists. Thankfully he still seemed to understand the rest of them when they talked, on a rudimentary level at least, like how a dog understood its master's commands. When they shoved Lyantree magic into him and asked him to cast, he did, but Olivaard wondered how long it would be before Wulfric simply ran off in one of the tunnels like some enraged and wounded animal, never to be seen again.

Of all of them, Olivaard was the only one who seemed to have retained the ability to think. The only purpose the others served was to increase their collective power when they cast spells.

"So…" Arsinoe started in, his voice raspy. "You failed. So…let's assess the root cause, shall we? Isn't that what you're so fond of, Olivaard? Haven't you told us over and over: 'To assess failure rationally, we must parse out the root cause?' Tell me, was it because you made a mistake on Brom's hair style? Did you make him three inches too short?"

"Shut up," Olivaard growled.

"No." Arsinoe's voice was barely audible in the still, close air of the tunnel, but to Olivaard it sounded like a screech. "You called Oriana the *queen*. Queen queen queen," he murmured. "Queen queen queen..." His voice dropped to a whisper. "Only the most formal and reverent Quad mate would call his fellow by her official title. Formal and reverent, formal and reverent... That is *so* Brom. That is the epitome of the little rule-breaking ferret. Well done."

"You are insufferable," Olivaard said.

Arsinoe rolled the back of his head side to side against the rock. "She wasn't even the queen yet when Brom died, you moron," he breathed.

Olivaard looked at Wulfric's short sword, but it was at last six feet away. Much too far to reach.

"We are going to die down here," Linza creaked.

"No. We will kill her," Olivaard said.

Arsinoe gave a lethargic chuckle. "Let's bet on that, shall we?"

Olivaard silently ground his teeth. This was what he had to work with.

What the two of them didn't know was that the game had changed. If they couldn't get free soon, it wouldn't matter if Vale could kill them. They would die anyway, as would everyone else in the two kingdoms. The world balanced on a knife's edge. The One Beneath had gnawed through the protections The Four had put in place. She was coming for her due.

If The Four couldn't get back to their tower soon—very soon—the One Beneath was going to own this land.

"We have allowed this little girl to imprison us. Us! We must end this charade."

Linza raised a white eyebrow.

"Yes, you're right, of course. Let's stop toying with her, shall we?" Arsinoe drawled sarcastically.

"We assumed our strength was enough to overwhelm her. It wasn't. We assumed her body would be torn to pieces by the forces she plays with. It wasn't. We cannot allow this to continue."

"What are you suggesting?" Linza asked.

"We call for help," Olivaard said.

Arsinoe sneered. "Oh yes. Let's do that, shall we?"

"Yes," Olivaard said through his teeth.

"And just who will come to *our* rescue?" Arsinoe said.

"The masters."

Linza raised both eyebrows now. "We cannot do that."

"We are out of time," Olivaard said. The words were bitter acid on his tongue. "We must throw all caution to the wind, because we won't have a tomorrow."

"But the masters have been taken by…Her." Linza's voice broke. She was seemingly unwilling to say the words: *the One Beneath*. Kelto's Beard, was Linza so scared now? "We felt Her break their bonds to us," she continued. "We know she has taken some of them."

"It appears we must, once more, make an ally of the One Beneath," Olivaard said.

Arsinoe gave a dry chuckle. "Oh, that will turn out well. I am sure She will trust everything we have to say."

"If She thought it would advance her agenda, She won't be able to help Herself."

"What are you saying?" Linza asked, her thin body as tight as a bow string.

"Much has happened this last month while we have been trapped," Olivaard said.

At that, Arsinoe raised his nearly-disconnected head.

"You've been in contact with the masters? I mean, recently?"

"I have." They had all been cut off from the two kingdoms while trapped down here. All save Olivaard. Their only possible glimpse of the world they once ruled was through Olivaard's mind probes. In the desperate battle with Vale, Olivaard had refrained from mind-probing anyone in his attempt to conserve strength. But he had broken that rule two days ago and had mind-probed Master Jhaleen without telling his Quad mates. He'd reached into her overthrown mind, pushed back the One Beneath, and read as much of Jhaleen's thoughts as he could manage before the One Beneath had shoved him out.

"Olivaard," Arsinoe said, serious for the first time. "What has happened in the two kingdoms in our absence?"

"Aside from the fact that the One Beneath has broken through enough to enslave the masters." Linza was positively whiny.

"That is now a problem for later," Olivaard said. "We have a more pressing problem."

"More pressing than the One Beneath devouring our world?" Arsinoe asked.

"That could still be averted if we could just escape," Olivaard said. "I had thought our latest attempt would prevail. I had hoped we would be well on the way to our tower by now. But the plan failed, and now we must address what is coming."

"And what is coming?" Linza asked.

"Queen Oriana received a message from Vale," Olivaard said.

Linza put her bone-thin fingers on the bridge of her nose, closed her eyes and let out a rattling breath.

"Well that's just perfect," Arsinoe growled. "Another member of Quad Brilliant."

"Royal is with her," Olivaard said.

"What?" Arsinoe snapped. "Royal? How is that even possible? They hate each other!"

"And," Olivaard said, "it's worse."

"How can it be worse?" Arsinoe demanded. He glanced at Linza, then back at Olivaard. "What is worse than two of her Quad mates coming to strengthen her...freakish abilities?"

"*Three* of her Quad mates coming to strengthen her freakish abilities," Olivaard said.

Arsinoe's jaw dropped. He caught it with his hand and shoved it back into place. "Not possible. Brom is dead."

"So we thought."

"What are you saying?" Linza whimpered.

"Brom has risen."

"Risen?" Arsinoe said in a high-pitched voice.

"From the grave," Olivaard supplied.

"No," Linza stated, like it simply was not true.

"How.... How is that...?" Arsinoe stammered. "Did he make a deal with the One Beneath?"

Olivaard shook his head. "I don't think so."

"Brom is dead!" Linza insisted.

"Master Jhaleen fought Brom—fought all of them—in Torlioch three days ago," Olivaard said.

"I take it she lost that fight," Arsinoe drawled.

"Tohn Gelu died," Olivaard said. "Jhaleen barely escaped."

"Gods, they could be here by now," Arsinoe whispered. "With an Impetu—"

"If Brom is alive..." Linza's voice was thin and fragile. Unlike Arsinoe, neither Linza nor Olivaard

277

thought for a second that Brom's resurrection had anything to do with the One Beneath. Quite the opposite.

Magic couldn't bring back the dead, even with the power of a thousand Lyantrees. The Four had tried. Magic could reanimate a corpse, but it could not resurrect a soul.

But the capricious force they called the Soul of the World could do it. It *had* done it. As the most powerful Anima in the two kingdoms, Linza had been the Champion of the Soul of the World for a hundred years. And as the Champion, she had been immune to death because of the Soul of the World. It had resurrected her half a dozen times. Olivaard and their other Quad mates had seen it firsthand. It was a unique power that, so far as Olivaard knew, was reserved only for the Champion of the Soul.

But if the Soul had resurrected Brom, it begged the question: Was Brom the new Champion of the Soul of the World?

If so, then powers Linza had leaned on for a century no longer belonged to her. It meant Brom was the most powerful Anima in the two kingdoms, not her. And it meant that Linza no longer had the protection of the Soul. She was now as vulnerable to death as the rest of The Four.

Of course, The Four could never know for certain, not until Linza…. Well, until she actually died.

During his Test of Separation, Brom *had* shown phenomenal talent. What if, in that final battle, he had surpassed Linza and no one had noticed except the Soul of the World?

It might also explain why Linza's powers were faltering.

"Brom *is* alive," Olivaard said. "I had hoped to kill

Vale, then deal with the rest of their broken Quad separately. Obviously we can no longer hope for that outcome. We've run out of time."

Arsinoe narrowed his eyes. "You have a plan already."

"Yes."

"If we're allying with the One Beneath, it's a desperate plan," Arsinoe said, no doubt preparing himself to hate it.

"Not allying," Olivaard clarified. "Manipulating. I suggest we alert the masters and let them know everything."

"What?" Arsinoe said, predictably. "That is a horrible plan."

"We need someone to stop Quad Brilliant from arriving."

"If we alert the masters, the One Beneath will send them straight here to kill us."

"Yes. I am counting on it," Olivaard said.

Arsinoe opened his mouth, then shut it, thinking.

Linza had said nothing for a long time, no doubt grappling with the shocking possibility that she was no longer the Champion of the Soul. Finally, she spoke. "But they'll have to go through Vale first."

"Exactly." Olivaard pointed at her. "And the rest of Vale's gods-be-damned Quad."

"Why would the One Beneath attack Quad Brilliant?" Arsinoe asked.

"She wants to eliminate us, true," Olivaard said. "But next to that, the last thing She wants is another Quad to oppose Her after we're gone. If I tell the masters everything, tell them that we're all in one spot, the One Beneath won't be able to resist. She'll want to wipe us all out at once. The Four *and* Quad Brilliant."

"And once we're wiped out, how does that help us?"

Arsinoe asked.

"Idiot," Olivaard growled. "We won't be here by then. We are going to rest until the very last moment. Then we are going to hit Vale with everything we have."

"I thought we already did that," Arsinoe said.

"Dammit, Arsinoe! We are letting this little girl intimidate us. She has gotten lucky so many times, and we are envisioning her as some kind of goddess. She's not. We're defeating ourselves! We hurt her badly today. She is at death's door. She has to be. If we can rally our strength and make one desperate final strike, we will break her."

"Like she has broken us, you mean?" Arsinoe held up his detached arm.

"Pity yourself once we escape!" Olivaard barked. "Until then, grow a spine. We have all forgotten what it is like to risk our lives, and that makes us weak. Vale has used this weakness against us time and again. She knows we're afraid to die."

"And the masters?" Linza asked. "How long would it take them to get here? How long do we have to rest before this big attack?"

Olivaard was silent.

"Gods, you already told them," Linza guessed.

"You bastard!" Arsinoe said. "Without asking us?"

"And what would you have said?" Olivaard demanded.

"I'd have said the last thing we want is alert the One Beneath that we're thrashed and ragged and stuffed in a cave!" Arsinoe shouted. "And I'd have been right!"

"She already knows," Olivaard said. "She has been breaking through our barriers for a month and we have done nothing. She has infiltrated our academy, enslaved the masters. Do you think for one second She doesn't *know* we are weak?"

Arsinoe glanced at his hands, brows furrowed as though he might think of an answer to that, but he said nothing.

"I alerted The Collector," Olivaard said. "He, Master Saewyne, Master Jhaleen, and a cohort of students are heading to intercept Quad Brilliant. After that, I'm sure the One Beneath will send Her newly infected minions to scour the forest for us."

"So we have until they kill Quad Brilliant to free ourselves and get back to our tower," Arsinoe said.

"Yes."

"Well, that's just perfect." Arsinoe threw his hands up in the air. "So your advice is to do what we've been *trying* and *failing* to do for the last month? Why didn't you just say so! How simple!"

"It is, in fact, that simple," Olivaard said. "If this ragged little urchin can pin us down like butterflies on a board, then maybe we don't deserve to survive."

"Oh great. Torture tunnel philosophy," Arsinoe said.

"We push her," Olivaard said. "We come at her again and again until she is dead. Or we are."

"An inspirational speech from our intrepid leader."

"Once we're back in our tower, you can talk about comfort."

"Once we're back in our tower, I'm never leaving again," Arsinoe said. "Let Wulfric run around in the woods if he likes. I'm done."

"For once, Arsinoe, we agree."

"So we just let the One Beneath loose on the lands?" Linza asked.

"What choice do we have?" Olivaard said. "I would love to take the long view, but the clock of our lives is ticking."

"What about Brom and the Soul of the World?"

Linza asked. She sounded like a little girl who was afraid of the dark.

"The One Beneath will kill him. And if not, we send him back to the grave after we kill Vale."

That seemed to make Linza feel better, though it probably shouldn't. If the Soul of the World had chosen a new champion, there was no guarantee it would simply choose Linza again after Brom died. Obviously, she'd already been found lacking. The Soul would likely choose some other Anima when Brom died, or resurrect Brom again.

But hope was a useful tool. Let Linza believe she could return to her former glory. As long as she stopped sniveling and focused on killing Vale, Olivaard didn't care what she believed.

"So the One Beneath destroys Quad Brilliant," Linza said.

"Yes."

"And we destroy Vale."

"And we destroy Vale," Olivaard growled.

4

BROM

BROM, ORIANA, ROYAL, AND FALINE rode all day at the same breakneck pace. Their mounts leapt over streams. They wove through rocky outcroppings like agile hares and pelted across open fields at a full gallop, drawing strength and power from Royal. Brom was sure that any other horse—one not augmented by an Impetu—would have collapsed by now, or tripped and broken a leg.

Royal rode in his saddle with a look much like Oriana's from this morning. His eyes were nearly closed, but his body moved with the galloping horse as if they were one creature.

Late that afternoon, Vale's forest hove into view and they reined in. Brom's horse whickered, stamping its hoof as if it wanted to break into a gallop again.

Brom stared at the forest, and he could scarcely believe his eyes. The entire horizon was Lyantrees, a green and purple wall that stretched on forever. His companions' mounted shadows reached across the rolling hills toward the forest as though pointing the direction.

"Am I the only one seeing this?" Brom murmured in awe.

The Hallowed Woods were the reason for the war between Fendir and Keltovar. The Fendirans considered the Hallowed Woods a holy place, treated it like a temple of their goddess, Fendra. The Keltovari prized the trees for their ability to be turned into weapons of incalculable value. Cured Lyanwood blades were stronger than steel and a third the weight, like the rare Lyanwood sword across Royal's back.

But most importantly, the two kingdoms warred over the Hallowed Woods—had fought bloody battles for decades—because the Hallowed Woods were the *only* place in the two kingdoms where Lyantrees grew.

When Oriana had told her story about sending an expedition to find a *new* Lyantree forest, Brom had imagined a grove, an unlikely—and small—cousin to the Hallowed Woods. But this... This could be every bit as large as the Hallowed Woods. By the gods, it could be larger. It seemed to go on forever.

"That's a lot of Lyantrees," Brom breathed.

Royal gazed at the stretch of green-scaled trunks and purple-and-silver leaves like he was staring at the goddess herself made real. He seemed shaken. The Hallowed Woods was a holy place to him. What must this endless sea of Lyantrees seem to him?

"How could no one know this was here?" Faline murmured, as stunned as the rest of them.

"You sent an expedition here?" Brom asked Oriana.

"I..." Oriana faltered. Royal and Faline both looked at her. Seeing Oriana falter was like seeing a fish flying.

"Did your man mention it was this big?" Brom asked.

"I did not…ask," she said. "Once the academic mentioned the writ of passage, I did not think about anything else."

"You weren't expecting this," Royal said.

"I expected a grove," she said. "Not…." She waved one of her elegant hands at the forest.

"How could this be here?" Royal whispered. "How could it even be here? All these years, how could no one have discovered this place?"

The question settled like a stone sinking to the bottom of a pond. It reminded Brom of another question they'd asked at the academy, one just as unlikely, a question that had led them to uncover the deadly secrets that had blown their Quad apart: In a hundred years, how could not one Quad have graduated intact from the academy? How could no one have ever noticed how odd—and horrible—that was?

"The Four," Brom murmured.

"What?" Royal rumbled.

"The Four didn't want us to know," Brom said. "It's the only possible explanation."

"You think The Four cast a spell over everyone in the two kingdoms?" Royal asked. "The spell that would be required to ensorcel everyone in the two kingdoms…. Could even The Four do that?"

"I think we are only beginning to see what The Four can do," Oriana said. "Though I find it unlikely that they would have cast a spell upon everyone in the two kingdoms. More likely they cast a spell upon the forest."

"Oh, just the entire forest," Royal said sarcastically. "How far do you think that goes?" He waved at the never-ending forest.

"What kind of spell?" Brom asked.

"I imagine it is a hanging Mentis spell that takes hold

of the mind when someone comes too close to the trees and causes a person to forget it," Oriana said. "Perhaps there is even a Motus component that causes them to flee in fear, inventing stories about dragons and other grumkins."

"This forest...." Royal said. "Even a full Quad is only capable of generating thirty-two Soulblocks. Would that be enough to span this entire forest? That's not even thinking about the power it would take to maintain it day after day. Even The Four don't have that much magic.... Do they?"

Oriana licked her lips, a nervous gesture Brom had never seen her make before. "I think the power required for such a spell suggests a possible answer."

"Stop talking like that," Royal said through his teeth. "If you know, just say it."

"I am *thinking*," Oriana snapped. "I suggest you try it."

Royal drew a deep breath, his chest swelling, and he clenched his fists.

"Okay, enough," Brom said.

"I suggest we camp here tonight," Oriana said, glancing at the setting sun behind them, which had already sunk halfway below the western horizon. "I believe it would be unwise to plunge headlong into the forest at night. There may be dangers to this place we aren't considering. A bit more...study may be in order."

"Do we have time to spend in study?" Brom asked.

"Much as I would like to reach Vale, we must reach her alive to do her any good. If there is power enough to hide this forest from the whole world, there is power enough to set traps to kill anyone who dares set foot inside."

"You're not going to tell us what you're thinking?

About the power required suggesting an answer to how they got the power required?" Royal said through his teeth.

"Bide, Royal. Set your restlessness to a task," Oriana said. "We may be glad we paused here."

Royal fumed, but they all dismounted, removing saddles, bridles, and saddlebags, and began making camp. Oriana stared at the distant forest like the answers were written in the air above it. Finally, after their camp was made—Royal had even crafted a fire ring—Oriana stopped staring, turned to them, and spoke.

"Since we regained our memories," she said, "I have considered many things. The reason for the Champions Academy. The deception of The Four. The reasons for...everything that happens in the two kingdoms. The Four could have changed the course of history at several pivotal moments in the last century. They did not. They have not interfered with politics—even the war in the Hallowed Woods. By Kelto, if The Four had wanted to overthrow Fendir and Keltovar both, they could have done it."

Brom followed her train of thought. "And we've accepted this because we thought they were benevolent caretakers."

"Which clearly they are not," Oriana said.

"Okay."

"So I ask myself," Oriana said. "Why haven't The Four overthrown the two kingdoms? Why don't they rule from on high? If they are the nefarious villains we've uncovered, why would they hold back?"

"Because they don't *want* to rule the two kingdoms," Brom guessed.

"It is the only possible answer," she agreed. "And it begs the question: why not? *That* is the question that stills my tongue, Royal."

"Why?" Royal prompted.

She flicked him an annoyed glance. "Most who rule are drawn to power. They are hungry for it. There would be no reason for The Four to resist dominion over Keltovar and Fendir unless, for them, it is a lesser conquest."

"Lesser than what?" Royal asked.

"Yet another question. I could only guess," she said.

"You're saying there is more power to be had elsewhere, other than the thrones of Keltovar and Fendir," Brom said.

"Vale summoned a dragon," Oriana said. "But dragons are a myth. Vale is fighting The Four by herself. But that is impossible. Where is she getting the kind of power it would take to do either of these things?"

"A…different source of magic?" Brom said.

"A different source of magic," Oriana echoed.

"Something that can only exist within a forest of Lyantrees…" Royal finally caught up.

"Perhaps." Oriana peered at the forest intensely. "But let us look at the truths as we know them. The Four, sometime in the last several weeks, vanished. And two weeks ago, my expedition found this forest. Those are our facts. They would indicate that whatever spell had been cast upon it had faltered by then. That, in turn, indicates that Vale had already attacked The Four. She forced them to abandon maintaining the forest's spell in order to focus on her."

"Or perhaps she destroyed the spell," Brom said.

"It would have worked well as a lure," Oriana said contemplatively.

"You think she lured them here?" Brom asked.

"I don't follow you," Royal interrupted. "How does

her destroying this spell explain how Vale had the power to attack The Four?"

Oriana held her chin and tapped a long finger on her lips. "The Four don't want the two kingdoms," she said as though thinking aloud. "But they put what we must imagine are enormous resources into hiding this forest. Now, Vale is entrenched here. That is not an accident. I must believe the power is somewhere within these trees. Some nexus of magic. Like the tower at the academy."

"And Vale found it," Brom said.

Royal looked confused. "She found a tower?"

"It need not be a tower. Or a castle," Oriana said. "It could look like anything."

"You're saying Vale found The Four's place of power here and stole it from them," Brom said. "And they came to kill her."

"You said she lured them," Royal said.

"That sounds like Vale, don't you think?" Oriana said. "When we first met in that crowded room at the academy, she found the biggest, most powerful-looking among us and stabbed him in the calf with her knife. Yes. I think she lured them."

Royal chuckled, a deep-chested sound. "That girl…"

"The woman is clearly insane," Oriana said, but there was pride in her voice as well.

"So there is a power nexus somewhere in that vastness," Brom said.

"Of some kind. Perhaps not a place, but a creature. Perhaps a warren of dragons that she somehow learned to control," Oriana said. "Perhaps dragons is what The Four were hiding and Vale discovered how to communicate with them, to command them."

Royal scratched at his beard. "If dragons live within this Lyantree forest, why have we never seen dragons in the Hallowed Woods?"

"Perhaps there are no dragons in the Hallowed Woods. Or perhaps they are there, hidden, either by nature or by command of The Four," Oriana said.

Royal shook his head. "I have traveled extensively through the Hallowed Woods. I never saw a dragon, nor any hint of a dragon. Besides, why would The Four allow the war in the Hallowed Woods to continue?" he asked. "Why not put the same spell upon the Hallowed Woods that they put upon this forest?"

"Why indeed," Oriana said, and she smiled.

"Every time you smile like that, you make it seem like the answer is obvious," Royal growled.

"Isn't it?" Oriana said. "The Four could have singlehandedly decided the War for the Hallowed Woods long ago. So if there is a war, they wanted a war."

"They wanted us fighting each other..." Royal whispered.

"It is possible their spell of forgetting falls only over one part of the Hallowed Woods, and while we focus on slaughtering each other in the western end, they keep the eastern end hidden."

"But why not just do for the Hallowed Woods what they have done here?" Royal gestured at the purple-and-silver trees, the bushy tops glowing with the golden light of the setting sun.

Oriana shrugged. "Who can say? Perhaps because the Hallowed Woods stands right between our two kingdoms. Perhaps they had not perfected this spell when we began fighting there."

"Now you're just guessing," Royal said.

"I am. But think of the war in this light: once we *did* start fighting, we made the Hallowed Woods the most dangerous place in the two kingdoms," she said. "Only

Keltovari soldiers and Fendiran warrior druids would dare enter. The war keeps everyone *else* out."

"They had a deterrent," Royal murmured. "And with us so focused on each other, who had time to explore the woods?"

"Perhaps," Oriana said.

"And Vale has dragons," Royal said.

"Allegedly," Oriana said. "In the end, only Vale can tell us—"

Royal leapt at Oriana, raising his muscular arms.

"No!" Faline drew her sword.

"Royal!" Brom shouted, but both he and Faline were too slow. They couldn't possibly match an Impetu at full speed. No *normal* in the two kingdoms could.

A blur, Royal rose up in front of Oriana, fists up above his head—

But he didn't strike.

Instead, a wide, steel spearhead protruded from the front of Royal's chest. He gasped and fell to his knees.

Only then did Brom see the long spear handle sticking out of Royal's back.

"They've returned," Royal said softly, blood trickling out of his mouth. He fell forward onto his face.

Brom snapped his gaze to the rolling hills behind them.

A thick, muscled human figure sprinted over the distant rise, holding a second spear in hand and moving faster than a horse at full gallop.

5

BROM

THE FIGURE WAS SO FAR AWAY she was little more than a speck of movement, but Brom knew her. He'd know that hulking, wide-shouldered silhouette anywhere. It was Master Jhaleen, and she'd taken down Royal before they even knew she was here.

Jhaleen vanished beneath another hill, but she was closing the distance fast. As soon as she came back into view, she'd loose that second spear.

"Pull it out," Oriana commanded.

"We must get you into the cover of the trees, Your Majesty." Faline grabbed Oriana's arm. Oriana shrugged her off.

"Pull out the spear," she repeated.

"He's dead!" Faline said.

"Do it now!"

Brom snapped out of his shock. Oriana was right. If Royal wasn't dead yet, if he had any chance at healing, they had to get that spear out.

"Faline, help me!" Brom grasped the haft. Faline leapt to the task and together they wrenched the spear from Royal's back. The big man jerked as it came free but otherwise didn't move. He wasn't breathing.

While Impetu magic imbued Royal with incredible powers of healing, it couldn't bring back the dead.

"That's as much as we can do," Oriana said. "Now, to the woods." She mounted her horse. There was no saddle or bridle, and she grabbed a fistful of the horse's mane.

Faline glanced at their packs of food lying on the ground. "Your Majesty, the food—"

"We just leave him?" Brom interrupted incredulously.

"There is no more time, Brom." Oriana wheeled her horse. "Fly like your life depends on it."

With a frustrated growl, Brom jumped on his horse. Faline was already mounted—having done so the moment Oriana did—and they left everything behind: saddles, bridles, food, Royal's horse and Royal himself. They galloped for the tree line. Oriana's silver and gold hair came loose, streaming like a banner behind her.

Just a moment ago, the forest had seemed close and enormous. Now it seemed terribly far away.

Brom's horse beat a frantic cadence on the uneven ground. They were moving so fast, so carelessly, he was certain his horse would break a leg and they'd both go down. Oriana and Faline rode bareback like they'd done it their whole lives. But Brom had barely learned to master a horse *with* a saddle and bridle, let alone without.

He clung to his horse's mane with white-knuckled desperation. He had never appreciated stirrups more than he did now. Each surge felt like it would launch Brom over the horse's head. He bounced and clenched and tried to hang on.

All the while, he felt an itch between his shoulder blades, certain that any second, Jhaleen's second spear would plunge into his back.

He suddenly wondered if all his bouncing atop the horse was a blessing in disguise. Even *he* couldn't predict his movements. Perhaps it was making Jhaleen hesitate before throwing.

Brom suddenly had another thought besides his inept horsemanship. Jhaleen's target hadn't been Royal. She'd aimed for Oriana, and Royal had intervened.

Brom yanked on his horse's mane and kicked his heels in, trying to put himself between Jhaleen and Oriana. But the horse barely moved at the fierce yank. It continued to run as though Brom were an afterthought, rather than its commander. Thankfully, Faline saw what Brom was attempting and did it successfully herself. The three of them rode in a lopsided line, with Faline close behind Oriana and Brom struggling to keep up.

"Calm yourselves," Oriana said in Brom's head. *"I have delayed Jhaleen, but the fight has only begun. There are others."*

"Others?" Brom responded through the mind-link.

"The Collector is here," Oriana said. *"He was going to interpose himself between us and the trees, along with a group of students from the academy, but we moved faster than they expected. There are five of them. And I sense three more further back."*

Eight Quadrons. One Quadron couldn't stand against eight, no matter how powerful she was.

"How did they know we were here?" he asked.

Oriana ignored the question. *"I will attempt a veil to make them overlook us, but for that to work we must reach the trees. If they catch us before then, it will be a fight."*

"Oriana—"

"Faline, you come with me," Oriana said.

"Yes, Your Majesty."

"Brom, once we reach the trees, you run ahead."

"I will not," Brom replied.

"Our sole hope now is for you to reach Vale. You cannot fight the masters or the other students."

"Neither can you. Not by yourself."

"Do not argue with me—"

"Fine. I won't." Brom said. He wasn't going to just leave Oriana and Faline to die at the hands of the masters. If they were going to die, they were going to go together.

"Vale knows the secret of the forest," Oriana said. *"She might be able to show you how to use that power. To re-invoke your power. Then you can—"*

"Forget it. Even if I knew how to find her, even if she could show me her new skills, and even if I could somehow wield that magic, I'd never make it back in time. We are a Quad. We stick together."

"You intransigent idiot," Oriana said, and she cut off the link.

The purple and green trees loomed before them, bobbing and bouncing as Brom fought to stay seated. He waited for someone to pop up before them in the tall grass, to block them from entering the trees....

But no one did.

Their mounts shot into the woods going far too fast. Gnarled, bent trees whipped past them. Brom tried to turn his horse to the left to avoid a trunk, but it went right instead. Brom slung sideways, and a low-hanging branch smacked him hard in the shoulder.

In a flurry of purple-silver leaves, he lost his seat and tumbled to the ground.

Oriana wheeled her mount.

"Your Majesty!" Faline protested.

"Quiet," Oriana said in their minds again. *"This is where we make our stand."* She dismounted and smacked her hand

against her horse's rump. The horse bolted into the woods. Reluctantly, Faline dismounted and did the same.

Oriana strode to Brom and crouched next to him.

"Are you injured?" she asked, still using the mind-link.

His head was ringing, and for a moment he couldn't remember which way was up. But the world righted itself and he got to his knees.

"Stay close to the trunk." Oriana pressed her back against it, facing the direction they'd come. Brom and Faline did the same. *"I sent images into their minds convincing them that we were a hundred yards further north than we are. That is where they thought they saw us plunge into the woods, and there they will search. Once they hear our horses galloping, they'll move south toward the sound. Let's not give them another sound to follow."*

They all stayed absolutely silent, waiting. Brom looked into the gloom of the forest. The sun was setting, and it was far darker in here than it had been on the plains. More than that...there was something in here. The pebble in his belly vibrated.

"There's definitely something in the trees," he thought to Oriana.

"Yes," she replied tersely. *"Quiet now. We dare not speak, even mind-to-mind. There is a Mentis among them."*

The pebble in his belly vibrated harder. He felt something coming from the trees, something faint, a...sense of power. The hairs on his forearms stood up.

The pebble always got agitated whenever Brom was in danger, but this felt different. The pebble wasn't just vibrating, it was pushing forward and to the left. Something was interacting with it, making it dance, beckoning it.

He peered in the direction the pebble wanted to go, and he caught movement. A young Champions Academy student wended his way through the woods in their direction, searching for them.

Brom put a hand on Oriana's arm. She glanced at him, and he gave the barest tip of his chin. Her gaze shifted and she spotted the student. Her lips tightened.

She touched Faline, and they all watched their hunter approach, but he seemed unaware of them so far.

The student walked with his eyes mostly closed, head up, like he was following the scent of a freshly baked pie.

Faline shifted subtly. Her dagger appeared in her hand, glinting in the dusky light.

She was going to kill the boy!

"Oriana," Brom spoke mind-to-mind to her. *"We can't kill him. He's just a student. Oriana, we were students once—"*

"Quiet!" she sent back.

The student raised his head like he'd heard an acorn fall. His eyes opened, and he spotted them where they crouched behind the bushes. He opened his mouth to shout—

Faline's dagger flew, taking the young man in the throat. With a shocked gurgle, the student fell face-first onto the forest floor.

"No!" Brom jumped to his feet.

Oriana grabbed his arm, and he half hauled her to her feet as she arrested his momentum.

"Quiet, dammit," she said into his mind. *"Reign in your passions, Brom. This is a deadly game, and we do not have the luxury of compassion."*

"Faline killed him!"

"It was him or us. Choose." She strode past the dead student, uncaring, and pulled Brom forward. Faline knelt by her victim, retrieved her dagger, and sprinted to get ahead of Oriana. The spy's bloody dagger dripped onto the forest floor as her hawk eyes searched the shadows for new threats.

Heartsick—his gaze never leaving the face-down student as they passed—Brom doggedly followed them, ducking under the low-hanging branches of the Lyantrees. Yes, he wanted to fight The Four. He'd even battle the masters, but he didn't want to hurt the Champions Academy students! As he wound through the thick foliage, he grasped a Lyantree branch to steady himself—

A tiny crackle of lightning zinged into him.

He staggered away, almost losing his balance, and stared up at the tall trunk. What was that? Had the tree attacked him? Its purple-silver leaves fluttered in the fading light, seemingly innocent.

With a shaky hand, he reached out and touched the tree again, expecting the crackling jolt, but nothing else happened. He grasped the branch with both his hands, but the sensation had gone.

He turned to tell Oriana...only to find that he was alone in the darkening forest. Oriana and Faline had vanished into the woods ahead of him, out of sight.

"Oriana," he called out through the mind-link. She didn't respond.

He jogged lightly ahead, trying to stay quiet and hurry to catch up. He ducked under branches and jumped over bushes until he was breathing hard.

Oriana and Faline were nowhere in sight.

"Oriana!" he said more forcefully, trying to feel her mind link. *"Oriana!"*

The pebble in his belly suddenly went wild.

At the same moment, Brom's toe caught on an exposed root. He stumbled, tried to catch his balance, and caught his other foot on a different root. He pitched face first into the dirt.

He rose up on hands and knees to see two boots

standing before him, protruding from beneath a black robe. Brom craned his neck up and looked....

...straight into the shadowed face of The Collector.

6

BROM

THE COLLECTOR'S HOOD was pulled low over his face, revealing his mouth and his black goatee. Cold fear climbed up Brom's back like a spider.

Brom knew exactly what an Anima could do in a fight against a *normal*, and he had no defenses against it. No matter what he might try to do, what punch or kick or stone Brom might throw at The Collector, the man would feel it coming before it landed. Even now, The Collector was probably reading Brom's soul like a map, seeing every possible pathway that led away from this moment.

"So," The Collector said. "You really are alive."

Brom swallowed, levering himself cautiously to a crouch.

"And you really have no magic," The Collector added.

"Maybe I do," Brom said.

"Then attack me."

"Maybe I don't want to attack you."

The Collector laughed. "I know you, Brom Builder. I know you better than you know yourself. That was my job as your instructor. If you had even a sliver of a chance of winning, you wouldn't be crouching there, waiting. I can smell your fear." His exposed mouth smiled, wide and flat.

It was no use trying to fool him. The Collector could read Brom's soul. Brom waited for the telltale despair that came from a soul-suck. He stayed silent, his heart pounding in time with that stupid, useless, bouncing pebble.

But the attack didn't come.

The Collector circled Brom slowly, seemingly without a care in the world. "Jhaleen *said* you had no magic. I confess I doubted her entire story, not the least of which was that you were alive. I thought the queen had muddled her mind. But it really *is* you." The Collector mused. "How did you do it?"

Brom slowly rose to his feet, still expecting The Collector's lightning-quick assault, but The Collector just kept circling.

Why was he waiting? Why didn't he call out for the others searching the forest?

"Are you the Champion?" The Collector suddenly whispered with such intensity that Brom's heart skipped a beat. It was as though The Collector didn't want anyone but Brom to hear it.

"Champion…" Brom whispered. "Champion of what?"

The Collector raised his chin. Deep within his hood, his black eyes glinted. "Tell me," he whispered. "And I will help you."

The statement struck Brom so oddly that he couldn't think of what to say. He would have thought The

Collector was trying to fool him, except the master held all the power here. There was no reason to cajole Brom, to set him off guard, to gain his confidence. If The Collector wanted to kill Brom, he could do it. Why play around with cryptic messages?

But the master's whisper sounded urgent. It sounded...desperate.

"You're not one of them," Brom whispered back. The Collector's dark, glittering eyes didn't glow green. Whatever had happened to Jhaleen and Tohn Gelu...somehow The Collector had avoided it.

"You must help me free The Four," The Collector said. "It's the only way to save this land."

"What?"

"Surely you know The Four are trapped here, somewhere in this forest," The Collector said.

"I know they're here," Brom said. "But I haven't come to help them. I've come to help *end* them."

"You're a fool," The Collector said through his teeth. "Do you know who the One Beneath is?"

"The One Beneath?"

The Collector hissed between his teeth in derision. "Ignorant child." His mouth twisted sourly. "Without The Four, the lands will look like this." He waved a hand at the trees, and Brom realized he meant the Quadrons and students he had come with. Those with the glowing green eyes.

"What happened to them?" Brom asked. "Who is the One Beneath?"

The Collector shook his head impatiently. "There isn't time to explain. The Four have been on the winning side of a secret war against the One Beneath for decades. Now their opponent is free, and if The Four die, the One Beneath will tear our world apart." Again, he gestured at the woods. "We'll all become slaves."

Brom swallowed.

"Tell me…" The Collector said intensely, as though he would push the words into Brom with his fingers. "Tell me you are the Champion. It's the only explanation!"

"I don't know what you're talking about."

The Collector's black eyes glittered. "How could you be the Champion and not know it?" he murmured.

"Tell me!" Brom demanded.

"Every generation," The Collector said. "The Soul of the World chooses her champion. It is always an Anima and this Anima has more ability than other Animas. This person can sink deeper into the Soul of the World. And…"

"And what?"

"And this person cannot die. The Soul will not let them."

The statement hit Brom like a fist to the chest. Since his awakening, he'd had no clue as to why it had happened. Had the Soul of the World brought him back?

"What does…the Champion do?" Brom stuttered out the words, his mind racing.

The Collector clenched his teeth, angry. "She fights for the world, for the Soul of the World. She stands against those who would pull apart the fabric of the lands."

"She?"

"Linza has been the Champion as long as I've been alive."

"So, one can be the Champion and still be a black-hearted murderer?"

"The Four are not villains, despite what you may think," The Collector said.

"They *killed* me!" Brom shouted.

The Collector looked nervously over his shoulder at the dark woods, cringing at Brom's shout, then back at Brom with rage in his eyes. "Do you want to die *again?*"

"They killed hundreds of students!"

"You know nothing, you little whelp. We trust in The Four because they are saving our lives every day. They are the only ones who can fight the One Beneath. Do you know what you have done? You and your friends have set in motion the end of the world."

"By surviving?"

"By threatening The Four. You cannot fathom the responsibility they carry. Whatever methods they must use, no matter how dire…those methods are justified."

"I don't believe that," Brom said.

The Collector sneered again. "What you believe doesn't matter. Life isn't some boy's tale about heroic Quadrons. It is about hard choices and bloody sacrifices."

"It's hard to believe the Soul of the World didn't choose *you* for her Champion," Brom said acidly.

The Collector recoiled like he'd been struck. "You arrogant little bastard." He clenched his fists and lunged at Brom—

A huge silver blur struck The Collector in the chest like a ram, tossing him across the small glade like a doll. The Collector cried out in pain and tumbled to a crumpled heap on the forest floor. The flying silver blur arced up, past the branches and out of sight.

Brom staggered to the side and caught his balance. He looked up, stunned, trying to follow the thing's movement, but it was already gone.

"Brom!" Oriana's voice suddenly entered his head.

"Oriana! Gods, where are you?"

"Where are you?"

"I fell behind and…you're not going to believe this. The Collector caught me—"

"He has you?"

"No, he's unconscious. But…I have another problem just now. There's a monster. A flying monster somewhere close by."

Brom heard the snap of a twig and spun, expecting to be struck by the same giant, blurred creature that had taken down The Collector. But it wasn't the creature. Those were actual human footsteps.

"I can't stay here," he said to Oriana. *"They're coming."*

"Come east. You'll see a large clearing. Kelto is rising so follow the moon. We'll be there. I can sense the minds around you closing in. Run, Brom. I'll try to confuse them. Run now!"

It was almost full dark in the forest, but he caught a glimpse of silver Kelto through the glade's gap in the foliage above. He made for the light—

And pulled up short.

On flapping, silent wings, a giant silver moth settled to the forest floor in front of Brom. Its wingspan must have been ten feet across, and its body was nearly as long as Brom was tall. Its wings settled on the ground, fully extended. It was mostly silver, peppered with oblong and asymmetrical purple spots. Its feelers, which looked like silver branches, tested the air in front of it, like it could smell him.

Brom's heart pounded. Cold sweat prickled on his scalp, and he knew instantly this was the monster that had laid The Collector low.

Those quivering, questing feelers looked like they'd been made out of…parts of a Lyantree. In fact, the entire creature looked like it could have been made from the stuff of a Lyantree. Its silver body was the same color as the silver edges of the Lyantree leaves. The tufts of black fuzz around its neck looked like the moss that grew at the base of the trees, and the almost leaf-shaped purple spots on its body were the same purple as the Lyantree leaves. Even its long, segmented legs looked like branches.

"What are you?" Brom murmured.

The creature skittered toward Brom, the jerky movement of an insect. He ducked away from it, using a tree as a shield. The creature turned as if to chase but stopped, silver feelers twitching. It seemed to track him as he worked his way through the forest. He gave it a careful, wide berth, but it didn't follow. Once he was past it and could follow the moon again, he ran for all he was worth. He gave the giant moth a quick backward glance.

It was gone.

But he could hear the voices of his human pursuers behind him now.

"Ahead," one of them said. "Just ahead. I hear them."

Brom abandoned stealth and ran hard as his pursuers closed in. He didn't have hope that he could stay ahead of them without Oriana's help. His lungs burned. He already tasted the copper tang of blood in his mouth, and his legs ached with the strain. Once, with his magic, he could have run all night. But he'd been buried, starved, nearly killed by infection, and confined to a bed for weeks. It was a wonder he could run at all.

He wended around thick green trunks, hopped over undergrowth, and burst into another small clearing. Kelto's pale light lit the tops of the trees and the flat stone that had caused the gap in the ever-present trees.

Branches snapped and leaves flew as Jhaleen burst through a thick tangle of branches to his left. A shower of purple-silver leaves floated around the massive master as her big boots skidded to a stop atop the stone. She breathed hard, and her glowing green eyes lit with a feral joy as she stared at him.

"Well, well," Jhaleen said. "I won't make the mistake of leaving you alive this time, little Anima."

She lunged at him—

The giant moth dropped from the sky like a falling log, right onto Jhaleen's head, driving her face into the hard stone. The moth flapped its huge wings once, surged upward, and fell onto the master again, smacking her head down with a sickening thud.

Jhaleen groaned, stunned, and the moth leapt at Brom. He flinched, but it stopped in front of him, feelers quivering. It skittered around on the flat rock, facing away from Brom and presenting its back. Its silver feelers leaned toward him over the top of its head.

Jhaleen groaned again. Blood trickled down her forehead, but her thick fist pushed against the rock as she rose to her hands and knees.

The giant moth skittered half a step forward, as though impatiently waiting for Brom. It seemed like…like the creature wanted him to jump on its back.

"This is crazy…" he whispered.

He ran and jumped onto the giant moth's back, grabbed the black tuft of hair behind its head, and it launched into the air.

"No!" Jhaleen shouted. Her shout was so loud, so close. She leapt at them and her outstretched fingers brushed Brom's ankle, just missing him, as the moth's wings pumped against the air. Cursing, Jhaleen fell back to earth.

The moth struggled to gain altitude, and plunged into the treetops at the far side of the clearing.

Wind roared in Brom's ears and leaves shot past them, but they broke above the forest's canopy into the night sky at last. He gasped, barely able to breathe against the speed of air rushing into him.

He dared a glance over his shoulder and saw Jhaleen far below, standing in the hole the moth had made in the leaves. Jhaleen snatched up a rock and hurled it at them.

The moth banked sharply left as though it could feel the missile coming, and the rock sailed harmlessly past. Then Jhaleen was gone from view, and the moth soared high above the purple and silver forest. The moon shone brightly to the east.

"Gods..." Brom murmured, staring around himself in wonder. The pebble in his belly bounced happily. "What *are* you?" he asked the creature. Its frond-like feelers quivered, leaning toward him, but that was the only answer he received.

"Oriana?" he reached out.

"Brom," she sent back. *"There you are. They brought more than one Mentis, apparently. I lost contact with you. Are you okay?"*

"You're never going to believe this..." he said. *"But..."*

He trailed off as he saw a break in the trees just ahead, a wide meadow just as Oriana had described. Oriana and Faline stood at the eastern edge, just outside the trees.

The moth descended silently. Ahead, perhaps a mile beyond Oriana's glade, lay another, larger break in the trees, shaped like an eye. A river flowed through it, splitting and rejoining around a perfectly circular island. It was as though something—or someone—had split the river intentionally, and carved the perfect little island in the middle.

"What am I not going to believe?" Oriana asked inside Brom's mind.

Entranced by the island, he didn't respond right away. That island was too symmetrical to have been nature's work. Someone had *made* that.

"Brom?" Oriana said urgently. *"Can you hear me? What won't I believe?"*

He reluctantly tore his gaze away from the eye-shaped clearing as the moth soared over the glade. Neither Oriana nor Faline had seen him yet, and they peered nervously to the western edge of the meadow, where they expected Brom to emerge from the trees on foot. They didn't expect him to come from above.

"This," he said as the moth dropped silently from the sky. At the last moment, its huge wings flapped hard, arresting their momentum and alighting smoothly on the grass. Oriana and Faline leapt backward.

Faline's jaw dropped and Oriana's eyes were wide, though she held herself with a rigid composure. Faline gripped her bloody dagger, her gaze flicking between Brom and the enormous moth.

Oriana cleared her throat. "Very well," she said. "You are correct. I would not have believed that."

7

BROM

"What..." Oriana cleared her throat. "Is that?"

"A giant moth," Brom said.

"Is it?" she said icily at his statement of the glaringly obvious. "Please explain what it is doing with you."

Brom quickly recounted the events of the past few minutes.

"The moth saved me from both of them. I think... I think it's made out of the trees."

"How..." Faline said. "Do you make a moth from a tree?"

Oriana held up her hand. "Faline, please."

"I think it's from Vale," Brom said. "It has to be Vale."

"I have been trying to reach Vale since we entered the forest." Oriana shook her head. "But I cannot. She's still blocking me. Or The Four are. Surely if she knew where you were and sent a giant moth to save you, she'd have the wherewithal to respond to a simple mind-link."

That was true. "Then I don't..." A sudden lightning strike of inspiration hit Brom. They were looking for some hidden base of magical power. But....

"Oriana, what if the power Vale has found isn't some tower or legion of mythical dragons, something *hidden* in this forest. What if it *is* the forest?" Brom said. "What if Lyantrees can do more than be cut down to make weapons? What if they can transform into living creatures?"

"Like moths," she murmured, appraising Brom's new friend.

"Or dragons," he said.

"We *must* find Vale," Oriana said. "Before it is too late."

"I think I know where she is."

"You do?" Oriana asked.

"When the moth flew me above the trees, I saw a space that looked...made. Crafted by something other than nature. A perfectly circular island in the middle of a river. I swear it looked like someone used magic to make it. It could be Vale."

"Or The Four," Oriana said.

"Either way, it brings us to the right fight."

"Agreed."

He glanced at the giant moth, which had remained quiet as they talked, and Oriana followed his gaze. The creature's feelers quested toward her, twitching. Oriana closed her eyes and opened them a second later.

"I cannot read its thoughts," she said. "It could have been sent by The Four for all we know."

"It saved my life twice. I'm feeling pretty trusting," Brom said.

"What a surprise."

"What's that supposed to mean?"

"That you are overly trusting."

"I was the first to trust *you* when we formed the Quad," Brom said defensively.

"You were also the first of us to die." She pressed her lips firmly together, then she sighed and gave a curt nod. "Very well. We trust the moth. Brom, you and I will find Vale."

Faline, who had been silent during the entire exchange, suddenly raised her head. "Your Majesty? What do you—"

"Faline, I need you for another task," Oriana said.

"I'm staying by your side, Your Majesty," Faline protested.

"You'll do as I command," Oriana said sharply.

"Your Majesty, your personal guard is dead, and I—"

"You will go back to Keltan," Oriana interrupted. "You will warn King Edmure and tell him everything that has happened here. Everything we know about The Four, about the green-eyed masters, about this forest. If Brom and I do not survive, the secrets we have unearthed must not perish with us. Edmure must know about the glowing green force that seeks to dominate us. He must know about the trickery of The Four. This is where I need you most, Faline. You must be my messenger, for there is no other."

Faline's eyes glistened and she raised her chin. For a second, Brom thought she would argue. Instead, she gave a curt nod. "Yes, Your Majesty."

"Good," Oriana said. "I am depending on you."

"Yes, Your Majesty," Faline said, this time with conviction. She bowed deeply, then turned to Brom and gave him a small smile. She switched to her peasant accent. "Don't go and kill yourself, eh love?" She hugged him tightly, then stepped back.

"Thank you, Faline," he said.

She winked, then she ducked into the trees and vanished into the darkness.

"Was that wise?" Brom asked after she was gone. "Her help might mean the difference between success and failure. We don't know what we're running into."

"Faline can do no more good here," Oriana said quietly. "Either Vale has the power to defeat The Four and all she needs is a push from her Quad. Or she doesn't, and we all die. Faline will not affect that outcome."

"You think we're going to die," he said softly.

She sighed. "This was a fool's errand from the beginning, Brom. What hope we had died with Royal. We gambled we could reform our Quad and take on The Four. We lost that gamble."

"Then why bother? Why not just run away or let the masters catch up with us?"

Oriana's indigo eyes glittered in the moonlight. "Because damn them anyway," she hissed. "The Four lured me to their academy with the hope that I might save my parents, and my mother died while I wasn't at her side. Because The Four put their invisible collar on me and yanked me about. Because they infiltrated my mind without my knowledge. No. If death is meant for me this night, then I shall die staring into the eyes of my enemies. I shall not scuttle away like a frightened roach. If we cannot win, we will make The Four suffer for their victory. We will make them remember Quad Brilliant."

Brom suddenly remembered why he loved Oriana. He remembered sitting in the mud with her at the river on the academy grounds, on that night when she had shown him how vulnerable—and how strong—she was. She'd shown him she was more than just an arrogant princess in a wealthy gown. She was implacable. She never gave up.

"Do you think you are up for that, Anima?" Oriana looked down her nose at him.

"What's another death among friends?" he said.

"Good." She glanced over at the moth. "Do you think it possible we might both ride your…friend here?" She didn't look excited at the prospect.

"I don't know," he said. "Let's try—"

The tree behind Oriana cracked, split, and half of it bent toward her, branches reaching out like arms. Brom lunged, intending to push her out of the way, but the moth was faster. It drove hard into both of them, shoving them clear. The tree's heavy, killing limbs crashed down right behind them, and Oriana cried out.

Branches cracked and purple leaves exploded all about. Brom tumbled and rolled to his feet, disoriented. He searched for Oriana and found her through the flurry of dirt and leaves. She had come to a stop against another Lyantree truck. Her eyes were tight with pain, and she gripped her bent knee with both hands. But she was clear of the reach of the suddenly animate, deadly tree.

The moth was not so lucky. It struggled, buried beneath the thick, scaly branches, crushed by the tree's bent trunk. The moth twitched twice, then stopped moving.

"No!" Brom shouted, tensing to leap to the moth's side.

"Brom!" Oriana's voice cracked like a whip, yanking his attention back to their still-present danger. Branches slithered toward them like tentacles. Brom danced back, narrowly avoiding one. A half-dozen branches slithered toward Oriana.

She scooted back on the grass, teeth clenched,

holding her right leg up. Her foot was twisted at an unnatural angle. Brom scrambled to her, hefted her into his arms, and staggered out of reach of the grasping branches.

"It's The Four," she said through her teeth. "I recognized Olivaard's mind. It's all of them. They moved the tree together."

"How can they do that?"

She shook her head. "I don't know." Voices rose behind them. The masters were coming. They'd heard the noise.

"Go, Brom," Oriana said tightly.

"What?"

"My ankle is broken," she said. "If you don't go, you will die."

"Then I will die," he said resolutely.

"Don't be an idiot," Oriana snapped. "There is still a tenuous balance of power here. The Four have not yet won, and if anyone knows why, it is Vale. She might yet hold the key to victory. Find her—"

"Oriana, I'm not leaving you."

The voices grew louder.

"Go, you fool," she commanded. "Go now, and I can buy you at least a little time."

Students of the academy, eyes glowing green, poured out of the woods on the west side of the meadow.

"They're here!" one shouted. They ran toward Oriana and Brom.

Oriana grabbed his wrist with her long-fingered hand, so tightly it hurt. "Go, Brom! Find her. Fix this." She turned her head to the approaching horde and her eyes flashed. One of the green-eyed students stumbled, grasping his head as he went down.

Brom hesitated. He could make a stand. He could go

to his death defending Oriana. *That* was what a Quad mate did. Lived together. Died together. To the end.

Except Vale was out there. She had unlocked the secret of the forest, a secret so powerful she might just be able to topple The Four. If he stayed here with Oriana, it was over. Everything they'd come to do would die with them. Their quest would be for nothing. But if he found Vale, there might still be a chance.

"Gods damn it!" Brom choked out the words. "I'm sorry, Oriana. I'm so sorry."

"Go, Brom. Go with Kelto's blessing." She gave a tight, rueful smile. "And mine."

He squeezed her hand. Then he let her go and ran into the woods.

8

BROM

BROM WIPED HIS SLEEVE across his tear-filled eyes as he sprinted into the forest. Royal…. Now Oriana….

He ducked branches, dodged trees. He jumped roots and pushed through underbrush. The scaly green trunks had turned black in the moonlight, like dragon legs thrust into the ground all around him.

He listened behind him for pursuit, listened for Oriana's final cry as they swarmed her. But the Queen of Keltovar never made a sound.

His feet pounded the soft forest floor. With every passing second, he felt the weight of his decision. Gods damn it, he shouldn't have left her! He ought to go back for her. What was he thinking?

What was he even *doing* here anymore? He wasn't a Quadron; he was just a *normal*. Even as a full Quad, it was a fool's errand to attack The Four. Oriana herself had said so. But now two of his Quad mates were dead. Quad

Brilliant was dead.

Gods, he didn't even know if the little island he was running toward was the right place to go. What if it was just some circular island in the middle of the forest, one that had always been there, one that had naturally formed? What if its existence meant nothing at all? In all likelihood, logically, Vale wasn't there.

And even if she was…even if she had the secret to defeating The Four, what did it matter? Killing The Four wouldn't bring back Oriana or Royal. It would be a pale and useless gesture.

He ought to just let the masters catch up with him and let this hopeless quest end—

A chill scampered up Brom's back as he realized how dark his thoughts had turned. Hopelessness, despair. These weren't his feelings…. This was an attack! A soul-suck!

"Linza…" he growled, and he forcibly pushed down his despair. As he reclaimed his own soul, he felt a brief, frustrated pushback, like a rat baring its teeth before scuttling back into the darkness.

The intense despair faded. Only then did he realize that the pebble in his belly was vibrating—that it *had been* vibrating for a long time now. He stopped, breathing hard, and tried to get his bearings. Silver moonlight filtered through the canopy overhead, lighting up the silver-lined leaves of the trees.

The island. He had to get to that island. When he'd caught a glimpse of it from the back of the moth, it had only been for a second, but it had been directly east. If he could just keep bearing in that direction, he should find that river, and the river would lead him to the island.

He headed toward the moonlight, bearing ever east.

He tried to remember how far it was. From that great

height, it had seemed close. Barely a mile. Surely he'd run that far already. Should he double-back?

The forest got thicker, and he wondered if this was natural or if The Four were at work again, trying to close the way. With every second that passed, he expected another tree to bend down and try to crush him.

He weaved back and forth, running northeast, then southeast. He didn't know what it took to bring one of those trees to life, but perhaps if The Four couldn't easily anticipate his route, it would make their attack more difficult.

His breath came so hard his chest hurt. He finally staggered to a stop, put a hand against one of the Lyantrees, and listened for his pursuers.

Nothing.

He peered up at the scant moonlight winking between the leaves. The moon was the key. The moon was the only constant he could count upon. If he used the moon, he could reach Vale.

The pebble in his belly bounced, but Brom ignored it. What was important was the moon. Vale was waiting for him to the west. And…what was he doing? Why was he facing east? No wonder he hadn't found her. He was walking away from her.

He turned around and headed west. He shouldn't be walking toward the moon. He should be walking away—

The pebble twisted, and Brom gasped.

Away from the moon…

Brom tried to think, but his mind felt foggy. Where did he need to go?

Away from the moon…

No! Wait. He needed to go *toward* the moon, didn't he?

He stopped. He was under attack again! Olivaard was

319

planting thoughts in his head. But...which thoughts were Brom's and which were Olivaard's?

Away from the moon? Toward the moon? Which way was the glade? East and west suddenly seemed exactly the same.

Brom leaned against the tree, breathing hard. How could he know which way to go if he couldn't trust his own thoughts?

A voice spoke from ahead of him. "You are *Alari's* mate?"

Brom started, fell on his side, scrambled to his feet, and brought his fists up. His chest pumped like a bellows, but he prepared to fight with the only weapons he had left.

A slender, brown-skinned Sacinto emerged from the shadows. Little nubs of branches protruded from his forehead. Brom had never seen a Sacinto before, but he'd heard a myriad of tales. He'd heard they were friendly. He'd heard they were killers. He'd heard they were myths. He'd heard they came from far away over the Coral Sea. He'd heard they sprouted from the ground in the Hallowed Woods.

"You are *Alari's* mate?" the creature repeated. Its tone was soft and seemed to blend with the light rustling of leaves.

"Who are you?" Brom asked.

"I am Tam," the Sacinto said. "I am friend to the *Alari*."

"I don't know what that means..." Brom said. "What's an *Alari?*"

"Ah," Tam said. "Forgive me. Her human name is Vale—"

"Brom!"

Brom spun around. Vale emerged from the shadows

between the trees, dappled in silver moonlight. She wore red breeches and a burgundy tunic. A fur-lined black cloak draped from her shoulders. Her hair was longer, braided. She looked like the queen of the forest.

"Gods! Vale, thank the gods, I found you!"

"Beware, Brom." She pointed at the Sacinto. "Beware of the Sacinto. He is an agent of The Four. Do not believe his lies."

Brom looked at the Sacinto, who continued to watch him with dark, somber eyes.

"Come with me," Tam said, as though he hadn't even heard Vale's accusation. "I will take you to Vale. She has been wanting you. You and the queen of stone houses and the tree runner."

Queen of stone houses and tree runner? The Sacinto must mean Oriana and Royal.

"Don't listen to him," Vale warned. "Olivaard is conjuring him to confuse you. The masters are closing in, and we must flee this place. Once we reach my island, I shall tell you how we are to defeat The Four. Take my hand, Brom."

Brom glanced at Vale, then back at the Sacinto.

"Come." Tam held out his hand. "I will take you to her."

"She's right here," Brom said to Tam, gestured at Vale.

Tam looked that direction, but his gaze didn't fall upon Vale. It went past her, to the right then the left, as though he was searching the darkness.

"Brom," Vale's voice cracked like a whip. "He seeks to deceive you. The masters are poised to strike. We must flee!"

Vale's face was as pert and mischievous as he remembered. Her clothes were clean, stylish. Her braids were well-tended, and they framed her face like she was posing for a portrait....

In the dream in Torlioch, Vale had worn scraps of cloth binding her breasts, leggings that were ripped halfway up her legs. There had been dirt smudges and dozens of cuts on her arms and face.

And the way she spoke...

Seeks to deceive.... Poised to strike.... Flee.... Those were words Oriana might use, but not Vale. That wasn't the way she talked.

"Oh gods," Brom murmured. Vale started toward him, hands out as though she would touch his cheeks.

"The Four," Tam said, as though suddenly realizing what was happening. "They are trying to take your mind."

"Do not listen to him!" Vale grabbed for Brom's head.

He leapt away, and she missed. He fled, bolting into the forest. Almost immediately, his mind felt clearer. The fog lifted, and his certainty returned. He wanted to go *toward* the moon. He needed to go east!

Tam drew alongside him, running easily. Brom's top sprint seemed a pleasant jog for the lithe Sacinto. He leapt bushes and weaved around trees with effortless grace, like he weighed nothing.

"Tell me, human," Tam said. "Are you the *Alari's* mate? Are you the one in her dreams? Are you Brom?"

"I am Brom," he huffed.

A wide smile spread across Tam's face. "Ah!" the Sacinto said joyously. "Come fast. It is safer on *Alari's* isle. We are in great danger here."

"Yes," Brom huffed. Tam put on a burst of speed, and Brom pushed his burning muscles harder, striving to keep up.

They left the edge of the forest and entered a wide,

moonlit glade, just like Brom had seen from above. Silver light brushed the grasses, lighting up the wooded island and the water flowing around it.

"She is there," Tam said. "She is—"

The Sacinto screamed and went down, as if a boulder had fallen on his head. He hit the grass face-first and slid to a stop.

"Tam!" A spike of fiery pain sliced into Brom's mind. His legs went limp, and he fell just like Tam had done.

Brom's limbs twitched, and he grappled with the earth.

Another pain jabbed him in the belly. This was stronger, harder, and horribly cold. It felt like he was being slowly cut open with a frosty dagger. He screamed, but it drove up, into his chest, into his neck, into his head and...the icy cold numbed the fire of the mind-stab.

He could think again, and he realized what the cold pain was. It was the pebble of his destroyed Soulblocks! Somehow, it was fighting the mind-stab. He felt the battle inside. The mind-stab wanted to immobilize him, but the pebble had become a spear, jabbing him forward.

Brom pushed himself up to his hands and knees with a moan of anguish and crawled toward the island. With every movement the ice cut deeper, a frosty knife slicing into his brain.

Hand over hand, knee after knee, he crawled toward the rushing water. Finally, he reached it and tumbled in.

As the water of the river engulfed him, the mind-stab vanished. He surfaced, gasping with relief, and the frosty dagger in his center slowly faded. The current dragged him downstream. He flailed, got his bearings, and grabbed hold of a rock sticking up from the water.

Now that the battle in his mind had ceased, he could think. His body came back under his control, and he realized the river wasn't actually so fierce. He stood up and regained his balance against the current by leaning on the rock.

He looked back at Tam, face-down in the grass only fifty paces from the river. Brom felt he should go back, help the Sacinto, but he knew that the moment he did, Olivaard would mind-stab him again. Something about this water offered protection. He could feel it.

He turned his eyes toward the island, which was a small Lyantree forest in itself. Vale was in there somewhere.

He gave one last look at the unconscious Sacinto, said a prayer to Kelto, then turned and strode through the water.

9

OLIVAARD

OLIVAARD LEANED BACK and gingerly rested his head—which felt like a thin-shelled egg about to crack—against the rock wall. Blood trickled down his arms from half-a-dozen splits in his skin. It was over. They were beaten.

"I tried..." Olivaard gasped. "He...has protection. I don't...know what it is..."

Linza said nothing. She kept her cowl drawn, like she didn't want her Quad mates to see how desiccated she was. As though they couldn't see her skeletal fingers and her bony chin as it flashed in the scant pearlescent light of Olivaard's ring. Linza had always looked like a wraith, but now she looked like a corpse that refused to die. She hadn't moved for several minutes.

The Anima of a Quad was supposed to bring vision, luck, and to find a sure path when none could be seen. And they'd had precious little luck since Vale had trapped them. Nothing had seemed to go their way. They had fought hard for every scrap of ground they'd gained. It was precious little, and they had not won through. They were still in these damned tunnels. Vale was still alive. Where usually The Four seemed to catch the lucky side of things, they hadn't this time. Not once.

They'd been fools to come out here into the woods in the first place, away from their tower, the source of their power, the stronghold containing all of their knowledge and artifacts.

But how could they have known? Vale was a gods-be-damned aberration! She simply shouldn't be able to do the things she was doing. How could they have known she would tap into the Lyantrees more profoundly than anyone in a century, more profoundly than The Four themselves?

Arsinoe sprawled flat on the ground. He was almost completely disassembled now. His parts lay close to each other but separate, like they'd been placed in the shape of a man and were ready for a child to glue together. Only his torso, neck, and head were still attached.

Each of The Four bore their marks, their physical changes. They were the prices paid to the One Beneath for their long lives: Linza's perpetual elderly appearance, the pestilence that crawled beneath Wulfric's armor, Olivaard's stretched body. But the clean, seemingly painted segmentation of Arsinoe's wooden-toy body was somehow more vile than all the rest.

"So…" Arsinoe's head said to the ceiling, "the mind-stab didn't stop Brom?"

It actually sounded like an honest question, rather than a taunt. Perhaps Arsinoe was too exhausted to lend inflection to his words.

"He made it to Vale's island," Olivaard gasped. "We cannot stop him from reaching her."

"But their Quad is broken," Wulfric growled. They had reanimated him with an influx of Lyantree Soulblocks, and a trickle still flowed through him. When it ran its course and returned back to the woods, Wulfric would collapse again.

For now, he was the only one still standing, though he leaned heavily against the rock wall. It was difficult to tell how damaged the Impetu was. His left hand was still wrapped in the bloody rag where he'd lost the two fingers, but aside from that, it was impossible to tell his physical state. He could collapse at any moment.

Olivaard glanced at Linza. She still hadn't moved. If not for the flicker of her Soulblocks deep within her chest, he'd think she was dead.

He nudged her with his elbow, and she hissed.

"We have run…" Olivaard gasped for a breath, "out of options."

"We are close to the surface," Wulfric said. "I can feel it."

They *had* made progress. It seemed like Vale was weakening, but they had all thought that before.

The girl had created a magnificent trap here—a combination of wards and illusions that, in the beginning, often had them digging in the wrong direction. She had dulled their efforts, made them expend their Soulblocks until they were dry. Then she'd forced them to pull an outrageous amount of magic from the Lyantrees for little effect and substantial personal harm.

But with this last effort, they had clawed ever closer to the surface. Due to her nagging hanging spells, left behind like snares in this benighted place, the magic of The Four had been weakened by half, but once they broke the surface, they would tear free of those bonds, and their power would double.

Once they were free of this infernal maze, they could take the fight directly to the little bitch, push a torrent of magic through Wulfric and send him at her like a meteor. Once above ground, he would stride through her damned river and break her little neck. Olivaard daydreamed about Wulfric's fingers wrapping around the girl's slender throat.

But that was only if they escaped the maze.

If even one of The Four fell, their victory vanished. Vale had tried to divide them, to slaughter just one of them. And she'd almost succeeded *three* times. Almost...

Olivaard finally spoke the words he'd been dreading.

"We must face the fact that our recent progress might be Vale toying with us, giving us a false hope while she wears us down. She might..." He trailed off, hating himself for what he was about to say. But if they were to have the slightest chance at survival, they had to face the facts. "She might simply be too powerful for us to defeat. From down here. From inside her trap."

Arsinoe raised his head at that. Wulfric's helmet swiveled to face Olivaard. Even Linza stirred, her bony chin moving beneath the cowl.

So much of the human spirit was bound up in what a person believed, and acknowledging Vale's mastery gave her even more strength. If Olivaard believed Vale would win, the rest of them would believe it, too. He didn't like being the one to say it aloud, but they were coming to the end of their rope. It was time to chance something that could kill them, and he needed them to embrace the idea.

He reached into the small pouch at his side and withdrew a teleportation coin. "It may be time to try this."

Wulfric shook his helmeted head, steel grating on steel. Linza went completely still, and Arsinoe laughed mockingly.

"So we failed. We're done. It's time to die is what you're saying," he said to the ceiling.

The first thing they'd tried to do when they'd plunged into these tunnels was, of course, to teleport out. Olivaard had flung a coin at the ground and empowered the trigger spell with a small jolt from his Soulblock, as he had done a thousand times before.

The portal had opened, a vision of the meeting room at their tower. Olivaard had almost stepped through when a black blur sliced over the opening like a giant headsman's axe. It was only for a second, but the portal had never done that before, so he had hesitated. He'd told Wulfric to put his hand through the portal to see if it was working.

The black blur sliced through Wulfric's hand like a razor, and two of his fingers fell onto the floor of the meeting room beyond. If he hadn't been an Impetu with lightning reflexes, he'd have lost his whole hand.

That was the first impossible thing Vale had done. She'd somehow rendered the teleportation coin deadly, unusable. Even Olivaard didn't know how she'd done that.

He had, of course, considered it might be a side-effect of the thick layers of spells Vale had put upon the tunnels, an accident that she hadn't seen coming. Through design or accident, though, Vale had closed off an easy escape. From that moment to now, everything had depended on The Four's ability to dig their way out of her hellish maze.

"You want to use the teleportation coin," Arsinoe said.

"Yes."

"I just wanted to clarify because the last time we used

it, it ate Wulfric's hand."

"I know it's a risk, but at this point, everything is a risk!" Olivaard stressed.

"You go first," Arsinoe said.

Olivaard frowned. "Arsinoe—"

He chuckled. "So you want to chuck one of us through the hole first."

"Not...entirely," Olivaard said.

"What do you mean not entire—" Arsinoe cut himself off. "No," he said.

"You are the only one of us who might manage it," Olivaard pressed.

"You want to send me through a piece at a time?" he blurted.

"Listen, Arsinoe. Listen to me. This may be the hidden victory we've overlooked. Wulfric can throw your pieces through the doorway one at a time, so fast the shadow won't have time to react. Once all of your pieces are on the other side, reassemble yourself within the tower, and then return with an arsenal of artifacts. And kill that bitch."

Arsinoe looked at Wulfric, who stood stock still, his helm's eyes dark and unreadable. Arsinoe glanced at Linza, her bony white chin the only visible part of her face beneath her cowl. He swallowed. "You both think this is a good idea?"

"No," Linza creaked. "I think it is the only idea we have."

"We're dying," Wulfric rumbled. "She's killing us."

"Oh fine. Oh, well and good," Arsinoe fretted. He swallowed hard and stared at the coin in Olivaard's hand.

"Arsinoe—"

"I won't survive if you just chop me up, you know. Each piece of me is...me. Each is alive and.... I'll still feel it! If my head gets chopped in half, I'll still die!"

"I don't intend for any of your pieces to get chopped. Like I said, if he throws them fast enough—"

"Fine," he cut Olivaard off. "Take my…." He glanced at the pieces of himself that were disconnected and lying on the floor. He hesitated. "Oh Fendra save me, take my hand." He pulled his left hand off with his right and tossed it to Wulfric, who caught it with surprising gentleness.

"I will throw it hard," the big man rumbled.

"I'm not going to watch," Arsinoe said, turning his head away.

Olivaard rubbed the coin between his fingers, then tossed it to the rock floor and let the magic flow through him, into the artifact.

A loud "clang" sounded, and the portal opened, an oval over six feet tall and three feet wide. Beyond it, they could see the meeting room at their tower. Just seeing it made Olivaard long for home, for the safety of the tower.

Black shadows sliced across the surface of the portal, and Wulfric stood immobile, watching them.

"Whenever you are ready," Olivaard said.

Wulfric grunted, seeming to study the pattern of the slashing black shadows, though to Olivaard they seemed random.

With a roar, Wulfric lunged toward the portal. His body blurred with speed, and he flung Arsinoe's hand with all his might.

Black shadow flashed.

Arsinoe screamed.

Half of Arsinoe's hand fell on the far side of the portal, onto the floor of the tower's meeting room, severed just below the fingers and flickering with a frenzied green light. The other half rebounded and landed at Wulfric's feet, the severed end crackling green as well.

Arsinoe screamed again. "Gods! Fendra damn you, Olivaard!" His torso thrashed and he whipped his head side to side, clenching his remaining fist. His legs weren't connected to him at the moment, but they quivered as though they could feel pain, too.

Wulfric stood, his shoulders slumped, defeated. "It is…too fast," he rumbled. "I am sorry."

Olivaard ground his teeth, staring at the damnable portal as Arsinoe's screams turned to breathy whimpers. The man used his good hand to grab his severed hand, and he reattached it to his wrist. The green light still flickered and fizzled.

Linza reached out a feeble arm and picked up a rock. She threw it at the portal in a petulant fit that Olivaard completely understood. The shadow passed over the portal's surface, slicing the rock just as it had sliced Arsinoe's hand. Rock popped and chunks fell to the floor in a shower.

Wulfric fell to one knee and the boom reverberated in the tunnel, drowning out Arsinoe's whimpers for a moment. The Lyantree magic they'd pulled to them was leaving. Wulfric would soon collapse back into his coma.

"I suppose…" Olivaard said, trying not to let his despair leak into his voice but failing. "We just keep digging like we've been doing. And we hope that Vale is as close to the edge as we are."

"No," Linza creaked.

"We cannot…. We cannot just give up," Olivaard said. "Not after all—"

"No," Linza creaked. "We don't keep digging the way we've been digging." She wiggled back and forth, slowly at first, and then her thin legs shifted, moving to tuck beneath her. Miraculously, the old bag of bones found the strength to stand. She tottered toward the portal.

Magic flowed through Olivaard as Linza pulled it from him, from all of them, from the Lyantrees far above them. She was going to cast.

"Linza, we have to conserve our strength," Olivaard said.

"Exactly," she said. She shuddered as the magic passed through her and she directed it with her will. Olivaard clenched his teeth and winced as the rips in his skin lengthened.

"Gods, really?" Arsinoe whined, feeling the damage as well. "Can I not have a moment to recover here?"

Stone flew from the walls, malleable under the power Linza commanded, and slapped onto the floor, becoming like clay and lifting the teleportation coin into an indentation she had formed. More stone flew and formed into a huge oval frame around the portal, smooth and polished, razor thin where it almost touched the portal. It was half a foot deep, the razor edge widening to a half a foot width at the back of the frame, with round handles sticking out.

"Linza, what are you doing?" Olivaard demanded.

The magic subsided. Wulfric crashed onto his face as if his strings had been cut, Arsinoe wailed, and Linza sagged, holding herself up by one of the handles she had just made.

"Pull…more…magic…." Linza said. "From the trees above. Pull more. Wake up Wulfric. We will need him." With a strength that belied her skinny body, Linza dragged one edge of her new stone-framed portal until it faced away from them, toward the rock wall.

"Wake him up to do what?" Olivaard said. "The portal doesn't work!"

"Yes…" Linza creaked. "It will…. It's the only thing

that will."

Shaking like an aspen leaf, Linza pushed at the back of the frame. It tipped...and fell against the wall.

Olivaard flinched as rock popped and crunched, the plane of the portal chewing into the wall, slicing it like it had sliced through everything else.

Olivaard's jaw dropped as he stared at the alcove the portal had just eaten out of the wall.

"It..." Linza creaked, "will work."

Olivaard wanted to kiss her. He closed his eyes and reached through the tons of stone above them, seeking with senses that could only detect magic. He went through stone, dirt, grass, until finally he felt the presence of the Lyantrees on the surface. He opened their Soulblocks, let the power flow down to them. Linza stood up straighter. Wulfric sat up again as the rich, powerful, deadly magic flowed into him. Arsinoe stopped whimpering, and his pieces slid toward his torso, completing his body.

"Yes..." Olivaard said. "Now, one last push. Let's take this fight to this whelp who thinks she can best The Four."

Wulfric roared, grabbed the frame and slammed it against the wall. Rock popped and flew, showering the floor with debris. The new tunnel was almost instantly deep enough for Wulfric to step inside. He angled the frame sharply, growled, and pushed the portal upward. Dust billowed out of the tunnel's entrance, and rock debris bounced and tumbled down the slanted floor.

For the first time in weeks, Olivaard smiled.

10

VALE

VALE HUDDLED AGAINST CROOKBRANCH, and tears slid down her face. She couldn't remember feeling anything but pain. Everything was pain. Everything she did came with pain, and her leaking eyes were just one more injury in a long list.

She told herself it was a good thing. The moment the pain stopped, it meant she had died, and The Four had won.

Only the magic from the Lyantrees kept her ripped and damaged body alive, and the fierce twist of irony was not lost on her. The same magic was also tearing her apart. She could only guess what would happen the moment she stopped using it. She feared she'd collapse in a bloody heap and would never wake.

In fact, she couldn't remember the last time she'd noticed her own beating heart, the pulsing of her blood in her neck. She listened now, felt for it, dove down through the stinging, rending pain to prove she was actually still alive and not an undead aberration propped up by magic.

Thump thump...thump thump...

Her heartbeat was still there. Good... That was good, wasn't it?

Fear washed through her as she realized she had been carrying on this inner monologue for some time now. She hadn't been fighting The Four. No. No no no...

Once The Four broke the surface, they could finally fight her on equal ground, and she would lose. She would lose almost instantly.

Only her constant onslaught had kept them at bay, and here she was daydreaming, thinking about her pain. She'd lost track of time. She didn't know how long she'd been just sitting here, thinking. For all she knew, she hadn't attacked them in an hour. Gods, could it even be a day?

She never cut her connection to the Lyantrees anymore. She wasn't even sure if she *could* disconnect from them. Sometimes she used the magic, and sometimes she didn't, but it was always there: a raging river in flood when she called on it, a calm lake buoying her up when she didn't.

Now she pulled the lightning into herself, let the raging river fill her. The rips in her skin widened, and she keened—a high, thin sound. But with the bright pain came the magic. So much magic. It allowed her to link the paths together: Mentis, Motus, Anima, Impetu. Once linked, she would dive deep into the rock, to focus her awareness on any sign of The Four—

"Vale...?" A voice broke through her drifting thoughts. A voice in the surface world, where her body was, not inside the Lyantrees or even in the rock beneath her.

Vale painstakingly pulled herself up from the rock and away from the lightning tempest of the magic roiling inside her. Her awareness slammed back into her body. The horrible pain came back, and she bit her lip to stifle a whimper. She'd bitten her lip so many times that it was bloody, and the metallic, coppery taste filled her mouth.

She opened her gummy eyes. A figure stood at the edge of the glade that encircled Crookbranch. Her vision was blurry, and she blinked until the figure came into focus.

Brom. Again.

"Gods, Vale…" he said, moving cautiously toward her like he stood on a pane of glass about to crack. He was thinner, his hair longer, his face covered with dirt smudges, and he had the beginnings of a scruffy beard. He looked altogether different than the last time she'd seen him.

"What have they done to you?" Brom fell to his knees beside her. He reached out his hand but stopped short of her cheek, hesitant, as though he was afraid to hurt her.

That's a nice touch, Vale thought. *Brom* would *do that. You're getting better.*

But she wasn't about to let Olivaard inside her mind again.

"Not twice," Vale croaked. She put a fluttery hand on Brom's chest—

And let the magic loose, a straight surge of electrifying power. Pure, raw magic could dismantle any spell. It would wash away Olivaard's illusion like suds in the rain.

She gave "Brom" all of her rage and all the magic she had. She twisted the stream into a Mentis mind-stab, a Motus heart-spike, an Anima soul-suck. Anything and everything to blow the illusion apart. If she hit it hard

enough, fast enough, with enough conviction, Olivaard
wouldn't be able to disconnect from her immediately.
The magic would ram into him far below. Maybe she
would get lucky and it would blow out his mind.

The Brom illusion screamed. Lightning hurled him
into the air like a rag doll. He hit the ground, rolled to a
stop, and fetched up against the base of a tree, limp.

The illusion lay still. Residual crackles of lightning
flickered around the body, racing over the fake Brom's
arms, back, and legs.

Vale stared, waited for the illusion to vanish. It didn't.

That wasn't right. That much magic would have
backlashed to Olivaard. It would have forced him to
abandon the illusion. Brom should have vanished....

The lightning still raced over Brom like it would have
raced over a real body.

"Get out of my head!" she shouted, and she sat up.
The pain lashed her like a dozen torturers whipping her
with a cat-o-nine tails. Her skin screamed, but she levered
herself to her feet anyway, biting her lip so hard she
tasted blood again. She wouldn't give Olivaard the
satisfaction of a scream. Not this time, she wouldn't.

"Go...away...." she growled to the limp body. "I
don't believe you. Get out of my mind!"

She took two steps toward the illusion. Her left leg
buckled, and she pitched forward onto her hands and
knees. The shock pulled at the rips in her skin and she
cried out.

When she raised her head, Brom's body still lay at the
base of the tree.

She closed her eyes firmly, felt for Olivaard's slimy
touch on her mind. She'd grown quite intimate with his
fetid presence. She would know it anywhere, but....

It wasn't there. She searched harder, feeling for even

the most subtle wisp of Mentis magic. She scoured the corners of her mind. Something…anything.

There was nothing. She opened her eyes again.

And Brom still lay there.

11

VALE

VALE'S MIND LOOPED, following a circular track that went nowhere.

If Olivaard isn't in my head, she thought, *Brom can't be here. But if Brom is still here, then Olivaard is in my head. Except Olivaard isn't in my head, so Brom can't be here...*

She crawled on her hands and knees toward him. Her skin pulled, wringing a whimper from her. One hand, then the next, until she drew up alongside the body.

A flicker of lightning raced over his arm, his leg, then the back of his head. With a shaky hand, she reached out and touched him.

He was warm. Solid. He seemed...real.

She yanked her hand back. Gods, what a perfect illusion!

His dark, wavy hair fell against his pale face the same way it used to when they lay in bed together. He was gaunt, like a Brom who had been through hell, but every other detail was right. His eyebrows. His dark eyelashes. That little mole just behind the left side of his jaw. That slender neck she had loved to kiss.

A knot of lightning twisted and writhed over his belly like two fighting cats, a node of power still churning within him, and she shuddered as she realized the chilling truth. The Four had constructed an automaton! A...golem with Brom's face. Where had they found the resources to construct such lifelike flesh? She couldn't fathom how they had—

An invisible hand squeezed her heart, and she gasped, abandoning her thoughts. That was a trigger spell! She'd imbedded dozens of them deep in the earth, warnings that would lash back to her and shock her awake if The Four passed them.

The Four were digging. They'd begun again, and she'd been so distracted she hadn't noticed until her trigger spell had been activated. They had already burrowed past her traps, past her wards.

Vale left Brom and staggered back to Crookbranch, reaching out to the Lyantrees to gather even more magic, to ready herself for her last stand—

An unbidden influx of magic filled her, rising from within. Euphoric lightning crackled in her belly, ready to be used.

Except this magic didn't hurt like the raw, ravaging kind she pulled from the Lyantrees. Instead of fire burning through her body and splitting her skin, this felt like taking a deep, satisfying breath of cool air. This was her own magic, meant for her alone, birthed from her own Soulblocks.

Her Soulblocks had expanded, like back at the academy when she'd stood next to her Quad mates. She snapped her gaze back to Brom when a breeze whooshed down on her, then again, rhythmic to the soft flapping of wings.

She craned her neck to look into the night sky, and a dark shadow blotted out the silvery moon of Kelto. Was that her dragon? But how? The great Lyantree beast lay inert at the corner of the island because it took an incredible amount of magic to bring it to life. She had been holding it in reserve for her last stand.

The flying creature descended, and it wasn't her dragon at all, but a giant moth made of Lyantrees. It landed softly next to her. Oriana sat astride it, clad in brown leathers like a common traveler. Her silver-gold hair fell past her shoulders like the mane of a Keltovari snow cat, but her expression was the same as ever: chin up, eyes glittering with her slashing intelligence, her mouth set in a determined line.

Vale stared, agape.

"Kelto's beard, girl," Oriana said. "The Four? By yourself? What do you plan to do after? Fly to the moon and punch Kelto on the nose?"

Vale clenched her teeth and readied herself to blast the woman like she had blasted the golem Brom. How were The Four doing this?

"Why didn't you come to me?" Oriana asked. "I'd have believed you. Once the writ of passage was triggered, I'd have believed you."

Oriana seemed peeved and haughty and demanding. Her inflections and her straight-backed posture were so authentic. How had The Four gathered enough strength to conjure these?

"You frightened my man so badly he fumbled your words," Oriana said. "He babbled about your dragon and that you were twenty feet tall. Your real message got lost in the drama you wrapped it in. You should have come to me directly."

A foreboding rose inside Vale like foul oil, submerging her heart and pushing into her throat. An Oriana constructed by The Four would have cajoled. She'd have tried to lead Vale from the island. She'd have promised safety.

This Oriana criticized, commanded. She told Vale what she *should* have done, just like the real Oriana would. Could this be....

No! It was another trick! Vale couldn't afford to let The Four fool her again!

"At the academy," she said, "you loaned me something. I came to you asking for assistance in drawing a man's eye, and you—"

"Ah," Oriana replied, and she instantly seemed to understand. "Olivaard has been at you. You think I'm an illusion."

"What was it?" Vale demanded through her teeth. "Speak quickly. The longer you wait, the more—"

"Lavulin perfume," Oriana answered. "You told me you were going to use it for a boy you had met in Master Saewyne's class. Which was lie, of course. You meant it for Brom."

For a moment, Vale couldn't breathe. That was correct. Every bit of it, and there was little chance The Four would know that information. Oriana had given Vale the perfume long before she and Brom had rattled the cage of The Four.

"Is it really you?" Vale murmured, and her beleaguered heart beat faster. "Tell me it's really you."

"I have come at your request. I even brought Brom," Oriana said. "Unless he ran into difficulties, he should have been here by now."

Vale looked over her shoulder at the body sprawled

on the other side of glade, and Oriana's gaze followed. The ball of lightning still crackled and twisted over Brom's belly.

Oriana's eyes narrowed. "Gods. Vale, what did you do?"

"I thought he was…. Gods, Oriana, I thought The Four had made him!"

"Kelto's teeth," Oriana cursed.

"But Brom is dead!" Vale wailed as she frantically hobbled across the glade like a wounded animal.

Gods, what have I done? Vale thought. *My beautiful Brom somehow escaped the Ragged Man and came back to me, and I've killed him—*

The ground shook, pitching Vale to her knees. An explosion of dirt erupted just across the river. She raised her head and realized in horror she had neglected the one thing she couldn't afford to neglect: she'd stopped paying attention to The Four.

In a shower of dirt and rock, they burst from the ground.

12

ORIANA

FROM HER SEAT ON THE GIANT MOTH, Oriana watched Wulfric erupt from the earth like a monstrous badger. He held some contraption that looked like a tall, glimmering stone shield. He tossed it aside the moment he emerged.

The thick man's corroded armor was covered in dirt and slime. He clenched his fists and roared at them from across the river. Though Oriana now hovered a dozen feet in the air, she thought for a breathless moment that the Impetu of The Four would leap straight into her face like a stone shot from a catapult, but he didn't. He stopped, hands on his armored knees, breathing hard inside his helmet.

Next, Linza's thin form scuttled out of the hole like a cockroach. Arsinoe leapt after, and he and Linza reached down and lifted Olivaard up.

The Four stood beyond the river, glaring up at Oriana, and she honestly couldn't think of what to do next. This wasn't some band of brigands preying on hapless villagers, after all. This was The Four, and their battle with Vale was of a magical magnitude that Oriana couldn't yet comprehend. Finally, Quad Brilliant was incomplete. They had spent everything to get here, including Royal's life and possibly Brom's.

The last time Oriana remembered feeling so outmatched was in the grips of the Test of Separation, and then she'd been prepared with a full night's rest and four full Soulblocks.

This time, her ankle was broken. She had used her first Soulblock and most of her second fighting the masters' mind-stabs before Brom's moth had rescued her.

Now the moth floated back down to the ground and alighted next to Vale. Oriana still didn't know precisely what the moth was, or why it protected her and Brom, but after all their misfortune, she wasn't going to question a bit of good luck.

To Oriana's surprise, The Four didn't attack. She felt no siege on her mind, no suck at her soul, no attempted manipulation of her emotions.

"They hesitate," Oriana said to Vale. Was it possible The Four were afraid?

Vale gave a croaking laugh, which turned into a cough, and she held a fist up to cover her mouth. The cough turned into a wracking fit, and Vale slumped to her knees. Blood covered her fist when she took it away.

"Vale!" Oriana said. She almost dismounted the moth, then remembered she couldn't walk. Her broken ankle was the size of a grapefruit. Once off the moth, she'd never get back aboard. Better to stay where she was. Better to stay mobile, with the ability to fly.

"It's almost worth it..." Vale rasped as the cough subsided. "...seeing them so twitchy. A little gift before we die."

"We are not going to die," Oriana said.

Vale glanced up at Oriana and forced a smile. "Oh, I have missed that overweening confidence, Oriana. Gods, I have missed you."

Every movement seemed to cause the girl pain. No *normal* could live with so many cuts on her body. Oriana was certain now that Vale was only standing because of the magic flowing through her, but would Vale still be standing after the magic had trickled away? Would it be like opening the fourth Soulblock?

"Get up," Oriana commanded.

Vale laughed again, and it again turned into a bloody cough. "If I could," she rasped, "I would." Instead, Vale slumped to the side, propped up against the ground by one thin arm. "I had one chance. Just one chance, and I failed. They are above ground now, and I cannot stop them for much longer."

Beyond the river, The Four clustered at the edge of the water. They peered between the trees like wary scavenger dogs, but still they didn't come ahead.

"You really have frightened them," Oriana said.

"Go," Vale croaked, and the word seemed to take the life from her. She slumped over Brom, over the spitting ball of lightning on his belly. "Take Brom. Take him and fly away. You can regroup, find a new…way to fight them…."

"And leave you here to die?" Oriana asked.

That bloody cough shook Vale again. When it subsided, she said ruefully, "Princess, I think you know I am already the walking dead. We studied the same books. We know how much magic a body can endure, and I have pushed far past that. I am impaled upon spears I have thrust into myself, and when I pull them out, that will be the end." She laid her head on Brom's chest. "I called you," she murmured. "But I called too late. You shouldn't pay for my mistakes. Don't make Brom pay. Take him and go."

Oriana painstakingly brought her broken leg over the moth's back, her swollen ankle bent at an awkward angle. She hissed at just moving it. The idea of standing on it made her feel faint.

Gritting her teeth, she slid from the moth and landed on her good foot. The impact sent a jolt of pain from her ankle all the way to her head. Black spots swam before her eyes, but she held onto her consciousness. She steadied herself, clung to the odd, fern-like ruff of the moth.

"No," Oriana said through clenched teeth, and she repeated what she'd said to Vale when they'd first bonded in the shadow of Westfall Dormitory. "You are my Quad mate. And I will not give you up."

Vale's head lifted. Tears stood in her eyes. "Oriana…. There is no victory here. We cannot—"

"Get up," Oriana said, standing on one leg, holding out her hand. "We finish this together. One way or another."

Vale glanced at Oriana's broken leg, then up at her face. "Calculate the odds, Princess. Save Brom. Face The Four later."

"No."

"You stubborn bitch," Vale hissed. "They're coming!"

Oriana forced herself not to look at The Four. She kept her gaze on Vale, hand outstretched.

"At the Test we faced horrible odds," Oriana said. "And I told you to leave Brom to his fate." She shook her head. "I was wrong. And I do not make the same mistake twice."

"Are you saying you made a mistake, Princess?"

Oriana gave a tight smile. "Fight by my side Vale, and when we survive, I will regale you with all my mistakes."

"Gods…" Vale gave a stiff smile. "That might actually be worth living for." She slapped a bloody hand into Oriana's, and Oriana pulled her to her feet.

Together, leaning on each other, they turned toward the river.

The Four started into the water cautiously, searching left and right for unseen traps.

She has terrified them! Oriana thought. *They look like timid children. Kelto's Teeth, this girl!*

Admiration swelled in Oriana's heart. "You've cowed them. If I die today, I shall die in awe of you."

"But I failed in my objective," Vale said. "I…wasn't strong enough to finish the job. As soon as they find out I am spent, their fear will vanish."

"Then perhaps now would be a good time to summon that dragon of yours," Oriana said.

Vale chuckled. "A very good time. But it's…too late for that."

"Too late?"

"I don't know if I have the strength to bring it to life again. It takes…so much magic."

"The dragon was a construct?"

Vale glanced up at her. "Surely you knew."

"How would I know?" Oriana said, annoyed.

"Because the moth. Because you made it."

"I? No."

"You haven't discovered the Soulblocks within the trees?" Vale asked.

Ah! That was the missing piece! Of course! "The trees have Soulblocks," Oriana murmured.

"You didn't know…. So who made the moth?" Vale asked. "Brom?"

"Perhaps we should save this debate for after we survive," Oriana said. "If you cannot summon your dragon, then perhaps you can tell me how to open the Soulblocks in the Lyantrees."

"I have…bonded with them. I learned their language." Vale glanced at Oriana with bloodshot eyes. "But it took weeks."

"Ah," Oriana said, disappointed.

"I suppose we'll just have to improvise," Vale chuckled, and it turned into another bloody cough.

The Four were halfway across the river now, staying close together. Their cautious pace increased.

Now that they were closer, the moonlight illuminated them better, and Oriana saw the devastation Vale had wrought. Linza was a skin-wrapped skeleton, with torn and ragged robes revealing her bony body. Olivaard wasn't much better, his tall form bent nearly in half. His normally droopy skin sagged like melted candle wax. Both he and Linza bore the same cuts on their hands and faces as Vale. Arsinoe was not cut, but his movements were jerky and wobbly, as though his ligaments were loose, and he cradled one wrapped hand against his belly. Wulfric limped, dragging his left leg behind him. An Impetu, limping.

"They look the worse for wear," Oriana said.

"Get ready," Vale said.

Oriana unlocked her third Soulblock, the last Soulblock she could use without dying. Lightning crackled through her, filling her body, filling her mind, lifting her up. Suddenly, everything seemed possible again. They *would* win this battle.

"Remember this," Vale said. "If I die, I will give you

as much of my magic as I can before I go. It will come fast and hard. It will hurt, but it will make you strong enough to fight The Four…or to escape."

"I'm not going anywhere. And neither of us is going to die."

"Here they come," Vale said.

The Four stepped out of the water, and they had stopped checking the shadows for threats. They didn't look anywhere but at Oriana and Vale. It appeared that they finally believed their own eyes: they were facing two broken Quadrons, and that was all.

Olivaard stabbed at Oriana's mind. It came fast and powerful, but she'd readied herself. His attack was a spear, but her defense was an iron shield.

Linza's soul-suck came next, but soul-sucks were most effective when the victim was caught unaware. Oriana rode the euphoria of her own magic and held Linza's despair at bay.

Wulfric broke into a run toward them, bringing the physical threat. As he reached land and passed the first tree, he snapped off a huge branch and wielded it as a club.

Vale laughed maniacally, and Oriana glanced at her in surprise.

Pure lightning burst from the girl, arcing toward The Four.

13

BROM

BROM JOLTED AWAKE to a paralyzing pain. He spasmed, arching his back and clawing at his chest. Spikes of lightning pierced him like a giant, hot sewing needle mending a rip, the thread dragging through his innards again and again. He couldn't breathe, couldn't....

Then the pain vanished. Sweating, gasping, he gulped for breath. The roar in his ears faded.

And he opened his eyes to the end of the world.

A thick cloud of dirt and leaves hung in the air, as though a tree had exploded. He smelled the rich, wet soil and the vanilla sweetness of tree sap. Bits of earth, green scaly bark, and purple leaves rained down, pattering on his head and arms.

Before him, giant figures surged in the haze, clashing with the thunderous impact of a falling drawbridge. Brom felt crackling magic passing between them; he felt it pass through him. The entire forest was charged with it.

The two behemoths locked together into a big, writhing mass. Tree limbs cracked and crashed.

He struggled to remember where he was, and the memories came back fragmented. Vale. He'd come for Vale. Royal and Oriana had died to bring him here, and Vale had attacked him when he'd arrived, had shot him with lightning.

She'd shot him with lightning.

He drew a long, thin breath as several realizations hit him at once. He *felt* the magic in the forest. He felt it crackling *inside* himself!

He felt the Soul of the World again, connecting him to the trees and the flowing river around the island, to the sifting dirt in the air and the solid earth beneath him.

The vibrating pebble in his belly had vanished, and in its place were his four Soulblocks, brimming over with magic. The first had already opened on its own, releasing lightning into his body.

His Soul of the World senses expanded his awareness, and he assessed the raging battle. This was a fight between Vale and The Four, and he had to get into it.

Six humans moved in the haze beneath the savage behemoths that crashed and fought each other. No…not just behemoths. Dragons. Those were dragons!

The magnitude of this magic staggered him. It was like a thousand Soulblocks had been opened to the very air, and…the dragons *were* the trees! They were made of trees, just like the moth. He felt the fierce magic twisting inside the dragons like a lightning storm of creation, rumbling and booming, holding each tree-dragon together, dictating its actions.

Brom opened his second Soulblock, adding its crackling power to the first. Lightning raced through him, lifting his soul up on the wings of euphoria, higher and higher until it seemed like he could see the entire battle from two dozen feet in the air.

The Lyantree dragons savaged each other, sending cracked branches and leaves spinning down.

The battlefield and its combatants came more into focus. Behind the larger dragon stood Linza, Arsinoe, and Olivaard, hands up like they were working in concert. Even further back, Wulfric picked himself up from the midst of the river. He looked as though he had been thrown, and his body had carved a trench through the earth to the center of the river. Clumps of mud dropped from him as he stood up. Water streamed off him, and he shook his helmeted head like it was full of bees.

Closer to Brom, just behind the smaller dragon, Oriana stood with Vale. They leaned on each other as though neither could remain upright alone.

Oriana had survived! Relief flooded through Brom. Somehow she had escaped the minions of the academy, but her ankle bent at an unnatural angle, horribly swollen.

The smaller dragon—which Brom surmised to be Vale and Oriana's dragon—was clearly losing. It was missing its front left leg and half of its left wing. The larger dragon—which Brom guessed belonged to The Four—was clawing, bashing, trying to get its massive jaws in a position to chomp through the smaller dragon's neck.

These past days Brom had been lost, uncertain, struggling like a moth in a bowl of milk. But now his confidence had returned in the crackling swirl of his magic.

He didn't understand the magic of dragons and trees, but he sized up the tactics of the fight. Olivaard, Linza, and Arsinoe animated the dragon and kept Vale's at bay, while Wulfric had been sent to thin the herd. To wreak havoc. To kill one of the women if he could.

Wulfric roared and charged again, and Brom knew exactly where he could be most useful.

An Anima was designed to handle an Impetu. An Anima had natural immunities to Impetu strengths. Oriana had unearthed that bit of arcana at the academy, and Quad Brilliant had proved her supposition during their primer against Quad Phoenix.

Brom leapt to his feet and sprinted toward the oncoming Wulfric, who headed for Oriana. Brom saw The Four's plan like a map laid out before him. Remove Oriana, gang up on Vale. That was the order in which they planned to strike.

Brom yanked his dagger from its sheath, leapt atop a low branch and launched himself at Wulfric like an arrow.

Wulfric was already in mid-air—in a leap of his own—when Brom hit him like a ram.

Brom saw it all happen in his mind's eye. He saw where his shoulder must hit, where his hand must grab, where his dagger must stab. He even saw the pestilent Impetu's eyes widen behind those thin slits in his helmet...

Then everything played out at lightning speed. Brom slammed his shoulder into Wulfric's right arm and jammed his fingers into one of the tight seams in the armor. He pulled, bringing his body up and slamming his knees into the Impetu's chest.

The impact spun Wulfric, altering his arc just enough to miss Oriana. Brom followed his fingers with his blade, thrusting the dagger into the armor's seam and slicing into flesh and bone. Wulfric screamed. Brom pushed off with his knees just as the big Impetu slammed into the ground.

Wulfric slid past Oriana on his face, throwing up a spray of mud and dirt, while Brom landed gracefully on his feet.

"Brom!" Oriana said, eyes squinched tight from concentration.

"Sorry I'm late," he said.

Wulfric scrambled upright, wildly grasping for the dagger stuck high in his side, but he couldn't reach it.

"Kkkk…. Kill you!" Wulfric growled. "Kill…. Kkkk… Kill…."

"Have to catch me first," Brom taunted. He'd done this same trick with Quad Phoenix's Impetu during the primer. The trick was to stay calm, stay loose, and let the Soul of the World guide his actions. And almost as important: Brom had to push the Impetu to lose his temper, to sink into his instincts and forget his rational mind. The ensuing rage would make Wulfric stronger and faster, but the Soul knew where he was going before he ever got there. And once Wulfric stopped thinking, Brom would lure him into a mistake.

Wulfric roared and charged, so fast he was a blur. Brom leapt at him, ducking and rolling beneath the surprised hand that almost grabbed him.

Brom slid to his feet again. He wanted to know how his Quad mates were faring, but he couldn't stop listening to the Soul of the World for a fraction of a second.

"You're getting old," Brom taunted.

Wulfric didn't charge again. He pulled that ridiculously wide sword from the sheath on his back. Metal scraped on metal and the Impetu crouched gracefully, moving sideways, stalking Brom. Wulfric grunted and snuffled like a beast. Words tumbled from his mouth in a mumbled string, but none of them were recognizable.

"You should have killed us when you had the chance," Brom said. "Back when we were innocent, when we didn't know what you *really* are."

Wulfric roared and lunged, but Brom was already sprinting. He didn't have much hope of actually killing Wulfric. Nothing was harder to kill than an Impetu. But if he could take the Impetu out of the fight long enough, Oriana and Vale might prevail against the other three.

Instead of going low, Brom leapt high this time. The sword sliced a half-inch below his boots. He landed and sprinted toward the nearest tree, which had a broken branch six feet off the ground.

He sailed onto the broken branch and, with the super-human agility from the magic coursing through him, launched off. Wulfric jumped after, and he almost succeeded in grabbing Brom a second time. Thick fingers scraped along Brom's back, just missing.

Wulfric slammed into the tree, impaling himself on the broken branch. The Impetu roared, blood leaking from below his helmet as he craned his neck down to see the thick Lyantree branch jammed through his armor and his body.

"If you're going to be so slow," Brom said, trying hard to sound conversational as he clambered up the tree like a squirrel. "Perhaps send Olivaard to chase me instead."

Inhuman grunts blasted from Wulfric's helmet, but no words. The Impetu pushed himself off the tree spike and landed on his feet. Blood streamed from the hole punched in his armor just below his ribs. Grunting like an ox, Wulfric glared at the bloody branch, grabbed it, and launched himself up the tree.

"Kkkk… Kill…" Wulfric gargled. "Kill you…"

"Maybe we could get you a cane," Brom said.

Brom kept the taunts coming, but he was reaching his limit. Even with his newfound magic, his breath came fast. His lungs ached. His arms burned. He wasn't an Impetu, after all, and the physical benefits of an Anima only went so far.

I can't maintain this pace... The thought slithered into his mind. *I'm going to make a mistake. I'll slip or miss a grab, then Wulfric will have me. He'll crack my bones and break my skull—*

Brom shook his head, trying to break the tendrils of the soul-suck, and climbed higher.

"Your first time was better," he shouted to Linza, who stood far below at the base of the tree. Brom grabbed the next branch, lifted himself up, put both feet on it and bunched into a crouch, readying himself for a mighty leap from the top of this tree to the next one over.

Just as Brom sprung, Wulfric's massive fist clipped his boot and cracked the branch in half, sending Brom spinning into the gap between branches.

With a cry, he twisted, trying to catch something, anything. His hand flung out and grasped a thin branch—

But it snapped under his weight, sending him spinning in a different direction, and he lost control. A branch smacked him in the side, spun him again, and another hit his leg so hard he cried out.

He slammed into the ground face first. He couldn't breathe, couldn't make his arms or legs work. He felt the soul-sucking despair from Linza slip past his defenses this time and coat his insides like oil.

Your little game is over. We have you now.

Brom's chest spasmed as it tried to remember how to breathe, and he shakily raised his head to find Linza hunched over him. Her hood had fallen back, and her bald, bony head looked like a skull with eyeballs bulging out of it. She shook with palsy as her thin arms reached for him.

"Give it…" she rasped. "Give it back…."

Brom looked past her for his Quad mates. He had pulled not just Wulfric, but Linza away from the fight as well. Vale and Oriana might be able to turn the—

No!

Vale was down, her bloody little form slumped on the churned earth. Her dragon had gone inert. The larger dragon controlled by The Four lowered its head and chomped through the neck of the smaller dragon. Then the larger dragon also went still.

The battle is over…. The despair soaked into him.

Even though Brom knew the dark thoughts were Linza's doing, he couldn't refute them. How could he overcome The Four now that his Quad mates had fallen?

"It's over," Linza rasped, repeating his thoughts aloud. "Now give me back what you stole, and I'll let you live."

Oriana crawled through the mud away from the dragons as Olivaard and Arsinoe limped after her, knives in hand.

Wulfric's huge, hoof-like feet shook the ground with a thunderous boom as he landed next to Linza.

Linza held up a hand to ward Wulfric away. "Wait…" she rasped. "I need him."

"Kkkk…." he grunted. "Kill you!" Wulfric raised the sword over his head and brought it downward at Brom.

14

BROM

THE MASSIVE BLADE ARCED DOWN—

A blurred body slammed into Wulfric, and the enormous sword jolted sideways, cutting through Brom's hair and nicking his ear before plunging to the hilt in the soft ground.

Wulfric flew as if shot from a catapult, knocking Linza down midflight. The blur that had launched him became Royal, his wild hair and beard sticking out in every direction.

Linza sprawled in the mud like a scarecrow, and Wulfric arced over the ground, smashing into the big dragon a hundred feet away. The dragon collapsed into a tumble of logs, burying Wulfric.

"Royal!" Brom gasped. The big man looked like he'd been thrown down a mountain. His beard and face were covered with dirt and blood. His tunic had been ripped away, exposing his hairy, muscled chest and arms. A pink scar ran at an angle from his clavicle to his ribs where the wide-bladed spear had taken him. Somehow he had survived!

At Royal's nearness, Brom's Soulblocks doubled, filling him with that sense of joy and invincibility that only a full Quad could bring. Quad Brilliant was complete again, and that meant....

"Vale is still alive," Brom murmured, craning his neck to look at the bloody little pile a hundred feet away. The Four couldn't afford to face a full Quad, and Brom knew they'd go for the easiest target like a pack of starving jackals.

Royal followed his gaze. "Vale?" he said, and he seemed to understand Brom's fear without any words exchanged. His big booted feet churned mud as he launched himself at the vulnerable Vale.

The fallen dragons had made a tangle of broken Lyantrees nearly twenty feet tall between Arsinoe, Olivaard, and Vale. Arsinoe clambered desperately over the thatch, trying to get to Vale first.

But Royal skidded to a stop in front of her, fists clenched. Arsinoe drew up short, hissing.

Linza extricated herself from the mud, gave a seething glance at Brom, then scrambled away on all fours like a spider.

Brom opened another Soulblock. Magic crackled into him, and he leapt to his feet. He wanted to chase her, but he stopped.

Impossibly, Quad Brilliant was back together. The last thing he should do was separate himself from the group. Linza's retreat could be a calculated maneuver to make him do just that.

Instead, Brom sprinted toward his Quad mates and fell to his knees beside Vale.

She was a bloody mess. Her face and her arms—her entire body—was covered with those horrible splits in her skin, some of them a foot long. She wasn't moving, and she didn't seem to be breathing.

"Vale…" he murmured. He glanced up at Royal. He could heal her, if he was quick, but right now Royal stood as an implacable guardian between them and Arsinoe. He was like a living wall with his inhumanly broad shoulders, his hulking arms and tree-trunk legs. His beard shifted in the breeze, but his body remained tense and ready for violence.

Perched on a log, Arsinoe bared his teeth like a cornered rat. He crouched there a moment as if he could will Vale's death without having to get close to her. Then, with a growl, Arsinoe danced back down the logs, away from Royal and back toward Linza and Olivaard. They all stooped like they were exhausted.

On the other side of the log pile, Oriana limped toward them, keeping her bent ankle off the ground and leaning on the many branches to keep herself upright.

The pile of logs shifted, one thudding and rolling down from the top, then another. Wulfric emerged between two giant trunks as he pushed them apart, growling and huffing. His armor was bent and dented, and blood seeped from slits at the shoulder, elbow, and waist joints. His square helmet was dented so badly it seemed impossible that the skull inside remained uncrushed.

"Well," Royal boomed in his thundering voice as he went to Oriana, lifted her in his arms like a doll, and brought her back to join Vale and Brom. "It appears we have a fair fight at last. No psychic hooks. No rigged contests. No lies." He held forth his thick hand and beckoned. "Come, demigods. Let us put *you* to the test."

Arsinoe reached Wulfric, who falteringly tried to rise, then fell back to sit hard on one of the logs. Arsinoe took hold of the man's thick, armored arm and helped him upright. They staggered back to their diseased group. The Four clustered together and glared across the distance.

"You have made a grave mistake," Olivaard warned.

"One of us did," Oriana said.

"Do not be proud, striplings," Olivaard said. "You've doomed the two kingdoms today."

"We have liberated them," Oriana responded in her queen's voice.

"Fools!" Olivaard hissed, reaching into his bedraggled, dirt-brown robes, and withdrew a coin. Royal stepped in front of Oriana just as Olivaard threw the coin at his own feet.

A loud *clang* sounded, and a shimmering portal—just like the ones in the mirrors at the Dome—appeared between Olivaard and Quad Brilliant.

Royal roared and leapt at The Four.

"Royal, stop!" Oriana snapped.

Royal might have reached them in a heartbeat, but he pulled up short at Oriana's command. The Four leapt through the portal one-by-one. It gave a loud *clang* again and vanished.

"Not right now," Oriana said softly to the frustrated Royal. "We are injured, at our limit. Let them go. There will be another time."

"There will never be a better time to kill them," Royal growled.

"And there will never be another time to save Quad Brilliant," Oriana said. "They fled. Savor that victory, my friend, and instead of harvesting four more souls, let's try to save one."

But even as Oriana said it, Brom felt his Soulblocks

flickering, diminishing, retreating from their doubled nature to their normal size.

"No! Vale!" he cried, holding her limp shoulders.

She was slipping away, and they could all feel it.

With a roar of denial, Royal leapt toward her.

15

VALE

VALE HEARD VOICES. Just warbling sounds at first, then words, then they came in a rush. Brom's voice. Oriana's voice. Royal's. Tam's. Arsinoe's as well. And Olivaard's...

"I love you..." Brom whispered.

"Vale," Olivaard said sternly, *"What are you doing?"*

"I will see you on the battlefield," Royal growled.

"Anything I want," Arsinoe whispered in her ear. *"I can do to you..."*

"We must run, Alari," Tam said urgently. *"The lyans tell us we must run..."*

"Surely you must know that you don't love *me..."*

"And so here we are," Oriana said. *"Precisely where we began..."*

Vale swallowed. It felt like a hawk clawing at her throat from the inside. She stifled a groan, a habit of silence she had learned long ago waking up on the streets of Torlioch.

Where am I?

Then she remembered. She was in the forest, battling The Four.

Except....

She wasn't in a forest. She was in some dark place with a shaft of light angling down in front of her.

She blinked, her eyelids fluttering against the brightness. Was that a shaft of light through a crack in a rock wall? Had The Four kept her alive and trapped her in her own tunnels as some kind of twisted punishment?

No.... They wouldn't dare do that. They wouldn't have toyed with her anymore. They'd have just killed her.

How was she alive? There was no way she and Oriana could have won that fight. They'd been overmatched in every way.

Moreover, the rips in her skin didn't hurt anymore. The agonizing pain was gone!

As her eyes adjusted, she saw that the light came from a thin slit in closed shutters.

Shutters?

She was lying on a bed with cotton sheets and a goose down mattress, in a room. And there were other people here with her.

They gathered around a table at the foot of the bed, talking. Though the voices in her head had been sharp and clear, these seemed distant for a moment; she had to focus on them to understand them. But slowly, the conversation became clear.

"It is a wonder you have survived this long," Oriana said.

"It *is* dangerous for a man," Royal replied, "having to save your life all the time."

"Is that what that was?" Oriana said. "I thought it was some Fendiran drama, playing dead to heighten the effect, rushing in to save us at the last possible moment."

"I admit, it took some time to get up after you abandoned me with a spear in my back," he said.

"I took the spear out."

He chuckled, a deep and comforting sound that pleasantly rumbled Vale's chest and filled her with joy.

"I bow before your arguments," Royal said.

"At last, he bows," Oriana said drily.

"You bowed to me first," Royal said.

"And I've been waiting all this time for you to return the favor," she replied. Her voice was pleasant and as carefree as Vale had ever heard it.

"Hey," Brom said, and both Oriana and Royal stopped talking. "She's awake."

Vale turned to her left to find Brom sitting at the edge of the bed. She'd seen him so many times in her dreams, but this time, it was *really* him. Brom, with his dark eyes, and wavy hair that kept falling in his face. And his slender, delicious neck. He sat by her bedside, reached out and touched her hand. She squeezed his fingers.

"Gods, I missed you," she croaked. Brom. Oriana. Royal. All of them together, in the same room, not fighting. It seemed a glorious impossibility. "I missed all of you."

Oriana and Royal both smiled.

"What happened?" Vale said, her voice barely above a whisper. The magic had nearly ripped her apart as she'd fought Olivaard's dragon. She remembered her dragon falling to its knees and Olivaard's pouncing. And that was the last thing she remembered.

"I lost," she murmured. "But I'm not dead."

"No," Brom said. "We're not dead."

"Well, not all of us," Oriana said, giving Brom a sly glance. "We're still not sure if Brom qualifies as alive or not," she said, but she winked. She stood up, came to the right side of the bed, and smiled gently down at Vale. She wore a blue cotton dress, simple and unadorned, with hooks-and-eyes up the front instead of buttons. At her neck was a white collar, curved on either side like two dollops of snow. Peasant's clothing. The dress of a farm girl.

Royal was likewise dressed, not in his typical Fendiran leathers and beaded tunic. Instead, he wore a dun-colored rough-spun shirt, laces open at the front exposing his hairy chest, as well as trousers and a single suspender over one shoulder.

"You did try your best to die," Oriana said. "But Royal is stubborn."

"He passed out twice trying to heal you," Brom said.

"Our Impetu, the fainter," Oriana said.

"I did not pass out," Royal rumbled, moving to stand behind Oriana. He towered over her, his big, bearded face and thatch of unruly hair sprouting like some hairy tree behind the beautiful queen.

"How long have I been...?" Vale asked, looking around. She didn't recognize this place. "Where are we?"

"Kyn," Brom said. "We've been here about four days."

"We're in your hometown?"

Kyn was at least a three-day ride from the Lyantree forest. She'd been unconscious for seven days?

"We had to sneak in," Brom said. "Royal and you and me through the back door while Oriana paid for the room. She had to conceal her hair, of course."

"Not a difficult task at the time," Oriana said. "It was brown with mud."

"But what about…The Four?" Vale asked. She was thoroughly confused. Before her battle with Olivaard's dragon, Oriana had been the only one standing. Royal was supposedly dead, Brom was dying, and Oriana had been all alone when everything went black.

"Gone," Oriana said, her pleasant tone turning hard.

"For now," Royal rumbled.

"Gone from here, at any rate," Oriana amended. "Back to their tower, no doubt."

"They still live…." Vale's failure burned inside her. "I tried so hard to break them. Their Quad, their hold on the lands. But it was all for nothing."

"Not for nothing," Oriana said.

"We are right back where we started."

"Oh Vale…" Oriana said with a sad smile. She descended gently, seating herself on the edge of the bed. "You broke them. You, alone. No one in the history of the two kingdoms was even truly aware of them—of what they really were. You not only uncovered their secrets, but you bested them. You stood against them and made them fear you. And when we all came together, they fled. *That* is not nothing." She reached out one of her long, slender hands and rested it on Vale's and Brom's intertwined fingers.

Royal rumbled appreciatively deep in his chest.

"But they'll regroup. They'll come after us," Vale said.

"No," Royal said. "We will come after *them*."

"I do not think they will be so eager for our next encounter," Oriana said.

"They're so strong," Vale said. "You don't know."

"Oh," Oriana said, not seeming the least bit perturbed. "I think I have an idea."

"They have greater powers within their tower," Vale said. "Greater than the Lyantree forest. I felt it from all of them. They longed to get back to their tower. There is something there that feeds them, something greater even than the Soulblocks of the Lyantrees...."

"We have some thoughts on that," Royal said.

"There is much to ponder. But for now, I think we can rest, rejuvenate ourselves." Oriana replied in her queen's voice, as though she had decided this conversation was over. "You, especially, can rest. In fact..." She stood up, smoothing the front of her farmer's dress, though the smoothing did nothing to flatten its wrinkles. The queen looked as out of place as a snow rabbit wearing a hat. "I think Royal and I are going for a walk. I've never been to Kyn before. I rather like it. The rolling hills. The farming fields."

"Really?" Brom asked.

"Utterly charming," Oriana said, and Brom beamed.

"Your shawl, milady." Royal took a strip of cloth from the dresser and handed it to her as he bowed.

"Another bow, Royal?" The cloth fluttered gracefully over her head as Oriana draped it and tied it beneath her chin, covering her silver-gold hair. "I believe that's two to my one."

"Take care, milady," Royal said as she walked toward the door and he followed. "You might fall in the water."

"Water?" Oriana said.

"By the river. When we get there. After I shove you in."

Oriana laughed, and Vale had almost forgotten what the queen's laughter sounded like. It was pure, like chiming bells. There wasn't an ounce of Oriana's rigid control in her voice when she laughed.

They closed the door behind them, and Brom turned back to Vale. He hadn't let go of her hand once since he'd taken it. And she had the vague impression that he'd been holding her hand all this time, every day since she'd fallen unconscious. She looked at their hands, then at the razor-thin scars all over her arms up to the point where the cotton nightdress covered them. Royal's healing job was well-done, but nothing would take away those scars. Part of her wanted a looking glass, to look at her face, to see its many cuts.

"You took on The Four all by yourself," Brom murmured, nudging her with his elbow. "Royal talks about you like a romantic figure in a Fendiran poem. And Oriana… She would watch you sometimes while you slept. I think you're her new hero—"

"I love you," Vale said, her heart lodged in her throat. She squeezed his hand. "I'm so sorry for everything. You were the best of us, and I left you there. You reached out to me…." Tears welled in her eyes. "You said we could beat them together, and I—"

He put a finger on her lips, stopping her guilt-ridden confession. "Hey," he murmured. "It's okay."

She pulled him to her and clung to him, holding him, burying her face in his neck and smelling the clean, honest scent of him.

"I love you," she repeated.

"Yeah," he replied, a catch in his throat. "I kinda thought so. I thought you did."

"I was an idiot."

"And maybe a bit of a bitch," he said.

She half-laughed and half-cried into his shoulder. "I'm so sorry."

"Ahhh," he said. "Bitches are the best."

"You…" She backed up so she could look into his beautiful eyes. "You never gave up."

"No," he said softly. "Never."

"You came to save me," she said. "You died, but you

still came back to save me."

"And a merry chase you made it, I can tell you. The next time you want to confess your love, maybe just tell me instead of, say, attacking The Four by yourself."

She laughed and hugged him tightly.

"Okay," she said. "I promise."

EPILOGUE

AYVRA

AYVRA RODE TO THE TOP of the hill. The city of Torlioch hove into view, squat and dirty in the setting sun. The Torlioch River flowed around the city, as though it didn't want to come too close.

She threw her braided ponytail over her shoulder and scanned the terrain. Ayvra knew a little about Torlioch, and nothing she had heard indicated it was anywhere near as civilized as Keltan. Knifings in the alleys. City guards who were more interested in lining their pockets than doing the bidding of the city's leader.

Of course, Ayvra had much in common with that breed now. She, too, had flaunted the express wishes of her queen. When told to stay in the safety of the palace, away from the danger into which her lover intended to ride, Ayvra had instead saddled a horse and pursued. Oriana was used to being obeyed, but in this case Ayvra simply could not. She wasn't going to sit at home safe while Oriana rode into danger. If Oriana needed help on this deadly journey, Ayvra was going to make certain she was at hand.

Ayvra had given Oriana a half-day head start. Oriana's Mentis abilities would be able to spot Ayvra if she was too close. But if Ayvra kept her distance for the first few days, the queen would relax. Then all Ayvra had to do was keep Reela and Dantolis from noticing her. They were good at what they did, but then so was Ayvra. She had practically been born on a horse, working with them on her father's farm from as early as she could remember. At fourteen, she'd assisted a local trapper, and he'd shown her the ways of the northern forests, how to find game, how to hunt them down and trap them. That had led to a job as a courier.

Ayvra had ridden back and forth between her hometown and Keltan a hundred times, had learned as much about horses as anyone, and she'd used her tracking skills to entertain her mind during the long journeys, piecing together the directions and even the stories of the travelers who had gone before her. Tracks could tell a lot about the type of horse a rider had chosen, about their personal style. Even, sometimes, about their personalities.

So Ayvra had stayed safely a half-day behind Oriana for the first two days, intending to close the gap later. She could follow Oriana's tracks across hard-packed royal roads or overland. Only the cobblestone streets of a city like Torlioch masked her lover's tracks, but Ayvra didn't need to enter the city. She just needed to watch it from a distance. She suspected Oriana wouldn't stay long in Torlioch.

And she was right.

Later that same night, Ayvra saw the riders leave to the east, saw Oriana's unmistakable cloak trailing behind her. Ayvra put out her little cooking fire, saddled her horse, and started after them. Following tracks by moonlight was a different kind of challenge. She looked forward to it.

The first night Oriana and her party stopped and buried two bodies.

Apparently, there had been a battle in Torlioch, and Ayvra cursed herself for not being there. It had happened so fast she hadn't even noticed. But neither Reela nor Dantolis had survived. Ayvra had watched as Oriana, the huge Fendiran, some thin boyish man, and an attractive barmaid buried the guards. Ayvra resolved at that point to make sure she never got more than an hour's ride behind them, although the big Fendiran frightened her. He seemed the type of man who would kill before talking. That, she was sure, was Oriana's Quad mate, the Impetu. The one Oriana had been worried might harm Ayvra.

She trailed them for days, dropping back as they crossed the open eastern plains and drawing closer as they hit the rolling hills. The Fendiran was so heavy, his horse made impressions she could have followed on a moonless night, blindfolded.

The days and nights passed, and all seemed fine.

When the group approached a forest larger than anything Ayvra had ever seen, everything changed. An army came running across the hilly terrain. Ayvra was stunned she hadn't seen them coming, hadn't even known they were close.

She had been preparing to set up her fireless camp when she heard them, felt the earth vibrate with the approach of many feet. She snatched her bow and leapt upon her horse, ready to race off and warn Oriana—

When Ayvra realized someone was behind her.

She gasped and wheeled her horse. She hadn't heard a

sound, but suddenly a boy of ten stood in her camp, barely six paces away from her.

His eyes glowed green in the dark.

He cocked his head, an oddly innocent gesture that caused her to pause. She didn't know whether to flee, fight, or ask if the boy needed help.

"You know the queen," the little boy stated.

That snapped Ayvra into motion. His glowing green eyes, his emotionless face, his serious tone…it was too bizarre, and Oriana had warned her there would be deadly magics on this journey. Ayvra dropped the reins and nocked an arrow in her bow.

"You are attached to the queen." Glowing green tendrils grew from the boy's fingers.

She pulled back the bow to shoot the boy, but a tiny tendril of green light touched Ayvra's temple from behind, and she gasped. She spun in her saddle, suddenly realizing with horror that another child—a girl of about the same age—stood behind her. That thin tentacle of magic was connected to her fingers.

Her arrow fell from the string, and the bow fell from her hands.

"No!" Ayvra screamed, snatching at the reins, but a whisper began in her head, telling her to calm down. Telling her everything was all right.

She fought it. For an excruciating instant, she tried to shove it out of her head….

But it was like trying to fight a crashing ocean wave. It smashed down upon her and carried her, spun her, owned her.

Ayvra let her fistful of reins go. The horse stamped and snorted, wanting to bolt, so she lifted her leg and dismounted. The horse galloped away, and the little boy walked up to her.

"You are perfect," he said. "You are exactly what we need."

"What's…happening?" Ayvra asked, and a single tear streaked down her cheek. She couldn't run. She couldn't make herself run.

"You don't need to worry about that anymore," the little boy said. "You don't need to worry about anything anymore…" His tentacled green hands reached up for her face.

Green light flashed, and Ayvra knew no more.

Mailing List/Social Media

MAILING LIST
Don't miss out on the latest news and information about all of my books. Join my Readers Group

FACEBOOK GROUP

AMAZON AUTHOR PAGE

AUTHOR LETTER

Tower of the Four, Episode 4: The Nightmare started as a prologue. That's all it was supposed to be. After Brom wakes up in his grave at the end of *Episode 3: The Test*, the next part of the story, naturally, was to follow his journey to rejoin his Quad.

But what had become of those Quad mates in the year Brom had been absent?

Well, I planned to show what had become of Oriana and Royal in the meat of the story. But Vale would only be seen at the very beginning. I planned to kick off the next episode with a brief, teasing bit, showing the reader that Vale had not only grown more powerful in the year that Brom had been absent, but that she was in serious trouble and needed her Quad more than ever.

So *Episode 4: The Nightmare* started as a one-chapter tease. But as I crafted the story of Brom's journey after he awoke, questions about Vale kept popping up.

How did she get to this new Lyantree forest? How did she amass enough power to attack—and hold—The Four? What was she doing before this happened? Aren't the readers going to want to know more about this? Is there a full episode there?

Those questions grew larger, and soon what had been a mild curiosity grew into a full-blown roadblock. I remember stopping in the midst of what is now *Episode 5: The Resurrection*, unable to continue because I might have skipped a critical element.

I walked away from the keyboard for half a day, puttered around in my yard, mowed the lawn, trimmed the weeds, threw sticks for the dog, and let my mind sort through the problem. I will often do this when I reach a stuck point. I'll go to sleep or go for a walk or watch a movie or whatever. Anything to take my mind directly off the problem while my subconscious goes to work in the dark.

I will also call my friend Chris and throw the problem at her feet like a tangled coil of ropes and pulleys. She understands my process so thoroughly that she has become a master at picking up those frustrating knots and unwinding them, showing me what I knew all along but was too stubborn to see.

Sometimes this unwinding takes days, even weeks. But Vale's was a pretty obvious problem, I suppose. It only took half a day.

In the end—just like Vale does in the story with her Quad mates, with the masters of the academy, with all those who underestimate her—my little urchin refused to be overlooked. And I'm so glad she stood up and shouted. *Episode 4: The Nightmare* is the best episode yet.

Now back to work. The *Tower of the Four* storm is picking up speed. Hold onto your hats.

-TODD

ALSO BY TODD FAHNESTOCK

Tower of the Four
Episode 1 – The Quad
Episode 2 – The Tower
Episode 3 – The Test
Episode 4 – The Nightmare
Episode 5 – The Resurrection
Episode 6 – The Reunion
The Champions Academy (Episodes 1-3 compilation)
The Dragon's War (Episodes 4-6 compilation)

Eldros Legacy (Legacy of Shadows)
Khyven the Unkillable
Lorelle of the Dark
Rhenn the Traveler (Forthcoming)

Threadweavers
Wildmane
The GodSpill
Threads of Amarion
God of Dragons

The Whisper Prince
Fairmist
The Undying Man
The Slate Wizards (Forthcoming)

The Wishing World
The Wishing World
Loremaster (Forthcoming)
Spheres of Magic (Forthcoming)

Standalone Novels
Charlie Fiction
Summer of the Fetch

Memoirs
Ordinary Magic

Short Stories
Urchin: A Tower of the Four Short Story
Royal: A Tower of the Four Short Story
Princess: A Tower of the Four Short Story
Pawns of Magic: A Tower of the Four Short Story
Here There Be Giants: *Fate's Dagger*
Talons & Talismans 2: *The Darkest Door*
Parallel Worlds Anthology: *Threshold*
Fantastic Realms Anthology: *Ten for Every One*
Dragonlance: The Cataclysm – *Seekers*
Dragonlance: Heroes & Fools – *Songsayer*
Dragonlance: The History of Krynn – *The Letters of Trayn Minaas*

ABOUT THE AUTHOR

TODD FAHNESTOCK is a writer of fantasy for all ages and winner of the New York Public Library's Books for the Teen Age Award. *Threadweavers* and *The Whisper Prince Trilogy* are two of his bestselling epic fantasy series. He is a finalist in the Colorado Authors League Writing Awards for the past two years, for *Charlie Fiction* and *The Undying Man*. His passions are fantasy and his quirky, fun-loving family. When he's not writing, he teaches Taekwondo, swaps middle grade humor with his son, plays Ticket to Ride with his wife, scribes modern slang from his daughter and goes on morning runs with Galahad the Weimaraner. Visit Todd at www.toddfahnestock.com.

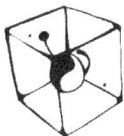

Made in the USA
Monee, IL
03 April 2023

30727801R00236